SHE COULD NEVER TELL HIM WHO SHE WAS.

"Is he alive?" Matt asked, his deep voice quiet.

"Alive?" Charlotte's heart had finally stopped thudding so hard. She was able to breathe normally again. "Who?"

"The man who shot you." The stark words hung there in the silent room.

Charlotte met his eyes, so dark and compelling. She couldn't begin to imagine what he was thinking. For a moment, the desire to ease her huge burden off her shoulders and share it with another human being was so fierce she had to bite her lips to keep from spilling it out. Telling the truth could be fatal, and yet she couldn't lie to him. She nodded once, jerkily. "Yes," she whispered, her voice trembling. "He's alive."

The grooves around his mouth deepened. His big fists clenched once, hard, and relaxed. It was the only movement he made. He became, if possible, even more still. "No one will ever hurt you again, Charlotte. You have my word on it."

PURSUIT

ELIZABETH JENNINGS

FOREVER

NEW YORK   BOSTON

Copyright © 2008 by Elizabeth Jennings
All rights reserved. Except as permitted under the U.S. Copyright Act of 1976, no part of this publication may be reproduced, distributed, or transmitted in any form or by any means, or stored in a database or retrieval system, without the prior written permission of the publisher.

Book design by Stratford Publishing Services, a TexTech business

Forever
Hachette Book Group USA
237 Park Avenue
New York, NY 10017
Visit our Web site at www.HachetteBookGroupUSA.com

Forever is an imprint of Grand Central Publishing.

The Forever name and logo is a trademark of Hachette Book Group USA, Inc.

Printed in the United States of America

First Printing: April 2008

10 9 8 7 6 5 4 3 2 1

*This book is fondly dedicated to
my husband, Alfredo
and to my son, David.*

ACKNOWLEDGMENTS

I'd like to thank my wonderful editor,
Karen Kosztolnyik
and fabulous agent, Ethan Ellenberg.

PURSUIT

PROLOGUE

Eight billion dollars.

All that was standing in the way of $8 billion was an old man dying of pancreatic cancer and his cold bitch of a daughter. Once Philip and Charlotte Court were dead, he could cash in. In about an hour, it would be a done deal.

Robert Haine ran his finger over the preliminary contract with the Pentagon. The figure was written in letters and digits, simple laser-produced strokes of ink on paper, but he found it impossible to lift his hand from the document.

Haine wasn't a fanciful man—indeed, being a cold-eyed realist had taken him far in life—but it seemed to him that the letters grew warm under his fingers.

Eight billion dollars. On May 30. He'd be a billionaire in three months' time. True, the money wasn't, strictly speaking, his. Strictly speaking, it belonged to Court Industries, or rather to Philip Court and his beautiful daughter, Charlotte. It would have been his by rights if Charlotte had married him. That had been the plan. But his careful courtship of her had gone nowhere. The tasteful expensive gifts, the flowers, the dinner invitations—all turned down.

Still, he was CEO of the company, and the Proteus Project was his. His baby, his idea, rammed through over the objections of the Courts.

Haine was now a mega-rainmaker. Billion-dollar contracts were the stuff of legend, and he'd suddenly become a man who could bring in ten digits, a man who had the power to move so much money it would take a train convoy to ship it in cash.

There was no going back. He couldn't lose this.

He was rich now.

He was good at being rich, too. He knew how to do it right. The Courts, both father and daughter, sucked at it. Fuckers had had money for more generations than he'd had hot meals as a child, and you'd never know it. Philip dressed in old, comfortable clothes and ancient shoes made by an English cobbler a thousand years ago. He'd once boasted that the ragged old tweed jacket he had on had belonged to his father. Robert had nearly gagged.

They had a huge three-hundred-year-old pile of bricks along the river that hadn't been renovated in fifty years. Everything in it was shabby. "Comfortable" they called it. There was no sense to it, either. Charlotte's watercolors were hung right next to the two Winslow Homers her great-grandmother had bought from the painter himself. The Homers were worth a cool $2 million, and Charlotte's watercolors were worth exactly zero since she didn't exhibit, but there they were—together on the same wall. Charlotte could have had all the jewelry she wanted, but all she ever wore were her mother's and grandmother's rings.

And Charlotte herself...with those cool gray eyes studying him, finding him wanting.

If she had accepted him in her bed, he'd have showered her with Bulgari rings and Damiani bracelets, but the little bitch wouldn't give him the time of day. Nothing he could do would catch her attention for more than a minute. He might as well have been a neutered dog. Here he was, saving her company for her, and she couldn't look at him for more than a minute without yawning.

There was nothing he could do to impress her. She didn't seem to give a shit that he'd taken the company from the brink of bankruptcy and had turned it around in five years. No matter that instead of a slow slide into bankruptcy, the end of a company that had been in the Court family since 1854, Court Industries had been turned into a leading-edge provider of precision equipment and that he'd worked eighteen-hour days for years to do it. He'd saved the Courts' asses, and they weren't even noticing. Philip Court was on a respirator, dying, and Charlotte Court didn't care about anything but her father.

What the fuck did she care if the company went under? She probably had enough socked away for life. Charlotte had a rich aunt in Chicago who'd left her a bundle she hadn't even touched. There was enough crap in that musty old mansion of theirs to keep her for a hundred years. No, Miss Cold Bitch would never know poverty and degradation, would never live in a trailer park. She had no idea how low you can fall and never would.

Well, she'd asked for it.

Charlotte had no clue that when she refused him first, then the Pentagon contract, she had suddenly made herself into a roadblock, a wall to his ambitions.

All his life Haine had been able to see the next step and the one beyond that and channel his energy in the direction he wanted events to go. It always amazed him that people could be so blind to consequences, not *see*. Haine could. He could war-game it so easily.

Philip Court was about to die—Haine checked his watch, the slimmest of Huguets—in about twenty minutes. Wasn't even murder, really. Just a little speeding up of the natural schedule.

Haine had outsourced that task to his chief of security, Martin Conklin, and his team. Conklin was scheduled to call in half an hour to say that part one of the mission was complete. Philip Court was dead in his intensive care unit. That was easy—who was going to do an autopsy on a guy dying of pancreatic cancer, wasting away in some elegant private clinic, listening to Mozart? Conklin—who was good at impersonations—would place the call to Charlotte. *Ms. Court, this is Sebastian Orvis at Parkwood Hospital. I'm afraid I have some bad news.* He'd then drive to the dangerous curve on Overlook, where Charlotte would lose her life.

Haine started rehearsing the solemn tones he'd use at the club, lamenting the tragedy over a vodka martini.

Well, you know how distraught Charlotte's been lately. Practically living in that hospital room. Beautiful young woman like that, it's not natural, spending all her time with a sick man. There had to be a reaction. Such a loving daughter, but she was exhausted. And you know what the road is like just above Overlook. That's a really tricky curve. Why just the other day, my car slipped and almost bounced off the guardrail at that exact point. Charlotte's never been a good driver. The car just spun out of control.

What a tragedy. What a waste. Court Industries? Why I guess I'll just have to carry on without Philip. That's what he would have wanted. Charlotte, too.

Haine trusted Conklin to run her off the road. He'd been trained and trained well in offensive driving.

The phone rang and Haine frowned when he saw the caller ID. It was way too soon for Conklin to be calling.

"Yes?" Haine answered. As always, no names. Not on cell phones, not on landlines.

"We got a problem." The cell-phone connection was lousy, crackling and hissing. Was Conklin *panting*?

"What?" Haine's voice was calm, but the hairs on his neck were standing up. This was supposed to be *easy*. It was just a thing that had to be done to get to the other side of the road, without any fuss.

"She was there already."

Every hair on his body was standing up.

"Bitch whacked me with the IV tree. A nurse got in the way, and I had to take her down, too. But I winged Court. Through the shoulder, I think. She's bleeding, I followed her trail out of the hospital, but she's gone."

Shitshitshit!!!

And then it came to him complete, like a storyboard.

"I'm going to have to go down to police headquarters. Can you meet me there?"

"Yeah. There's going to be fallout, though. The old guy's room is a mess, and there's a dead nurse outside."

Haine was thinking fast. He had ten men in CI's Security Department to deploy. He'd hired well. They were loyal to him, not the company.

"Don't worry about that. You'll be meeting up with Vaneyck, Oakley, and Ryan outside police headquarters.

Stop Charlotte from getting into the police station. Use any means you want, but make sure she doesn't get through. No matter what." Conklin would know exactly what he meant. "Send the rest of the men to the Court mansion. Don't let her get in. The gun you shot the nurse with—is it untraceable?"

"Of course." Conklin sounded shocked.

"What is it?"

"Smith & Wesson 908."

Perfect, Haine thought. It only weighed twenty-four ounces and had a small grip. The kind of gun a woman would choose.

"Wipe it down. Did you load the magazine like I told you?"

"With latex gloves? Yeah."

Okay. There would be no fingerprints on the weapon traceable back to Conklin. Now they needed Charlotte's fingers. With or without her hand attached.

Haine war-gamed the new version. For the benefit of Chief Brzynski and that new anchorwoman on WRCTV, the cute one with the tight ass, what was her name? Anna. Anna Lorenzetti.

Poor Charlotte, I guess she finally just... broke down. Maybe I should have seen the signs. She told me a couple of months ago she felt hunted, there were enemies everywhere. She even told me she'd acquired an illegal weapon. A Smith & Wesson, I think she said. She's been acting very erratically, Anna. Said she hadn't slept well in months, and she was looking very poorly.

Who on earth could imagine it would come to this?

I sent my head of security to check on how Philip was doing in the hospital. We miss him very much at the office. Conklin said he caught Charlotte smothering her father with a pillow. I guess she just couldn't stand to see him suffer anymore.

I'm sure she wasn't herself when she shot that nurse. The stress was just too much for her.

Here a slow sorrowful shake of the head. Sad, pensive expression.

What a waste, Anna. What a terrible waste.

Wonderful story. Played very well. It would play particularly well with Chief Brzynski. A month ago Haine hinted that Brzynski could count on a 200K-a-year job with Court Industries after retirement. It was all in place.

Now all that was missing was a dead Charlotte.

"Take her down, Conklin. I want men around her house and in a perimeter around police headquarters. Tell your men to shoot on sight. Make sure you get to the body before the cops do and plant that gun on her. Fold her fingers around it. Say she was drawing on you and you shot in self defense." Haine stopped and did some calculations. The amount had to be just right. Enough to be a strong motivator but not so much they'd be too eager to take precautions. "Tell the men there's a thirty-thousand-dollar bonus for the one who bags her."

Haine disconnected and started dressing to go out. It was snowing. He hesitated a moment. The cashmere Armani overcoat would get soaked. Better to go with the Shearling.

CHAPTER ONE

Fill it up!"

Charlotte Court buzzed down the window of her maid's SUV and shouted over the howling wind at the gas-station attendant. She was shaking with shock and pain and grief, huddled in her down jacket against the icy sleet pinging against her face.

Underneath the jacket, blood was seeping out of the makeshift bandage she'd packed against the bullet wound. Her heart was also bleeding grief for her father, still and dead on his hospital bed, murdered by one of Robert's minions. Of the shocks of the past two hours, that was the worst—knowing her father was dead.

She needed a safe place to hole up. Robert's men had been at the police station and had surrounded her home. The profile of an armed man outside the gates of her home had been visible against the dying light. Whatever was going on, she needed to get away from Robert, get medical attention, then call in the murder of her father and the attack on her life to the FBI.

A motel was a possibility. She was driving her maid's SUV. Moira had even left her brand-new American passport in the glove compartment, so she could check into the hotel as Moira Charlotte Fitzgerald. Then from there she could call...

Charlotte jumped as a face with a straggly moustache plastered itself against the passenger-side window. "That'll be seventy bucks, ma'am," the man screamed against the wind.

Charlotte bumped her left shoulder against the door in turning toward her purse and nearly blacked out from the pain. She had to breathe slowly through her nose until the worst had passed. Thank God she was wearing black. Blood from the wound had seeped slowly through the down jacket and left a red, wet sheen on the left-hand-side door.

No credit card. Whatever Robert was up to, he had the resources to track credit-card payments. So she handed most of the small amount of cash she had over to the attendant and drove around to the side of the station.

The restrooms were way in the back, past rows of shelves with junk food, soda pop, maps, and movie magazines. Were there any OTC medications? A couple of aspirin might just dull the pain a little. Or even better, ibuprofen.

She heard her father's name mentioned and another stab of grief nearly brought her to her knees. Her eyes welled, her heart thumped painfully at the thought that she'd never see her father again.

Then another name caught her attention.

To her horror, someone was calling her name! Charlotte cringed, ready to run, when she realized that except for a very bored young teen bopping her head to the beat of an iPod, she was alone in the shop.

What...?

Her name was being blared from the TV fixed to a bracket high up on the wall. There was a big-hair female anchor. A photograph of Charlotte was in the upper-left-hand corner of the screen.

Police are on the lookout for Charlotte Court, heiress to Court Industries. She is wanted for questioning in the death of her father, Philip Court of Court Industries at Parkwood Hospital and the shooting death of Imelda Delgado, a trauma nurse at the hospital. Police warn that Ms. Court may be armed and must be considered dangerous. Anyone sighting Ms. Court is warned not to approach her but to contact the authorities at...

Oh my God! She was wanted for *murder!* Not only did she have to escape Robert and his goons, she had to avoid the police! *Armed and dangerous.* They'd shoot her on sight. And worse—Robert was friends with the chief of police. If she were in custody, he'd find a way to get to her.

Charlotte made it back to the SUV, gasping with panic. She pulled out of the gas-station lot as quickly as the ice on the road allowed and headed west, hoping to make it across the state line before she fainted.

By nightfall, Haine was pacing, impatiently waving away his housekeeper's offer of dinner.

The bitch had gotten away. He didn't know how she had done it, but she'd disappeared off the face of the Earth.

She couldn't get far, though. She hadn't been back to Court Mansion, so she wouldn't have much money. The instant she used her credit card, they'd be on top of her.

He'd spent the day at police headquarters, and an APB had been put out for one Charlotte Court, suspected of murder, considered armed and dangerous.

The state police would be alert, but Haine trusted Conklin's men more than he trusted the police. Conklin's men were good—they were fast, and they were ruthless. They'd find her first and deliver a corpse.

It wouldn't be long. Charlotte was wounded and on the run, the object of a manhunt.

No, Haine thought with a slow smile. A womanhunt.

Somewhere in Kansas
Crest Motor Court
February 24

Charlotte Court stared at her pale, exhausted face in the cracked, spotted bathroom mirror. Her skin was paper white, except for the patchy red fever flags on her cheekbones. Whatever her temperature was, she didn't want to know. All she knew was that it was high. Fever floated in her veins, making her light-headed, slightly hallucinatory. For a moment, there were two white-faced Charlottes reflected in the dark-spotted mirror with the backing nearly completely eaten away on the left-hand side.

The only good thing about looking like someone about to circle the drain was that she bore no resemblance whatsoever to the photograph that until two days ago had been broadcast over every TV station on Earth, it seemed. The photograph had been taken at the Red Cross charity ball, and she'd spent an entire day at Elizabeth Arden's in preparation. The white-faced woman staring back at her in the mirror bore no resemblance to the polished, coiffed, bejeweled, heavily made-up woman in the photograph.

Right now, she looked ten years older, ten pounds lighter, and $10 million poorer than in the photograph. Last night, somewhere in Illinois, she'd washed her hair one-handed. The motel's hairdryer didn't work, so she'd fallen into bed with her hair wet. It was a universe away from Pierre's frothy coiffure, which had taken him all afternoon to concoct before the charity ball.

The Red Cross ball photograph had migrated all over the newspapers over the past four days. It had been front-page, above-the-fold news the first day. Then it had slipped to below the fold, then onto page three, from color to black and white, and had finally disappeared altogether while several other news cycles cranked their way through the public consciousness.

The story of Charlotte Court, double murderer, had become a low background hum by the time she made it to Chicago.

That was good because she didn't have the strength to do much more than keep her head down whenever she saw a security camera. And she'd run out of money.

She'd almost run completely out of cash and had coasted to her Great Aunt Willa's street on fumes. Great Aunt Willa, bless her heart, had passed away at Christmas, leaving everything she owned to Charlotte, who had been unwilling to leave her father to settle the estate. Great Aunt Willa had been rich and, even better, crazy as a loon. One of her eccentricities was to always keep vast amounts of cash on hand. What she called "walking around money."

Charlotte had the keys to Great Aunt Willa's house—technically her house, now—because she'd been meaning to take a quick trip to Chicago when her father's health allowed it, and it never had.

After a morning's search, she found Aunt Willa's stash. A little under fifty thousand dollars in cash in four shoeboxes in Aunt Willa's walk-in closet that could have housed a family of four.

As she closed the door of the big mansion behind her, she vowed that she would one day return, with a cleared name. Her next step was a Western Union wannabe in a poor part of town, where migrant workers sent their wages back home to their families. She chose the scruffiest remittance counter she could, with the most bored-looking employees.

They didn't even question it when Moira Charlotte Fitzgerald sent nine thousand to Moira Charlotte Fitzgerald in Warrenton, New York. The same for another remittance agency several blocks away. In all, she sent Moira eighteen thousand dollars, which is what her SUV had cost her.

She'd made off with Moira's pride and joy. Moira had saved two years for that black monster. Charlotte couldn't live with herself if she didn't pay Moira back.

Once she'd wired the money, she put the two receipts in an envelope and mailed them to Moira's home, disguising her handwriting. The process exhausted her.

Her only consolation was that, after buying a second-hand huge, shapeless, hooded down coat in a Goodwill that reached to her ankles, a black wool watch cap and enormous sunglasses, her own father wouldn't have recognized her.

Security cameras were everywhere these days, she knew. So if by chance she was on film somewhere, the camera had caught images of a woman moving so slowly she could have been eighty years old, dressed in a shapeless coat, with a hood and sunglasses. No one could ever have recognized her as Charlotte Court.

Time and distance from Warrenton were taking her farther and farther away from immediate danger. And the shoulder wound was making her look less and less like Charlotte Court, heiress and socialite.

That was the good news. The bad news was that the wound had become infected, and the infection wasn't showing any signs of going away.

Exhaustion made her sway slightly. She clutched the dirty edges of the washbasin for balance. One look at the moldy Fungus City pad in the plastic shower stall had her opting for a sponge bath. The faucet yielded up a reluctant gurgle of yellowish, warmish water. By the time she finished cleaning up, she could barely stand.

Oh, God, she missed her father fiercely. Of course, he wouldn't have been much help in this particular instance. Philip Court was—had been—notoriously impractical. He wasn't too good at dressing bullet wounds or evading cops, but he knew how to comfort. Her father seemed to have had a book to recommend for every life event. She couldn't count the times she'd felt better just by having him hug her and fix a cup of tea.

A single tear ran down the pale, drawn face in the mirror. If she dwelled on how much she missed her father, she'd lose the last of her reserves, and there was still one more task to face before she could sleep, though bile rose in her throat at the thought.

She stood naked in the bathroom, feet curling on the cold, damp tiles.

Charlotte stared at her shoulder, at the bloodstained gauze that had been pristine white that morning, hating what was coming next. The first time she'd tried to tough it out, tearing the bloody packing off in one decisive, painful rip, she'd woken up half an hour later on the bathroom tiles with a huge bump to her head.

Still, experience told her that it was better to do it in one go. Her right hand lifted to her left shoulder and with a decisive, painful rip, she tore the bloody packing off and clenched her teeth to stifle the scream. The fiery pain made her head swim and her stomach clench. Luckily, there was nothing in her stomach to throw up.

It was worse than yesterday. She leaned forward and examined her shoulder carefully in the mirror. Yes, it was definitely worse. The wound hadn't closed completely yet. It still suppurated sullenly, blood leaking out at a slow but constant pace. Part of it had scabbed over, but she could see pus at the edges of the scab. The skin was raw and red, inflamed and painful to the touch. To her horror, she could see a small streak of red angling downwards.

So far she'd managed without stitches, but the infection was getting out of control. At a loss for antibiotics, she'd remembered going to a farmer's supply store when her collie, Yeats, had caught his paw in a hunter's trap. The store hadn't blinked at selling her antibiotics over the counter. So Charlotte had stopped that morning in one of the thousand anonymous small farming towns in Illinois and had bought antibiotics for a nonexistent collie weighing sixty pounds. That way all she had to do was double the dosage the friendly man behind the counter had given her.

She'd stopped at a supermarket to buy candy, fruit juice,

bandages, and the largest size possible of Ziploc bags. Opening one of the bags, she filled it with the first of the three plastic bottles of hydrogen peroxide she'd bought at a drugstore.

Gritting her teeth, she raised the hydrogen peroxide-filled Ziploc bag until it was slightly higher than her shoulder, leaned forward into the sink, and punctured a corner of the bag with the sharp end of the pencil the hotel provided. Immediately, a gush of liquid poured out, hissing and bubbling at contact with her skin, irrigating the wound. Charlotte wanted to scream with pain but didn't dare. She didn't dare do anything that would call attention to herself.

It was like being stuck through the shoulder with a red-hot poker. It actually hurt more than when she'd been shot. Then she'd been filled with adrenaline, so enraged at witnessing her father's murder, then so panicked at realizing that Conklin was trying to kill her, too, that she'd barely felt the bullet going through.

Right now, though, it felt as if all the pain in the world had rolled into a fiery ball that had found a home in her shoulder.

Her left hand, slippery with blood, slipped on the rim of the dirty washbasin. She clenched harder, until her shaking knuckles turned white. It would have helped to use both hands to squeeze the bag, in order to increase the water pressure, but she had to hold on to the basin or fall to the floor. She filled the bag again and lifted it. The face looking back at her in the mirror was now gray, with huge beads of sweat on the forehead. Bracing herself, she irrigated the wound again, locking her jaw against the scream that tickled her throat.

Again and again she filled the bag until the liquid from the wound ran pale pink in the sink instead of bright red.

The pain was blinding. Her hands and knees were shaking by the time she'd finished. Though she could barely stand up, there was more still to do.

Opening the packet of antibiotic powder for dogs, she sprinkled it liberally over the wound, hoping against hope that her physiology was close enough to that of a dog to kill the bacteria. By the time she'd finished putting packing on the wound and taping it, she was trembling so hard she could barely stand up.

There was still one thing left to do—clean up the bloody mess she'd made. Using the towels to wipe off the blood would have been stupid. Instead she used up an entire roll of toilet paper, flushing it all down the toilet.

It was possible that if some crime-scene analyst were to examine the bathroom, he'd find plenty of DNA, but Charlotte was certain that unless she did something to call attention to herself, it would be all right. Tomorrow the cleaning crew would come in with bleach and eliminate all traces.

By the time she was finished, Charlotte was exhausted and sweaty and whiter than the dirty sheets on the bed. She knew she needed some food, something warm and solid in her stomach—or even just something warm like tea or hot milk—but there was no hope of that. Going out for something was simply beyond her, not to mention the fact that if she ate another fast-food hamburger, she'd throw up. And the Crest Motor Court definitely did not run to room service. She'd chosen it specially because it was the most depressing and desolate motel she could find.

Luckily, it wasn't far from the bathroom to the bed. She hesitated just a moment by the side of the bed, every fastidious cell in her body rebelling against lying down on the stained counterpane, but it was either lie down on a bed a thousand traveling salesmen had slept in or fall to the floor and sleep there. It was a toss-up as to which was dirtier.

Charlotte turned her head on the lumpy pillow and examined the room. Faded wallpaper, scratched Formica desk, and broken-backed chair. A TV set that only caught three channels. It was almost exactly like the other four motels she'd slept in, only worse.

Where was she? Somewhere in Kansas, that much she knew, though she had no idea where or what the name of the town was. It had been a long, frightening blur of Denny's and Motel Sixes and used-car dealerships from Chicago to here. One town had blended into another. She wouldn't even have known she was in Kansas if it hadn't been for the big ENTERING KANSAS sign.

She still didn't have much of a plan in mind, other than staying off the interstates and moving south, away from the vast cold front that gripped the Midwest. She was so weak and feverish, she knew instinctively that staying in the midst of a record-breaking blizzard would kill her.

She didn't want to be in Kansas. She didn't want to be anywhere, except back at home, caring for her father.

And while she was at it, wishing for impossible things, she wished it were five years ago, instead of now. Before her mother had died in a car crash. Before her father had fallen ill. When she was young, studying art, without a care in the world.

She lay back, shaking, trying to ignore the ball of fire

in her shoulder. Charlotte stared up at the ceiling, dry-eyed, too tired to cry, too weak to move.

Tonight, somehow, it took forever for the pain medication to kick in. She glanced down at her shoulder, saw a pinprick of blood, and closed her eyes briefly in despair. Blood was already seeping through. In a couple of hours, it would spread in a bright red lake over the bandages. She had to put on extra packing and stick something under her if she didn't want the maid to find blood on the bed and possibly remember it. If the police for some reason came around to canvass hotels and motels, maids couldn't be expected to remember the hundreds of anonymous bodies that transited through their rooms, but they could certainly remember having to clean up blood.

She had to get up. *Now.* Though her mind gave out peremptory orders, whipping her into a state of action, her body just sank deeper into the mattress.

Charlotte lay on the bed, completely hollowed out with fatigue and blood loss and despair. The dark wings of desperation fluttered in her mind.

The motel was close to the highway, and the sounds of heavy traffic filtered in from the window. It was raining so hard she could hear the hiss of the tires plowing through the water. A siren sounded in the distance. In the next room, a man and a woman were arguing, voices shrill.

You goddamned son of a bitch! a woman's voice in the room next door screamed, voice sharp and high with hysteria. Charlotte had never heard that raw note in a human being's voice before.

The dull thunk of an object hitting the wall behind the bed reverberated through the room.

This was a world she'd never been in before. An airless, dark world of despair. Charlotte felt like she'd fallen into a deep well, cut off from the rest of humanity, cut off from the rest of her life.

Robert Haine had done this. He'd stripped her of everything she had and everything she was. He was responsible for the death of her father and Imelda Delgado, the sweet-faced Filipina nurse who'd been so kind to her father, and he'd managed to cast the blame on her. The Courts had stood in his way, and he'd cold-bloodedly eliminated them.

This was about money. It had to be. It was what motivated Robert, what made him tick. Money and sex.

He'd certainly tried hard enough to get her into his bed.

If she hadn't been so busy looking after her father, she'd have started a campaign with the board to get rid of him. But he was a successful manager, the board members were delighted because the shares went up, and Charlotte hadn't cared enough to mount a campaign when she was losing her father, day by day.

Now she'd lost her father forever. She hadn't even been able to attend his funeral. One more thing Robert had taken away from her.

How could she ask for help? Robert had run amok. If he was willing to kill her father and was gunning for her, he'd be perfectly willing to hurt anyone she turned to for help. She was on her own.

She ached with pain at the loss of her father. For the very first time in her life, there was no one to turn to. And no one knew where she was.

She realized, with a start of surprise, that she'd always been . . . reachable by the people who loved her, all her life. Her parents and friends had always had a phone number. The closest she'd ever been to being out of touch was a cruise in the Caribbean two years ago, in places where her cell didn't have coverage for a couple of hours.

All her life, she'd been tied by bonds of love and affection to everyone around her. This new place she was in— barren and bereft of human contact—felt exactly like hell must feel, only cold.

Charlotte shivered, partly from the chill of the room, partly from the fever that was burning in her veins.

The fight next door was escalating. There were ominous bumps and thumps, voices raised in anger. The snatches of words she could hear were vicious. Even though she didn't catch what they were arguing about, it didn't matter. The tone was enough to know that it was primal and primitive. Another sharp blow to the wall so hard she could feel the vibrations. She only hoped it was an object and not the woman's head.

Charlotte couldn't call the police or even call down to the front desk without calling attention to herself. She started at the sound of glass shattering. Perhaps a replica of the big, cheap porcelain lamp base on the desk. Suddenly, the woman's voice wailed, notes rising in a hair-raising sound of animal despair.

They could trace 911 calls. Charlotte knew this from a thousand TV crime shows. How could she call in an emergency without—

Suddenly the raucous voices stopped and for a heart-rending moment, Charlotte wondered if the woman had been knocked unconscious. Or, worse, killed.

It took her a second to recognize the sounds now coming from the room, they were so different from the sound track of violence she'd been listening to for over a quarter of an hour. Low moans, murmurs...

Suddenly, the bedsprings of the bed next door started creaking in a fast, regular rhythm. Soon, the headboard was banging against the wall in brutally hard slaps accompanied by grunts.

Oh, yeah, baby, the woman moaned. *Oh yeah, give it to me*.

Violent sex had replaced the violence.

For a moment, worry about the woman next door had almost made her forget about her shoulder, but the instant she realized that the woman wasn't in danger, the pain came rushing back, like a flood that had been temporarily dammed. It was alive, the pain, like another being in the room with her.

She reached for the bottle of pain medication. Charlotte held the bottle in her good hand, turning it slowly. A normal white plastic bottle with a childproof top, colorful label, promising pain relief from toothache, migraines, and menstrual disorders.

No mention whatsoever of gunshot wounds.

She swallowed three pills dry, one after the other, and lay back, good fist clenched around the plastic cylinder, waiting with slow thuds of her heart for the pills to take effect. It occurred to her, as she held the bottle, the plastic slowly warming up in her hand, that the bottle was full. It was entirely possible that swallowing the contents of this little bottle would yield up permanent pain relief. Maybe a way out of all her troubles was right here, in a white bottle in her clenched fist.

It would be so easy, too. Much much easier than trying to tend a wound on the run, much easier than driving ten hours a day in a frantic rush away from danger and toward nothing.

Charlotte dangled the plastic cylinder in front of her eyes. Even holding the bottle up—maybe an ounce of weight—made her hand tremble. Over-the-counter medication was probably calibrated to ensure that even a full bottle would not be a suicidal dosage. But she was weak from blood loss, had no food in her stomach to absorb the medicine, and weighed much less than the average person.

It might work.

Swallow all the pills and lie back and wait for her life to drain away together with the pain.

Life as she knew it was over, anyway.

Her father was dead. Robert and his goons were out there, waiting to kill her. How could she turn to the police for protection when she was wanted for murder? The evidence Robert had planted must have been very convincing for a manhunt to have been organized that quickly.

It was all too overwhelming, too horrible. The future was an unknown abyss in front of her, dark and menacing and feral.

Opening the bottle one-handed, she shook out another three pills, popped them in her mouth and swallowed them. She could feel each individual pill as it went down. Lifting herself up slightly to be able to swallow made the pain in her shoulder explode in a fierce ball of fire, and she gasped and jerked, all the pills in the bottle spilling out onto the dirty counterpane. Tears of pain sprang to her eyes. Angrily she wiped them away with the heel of her hand.

Next door there was a loud male shout, a groan, and the bed-thumping stopped. Almost immediately afterwards, there was a sharp slap, and the woman's voice rose again. "You *bastard!* How could you?"

Well, the postcoital glow sure hadn't lasted very long.

Charlotte stared at the ceiling. There was a crack running across it, barely visible in the meager light of the twenty-watt bulb. At one point the crack split, like a river.

She stared and stared, fingering the pills, one by one. There were thirty-three of them. Enough, perhaps, for the job.

She could do it in ten swallows. Might even be pleasant—drifting lightly above the agony of her shoulder and the squalor of the motel room, feeling the pain slowly recede as the shadows drew closer. Drifting softly, gently, on waves taking her far far away. And at the end, peace.

Robert would win, then, though. He'd be getting away with it—getting away with snuffing out the life of her father. Getting away with trying to pin it on her. He'd find a way to inherit Court Industries and live happily ever after, with his loathsome titanium golf clubs, Porsches, and Hugo Boss shirts.

He'd be delighted. She'd be solving all of his problems in one stroke.

Slowly, so as not to wake up the fierce giant living in her shoulder who took huge bites out of her flesh, Charlotte fingered the pills once more.

She couldn't let Robert win, she simply couldn't.

One by one, by touch alone, she slid the pills back into the cylinder, the little rattle as they hit the bottom sounding almost loud in the silence of the room. Thirty-three.

She stared, dry-eyed, at the crack in the ceiling until the chemical darkness came to take her away.

CHAPTER TWO

VA Hospital
Leavenworth, Kansas
February 24

Fifty miles away, Lieutenant Commander Matthew Sanders opened his eyes and stared at the ceiling. It was painted puke green and had a big crack running through it.

Opening his eyes and staring at the ceiling was Matt's newest, latest skill and was a huge step up from lying flat on his back in a coma, which is what he had been doing up until a month ago. It was an even huger step up from dying, which is what he'd done on a lonely, sun-blasted Afghan plain.

His heart had stopped four months ago, when he and his men had been exfiltrating from a series of caves at the foothills of the Hindu Kush. They'd destroyed close to a million pounds of ammunition and were running for the Huey swooping in to the prearranged exfil point. Matt was hustling his twelve men into the safety of the helo. *Five, six, seven* he counted in his head. He had one foot on the skids to pull himself in after the last man, when his blood ran cold.

A nest of tangos, lying in wait behind a hill, rose up out of the dun earth seven hundred yards away, scattering clods of dirt and stones. What had the hair on the back of his neck rising was the profile of the Al Qaeda terrorist at the top of the hillock. Matt had superb eyesight. Even through the dust kicked up by the helo's rotors, he could easily make out the RPG-7 on the man's scrawny shoulder. A Soviet-made rocket-propelled grenade.

Helicopters are swift and agile and have only two moments of vulnerability—at takeoff and while hovering. The pilot was hovering, had to, for the men to scramble on board.

Men were still clambering onto the cargo deck of the helo. It would take the pilot at least two minutes to pull out of range since he had to wait for the last man to board. RPGs don't operate at distances greater than a thousand yards, but by the time the pilot got them out of range, the RPG would have shot them down.

Matt had watched a Black Hawk with close friends in it go down over Fallujah, brought down by an RPG. It was not going to happen again. Not while he could do something about it. Not to his men. Not on his watch.

"Lorenzo!" he shouted over his shoulder. "Your SR-25!"

Sgt. Dominic Lorenzo, the team sharpshooter, automatically reached behind him for his heavy sniper rifle in its scabbard and handed it down. As Matt took the rifle from him, he saw Lorenzo's eyes widen as he realized what was going down.

Lorenzo could never get a shot off at that distance from the heavily vibrating Huey.

The last man was in the helo. Matt slapped the skids.

"Get out of here! Go go *go!*" he screamed over the

noise of the engines as he went down on one knee in the dust, sighting through the Leopold VX III scope. Once, a long time ago, he'd been a sniper. Sniping skills are perishable, but he'd kept his up.

Time went into combat slo mo. The dust and the noise and the confusion disappeared as he made the world narrow, then disappear. This shot mattered. It would be his last shot in this lifetime, and it had to be perfect. The old sniper's mantra. *One shot, one kill.*

Shooters shouldn't have to shoot twice. In this case, he wouldn't have a second chance, anyway.

High low angle rule, he reminded himself. A rule he'd drummed into his recruits' heads. Shooting up, aim high, shooting down, aim low. He was shooting up.

He'd been running, and he knew his heart rate was topping 145 beats per minute, that red zone where motor skills drop, hearing is lost, and tunnel vision sets in. He'd trained for this and knew what to do, only it took some time. It would be a race to the finish because the tango was ready to fire.

Matt needed his heart rate at 80 bpm, and he needed it there *now.* He rolled his shoulder muscles and took two deep breaths, relaxing all the major muscle groups as he shouldered the rifle.

He was at a disadvantage. All of this worked in training and on the range. He'd trained his body to obey his cortex instantly. But the midbrain—the animal part of him that valued personal survival above honor and duty—was going haywire. It knew perfectly well that he was preparing to die, and it didn't want any part of this. Matt wasted two perfectly good seconds tamping the midbrain monster down.

He breathed in and out, bringing the heart rate down 20 bps with each breath. He had to shoot between heartbeats and between breaths.

Now! He breathed slowly, in and out. In and out. In. And. Out. In and—he pulled the trigger—out.

Seven hundred yards away a tiny figure flung its arms up and fell backward, taking the RPG with it. Fifteen other men on the hillside shouldered their rifles.

It was the last thing he remembered. He spent the next three months in a coma and the month after that lying on a hospital cot staring at the ceiling, counting the cracks and water stains.

Later, he was told that Fred "Goat" Pierce, who'd grown up on a ranch in Texas, had lassoed him just as he was crumpling to the ground. His unconscious, bleeding body had dangled for long minutes from the helo as the pilot banked and hauled ass out of there. He flatlined once they got him up onto the cargo deck, his system closing itself down in shock at the massive blood loss from five bullet wounds. He lost almost two pints of blood in the first minutes, and his heart had stopped beating by the time the medic, Morrison, got to him.

Morrison refused to give up on him. He defibrillated him and pumped four bags of plasma into him, keeping him stabilized until they got back to base. He'd been airlifted to Ramstein, where a team of surgeons worked on him for eighteen hours straight, and when his vital signs had stabilized, he'd been airlifted—still in a coma—to the VA hospital.

He'd first opened his eyes a month ago. He remembered the deep bass *whump whump whump* of the Huey's rotors. He awoke to the sound of the EKG machine beeping and an orderly swabbing the corridor outside his room, softly singing a blues song.

It had taken Matt several sweaty minutes to realize that he was alive and in a hospital and hadn't been tossed into some scary hell reeking of disinfectant with puke green walls and cracked ceilings.

There was someone else in the room with him—a silent figure almost completely wrapped in bandages from his head to the two stumps that ended about seven inches below his torso. Only his nose and his fingertips were visible. A jarhead, a nurse had said. Victim of an IED in Iraq. Double amputee. In the week that Matt had been awake, the jarhead had shown no signs of life other than a few weak moans in the night.

"You okay, buddy?" Matt asked the man softly, as he had every morning since he'd come back to life. That was his second brand-new skill—talking. The first day out of the coma he'd been unable to articulate any words. He'd think the words, but all that would come out of his throat were raspy, guttural sounds, like an animal. It had terrified him, almost as much as the fact that he couldn't move much more than his fingers and his toes.

As always, the figure next to him swathed in white didn't answer. He wasn't hooked up to any machines. He had a drip of a clear solution going into a tube that disappeared into one bandaged arm and a catheter coming out of his groin took the liquid back out. White in, yellow out.

When Matt had asked the nurse how long his roommate had been in a coma, she'd replied that he wasn't in a coma, he was "clinically depressed." Well...*yeah,* Matt had thought. What else can you be in a clinic?

Matt had got over his own depression. Matt had big

big plans for today. Huge, ambitious plans. He was going to get out of this hospital bed and stand on his own two feet, by God. Right now, standing up was the most thrilling thing he could imagine, the most ambitious plan his exhausted mind could encompass.

In the Teams, Matt was the company tactician and strategist. He'd always been good at thinking ahead several moves, planning actions while always keeping the overall goal in sight. He could see the next step and the one after that, as clearly as if he were looking into a crystal ball. He planned missions down to the tiniest detail so that when the plan was put into action, it was as if he'd already lived it.

Not now. Not lying flat on his back on a hard cot in room 347. Now his horizon was totally shrunk to today, to getting through each pain-filled hour. Up until now, making any kind of a plan had seemed impossible— something other people did, not people with broken bodies on hospital beds.

Well, he was going to start grabbing his life back. He knew the hospital schedule by heart. Some black sludge, powdered milk, and a stale Danish had been served up, about a hundred on the Crap Scale, worse than the worst MREs he'd ever had to eat in the field, and just as guaranteed to gum you up for life.

Nurse Ratched, who'd been assigned to him as part of the VFW's ongoing effort to make his stay memorable, had cranked his bed up and insisted on waiting until he'd choked down every bite of the Danish, though it tasted like cardboard, and swallowed every drop of the coffee that tasted like what Helmut Dietmayer used to call Lutheran Church Basement Coffee.

Nurse Ratched—actually, her name was Doris Barnes, R.N., as the badge stuck on her flat chest indicated—would be back in half an hour to wash him, a humiliating ordeal he endured daily. He was treated like a piece of meat—uninteresting meat at that. Everything about being here was humiliating, starting from the appalling weakness he felt. Well, Matt thought, it's time to change all that. He had half an hour. With a little luck, Nurse Ratched would come back and find him standing on his own two feet, like a man.

And then he'd go to the head all by himself and burn the bedpan. Or rather, since it was plastic, toss it out the window.

He had it all mapped out in his head—throw off the covers, grab the overhead rails for traction, scoot his legs to the right and over the side of the bed, and slowly stand up, holding on to the side of the bed for balance.

That was the theory and that was the strategy and that was the mission—slide legs out of bed, put legs on floor, stand up. He had half an hour to do it in.

Go!

Grim-faced and determined, Matt threw back the covers. Or at least, he tried to. Damn things weighed a fucking ton. It took him three botched attempts. Such simple movements, even an idiot could do it. Clutch the covers, and swing the arm up and to the left. Nothing to it. But his hand's grip was weak, and his arm faltered halfway through each swing. He ended up entangled in the top sheet, blanket, and light cotton cover.

Even this light exertion had him breathing heavily from exhaustion and frustration. *Goddammit! I can do this!* He swung his arm again and again until the sheet and blanket and cover were entangled around his knees. In frustration, he tried to kick them down to the bottom of the mattress, moving his feet frantically, making a bigger mess.

He stopped and breathed, enraged and panicky. This part was supposed to be *easy*. This was only the first damned step to getting up. If he couldn't manage getting free of the blanket...

Stop! He ordered himself. He had to stop and regroup before he ran completely out of strength.

Jesus. Getting out of bed. How hard can it be? He was thirty-four years old. He'd done it over twelve thousand times in his lifetime. Even an idiot could get out of bed.

An idiot, maybe, but apparently not him.

Matt pressed the button on the side of the hospital cot and listened to the quiet motor purring as it lifted the head of the bed up. He raised it to its full extension. Maybe sitting up would help him. Sitting up was another nifty skill he'd just relearned, thanks to the hospital bed. Sitting up gave you a whole new perspective on the world as compared to lying flat on your back. Yesterday, he'd actually fed himself some watery soup while sitting up in bed.

Man, he was on a roll.

He looked with hatred at the tangle of sheet and blankets at the bottom of the bed and devised a strategy for dealing with it. Craftily, he slowly bent his knees and pulled his legs up until his feet cleared the tangle and were planted in the middle of the bed. Then he pushed them back down again, pushing the tangle of sheets and blankets to the bottom of the bed. *Smart move, Sanders*, he congratulated himself.

Glancing at the figure in the bed next to his, at a man who would never again in this lifetime stand on his own two feet, Matt thought—*this is for you, buddy*—and twisted his torso and straightened his legs until they dangled over the side of the bed. Moving hurt like hell, and he had to stop to get his breathing under control. His quick pants of exhaustion were loud in the quiet room. Eventually the walls stopped spinning, and the pain subsided enough for him to get a grip on himself. He sat on the side of the bed, trying to breathe regularly and trying to steel himself for what came next.

It had to be soon because Nurse Ratched would be coming in to measure his blood pressure and temperature and give him an antibiotic jab in about fifteen minutes and Matt wanted to be on his feet when she came in. It was a matter of pride—pride and, yes, his goddamned manhood. Men stood on their own two feet.

He sat and contemplated the floor for long minutes, studying the waxy green linoleum as if all the answers to the questions that had puzzled mankind for centuries could be deciphered in the dark green streaks veining the floor. He barely recognized himself. He wasn't an impulsive man—in fact, back in the day, he was known for his patience and self-control—but by the same token, once he'd taken a decision to do something hard, he immediately took action, and he didn't stop until he'd seen it through. He was patient but he was also pigheaded.

Sitting here bare-assed on the side of the bed with his bare feet dangling from the bed, Matt didn't recognize himself.

Just do it.

Bracing himself on his hands, he scooted closer to the edge of the bed, the open white coat opening even farther, but who the shit cared? His buddy in the next bed had his eyes closed, and it sure as hell wasn't anything Nurse Ratched didn't see every day. Didn't wipe every day, to his shame. He slid closer and closer to the edge until his feet touched the floor, the first time his feet had touched anything but sheets in four months.

Matt closed his eyes for a second and sent up a swift soldier's prayer—*just let me get through this next part and then I'll be good*—and stood up.

And fell flat on his face. No matter that he'd locked his knees and had visualized like crazy standing up, his legs simply wouldn't hold him, not for one second. He went down like a felled tree, and was splayed facedown on the floor.

It hurt, but that was okay. Pain was okay, he'd always had a high tolerance for pain, and, anyway, pain meant you were alive. *Pain is your friend* was drilled into SEALs daily. So he could deal with the pain. What he couldn't deal with was the humiliation of being sprawled on the floor with no idea of how to get back up. He turned his head sideways and looked up at his bed. As high as Mount Everest and just as unscalable.

Matt braced his hands beside his head and tried to lift himself up, but he couldn't do it. Simply couldn't. He pushed with his arms until they trembled with fatigue, until sweat poured down his face and back, until his breath came in hot, painful pants.

He rested for a moment, hands still braced, still in the position for push-ups.

Fifteen years ago, a lifetime ago, on his first day of BUD/S, the instructor, a nasty old son of a bitch called Blackie, screamed *Drop you motherfuckers!* to the recruits so often Matt could still hear him.

That first day on the grinder, he'd cranked out 450 push-ups together with the other recruits. He'd vomited that night, and the palms of his hands were raw and bleeding, but by God he'd done it. He'd been young and healthy and strong, at his own personal peak.

Matt could hardly remember that young man, so strong and healthy. Gone, together with his career. What was left was a large husk of a man—no, not a man—a *thing*. A thing that couldn't even get itself up off the floor. He burned with humiliation at the knowledge that Nurse Ratched was going to come in and find him on the floor, bare-assed, unable to help himself in any way.

A drop of salty liquid from his face fell to the linoleum with a faint *splat*. He didn't know whether it was sweat or tears, and he didn't care.

CHAPTER THREE

San Luis
Baja Sur, Mexico
March 3

He had died and come back to life. Just like her.

The woman who had once been Charlotte Court watched the big man make his slow way across the beach. Like her, he was a pitiful broken thing. A tall, big-boned man, he was covered in scars and burn marks. He was emaciated, the broad shoulder bones sticking out cruelly, the skin tautly stretched over his big rib cage, the ribs brutally outlined. He limped, each step slow and painful.

She was on her terrace in her own little refuge. She'd arrived three days before and had slept for twenty-four hours straight. Without nightmares for the first time in what felt like forever.

San Luis, Baja Sur. It had found her, she hadn't found it.

She had run out of gas and steam here at this perfect little town. A cheerful jumble of painted wooden shacks and adobe houses by the sea, populated by friendly Mexicans and enough expatriates so she wouldn't stick out like a sore thumb. The Americans were aging hippies, artists, beach bums, retirees. Laid-back and tolerant. No one asked questions, no one showed any curiosity at all about what she was doing there. It was very possible a few were runaways like herself.

San Luis had several small grocery stores with luscious fruits and vegetables, a number of cantinas serving excellent food, and several art supply stores. Everything she needed. Plus miles and miles of uninterrupted sandy beach.

Get out of the country, had been her first thought that morning in Kansas. *Mexico. Or Canada.*

The Midwest was in the grip of the coldest winter since 1931, as all the newspapers trumpeted.

Mexico, definitely. She needed sunshine like she needed air. Her very bones were chilled. Easing through the bottleneck at the border crossing had been excruciating. The border guard had nearly given her a heart attack when he'd spent long minutes scrutinizing Moira Fitzgerald's passport. There'd been another terrorist alert and the guards were spot-checking the cars coming through.

Charlotte could feel the blood oozing into the packing gauze. She had on a white tee shirt she'd bought in a package of ten from a supermarket outside Chicago, to be worn under a cheap scratchy sweater. She'd taken the sweater off without thinking. Soon, the blood would seep through the gauze, staining the tee shirt. The guard would surely notice. Her shoulder throbbed. The blood would be showing any minute now.

Charlotte was used to schooling her face to impassivity so she knew she looked relaxed, even bored, while under the cotton tee shirt her heart was racing. Nervous sweat trickled down her temples but she didn't wipe it away. The guard would just assume she was the usual *gringa* who couldn't deal with the heat.

He was leaning with one arm on the sill of the driver's window, studying her passport, then looking intently at her.

The woman in the passport photo, Charlotte's maid Moira, didn't really look like Charlotte. The face in the passport was round and Moira had light brown hair. Charlotte's face was slender and she was blonde. But police officers were used to women changing their hair color and losing weight. To a not-very-attentive eye, she and Moira shared a look—young, healthy, attractive, well-groomed.

Charlotte couldn't smile to make herself look more like the woman in the photo. Simply couldn't. She didn't know how to anymore. So she sat very still behind the wheel of the SUV, staring straight ahead while the guard decided her future.

"*Guapa*," the guard murmured, handing her the passport back. *Beautiful.* She relaxed the sweaty death grip on the wheel by a fraction.

He was flirting.

Charlotte's breathing slowed, and panic loosened its hold on her brain. She turned her head. She should smile at him, flirt back a little. It would be expected, after all. A harmless little exchange between a man and a woman who would never see each other again.

He was an attractive young man, with glossy black hair, healthy olive-toned skin, and sparkling dark brown eyes.

She couldn't flirt, couldn't smile, couldn't do anything but simply look at him. After a long moment, he stepped back and gave the roof of the car a slap, indicating she was free to go.

She shot out like a bat from hell, heart racing, driving for nine hours straight through the desert until she was so exhausted she found herself weaving across the center line at dusk. She had to stop or she'd kill herself. She turned off at the next town, San Luis, nestled along the rim of a long, curving bay.

And the miracles started happening.

San Luis was lovely at dusk, the dying sun's rosy light gentle and kind to the many ramshackle buildings. As the big red disk of the sun slipped beneath the Pacific, Charlotte stopped in the main square overlooking the beach.

CANTINA FORTUNA, a wooden sign read outside an adobe tavern.

Yes, please, Charlotte thought. *I need all the luck I can get.*

The cantina was run by a boisterous Mexican family, overlooked by the all-knowing black eyes of a short, stout elderly lady. She took one look at Charlotte, and without a word, sat her down on a bench and started bringing food. Tacos, bocadillos, burritos, albondigas.

At first, Charlotte had looked at the heaps of steaming, fragrant food in despair, her stomach clenching.

"*Comes, mujer,*" the elderly lady said gently, and put a fork in her hand. *Eat, girl.* Charlotte dug into the tastiest burrito she'd ever eaten, taking tiny bites at first, uncertain how her stomach would react.

It reacted enthusiastically. She hadn't had a warm, home-cooked meal in what felt like forever, simply grabbing what junk food she could while on the run.

The elderly lady sat across from her, watching her eat, until a family member came up to say, *Ayudame, abuelita. Help me, grandma.* Charlotte's high-school Spanish was suddenly there, in her head, as if it had been waiting all these years to be of help.

The *abuela* came back at regular intervals; she would check Charlotte's progress through the food, grunt with satisfaction, then leave again.

When Charlotte finally sat back, so stuffed she couldn't eat another bite, the *abuela* carted out a huge platter of tropical fruit. Mangos, guavas, pineapples, passion fruit, and papayas. Charlotte could smell the fruit from across the room, sweet and tangy. It all looked so luscious, but her stomach protested.

"Thank you." She looked up at the little old lady. "But I simply can't eat any—"

"For later," the lady replied in surprisingly good English. "Or for breakfast. You're going to have to stay the night in San Luis, *es verdad*?" She nodded at the dark window. "It is night now. The next town is a good hour's drive away. You're too tired to drive. You're going to want a room for the night."

Charlotte hadn't even thought that far ahead, but she realized that the old lady was right. She'd loosened the tight grip on herself that had allowed her to keep going. There was no way she could drive tonight. Already she could feel the waves of exhaustion coming at her and knew she was close to collapse.

"Yes," she murmured. "I'd love a room for the night. If you know of one." The town had seemed too small for a hotel, but maybe there would be a small pension or a bed-and-breakfast.

"How long do you want to stay?" the woman asked.

Charlotte looked around. The place was so warm and welcoming. She felt so at peace here, with the dim sound of the ocean's waves a backdrop to the friendly clatter. Charlotte looked into the old lady's dark, kind eyes and blinked back the tears. She'd been running for so *long*.

"Forever," Charlotte whispered, before she could stop herself.

"*Bueno*," the abuela said crisply. "Get your luggage and follow me."

Charlotte's legs felt like rubber as she got up from the table. Her head swam, and she had to hold on to the back of the chair for a moment. A stout arm around her waist steadied her. Charlotte forced her knees to stiffen. "*Gracias*," she murmured. The old lady nodded and let go.

Charlotte's car was right outside. The old lady didn't blink when all Charlotte got out of the car was a cheap rucksack. It contained some toiletry items she'd bought at a drug store, a nightgown, a clean change of clothes, and the cash she'd taken from her aunt's house in Chicago.

The old lady walked up a flight of stone stairs by the side of the cantina, then turned to the right, along a packed-earth strip too narrow for cars. Another flight of stairs and she was opening the door to a house with a large tiled terrace in front. It looked out over the ocean, a huge, black, heaving expanse on the horizon. The woman flipped a switch by the door, and Charlotte blinked at the gemlike colors.

"Enter, *mujer*," the woman said gently from inside.

Wonderingly, Charlotte stepped in.

The house was small and simply furnished with wooden rustic furniture. A hand loom was in the corner, the fruits of that loom lying on the floor, over the back of the small couch, hanging on the walls as tapestries. All in bright bold Aztec designs. A narrow arch led into another room, a potter's room, with a throw wheel in the center. Bright blue wooden shelves filled with exquisite ceramic plates, each different, covered one entire wall.

In an instant, Charlotte's soul lifted. It was an artist's room, a place of creation. The whole house looked as if its owner had just stepped out for a breath of fresh air.

"This house is lovely. Who lives here?"

"It belonged to a good friend. Janet. She lived here for ten years. She died last month. It's been empty since then. Now you can live here if you want."

The tears were threatening again, but she couldn't allow herself the weakness. The first tear to fall would become a flood. So Charlotte opened her eyes wide to keep the tears at bay, a trick from childhood, and said softly, "I'd love to stay here."

"*De acuerdo.*" The old lady moved briskly around the small house. "The bedroom is through there, there are clean sheets and towels in the closet, and there is still some coffee and supplies in the kitchen. I'll have my grandson bring the fruit over right away so you can have it for breakfast." She put her rough, stubby hand on Charlotte's arm. "*Buenas noches, mujer,*" she said, and was gone.

A few minutes later, a grinning twelve-year-old knocked on her door with the platter of fruit. Charlotte put it on the table. The scent of ripe tropical fruit filled the air.

It wasn't until she'd stripped to take a shower that she realized that she hadn't paid for dinner and that the old lady hadn't mentioned money once.

The shower was primitive, but it worked, and she felt as if she were washing more than the day's grime off as she stood under the lukewarm spray, careful not to soak the bandages on her shoulder she'd changed at a service-station bathroom. Charlotte barely had the strength to put on her nightgown and slip beneath the bright green and red hand-loomed bedspread before falling into the deepest sleep of her life.

She slept for twenty-four hours straight.

For the next two days, Charlotte slept and ate and slept some more. Late in the morning of the third day, she took a little walk around the town. It didn't take long. There might well be tourists later on in the season, but for now, San Luis seemed to be mainly a fisherman's village and an artist's colony. There were as many galleries selling watercolors and ceramic ware as there were food and fish shops.

Charlotte bought basic art supplies, some bread and cheese, and a bright pink hand-knitted sweater.

The little outing exhausted her. She changed the bandages on her shoulder when she got back to the house, fell into bed, and slept for another hour. When she awoke in the early afternoon, she felt weak, but refreshed.

The azure sky outside the bedroom window was streaked with pale pink tendrils. The color was so entrancing, Charlotte was seized with the compulsion to capture it. In her long trek across the country, she'd been pushed to the edge and had barely survived. Painting, drawing, or even stopping for a second to admire beauty had all been beyond her. Now that she was at least temporarily safe and rested, the craving to draw was almost overwhelming.

She opened a bottle of white wine she'd found in the cubbyhole off the kitchen that served as a pantry, and poured herself a glass. Armed with wine, sketchpad, and a box of oil pastels, she went out to the tiled terrace.

And that was when she saw him.

A lost, broken soul. Just like her.

The sun was starting to sink toward the horizon as he made his slow way across the beach on crutches with arm cuffs. His progress across the beach was painful. He leaned on the crutches so heavily they sank deep into the soft sand as he walked, and he had to work to pull them out. He didn't have the strength to pick his feet up, simply shuffling and kicking up puffs of sand with each step.

He was wearing only ragged cutoffs and sandals, unheeding of the chilly evening.

It took the big man forever to cross the beach, one slow, agonizing step at a time. He stood at the water's edge, swaying with fatigue.

He was outlined against the blue of the endless ocean, a huge man, but a pitiful wreck. Charlotte could pick out red, scarred welts on those broad shoulders. He'd had surgery recently, the stitch mark scars clearly outlined on his wide, bony back.

To Charlotte's astonishment, the man toed off his sandals, dropped the crutches and walked toward the sea. She leaned forward, wine, sketchpad, and colors forgotten.

He walked slowly, painfully into the water. The wide beach was empty, little wavelets lapping at the shore.

Charlotte's chest was so tight it hurt to breathe as she sat on the edge of her chair, watching the big wounded man as he waded into the water, a broad dark figure outlined in fiery red as he walked straight into the sun. She stood up, ready to rush toward the water.

Don't do it!

Charlotte sent the fierce thought his way. She knew exactly how much it hurt to live, how deeply desperation could cut. Those scars spoke eloquently of pain, the kind that went deep and lasted a long time, the kind that left scars on the heart and soul, too.

When the water reached the man's chest, Charlotte rushed to the steps that would take her down to the beach.

She was a mediocre swimmer and had barely managed to pass her Red Cross beginners swimming course. The man was big, and, even as thin as he was, he'd be heavy. She had no idea if she could save his life if he was intent on suicide, but she knew she'd try.

To the right was a long wooden quay where the fishermen moored their small boats at night. The boats were still out, the quay was deserted. The man dipped beneath the water, but before Charlotte could panic, he resurfaced. She could see his dark head pulling even with the quay.

Something about the way he moved in the water showed that he could swim, and swim well. His movements were slow but elegant, like her swim instructor's had been.

He swam slowly out past the quay, turned right, then right again toward shore, circling the quay. He wasn't heading out to the open sea to drown himself. She let out her pent-up breath and sat down again.

Charlotte watched, puzzled, as he slowly turned back and rounded the quay once more. And again. And again.

Finally, she realized what he was doing. He was swimming the equivalent of laps, around a recognizable goal. On the tenth trip around the quay, he swam all the way back in to shore.

When he stood, she could see that he was exhausted, face pale, jaws clenched against the pain. He walked slowly out of the water until he reached the sand. To her astonishment, instead of picking up the crutches and limping back into town, he dropped to his knees, then onto his face.

She stood again, ready to rush to his rescue, when she saw his big hands brace against the hard-packed sand. He slowly, slowly lifted his torso up, one painful inch at a time. It was excruciating to watch. His hard, lean muscles quivered with the effort, sweat covering his face though it was a chilly evening. When he let himself back down, he lay facedown in the sand for a good ten minutes, panting. Then he did another push-up.

And another.

And another.

It took him half an hour to do a set of ten push-ups, muscles straining, heartbreakingly slowly.

It was the most valiant thing she'd ever seen.

Charlotte stayed on her terrace and watched over him as the sun slowly sank beneath the sea. Inside, she was cheering him on, as if they were joined. As if his victory in some way meant that she, too, in the end, would prevail. When the last rays of light were draining from the sky, he sank to the sand one final time, lungs bellowing in and out, sweat staining his back and shoulders.

He lifted his head and looked straight up at her. His eyes were dark and piercing, jaw muscles clenched, deep lines of pain and effort bracketing his mouth.

Then, unexpectedly, he grinned in triumph.

Through sudden tears, Charlotte felt her lips tilt upward as she smiled back.

It felt so good to smile again.

CHAPTER FOUR

Warrenton
April 25

After Charlotte escaped, it had taken Haine two full days to calm down. For forty-eight hours he was unable to sleep or to eat. He even found it hard to breathe, to expand his lungs against the tight bands of steel encasing his chest.

No one could tell he was panicking because he'd been moving all the right pieces in all the right places. Everything was in place. All Haine had to do was sit back and wait for his men to come up with a dead Charlotte.

It didn't happen.

Charlotte had no money, and she'd been wounded. *Where the* fuck *has the bitch gone? And how can she stay hidden for two full months?*

Haine was sitting in his original Frank Lloyd Wright chair in front of the fire, frowning at the printout of an e-mail from Nat Lawrence, his man in the Pentagon.

Support for the Proteus Project is starting to wane, Lawrence wrote. Lawrence had handed over several hundred thousand dollars under the table to a colonel and a two-star general in charge of appropriations. It was all set—until the shit had hit the fan.

The corporate structure of Court Industries was under question, and the Pentagon couldn't commit the money necessary for Proteus unless it was certain that the company was solidly behind the project.

This was it.

Haine had one card left to play. He reached for the phone.

San Luis
April 25

Charlotte watched over him every day after that. She took her sketchpad out on the terrace and drew while he slowly and painstakingly put himself back together. She never left her terrace while he was on the beach, keeping him always in sight. In some crazy way, she felt she was keeping him safe.

The second afternoon, he swam fifteen laps and did fifteen push-ups. It took him two and a half hours. When at the end he picked up his crutches, he moved excruciatingly slowly, as if in great pain.

Matt, his name was. Matt Sanders. He was staying with the American owner of a dive shop farther up along the beach. Both of them were former soldiers, Navy men. Matt Sanders had been badly wounded in Afghanistan. He'd received a chestful of medals for bravery, awarded while he was still in a coma. He had spent four months in a VA hospital and had only been released in late February.

Charlotte didn't ask anyone for this information. It came her way in snatches, as she drank coffee and ate *polvorones* at the Cantina Fortuna, bought oranges and lemons from the greengrocer, and an easel and paints from the art supply shop.

Charlotte didn't want to ask anything about the man— Matt. She didn't want to meet him or talk to him. Everything she needed to know, she knew already. He'd been through hell and survived. Just like her.

Without a word, they developed a routine. She would sit and watch over his exercises, silently cheering him on. After a month, he was in better shape than most men and still pushing himself harder. After two months, he was stronger than any athlete she'd ever seen.

One evening, he went for his daily swim carrying a steel spear into the water. Charlotte watched curiously as he swam out toward the horizon. He swam for an hour every day now, far out into the bay, but never so far that she lost sight of his sleek dark head. He came out of the water with three fish spitted on the spear.

The next morning, she found two bream in a wicker basket on her porch.

The morning after, a fistful of wildflowers in an empty soup can.

She brought the flowers to her face and breathed deeply. There were sprigs of rosemary and sage together with the flowers, and the scent was heady. The wild bouquet was lovely, a delicate hint of spring.

Spring.

She'd survived the winter.

Humming, Charlotte spent the entire day painting watercolors of the can of flowers in a shaft of sunlight. She did eight of them, capturing each incarnation of the flowers as the quality of light changed. But she knew which one was for Matt. The first one, luminous with the early-morning light and hopefulness.

After dark, she made the short walk and slipped the watercolor under the dive shop door. She was smiling as she walked back to her house.

Two mornings after that, she found a conch shell outside her door. As big as her hand, rosy and convoluted. Utterly perfect.

She brought it to her ear and listened to the endless ocean pulsing inside.

It was an oil painting this time, and she worked on it for two days straight. When she was finished, she placed it on the table and stood back. It was a small masterpiece, without a doubt the finest thing she'd ever done. The conch shell in the painting glowed against the dark wood of the table, catching all the light in the room, so beautiful it hurt the heart.

That night, the painting wouldn't slip under the door of the dive shop, so Charlotte simply leaned it against the wall beside the door. If Matt or his dive-shop-owner friend found it, fine. If someone stole it, then that someone would have something beautiful.

It didn't really matter.

All she knew was that each quiet, serene day painting and watching over her wounded warrior was a day in which she grew stronger. She didn't know how, and she didn't know when, but one day she'd clear her name and avenge her father's murder.

One day, the weather turned unexpectedly cold. The water was gray and choppy.

Matt had taken to long runs along the beach, at times in full gear and combat boots. Back and forth, back and forth on the packed wet sand. It looked hard and useless, but Charlotte watched over him anyway. If that was what he wanted to do, she would wish him godspeed.

This afternoon, with the sky pewter gray and the water white with squalls, he ran back to the quay and, to Charlotte's utter astonishment, ran straight into the ocean. Fully dressed and with boots on.

She would have sunk like a stone if she had been dressed like that, but he bobbed up and started swimming powerfully.

Roiling black clouds gathered on the horizon, where usually there was a friendly setting sun at this hour. Sheet lightning lit the underside of the dark clouds.

Matt made out for the open sea with strong, regular strokes.

The rumble of thunder echoed throughout the bay. Lightning flickered like a dragon's tongue.

The sky lowered as wisps of fog came in. Charlotte's heart started pounding as she watched Matt's dark head moving steadily out to sea.

It became harder and harder to keep track of him as the waves rose and roiled. She'd been watching him from inside the house—it was too cold to stay out on the terrace—but all of a sudden she lost him. Anxious, Charlotte went out onto the terrace.

Matt was nowhere to be seen. Charlotte scanned the horizon. She'd often lost sight of him for a moment or two, but he had always reappeared almost immediately, regular as clockwork. This time, she searched the sea in vain.

Charlotte grabbed a sweater and hurried down the stone stairs to the beach, scanning the sea desperately. Hurrying across the damp sand, she searched the long, curving beach. Maybe he had swum back, realizing it was insane to stay out in the ocean in this weather.

Both ends of the beach were shrouded in fog. What she could see of the beach was bare and empty. As was the heaving ocean in front of her.

It was absolutely unthinkable that Matt should die. He had come through too much, been far too courageous in putting himself back together, to die now.

She wouldn't stand for it. Matt needed to live.

The waves were increasing in intensity, whitecapped and curling. There was no way she could watch for him on the beach. She needed to be higher up to be able to scan the horizon for that sleek dark head.

Charlotte made for the quay at a run. A few short steps up, then she was sprinting along it, feet pounding. She reached the edge and stood on tiptoe, searching anxiously for any sign of Matt. She wiped her eyes clear of tears. Tears wouldn't help anyone. Certainly not Matt. She needed to be dry-eyed and clearheaded.

He was nowhere to be seen. A bright bolt of lightning streaked down from the sky a few yards away, followed immediately by a clap of thunder so loud it deafened her. Oh, God, there was no way anyone could survive in the sea in this weather.

"Matt! *Matt!*" she screamed, but the rising wind bore her voice away. "*Matt!*"

Charlotte leaned against the weathered wooden railing, searching desperately through the fog and wind-driven ocean spray. She scanned the horizon, again and again, and saw only whitecaps and oily sea.

When she leaned more heavily against the railing, there was a piercing crack of thunder. Only it wasn't thunder.

She fell against the dark hard ocean surface with a sharp slap, which took her breath away. In an instant, she was sinking.

She couldn't see, couldn't breathe. However desperately she clawed, she couldn't seem to rise up, toward the surface and air. Her right leg couldn't move. Her pants were caught on a heavy plank that had broken off the quay and was sinking, taking her with it. However hard she writhed and grasped, she couldn't free herself.

Charlotte fought and fought, but the gelid water froze her fingers, slowed her muscles. She was sinking fast. Her movements stilled when she realized she was going to die in the cold dark waters of the ocean.

It had all been in vain. She would never avenge her father's murder or clear her name. All the pain and effort to escape and make a life for herself until she could return—all useless. It was over. She was going to die at the bottom of the Pacific Ocean. Robert Haine had won, after all.

Her muscles relaxed, and she drifted farther toward the bottom.

Something big, moving fast in the water, caught her eye. Bubbles rose and something hard caught her waist, propelling her upward. She was rising quickly, but it wasn't quickly enough. Her lungs were starved of oxygen. She took in a deep breath in the exact instant she crested the surface.

She choked desperately for air as something moved her quickly through the roiling sea toward shore. Her throat could barely let air in. Her lungs heaved uselessly, trying to pull in air and meeting only the swollen tissues of her throat.

Cold water was replaced by cold air against her skin. It

took her a moment to realize that they'd left the water. She was placed facedown on the cold wet sand, a strong force pressing rhythmically on her rib cage.

Charlotte coughed, feeling the harsh tang of seawater coming up as she vomited. She shivered and breathed shallowly. A hard hand thumped her back, and she retched seawater again.

At the first harsh indrawn breath without choking, she was suddenly airborne, carried away in strong arms. She clung, shaking, tears stinging her eyes. She'd never felt his touch, but she knew instinctively who it was.

"You came," she whispered.

She heard his deep voice for the first time. "Of course, sweetheart."

Lieutenant Matt Sanders's heart nearly stopped for what would have been the second time in his life when he saw his Guardian Angel fall into the freezing wind-whipped ocean.

She wasn't a good swimmer, he knew that. He'd watched her from up on the hill as she waded gingerly into the water. She always stayed close to the shore, paddling around a little where she could touch before getting out. When he'd seen her fall in to the roiling, steel gray frigid water with a heavy plank caught on her pants, he thought his heart would stop once again, just as it had in the Hindu Kush.

He held his Angel high in his arms as he rushed up the wooden plank path leading from the beach to the town. She tightened her arms around his neck, shivering and sodden. "You came," she whispered shakily into his neck.

"Of course, sweetheart." Matt shifted her in his arms,

frowning. She felt nearly weightless. He knew she was slender, but in his arms she felt so delicate, so fragile. She was shaking so much he was afraid she'd break a bone and held her more closely to him. He was sodden, too, but he had a lot more body mass and could radiate some heat to her.

His Guardian Angel lifted a slender arm and pointed toward a flight of stairs. "Over there," she murmured, "and to the right." The words came out slurred as she tried to keep her teeth from chattering.

Matt nodded. He didn't need to be told where she lived. He knew. Just as soon as he could climb stairs in the dark without risking falling flat on his ass, he'd walked over to her little house in the dead of night. He had stood outside her door more nights than he cared to think about. Oh, yeah, he knew where she lived, his sad-eyed beauty.

Charlotte Fitzgerald. A beautiful name for a beautiful woman. She'd been watching over him these past two months, willing him to make it. He'd come back to life thanks to her. He'd always been a hard man, and he'd been determined to come back even harder after dying, but he almost gave up, that first day in San Luis. He'd always been so strong, and his weakness had scared the shit out of him.

Then he'd seen this beautiful, sad woman on a terrace, looking down, and he'd felt waves of support coming from her. As if she knew what he was doing because she'd done it herself. As if she was willing him with everything in her to succeed.

Dying fucked with a man's mind. Matt knew in his head he'd been handed a second chance at life in the hospital, but he hadn't known it deep inside until the woman he'd come to call his Angel watched over him as he put himself back together again, broken piece by broken piece.

"Here," she whispered, as they reached her terrace. Matt made it to her door, bending slightly to open it with her in his arms. Inside, it was as if he'd spent all his life there. Somehow, he knew exactly which couch to put her on—the one with the brightly colored blanket covering the back. He somehow knew where the bathroom was and in a second he was out with a big thick towel.

Matt knelt in front of the couch and started toweling his Angel dry. The wild shivering continued, and he looked her over carefully, worried, as he rubbed her arms. He was a SEAL, a Navy diver. He'd seen hypothermia before—one of the deadliest dangers a soldier could face—and knew it could be fatal fast.

Frowning, Matt held her wrist for a moment, judging pulse rate and temperature. Pulse weak and slow. Core temperature about 92°. In a heavy man, the chances of total recovery were good, but she was slender. Thin people lost body heat faster.

She needed to get out of her wet clothes, right now. Cold wet clothes are a wick for body heat. He had to get her warm and dry. Then he needed to get some hot liquid and sugar into her.

"Charlotte," he said, keeping his voice low. It took her half a minute to respond.

"Yes," she whispered after a moment, as she looked up at him. She didn't question that he knew her name.

She was focused on him. Good. She seemed alert, though slow to react. She was shaking wildly.

"I need to get you out of your clothes. They're wet, and they're keeping your temperature down. It's dangerous for you to stay in them. Let me help you. I'll put the blanket around you and go get some dry clothes for you to put on."

She nodded—more a jerk of the head than an assent—and he bent to grab the bottom of her cotton sweater, tugging upward. She obediently lifted her shaking arms, the wet sleeves falling away from her delicate wrists. Matt pulled her sweater off, turned her slightly to undo her bra. And froze.

He couldn't move; he could barely breathe as he stared at her shoulder.

Hypothermia dulls the senses, slows the mind. Charlotte was only now realizing what had happened, what she'd shown him. He could see her registering his shock.

Her face went white, bone white, even her lips. She shuddered once, hard, and cringed away from him.

They stared at each other, her light gray eyes meeting his dark ones. Her pupils were so dilated with shock only a silver-blue rim remained. A shaking hand covered her mouth.

She looked utterly terrified, as if he were the symbol of death itself. And he was. Humans are essentially animals and like any animal in the wild, she was picking up on the waves of deadly rage coming off him. Death was in the room. Death for whoever had done this to her.

He was a soldier, he knew what that scar was. He'd seen hundreds of them. He had several himself.

Some fucker had shot his Angel, and recently.

CHAPTER FIVE

Warrenton
April 25

His name was a whisper on the wind, mentioned only at midnight, when the lights were low and the whiskey flowed, when ties and tongues were loosened. Haine had heard the stories, different versions of them, in Atlanta, in San Francisco, in Miami.

Depending on who you talked to, the man was a former CIA agent, a former SEAL, an ex-Ranger or that deadliest of Special Forces soldiers, a Delta operator. Depending on who you talked to, he was six-foot-six and blond, five-foot-eight and dark-haired. He was black, he was Hispanic, he was Irish.

He had gravitated to the one place on Earth where he could hide in plain sight what he was—a predator. Uncle Sam spent twelve years training him in the fine art of murder. Uncle Sam was good at that. The US government had actually given him the money, the training, and the weaponry to turn himself into what he'd been born to be—a killing machine.

The thing was, though, that the US government expected

its soldiers to have an off button, and he hadn't been born with one. After a couple of episodes which had to be hushed up, he'd been given a dishonorable discharge because a court-martial would have been too messy.

Haine knew of him only by his nickname—Barrett. Not because it was his name—no one knew the name he was born under—but because of the big .50-caliber sniper rifle he was so good with.

It didn't matter what his name was, only what he could do.

Barrett solved problems. If someone was standing between you and what you wanted, Barrett took care of it for you, for a price.

One night two years ago, in an exclusive club in Dallas, Haine had listened, bored, while a prospective client named Jerry Dunne ranted about his castrating bitch of a wife who was hell-bent on wiping him out financially during a particularly bitter divorce. According to Jerry, Mrs. Jerry had lawyered up with the Devil Incarnate, and Jerry was staring ruin in the face. Then Jerry's voice had lowered dramatically and he'd leaned forward, with the sly stupid expression of the very drunk, to confess that he was calling in Barrett to get rid of his problem.

Haine's heart raced as he casually asked how Barrett could be contacted. Five minutes later, Jerry was snoring in a drunken stupor on the leather banquette of the club, and Haine was tucking a slip of paper with instructions in his pocket.

He pulled that slip out now and moved to his laptop.

Barrett was clever. His clients contacted him by e-mail, over a Web-based e-mail site. The clients and Barrett all had the same user name and password, and they had access to the same e-mail account.

Haine logged on and wrote his message but didn't send it.

An hour later, Barrett logged on, read Haine's message, deleted it, and answered. Haine read it and deleted it. Since the drafts were never sent, no server kept a copy. It was perfect, it never went anywhere, and was utterly untraceable.

How much? Haine had asked at the end.

Four hundred thousand, Barrett wrote. *Two immediately and two upon delivery. Plus expenses.*

Haine lingered over the keyboard, hands trembling. He had stock options, slated to vest in September. Court Industries stock would probably go up to $70 a share after the Proteus Project was approved. He'd make $24 million. *Spend money to make money.* The oldest economic law there was.

Deal, he keyed.

I'll be there by midnight tomorrow, Barrett wrote.

San Luis

Shock shuts down the human nervous system. It drains blood away from the periphery to the vital organs in a last-ditch attempt to protect the center of the human body, the heart and lungs. While in a state of shock, a person is struck blind, deaf, and dumb. Totally helpless and vulnerable, unable to react in any way.

Matt had learned in hard places never to react to surprises. Nothing could shock him, nothing could slow his reaction time.

Matt made sure his men trained for real-life shocks.

They trained with thousands of rounds of live ammo whizzing right over their heads. They were subjected to flashbangs—2 million lumens of light and 180 decibels—designed to stun normal people. Matt worked himself and his men until they could recover in a few seconds from shock.

But his Angel wasn't a warrior, trained to overcome shock in a matter of seconds. She was a woman—a beautiful woman who'd been shot. By a 9-mm caliber weapon, judging from the entry wound.

Crazy as it seemed, it was a battle wound. It hadn't been dressed, except in the clumsiest of ways. The only other kind of gunshot wound like that Matt had ever seen had been in the field, far from a hospital. And even then, a medic had at least stitched up the wound.

One of Matt's former buddies had gone into law enforcement in St. Louis and over several beers had given him a quick course in wound ballistics. Matt could read what had happened to her as clearly as if he'd been there himself.

She'd been very, very lucky. The bullet had caught her in one of the very few places on her slender body that wouldn't shatter a bone, nick an artery, or penetrate a vital organ. Matt had taken a bullet through the fleshy part of his upper arm, but he had a lot of body mass in his biceps and it hadn't done much damage, besides blood loss and pain. If a bullet had caught Charlotte in her biceps, the shock wave would have shattered her humerus, requiring amputation. Without medical attention, it would have turned gangrenous. As it was, the slug had penetrated the soft tissue of her left shoulder.

The firing gun had been farther away than three feet, because there were no signs of stippling, which would mean muzzle contact. She hadn't had medical treatment. Though the wound wasn't infected now, he could tell it had been infected for a long time. There was only one possible reason for a young woman not to seek medical attention for a bullet wound.

His Angel was a woman on the run.

Matt had absolutely no idea what or who she was on the run from, but the running stopped right here, right now. She wouldn't have to run anymore. Someone had hurt her, and badly. No one would ever hurt her, ever again.

She was still in a total state of shock, unable to react. There was no blood in her face or in her hands. At this moment, if she were cut, she wouldn't bleed. The blood had pooled to the core of her body in instant defense.

If he had been her enemy, she would be at his mercy. He wasn't her enemy, but she didn't know that. Couldn't know it. He probably looked like he was, though.

Charlotte was so frightened of him, she was finding it hard to breathe. At the moment, he knew, she wasn't reasoning. She probably didn't even fully realize who he was. To her, he was a large, strong, dangerous man a hand's span from her, a woman who'd known violence at a man's hands.

Matt remained utterly still, moving only his lungs, a trick learned on the battlefield. He put on an expression so neutral it was as if he were alone in the room. He unfocused his eyes and looked past her. He had excellent peripheral vision, but she couldn't know that. All she knew was that he wasn't staring at her.

It worked. A tiny bit of color came back into Charlotte's face and lips. She'd stopped breathing for almost a minute and resumed again, taking in great gasping gulps of air.

She was shaking wildly, part fear, part the effects of the fall into the freezing water.

The physical effects needed dealing with first. She was wet and freezing, and the longer she stayed in that state, the more dangerous it was. Later, he could take care of the psychological effects of her shock, but right this instant, she needed warming up, and fast.

"You need to change your clothes right now, sweet-heart. You need to get into something warm and dry." Matt kept his voice neutral and toneless, as if he were casually discussing the weather. *Nice day today, though it might rain later on. You will die of hypothermia if you don't get out of those cold wet clothes fast before your heart gives out.* He held the brightly colored blanket up between outstretched arms, curving it around her and providing a screen.

Charlotte stared at him for a long moment, white-faced. He hoped to God he wouldn't have to strip her himself. He would if he had to, of course, but in her panicked state of mind, she'd take it as an attack. But after a minute, she jerked her head in a nod and in short stiff movements, she slid her unhooked bra, pants, and panties off under the colorful blanket, wrapping it around her. The clothes lay in a sodden heap at her feet. Matt realized what an act of courage it was for her to strip while he was there in the room with her.

Charlotte's faith in men must have been shattered, yet something, some bond between them had been forged over these past two months, and it somehow held, because she trusted him. Enough at least to strip, even under the blanket.

Matt stepped back, almost imperceptibly, so she would

have the sensation of space. Keeping his face and his movements smooth was one of the hardest things he'd ever done in a lifetime of hard things.

He wanted to howl, he wanted to punch his fist through the wall, he wanted to hurl things and hear them shatter. He wanted to kill him, the man who'd hurt Charlotte, whoever the fucker was.

None of it showed, in any way. He wouldn't let it. It was damned hard masking his feelings, though, and he wasn't used to it. Soldiers didn't have to pretend. He was used to doing what needed to be done without second-guessing himself and without hiding anything from anyone.

"Where can I get some clothes for you?" He could see which room was the bedroom, but having her tell him would give her back some sense of control.

She bit her lip, watching him cautiously. A slim hand emerged from the blanket tightly wound around her. She pointed with a trembling finger. "There." Her voice was low and shaky. Without a backward glance, Matt left.

In her closet was an unusually small collection of clothes for so beautiful a woman. In Matt's experience, the prettier the woman, the more vain she was. But Charlotte seemed to be immune to normal female vanity. The bedroom closet held only basics and few of those, all clean and ironed and neatly hung. He chose wool pants, a light cotton sweater, and a heavy wool sweater to pull over that. She needed layers of clothing. In a drawer, he found a neat pile of clean white underwear. Nothing fancy. No lace, no spandex, no thongs, nothing sexy, just plain white cotton. He chose a bra, panties, and two pairs of warm socks and grabbed another big dry towel from the adjoining bathroom.

She watched him carefully, out of big, wary gray eyes, as he crossed over to her.

She was so friggin' beautiful. That was part of the fascination he felt, but not all of it. He'd bedded good-looking women before—though none with Charlotte's otherworldly beauty—and left the bed without a second thought. There was something so special about her. That air of mysterious remoteness, a woman on a hill that had to be conquered.

Matt had spent his days canvassing San Luis for news of her, though there was precious little to be had. She'd just appeared one day, a few days before his own arrival. Or rather, she just appeared one night, according to Mama Pilar, the woman who ran the Cantina Fortuna with an iron fist. After doling out that small bit of news, Mama Pilar clammed up tight, and what little charm Matt could muster wouldn't work to make her open up. He had the distinct impression Mama Pilar was protecting Charlotte, and now he realized why. Charlotte must have been very sick when she arrived.

Matt hadn't approached her yet, not until he was sure he could be more than a broken, futureless, jobless man. When he arrived in San Luis, he was a wounded wreck of a man, a former naval officer with a small pension, no job, no immediate prospects, not even a healthy body to count on.

So he'd bided his time—and he'd nearly lost her to the stormy sea.

Well, now that he'd found her, he wasn't going to waste another second. He'd been handed a second life, and he wanted Charlotte in it.

She was sitting on the couch, watching him. Matt was glad to see that the shock was diminishing, as was the wild shivering. Luckily, she hadn't spent that long in the water. Once she was dry and he had something hot and sugary in her, she would start recovering.

He didn't know whether she'd recover from his discovering her secret, though. She was perched on the edge of the seat as if poised to make a run, as if she could escape him if he chose to attack. The idea was so ludicrous he would have laughed if there had been anything even remotely funny about the situation.

He had her dry clothes in a neat pile and put them on her lap, making sure he didn't touch her bare skin anywhere. "Here you go."

She covered the clothes with a hand. "Thank you," she said quietly.

"Dry yourself completely and put those on now." If there was one thing Matt knew, it was how to put command into his voice. Charlotte nodded.

He went into the kitchen, taking his time preparing tea, making noises so she'd know he wasn't looking. The kitchen was as tidy as the bedroom. She didn't have much in the way of food supplies, but there was plenty of fresh fruit and vegetables, neatly put away. When he came back in with two steaming mugs of tea, she was dressed, her hair was almost dry, and the worst of the shivering was over.

She was tougher than she looked, his little Angel.

"Here, drink as much as you can, as quickly as you can."

Charlotte took the mug from him, but her hands were still cold and awkward. The mug shook. Matt placed his hand under hers, steadying it. "Drink now."

She sipped, gingerly at first, wincing as the heat filled her mouth. By the time she'd finished the cup, her skin had lost that bone white color that had frightened the hell out of him.

Matt drank his own tea, fortified by a healthy dollop from the bottle of whiskey he'd found on a sideboard.

She'd avoided looking at him, but now she raised her eyes over the cup. Her expression was stark, white lines around that luscious pink mouth. "I can't talk about it," she whispered.

He nodded his head carefully, as if what she'd just said was the most reasonable thing in the world.

"Okay." He kept his face bland, determined not to spook her. She was sitting on the edge of her seat, in flight-or-fight mode. She wasn't going to flee and she wasn't going to fight. He wouldn't let her do either one.

Most people thought soldiers were wild, gung-ho types fueled by rage and hopped up on adrenaline. Not Matt's kind of soldier. Toughness took many forms, and patience was one of them. He'd once slow-crawled for three days past an enemy encampment. An inch an hour with a seventy-pound combat pack on his back, with no food and a sip of water every four hours.

Right now silence and stillness were what were called for, so he didn't talk and he didn't move.

CHAPTER SIX

Warrenton

Barrett arrived exactly at midnight.

The Philippe Starck clock on the mantelpiece had just sounded the hour when the bell buzzed.

Taking a moment to straighten his tie in the pier glass in the foyer, Haine schooled his face to impassivity, then opened the door. Haine studied the man on his doorstep.

No one had gotten it right.

The whispers in the dark of the night had all been of an extraordinary man, a man who looked like a predator, a stone-cold killer. The man standing before him now could have been an accountant or a low-level civil servant. The only hint at something extraordinary was the whipcord resilient thinness—the same build Olympic track runners or Tour de France bike racers had. Other than that, he was ordinary-looking. Normal, mild-mannered guy, you'd think, then you'd turn your back and forget him.

Only his eyes were frightening. Flat and a blue so pale they almost looked white in the dim light.

Haine had thought it would take at least a quarter of an hour to get down to business, starting with "how did you get my name?". But the man didn't bullshit around. He walked in with a battered leather suitcase, sat down on an armchair in front of the fire and waited, expressionless.

This wasn't the normal business world Haine was used to. Haine knew that he was a natural predator himself, which was why he always won in business. But he operated in a tame business environment, where making a killing meant raking in a lot of money, not leaving shattered bone and spilled guts behind.

This was an entirely different arena.

The maid had laid on a fire that had burned brightly all evening, but had died to just a warm welcome glow in the stormy night. Haine brought two cut-crystal glasses of Glenfiddich and handed one to Barrett. Two men sitting in armchairs, one very fit, but other than that unremarkable. Two men sipping whiskey in silence.

"Who?" Barrett asked. It was the first word he'd spoken.

Robert leaned over to the Gio Ponti side table to get two files he'd prepared, then reached forward to hand the first one to Barrett. "This woman here. Her name is Charlotte Court. She's probably using a pseudonym now."

"Time line?"

Haine could remember every single word at the end of Lawrence's e-mail.

General Norton says that if Court Industries isn't in a position to move ahead with the contract by the end of June, the deal is off, and they are going to Mason Technology in South Carolina.

"June 1," he answered. "Her body must be found by the first of June."

He would need at least a month to clear things with the board. With Philip and Charlotte out of the way, legally dead, the board would be easily persuaded to make the deal of a lifetime, and the Pentagon contract could go forward.

Barrett nodded and opened the file. "Better get started, then."

Haine sat and drank whiskey while Barrett carefully studied the file. It was a big one, most of it dating back to two years ago when Charlotte had moved back to Warrenton from Florence, Italy, where she'd been studying art, when Philip was diagnosed with pancreatic cancer.

At the time, Haine had been ecstatic over his good fortune. Philip Court, the owner and majority shareholder of Court Industries, was a weak man, interested more in writing some stupid scholarly book than in the company that had been in his family for almost two hundred years. Philip had given Haine a free hand in running CI. And then it turned out that Philip's daughter—who held a hefty package of shares herself—was a beauty.

Perfect. Haine could marry the daughter and acquire a big share in the company without spending a cent. And he could proceed with *Proteus*, which would make him megarich. He was earning good money as CEO, but nothing like what Proteus would make him.

Haine had never met a woman he couldn't seduce. He knew all the tricks both in and out of bed, and it wasn't until he'd spent months watching Charlotte turn up her nose at him and leave a room as soon as he entered it that he finally admitted to himself that she couldn't be seduced. Not by him, anyway.

But before he'd reluctantly given up on getting Charlotte to marry him, he'd studied her just as hard as he'd ever studied a company prospectus. His file on her was as complete as he could make it.

The photographs had been hard to get. Charlotte was a private woman and had never figured much in the society pages, though as a Court of Court Industries she could have, of course. She could have done anything she wanted to, though apparently all she wanted was to study art.

Many of the photographs had been taken by Robert himself, and in most of them, Charlotte was looking either bored or annoyed. Some of the photographs had been lifted off the Web, posted there by the charities she supported and the three weddings she'd attended as a bridesmaid. In those photographs, she was radiant.

"Looker," Barrett said, flipping through the pages.

"Yes." Haine nearly sighed. Maybe he should have tried harder to seduce Charlotte.

"Lookers have a harder time hiding." Barrett closed the last page and held out his hand.

The second file was entirely press clippings, all from the past two months. Dozens of articles from the first few days, then fewer and fewer as the days went by. Nothing new was being reported, and the Court news cycle ended, to be replaced by other news cycles. The worst winter weather since 1931. A plane full of high-school band players going down over Tampa. A new congressional scandal.

Barrett carefully read every word of every article, sat very still for about five minutes, his pale blue eyes unblinking, then went over every article again.

Haine knew that he was reading the police and newspaper versions of events. They'd constructed a story line with a lot of help and input from him.

Charlotte Court, in the throes of a nervous breakdown

after being a caregiver for two years, had smothered her ailing father with a pillow and been surprised in the act by the Court Industries head of security, Martin Conklin, who had come to pay his respects to Philip Court in the hospital. Charlotte Court nearly cracked Martin Conklin's skull open with the IV tree and shot and killed Imelda Delgado, an ICU nurse, in a desperate attempt to get away.

Charlotte had told Robert Haine, CEO of Court Industries, that enemies were following her and that she had been forced to procure a gun for herself. There were several interviews with Robert Haine, where he blamed himself for not recognizing in time "the enormous pressure Charlotte was under."

Though the police authorities put out an APB, Charlotte Court simply disappeared off the face of the Earth. Friends of Charlotte Court expressed utter shock at the events. They all knew she was under stress due to her father's long, lingering illness, but no one believed that she was capable of killing her father and a nurse.

Haine had even found an expert that the newspapers could quote.

"Long-term caregiver stress has only recently become recognized as an illness in itself," says Norbert Leonard, Rifkin Professor of Psychology at Stanford University, author of a recently published study on caregiver stress: *Close to the Brink: How Caregiver Meltdown Occurs and What You Can Do to Stop It.* "Clearly, Charlotte Court was able to put up a façade of functionality but the inner stresses concomitant with two years of caregiving led to a major breakdown. We call caregivers 'hidden patients.' The Task Force on Caregiver Stress, which I head, has carried out blood tests on four thousand caregivers, and by the second year of caregiving cortisol levels rise by 40 percent. Cortisol is the stress hormone, which interferes with linear thought and impulse control."

Barrett finished his reading and lifted his eyes. "How did she get away?"

It still rankled. Haine worked hard to keep a flush from rising to his face. "Well, you read it. She—ah—grabbed the IV tree and swung it against Martin Conklin's head. There's no way he could have foreseen that. It's right there in the articles—"

"No." Barrett's voice was calm and firm. "Charlotte Court clearly is a resourceful woman. What I meant was—how did she get out of Warrenton?"

"The police checked airport departures, Amtrak departures, and Greyhound departures. So did we."

Barrett looked away, then back. His eyes were unfocused, and he spoke as if to himself, as if in a light trance. His words came out slowly, as if he were reading what he was saying as it scrolled across a screen. "She knows she can't take public transportation. She's too well-known in Warrenton. There was bound to be somebody who would recognize her, either because of who her father was or because of her charity work. And public transportation has an end point. Find out where she got on, and you know where she got off. Or at least you can backtrack to the jumping-off point. So she needs private transport. Somehow she has to get away without being seen by anyone who can report later to the police. One possibility would be a private plane." Those pale blue eyes focused intently on Haine.

At least Haine had an answer to that one. He shook his head. "There was a snowstorm that night. All planes were grounded from 5 P.M. onward, both commercial and private. Martin was coldcocked around 5:15 P.M." Every time he thought of it, Haine shivered with rage. At the bitch herself, but at Conklin, too. He'd failed miserably, and so Haine was forced to deal with this contract killer with the cold pale eyes and was going to have to fork out an indecent amount of money, so he didn't have to do what Conklin should have taken care of in the first place.

Barrett tilted his head back against the high-backed armchair, eyes slightly unfocused again. "Then she has to use a car. An SUV could make it out of town. Roads are cleared before runways."

"Except she didn't own an SUV." Haine ground his teeth. The little bitch had joined an association to lobby for the banning of SUVs the week after he'd plunked down $45,000 for a Tahoe. The little lecture she'd given him about road safety and gas emissions in her cool soft voice still rankled. "She drove a Prius. A blue Prius."

"So how did she get to the hospital?"

"Don't know," Haine shrugged irritably. It was the question everyone asked. It had chilled him at the time to think that his plan wouldn't have worked in any case. Conklin had been on the lookout for a light blue Prius with a specific tag number. In the bad weather, he wouldn't have been able to make out the passengers of passing cars and wouldn't have been looking for Charlotte in another car anyway. "Not a taxi. The police checked. Someone drove her?"

"Maybe." That faraway tone was back again. "Maybe not. Maybe she borrowed someone's car. Then she catches your man killing her father. He's about to shoot Court when she takes him down and escapes, though he gets off a wing shot."

"Yes," Haine gritted. A small sun of humiliation and resentment burned brightly in his chest. Sitting still under that calm, flat scrutiny was unsettling. He got up to put more wood on the fire.

"So she gets in the car she came in and goes…to the police," Barrett continued softly. "That's the logical step. Why doesn't she take it? Why not go to the police and report what she's seen? Because"—he closed his eyes again—"because you're there already. Maybe with several of your men, already talking to the police chief. Maybe she recognizes some of your men. They're armed, and she knows they're dangerous. She understands what's happening. So she goes home, and you have men posted there, too." He opened his eyes. It hadn't been a question.

Haine nodded. Barrett's reading of what happened was eerie. It was as if he'd been there and had seen what went down.

"She's wounded, bleeding, on the run. She needs to get out of town." Barrett was silent for almost five minutes, silently drumming his fingers on the armchair. The fire against the far wall crackled. Haine jumped when a log crumbled into a pile of ash, shooting sparks up the flue. Barrett didn't move a muscle. If his eyes hadn't been open, Haine could have mistaken him for dead.

"I need to get inside the house. I need to get inside her head, find out what she likes and what she doesn't like. What kind of resources she'll have, where she might be headed. I assume that won't be a problem?" He turned that flat pale gaze to Robert.

Pending Charlotte's reappearance, Court Mansion was closed off by the police. But the chief wasn't about to deny him a small favor.

Robert nodded. "Yes, I can get the keys. We can go over there whenever you want."

"Right now. I'll need a couple of hours to go through her things. When I know her, I'll know where to find her."

"I can drive you over right now, if you want."

"I'll take my own car. Now, let's talk terms."

"Okay." Haine sat up straighter. "I need a dead Charlotte Court found and identified by June 1. It has to look like an accident, the cause of death something that will hold up as an accident even with an autopsy. Is that clear?"

"Perfectly." Barrett nodded his head once, gravely. "So. These are my terms: $200,000 now and $200,000 upon completion of the mission. Plus expenses. And since you're not giving me much time, expenses will pile up. It won't come cheap." He looked hard at Haine.

Shit.

Haine was putting himself entirely in this man's hands. He nodded.

Barrett rose smoothly, with the grace of an athlete. "You've just bought yourself a very beautiful corpse, Mr. Haine."

San Luis

Charlotte was so cold. It felt as if she would never be warm again.

Matt had made her change into warm, dry clothes and

drink hot tea with so much sugar in it, it was a miracle she didn't plunge into a diabetic coma on the spot. It all worked to bring her head back from the brink, though her body wasn't warming up yet. The deep, convulsive shivering had stopped, but tremors still shook her. She was still cold inside, a deep, painful chill, as if her heart had been packed in ice.

He knew.

Of course he knew. Those dark eyes were intelligent, observant. He'd put it all together. Charlotte had watched him do it, heart beating wildly in her chest, wondering if she was going to have to run for it again.

Somehow, though, she knew she could never escape from Matt. It had been bad enough running away from Haine and his goons. Matt was an entirely different animal. Quiet, strong, and observant, every inch a warrior. How could she possibly be a match for him?

Martin Conklin, Robert's preposterous head of security, had always posed as a real tough guy, letting everyone know he was a former soldier.

Conklin must have seen *Patton* a gazillion times because he affected a George C. Scott swagger. All that was missing was an ivory-handled revolver. His men, too, affected that hard-as-nails security-staff look, running around with close-cropped hair shaved to the skull along the sides, pitch-black Matrix sunglasses, and curly little wires running from the earpiece down into the collar. They spoke into their wrists in a sort of military jargon, and tended to say things like, "Roger that" or "Ten-four."

Charlotte thought they were ludicrous, all of them. She also thought it an utter waste of company money keeping such a large contingent of security staff. Her father had, too. While he had still been capable of taking an interest in the company, he had spoken to Robert a number of times about it.

She had been right in her assessment of the idiots. The security staff couldn't have been that good because, in the end, she'd managed to escape from both Martin Conklin and his men.

She could never escape from Matt Sanders if he chose to attack her. He didn't have to strut his toughness. He was the real deal. She'd seen his toughness and strength for herself. It was real, and it wasn't just physical, it was mental and spiritual as well, bone deep. The man was formidable in every way.

He was watching her calmly, not moving a muscle. His dark eyes were alive, aware. If it weren't for that, she could almost think him a wax figure. She had the impression he could see right inside her head. There wasn't anything she could do, nowhere to hide, nowhere to run. Matt Sanders would know if she was planning on bolting as soon as she knew it herself and would already have taken steps to stop her.

Right now, though, he was taking pains to be utterly unthreatening. He was so still he hardly seemed to be breathing. Yet, when he'd seen her scar, something frightening had come into his dark eyes, something feral and uncontrolled.

A bullet wound, clearly without medical care, could only mean one thing. She was a renegade, on the run.

"I can't talk about it," she said again. "There's nothing I can say." The words came out in a rush, impossible to stop, the stark truth. She covered her mouth with her hands, shaking, wondering what was going to happen next. They stared at each other wordlessly. Charlotte could feel the blood pounding in her veins, the adrenaline pumping, her hands and feet prickling. Her body was uselessly preparing to flee, though there was no place to escape to.

A full minute went by, while her heart thumped madly in her chest, so hard it actually hurt. Matt's eyes fell to where a vein throbbed in her neck, then rose again to meet her gaze. He nodded once, gravely, accepting what she was saying.

Charlotte drew in a deep breath, only then realizing she hadn't breathed for almost a whole minute. She felt as if her life hung in the balance.

Matt Sanders had been a military officer, which wasn't far from being a law enforcement officer. For all she knew, if he discovered her identity, he would hand her over to the American authorities.

No, she could never tell him who she was.

"Is he alive?" he asked, his deep voice quiet.

"Alive?" Charlotte's heart had finally stopped thudding so hard. She was able to breathe normally again. "Who?"

"The man who shot you." The stark words hung there in the silent room.

Charlotte met his eyes, so dark and so compelling. She couldn't begin to imagine what he was thinking.

For an instant, the space of a breath, Charlotte was fiercely tempted to tell him the truth. Simply lay her burden down. Put the whole mess into those large, capable-looking hands. It was so incredibly tempting. For a moment, the desire to ease her huge burden off her shoulders and share it with another human being was so fierce she had to bite her lips to keep from spilling it out.

Telling the truth could be fatal, and yet she couldn't lie

to him. She nodded once, jerkily. "Yes," she whispered, her voice trembling. "He's alive."

The grooves around his mouth deepened. His big fists clenched once, hard, and relaxed. It was the only movement he made. He became, if possible, even more still. "No one will ever hurt you again, Charlotte. You have my word on it. I'm going to sit next to you now. Is that all right?"

Oh God. Matt Sanders seemed to exert a magnetic field around him from where he was, a few feet away. If he sat down next to her, she'd fall right into it. Still, she hadn't the nerve to deny him anything.

"Okay," she whispered.

He sat down on the couch, far enough away so that they wouldn't touch. His heavy weight made the small, cheap couch's cushions dip deeply. Even sitting far enough away that she'd have to reach out for him intentionally to touch him, she could feel his body heat. He'd been in that freezing water, too, and his clothes were still slightly damp, but somehow his big body managed to generate heat.

"Give me your hand." Startled, Charlotte looked down at his outstretched hand. It was large, strong, tanned, rough-skinned. He didn't say anything else, just sat there calmly, large hand turned palm upward.

His big hand was rock-steady, unmoving. An almost unbearable temptation.

How long had it been since she'd felt a man's touch? It had been over two years since she'd even been out on a date.

So long. So very long.

The last male hand Charlotte had held had been her father's. Her father's hand had been bony, emaciated, with crepelike skin and dark age spots on the back. Toward the end they'd been deeply mottled with the bruises from the IV lines.

Matt's hand was nothing like her father's. It promised a strength she desperately needed, warmth and reassurance.

Touching this man was crazy, but she suddenly craved his touch more than anything else in the world. She had seen with her own eyes how strong and powerful he was. She desperately wanted a connection to all that strength and power.

Charlotte pulled her hand out from under the blanket, watching his eyes. His face was expressionless as he looked at her. He made no move toward her, just waited patiently, large hand open to receive hers.

Slowly, as if she were pushing her way through something much heavier than air, through a dense compound of time and desperation and fear, Charlotte reached a trembling hand out to him. A breath away from touching him, she stopped, fingers trembling. Matt waited, unmoving. He looked as if he could wait forever. Finally, Charlotte laid her hand in his, tentatively, shaking inside. From cold. From exhaustion. From fear.

He looked down at their two hands. The contrast in color and size was so great it was shocking. His hand was almost double the size of hers and much darker in color. It was so different in its size and shape and texture, it was almost as if the two hands belonged to two different species. He raised his eyes from their joined hands to meet her gaze. Slowly, so she had time to protest or remove her hand if she didn't want this, his hand curled up as his other hand covered hers in a warm, gentle clasp.

His grip was so warm it felt like a painless fire. The warmth made her cold hand tingle. She'd been so tense it had hurt to breathe, but that tight steel band around her chest loosened slightly. She took a deep shuddering breath, filling her lungs completely for the first time since the fall into the water.

There was a tiny ball of warmth that was her hand encased in his. It wasn't enough to dissipate the icy chill in her bones but it was enough to remind her system of the idea of warmth. Being frozen with shock—from the spill in the ocean and from the exposure of her terrible secret—had numbed her feelings. But with his warm touch, the icy grip of shock loosened, and with it her self-control. Despite her best efforts, a lone tear tracked down her cheek.

Something—some strong expression—crossed his face. His jaw muscles jumped.

"Ah, shit," he said, the deep voice soft and low, and reached over to pick her up. He didn't ask permission, and he didn't grab at her. He just lifted her up as if she were weightless and a second later she was sitting on his lap, his arms around her. He wrapped the colorful blanket around her. She trembled at his touch.

"No, I can't—you—" She couldn't even get the words out, she was shaking so hard, trying to hold back the tears.

Crying wouldn't help in any way. Crying wouldn't bring her father back. Crying wouldn't get her life back. Crying wouldn't help her figure out how to prove her innocence.

Charlotte knew all that, knew it deep in her bones, but the double shock of almost dying, and now being encased in Matt Sanders's warm, strong arms acted on her like a whiplash, and the tears were lying in wait, in a hot ball in her chest.

He eased her head down on his shoulder with a gentle

push and stroked her still-wet hair away from her face. Charlotte shook, the hot ball rising in her throat.

"It's okay." His voice was so deep she could feel the vibration of his words in his chest.

She shook her head sharply. *No*. No, it wasn't okay. Maybe it would never be okay again.

He smelled of the sea, of musk and man. Though his clothes were still slightly clammy, she could feel his body heat beneath the fabric. His skin warmed hers wherever they touched. Her forehead lay against his neck, right hand braced just above his heart. The beat was strong and slow, the beat of an athlete.

She felt warm and safe for the first time since that terrible night.

He shifted her slightly in his arms to pull the warm blanket around her more tightly, and her hip came up against a steel rod. It took her a full minute to realize that it was his penis. His erect penis. His very *big* erect penis. Startled, Charlotte lifted her head from his shoulder and met his eyes. The corner of his mouth lifted very slightly.

"It's okay," he repeated.

She held herself very still, barely able to move in the blanket encasing her like a cocoon. She shifted again, her hip rolling over him, and felt the ripple as his penis reacted to her touch. Even through her clothes and his, she could feel him lengthening.

A wave of pure heat rose from her loins in response. The heat took her totally by surprise. It had been so long since she'd felt anything like sexual heat, it took her a moment or two to even recognize it. It was like a little sun blooming in her belly, the warmth spreading instantly outwards. Every slight movement she made affected him, she could feel it. When he moved to tighten his arms around her, his penis surged against her hip.

He wasn't making demands, or pushing up against her. He made the situation a simple one—he was aroused but wasn't going to do anything about it.

She wasn't going to, either. The flash of heat was like a long-ago reminiscence of when she had been a normal young woman. There wasn't anything remotely normal about her life now. She couldn't even remember how you were supposed to respond to something like this. Even if she wanted to do something, act on the unexpected, unwelcome heat, she couldn't.

Charlotte was beyond a normal life. Beyond the healthy response of a woman to an attractive man. Dating, courtship, sex. All of that seemed like something people on another planet might do, not her.

Maybe on Earth, a man and a woman could meet and act on a strong tug, but not where she lived. Two months ago, Charlotte had moved to a planet of her own, spinning in deepest space. Pluto, maybe. Big and dark and silent and airless.

It was warm on her planet now, though. In her dry clothes, inside the blanket, surrounded by an immense amount of hard, warm man, she could feel muscles relaxing that had been tense for over two months. Charlotte shifted until she was turned more fully into his arms, laid her head down on that massive shoulder, and closed her eyes.

CHAPTER SEVEN

Warrenton

Three thousand miles away, the man known as Barrett emerged from Robert Haine's luxury condo. Head down, he breathed in the frigid night air, longing for summer. Soon, very soon, he'd be warmed by the Caribbean sun. If Barrett never saw upstate New York again in his lifetime, he'd be happy.

Barrett had excellent peripheral vision. He could see the CCTV surveillance cameras with motion-detector software swivel to follow his progress, but he knew how to hide his face for surveillance cameras. Haine thought he was so impregnable with his fancy security equipment. The fucker had no idea. Barrett's biggest weapon right now wasn't his Barrett sniper rifle, his MC5, or the four pounds of Semtex, all of which he had back in his hotel room, in hidden compartments in his luggage.

No, Barrett's secret weapon was right there in his shirt pocket, in plain sight—a voice-activated microbar digital recorder with voice-recognition software disguised as an MP3 player. He'd digitally remaster the recording back in the hotel with his laptop, disguising his own voice and keeping Haine's voice intact. Together with the micro-camera in his third shirt button, it was enough to take to any DA in the country and get an indictment in five minutes.

Barrett smiled as he drove sedately away, refraining from giving a one-finger salute to the surveillance cameras.

Four hundred K for a hit made him probably the best-paid assassin in America. The four hundred K topped up his bank account very nicely and put him right over the top of his self-set goal of $5 million in savings.

But Haine's contribution to Barrett's personal pension plan didn't stop there.

Barrett was going to make a neat and tidy little package of evidence and put it in the vault of a bank just around the corner from Feeb Headquarters in DC with instructions to forward it to the FBI should something happen to him. And let Haine know he had it.

Oh, yes, Haine would fund his retirement nicely. Barrett would make sure Haine won his big Pentagon contract, because if he did, Barrett figured Haine would be good for a million a year, easy.

Barrett had twenty little packages, just like this one.

Much better than any 401(k).

Now all he had to do was find this woman, Charlotte Court. That was the hard part. Killing her would be the easy part.

San Luis

She fell asleep like a child, between one breath and the next. Matt had never been around kids and had no brothers or sisters or even cousins to give him secondhand experience, but his married buddies told him that's what happened. When kids ran out of steam, they dropped to sleep in a second, sometimes right in their tracks.

Charlotte did just that, her muscles relaxing in an instant.

Matt felt the pulse at her wrist. It was slow, but the fact that he could feel it was a good sign. Below a body temperature of 91° the radial pulse disappears. He judged her temperature to be about 95°. In an hour's time it would be 96 and by morning her skin temperature would be back up to 98, with a core temperature of 98.6. He had every intention of being there in the morning to make sure of it.

She dropped off to sleep like a child because she was shocked and exhausted, but also because she knew she was safe. She was a woman who'd been in danger and that fired up all the senses. Animals who were prey had keener senses than the predators; they had to.

Charlotte had been in combat mode, all senses firing all the time. Judging by the state of the undressed wound, she'd been in combat mode for about two months now. Battle-hardened warriors who trained daily for the stress of combat found it hard to sustain two straight months of imminent danger and vigilance without bleeding off the stress in some way, let alone a young woman who couldn't have trained for it.

He knew exactly how she'd survived. By sleeping lightly, if at all. By being mindful of her surroundings at all times, ready to take flight at the first untoward movement. By keeping her adrenaline levels dangerously high, so high that the by-product of adrenaline, cortisol, would eventually ruin her kidneys.

His men were self-selected to be able to handle the

worst life could throw at them. Most actually thrived in dangerous situations.

Few people outside Special Forces realized that with the kind of men the armed forces recruited, keeping them on an adrenaline high wasn't difficult. Men like SEALs were hardwired for the hunt. They thrived under stress, with adrenaline-tolerance levels that would kill any other kind of man. What was hard was turning them off.

Humans fighting for their lives are reduced to animals, with the swift instincts of the wild. But few animals can survive that kind of stress without the ability to switch off when they can. The part of Charlotte's brain that was older than conscious thought was telling her she was safe with him. Falling asleep in his arms was her body telling him she trusted him.

I can't talk about it.

Her head didn't trust him though, not yet.

Eventually it would. He'd make sure of it. The promise he'd made to her was real—as long as he was alive to draw a breath, no man would ever hurt her again.

To keep that promise, he needed to know what the danger was, so he could guard against it. Her head would catch up with her body sometime soon, and she'd tell him everything. Her body would tell him when that happened before she knew it herself. Body language was infinitely easier to understand than the convoluted human brain. Particularly the female brain, which he'd never figured out.

His body was talking to him, too. Loud and clear. Couldn't be louder, couldn't be clearer. He wanted this woman, with every cell of his body. The danger she was in just made it come more sharply into focus.

Matt looked down at the woman in his arms.

She is so fucking beautiful.

Her hair was matted, lying in clumps that were still slightly wet with the ocean's salt water, looking darker than usual because of the damp. Matt knew that once it dried, her hair would return to the silvery platinum that looked like moonlight in the sun.

She was still very pale, though not that terrifying bloodless wax color she'd had when he'd fished her out of the water. Her soft lips were slightly rosy now, not a cyanotic blue. The cartilage of the nostrils was no longer pinched and transparent. For a heart-stopping, horrifying moment on the sand, he'd thought she'd died. She looked almost normal now, tired and wrung out, to be sure, but normal.

Matt studied her features, though he didn't really need to. By now her face was hardwired into his brain, he'd thought and dreamed of her so much.

He'd never been this close to her before, able simply to look his fill.

He'd never held such a beautiful woman in his arms. Anyone who looked like that was in the movies or already married, usually to some rich guy who could afford the best. A woman like Charlotte was completely unavailable to someone like him.

Most women had physical flaws; they were only human, after all. Makeup and hair covered a lot of defects. Once a woman was even just a little over on the pretty side of the scale from absolute dog to gorgeous, she used those mysterious arts women were somehow born with to fluster the eye and make you think she was even more beautiful than she was. He'd woken up many a time next to a woman who'd seemed like a looker in the darkness of a bar simply because she'd acted like one, only to find out in the morning that the looks were tricks of light and makeup and behavior.

No tricks here, none at all. Charlotte didn't have any makeup on and from what he'd seen in her bathroom, didn't even seem to own any except a lone tube of lipstick. She didn't dress to allure, and she wasn't a flirt.

Her beauty was all hers: fine features, good bones, perfect skin. Nothing short of death could wipe it out.

Death. Matt frowned. She'd come pretty close to it twice. She'd have drowned this afternoon if he hadn't got to her in time. And the bullet wound—pure blind luck there. An inch to the left and it would have shattered her shoulder bone, an inch to the right would have nicked the aorta, causing her to bleed out in about four minutes. Any lower, and the bullet could have pierced the heart, which would have dropped her stone dead.

Like him, she'd cheated death.

If she had died of her bullet wound, had been in the cold ground for months, would he even be here today?

Maybe not.

Matt thought about it long and hard in the quiet of the night, while she lay in his arms, fast asleep, breathing so lightly the blanket didn't move.

He had been so sick at heart the day he'd arrived in San Luis. He hadn't died in Afghanistan, and he hadn't died in the hospital. He'd fought to live with every cell of his being, with every painful breath he took. He'd fought death as if it were his personal enemy, throwing everything he had at it, unwilling to concede defeat.

But that day, the day he'd arrived in San Luis, he'd seriously considered swimming out to sea, as far as his strength could carry him, knowing he could have no hope of swimming back. He loved the ocean, always had, and it was fitting that he would simply let the ocean take him. For the first time in his life Matt had contemplated suicide that day. Just ending it. It wouldn't have been hard at all.

Not even in the hospital had Matt lost hope. Every day had brought a small, minor victory, one step at a time away from death until he was finally released.

Being away from the hospital environment for the first time had scared the shit out of him. Hospitals were prosthetic environments, designed to make up for what the human body had lost. Outside the hospital, Matt finally realized how far he still had to go to be a functioning man, if he ever made it back.

An old teammate, Lenny Cortes, had repeatedly invited him to stay in San Luis, Baja Sur, where Lenny ran a diving shop. Sunshine, clean air, the ocean. Lenny'd promised all three—exactly what Matt needed.

Then he encountered his first obstacle. For the first time in his life, getting somewhere was a problem. All his life, if Matt needed to go somewhere, he'd simply go. No question. Into the jungle, to the Arctic, across a desert, he could do it. He could drive just about anything that had wheels, including tanks. He could fly anything smaller than a 707, including helos. If there wasn't motorized transport available, he'd walk if he had to. Matt had never doubted his ability to do anything he wanted to do, or go anywhere he wanted to go.

And yet after his release, there he was, unable to get his miserable carcass from the VA hospital in Leavenworth, Kansas to Baja, California. Lenny, who'd lost his spleen and his hearing in one ear when a mine blew up, knew his problem. Matt hadn't had to say anything at all. Lenny'd sent a plane ticket to San Diego and had come to pick him up at the airport and driven him down the same day.

Matt had arrived utterly exhausted, completely drained from the plane trip and car ride. He'd been strong all his life and had no anchor to hold on to in this new life as a weak man. He didn't recognize himself, and he didn't recognize this new world he was in.

Even crossing the beach to get to the water that first afternoon had been an enormous challenge. He'd almost called it quits then and there.

Wading into the ocean, the temptation just to keep going, to swim as far out to sea as his strength would take him, knowing he wouldn't be able to make it back, had been ferocious. And that had been when he'd seen her— his Angel.

A beautiful woman on a terrace above the beach, watching him. There was sadness and knowledge in her gaze, as if she understood everything going through his head. Which was crazy. Even *he* didn't understand everything going through his head. But there had been an unmistakable connection, magnetic waves almost visible in their strength, connecting them.

In the ocean, when he'd been tempted just to keep going, he stopped and trod water for a moment, looking behind him. She'd been poised with her hand on the railing, ready to rush to his rescue. He was as certain of that as he was of the fact that he needed to expand his lungs to breathe. The mysterious beauty was totally prepared to run across the beach, throw herself into the water, and do her damnedest to save a life he was contemplating throwing away.

Later, the first time he watched her in the water, the

hairs on the back of his neck rose when he realized she could barely swim. She weighed a hundred pounds less than he did. If he'd given in to weakness and sought his own death, she'd have died trying to rescue him.

Beautiful and valiant.

Matt looked down at the woman in his arms. Even in her sleep, she looked troubled. She *was* trouble, every gorgeous inch of her. She carried trouble about her like a shroud. Now he was beginning to understand that aura of sadness she carried with her like smoke.

He didn't know the details of her story, but he didn't have to because the basics were so clear. Someone had tried to kill her. If she was here in San Luis, she was in hiding. Which meant someone was still after her, still trying to kill her.

She was walking, talking trouble.

Matt had never backed down from trouble in his life.

Charlotte stirred in his arms. She frowned and turned her face more tightly into his shoulder, small breasts rubbing against him. Matt clenched his jaws, because the urge to touch her, caress her, was almost overwhelming.

Much as he loved holding her, Charlotte would be more comfortable in her own bed. Matt rose with her in his arms and carried her into the bedroom. Bending to put her on the simple queen-size bed, his arms didn't want to let go. She had one slender hand on his arm, and it took a real effort to lift away from it.

He tucked her arms under the blanket and went out into the living room. He picked up the phone, spoke quietly to Lenny, then hung up. Lenny would be quick. Matt could have gone himself up to the small apartment behind the dive shop he shared with Lenny to pack his own bag, but he was reluctant to leave Charlotte even for a minute. Suppose she woke up suddenly and found herself alone? She'd almost died that afternoon. She'd be weak, disoriented. Frightened.

No, better to ask Lenny for a favor and put up with Lenny's knowing looks. Lenny'd find out soon enough anyway that he was going to spend the night, and the night after that. Everyone would. San Luis's population was broad-minded and tolerant, but that didn't stop everyone from knowing everyone else's business if they wanted to.

Matt had every intention of moving into this house and moving into her life.

While waiting for Lenny, Matt took a good look around. He'd absorbed a lot about the room when he'd carried Charlotte in, but now that he didn't have worry for her eating up the forefront of his brain, he had a chance to wander around the big room and really look.

He'd known she was talented by the lovely watercolor and stunning oil painting of the conch shell she'd given him. Waking up that morning to find the watercolor slipped under the door had blown him away. It could only have come from one person, and he'd known it the instant he held it in his hands. The delicacy could only be hers. And the conch shell—when Matt saw the small exquisite canvas outside the door, he'd been humbled by the gift. It hung over his cot in the place the Mexicans often hung crucifixes.

He could see now that Charlotte was an incredibly gifted artist. Her house was filled to the rafters with sketches, watercolors, pastels, and oils on easels.

Matt walked slowly over to a big portrait on an easel and stood looking at it. For an instant he tunnel-visioned, just like in combat. The painting was that compelling.

The world shrank to this flat square of canvas—a life-size portrait of a white-haired elderly man sitting erect in a straight-backed chair, wearing an old, tattered jacket. The old man stared back at him, as alive as if he were about to start speaking. He'd be an interesting old coot, too. The refined, wrinkled face was lively with wit and intelligence. The white hair had once been a platinum blond, the irises were gray-blue, and the features were a male replica of Charlotte's. Her father? Grandfather? An uncle?

Behind the old gentleman, in intriguing shadows, was a bookcase filled with books. Books were piled haphazardly on a shadowy table by the chair. The man's right elbow rested on another pile. The portrait was so alive Matt felt as if he knew this man, could see inside his soul. Matt was sure the man had a sense of humor. He loved books. He wasn't stuffy—the messiness of the library and the old jacket told their own tale.

Matt was thinking about him, wondering who he might be, when he heard a discreet knock on the front door.

Lenny stood on the front door stoop, all six-four of him, rain dripping off his hooded slicker. Matt stepped back as Lenny entered.

"Here you go, man," Lenny said, handing him his kit. Matt knew it would have clean sweats, old sweats doubling as pajamas, jeans, a turtleneck sweater, clean underwear, dry shoes, soap, his razor, and his Glock 19, because Matt hated being unarmed. Just as he'd requested. Lenny had always been good at following orders. "Really shitty weather."

This from a teammate who'd swum under the Arctic with him, who'd sat out a tropical monsoon for two days under a banyan tree, unmoving, waiting for a chance to take out a terrorist.

"Thanks." Matt clapped him on the back, subtly angling him back out the door, but it wasn't working. Lenny turned himself into a wall, a big flesh-and-bone wall. He pushed back his hood and looked around curiously. "Wow, lady's a real artist."

"You're dripping." Matt tried subtlety. You never knew.

"Hey, no prob, dude." Lenny took the slicker off and hooked it over the doorknob, looking around with interest, showing every sign of wanting to stay.

So . . . subtlety wasn't going to work.

Matt rolled his eyes. "Don't you have somewhere you have to be?"

"Nope." Lenny sounded cheerful as he snagged an apple from a bowl of fruit. "Dude. Weather's too bad for anyone to want to scuba dive or hire a boat. You know that. Just look out the window."

Yes, Matt knew that. He also knew that he wanted Lenny gone. "You get everything?"

Lenny didn't answer. Of course he'd gotten everything. Matt knew it was a dumb question.

Lenny met his eyes. "What's going on?"

Matt's jaws clenched. "She almost drowned this afternoon."

Lenny didn't even ask who "she" was. Lenny's light blue eyes bore into his. "Hey, bad karma, man. But why are you still here?"

"She risked hypothermia. I'm staying here to make sure she's all right."

"Uh-huh." Lenny was making the rounds of the room, looking at each and every work of art on the walls and on tables. "The fact that you're dying to get into her pants has nothing to do with it, right?"

"Lenny..." Matt growled.

"Hey, man." Lenny raised his eyebrows. "Don't shoot the messenger. "

"The messenger should go home. Now."

Lenny splayed a large hand over his heart and looked wounded. "Gee, do you mean you don't want me here?"

"Bingo."

"Tough shit," Lenny said cheerfully and continued walking around, fingering watercolors, touching the pastels and color palette, frowning over the oil portrait. Matt gritted his teeth, waiting it out.

"Hey." Lenny's big hand hovered over a sketch. "That's Pepe, Mama Pilar's grandson. You know—that cute kid that always gets into trouble?"

Matt walked over and looked down at the big sheet of drawing paper. "Yeah, that's Pepe all right."

The kid *was* cute, but in the time Matt had been in San Luis, Pepe had managed to break a hornet's nest with his beach shovel, get his head stuck between the bars of the fence surrounding the Cantina Fortuna, requiring two welders to free him, and get lost a few weeks ago. The entire town had turned out to look for him, the cries of "Pepe! Pepe!" echoing off the adobe walls. He'd finally been found asleep under a car with a melted ice-cream cone beside him.

The quick sketch was perfect, somehow managing to show Pepe in perpetual motion, as he was in life. Matt couldn't figure out how Charlotte had done it, how she managed to catch on paper the little scamp, but there he was. There was no way any human being on the face of the Earth with half a heart could look at the sketch and not smile. Next to the sketch was another one, just a few strokes, but he could tell it would be a portrait of Mama Pilar.

"Wow, that's talent." Lenny shook his head, bit the last shred off the core of the apple and tossed it one-handed into the wastepaper basket. "Picasso-ette." He chuckled at his own wit, the smell of beer and tequila coming off him.

Matt loved Lenny like a brother, but Lenny scared him shitless. Lenny was what he would become if he wasn't careful. When he'd been forced to leave the Teams, it was as if Lenny stopped living. He'd moved down to Baja Sur, opened his shop, and simply drifted through his days skippering and renting scuba equipment. He had no intention of expanding or of adding to the business. From what Matt could see, Lenny had no plans beyond the next beer.

Matt was by nature intensely mission-driven. He had to have clear goals he believed in and a plan to achieve them. He needed that like he needed air and water.

All SpecOps warriors were hardwired the same way he was. Or so he thought. You don't get through the training, you certainly don't get through Hell Week, without wanting it with every atom of your being, without focusing on that one goal to the exclusion of all else. That kind of drive carried over into life. Matt didn't know what the hell he was going to do with his life once he'd completely healed, but it wouldn't be what Lenny was doing. Lenny ran his dive shop and boat rental agency with a light hand, doing the least work possible merely to survive economically. He didn't even advertise, relying on satisfied customers and word of mouth to get by.

Matt didn't want to just get by, spending days soaking

up the Baja sun, drinking beer, and skippering boats so rich guys could do a little trophy fishing. He didn't want to drift. He wanted to *do*. But do what?

He shook his head irritably at the thoughts circling his head. Well, right now his mission was to get rid of Lenny, check on Charlotte, finally take a shower and change, check on Charlotte, dig up something to eat, check on Charlotte, and get some shut-eye—after having checked on Charlotte.

Lenny was engrossed in a small oil painting on a wood panel. Matt had noticed it, too. Sunrise painting the *Pintados*—the rocky outcroppings a mile down—a pearly rose. He'd admired the scene himself many times during his early-morning swims.

Charlotte had captured the mood of the ocean perfectly. Matt had spent all his life in the ocean and more hours than he could count swimming. She couldn't possibly know the water like he did and yet—and yet she'd caught it perfectly. That breathless moment as dawn rises over the water, and for a moment you forget that humans exist. You could almost imagine the Earth as one huge blue ocean spinning in black space.

She'd caught that, all of it. The mystery and the sense of awe. How did she do it?

"Pretty," Lenny said.

It wasn't pretty. That was a dumb word, meaning nothing. The painting was gorgeous, magical...Matt bit his lip. Those were dumb words, too.

"Does she sell this stuff? I bet she could make a bundle." Lenny put down the wooden frame and picked something else up. "Hey, dude, that's you. Really good likeness. *Man,* she's sweet on you. You've almost got more muscles in here than in real life."

Matt looked over, and the hairs on the back of his neck stood up. It *was* him. A line drawing with a few strokes of earth-toned pastels. She must have sketched it from the terrace—a view of him in profile as he stopped for a moment on the beach before diving into the ocean. He was outlined against the dying sun. He had on swim trunks and held his spear. It must have been the day he'd gone fishing and caught three bream. He'd left two of them on her doorstep.

She'd caught the essence of him. He looked elemental, like a warrior at the dawn of time. The emotion in the drawing reached out like a punch to the stomach.

Matt bit his lip. He hated this. He hated having Lenny paw through Charlotte's stuff. There was so much feeling in her artwork—out-and-out love for the elderly gentleman in the portrait, affection for Pepe and Mama Pilar. For him, maybe . . . admiration?

It was like reading someone's diary, it was that intimate. Matt took the drawing from Lenny's big paw and placed it facedown on the dining table. "I really need to shower, ace. I got soaked this afternoon fishing the lady out of the water. I'm cold, my clothes are still wet, and I'm hungry. So . . ."

"Scat," Lenny said amiably. He shrugged broad shoulders. "You got it." He leveled his hand and made an imaginary pistol with forefinger and thumb, aiming it at Matt. "You need anything, call. I mean it, dude. Anything at all, and I'm on it."

"Will do." Matt tried to hide his relief as he picked up Lenny's slicker and handed it to him. It had stopped dripping, but there was a puddle on the floor. There was no getting round it—Matt was going to have to mop up the mess. Charlotte kept a neat house. Mopping was not Matt's favorite activity in the world, but he'd done enough of it in the Navy to know he could do an efficient job of it.

By the time he scouted out the pantry, found a mop and pail, and walked back into the living room, Lenny'd gone. The space felt better. As Matt squeezed the mop and attacked the mess on the floor, he realized that Lenny's presence had unsettled him on a lot of different levels. It had felt . . . wrong, somehow. Invasive. As if the house was meant for Charlotte and him, and Lenny's presence was an intrusion.

Matt put the mop and pail neatly away, just the way he'd found it, and rummaged in his kit. He pulled out his weapon, clean and smelling of gun oil, just as he'd left it.

Matt hefted the weapon, liking the heavy feel of it. His hands held the muscle memory of the tens of thousands of rounds he'd shot with it.

Lenny was gone. He was armed again.

Matt felt a drop in the tension knotting his muscles. He grabbed clean underwear and his sweats and made a detour to the bedroom to check on Charlotte before heading for the shower.

She was in the exact position he'd placed her in. She hadn't moved an inch, so soundly asleep it was as if she were unconscious. He knew, without knowing how he knew, that she hadn't been sleeping well. Close up, there had been lavender bruises under her eyes. He wanted them gone. He wanted to get rid of those two small furrows between her eyebrows. He wanted the wariness in those gray eyes gone.

A matted lock of hair curled over her cheek. Matt reached down to brush the curl away, behind her ear. The back of his finger lingered for a moment against her cheek. It was so soft, it seemed like another material, not human skin. She wasn't in REM sleep, her eyelids were unmoving. He had to look closely to see the blanket move slightly with her breathing. She could easily have been dead.

Another twenty seconds, and she would have been. Matt shuddered at the thought.

She'd been looking for him. It was her cries that had made him look up in the water. The weather had become too extreme even for him, and he'd been heading back to shore when he'd heard his name on the wind. It had been Charlotte, standing on the rickety quay, searching the water, calling his name. If he hadn't plowed through the water at his own personal swim speed record, she'd be a lovely corpse right now instead of a beautiful, live woman.

Matt pulled the blanket farther up over her arms, his hand cupping her shoulder briefly. When he finally straightened, he stood and looked down at her for a long time.

He knew what he wanted. But he wasn't going to get it. Not right now anyway.

Sighing, Matt headed for the shower.

CHAPTER EIGHT

Warrenton
Early Morning, April 26

There's money here, Barrett thought, as he followed Robert Haine up the wide stone steps of Court Mansion. Big money. Old money. And class, the kind money couldn't buy.

Haine clearly knew his way around the place. He had had keys to the big wrought-iron gates a hundred feet back and he was now pulling out a set of keys for the big oak front door.

Haine's hand was trembling. He shifted so Barrett couldn't see that it took him three tries to open the door, but Barrett noticed, of course. Noticing details was what he was about.

Haine was under a lot of pressure. He was trying to hide it, but walking up the steps of Court Mansion had dialed the man's nervousness way up.

Haine smelled, too. Underneath an expensive cologne and the smell of cashmere and freshly laundered virgin wool was the sweat of fear, unmistakable. Barrett had smelled every permutation of it over the years. Haine was deeply, intensely frightened.

Haine finally got the locks open and pulled the heavy

door wide, flipping on the hallway and porch lights as he entered a few steps into the massive lobby. He held out an arm to him in invitation—*you first*. Barrett walked through. Haine made to follow, but Barrett suddenly stuck out his arm, like a bar of iron. Surprised, Haine tried to push against him, but he didn't stand a chance.

Haine had gym-honed muscles. Barrett had battle-hardened muscles.

"No," Barrett said without turning around. "I need to be on my own in here."

He had to flatten his mind out, make it blank, drive all sensation out of his body to concentrate fiercely on what this house could tell him about Charlotte Court. He needed a handle on the prey. For the next hour or three hours or however long it took, Barrett would turn himself into a human recording machine, filing away even the smallest details, to be taken out and pondered over time as he narrowed the hunt.

It was the first rule of battle—scout out the terrain—and he had to be alone to do it. He couldn't concentrate with this asshole around.

Foolishly, Haine continued to push against his arm a little, as if to dislodge it and enter the house with him.

Barrett turned then and looked at Haine. Just looked.

"Okay," Haine said, finally, holding up his hands and backing a step away. "Okay. But you can't disturb anything," he said, petulantly, as if giving in to an unreasonable request.

Barrett closed the door quietly in his face and entered Court Mansion. It was going to be a long night.

Haine had to walk around the gardens of Court Mansion for a couple of hours to calm himself down. Just seeing the entrance hallway and the glimpse into the huge living room past Barrett's outstretched arm made his heart pound painfully. Through the open hallway door he'd glimpsed the high back of Charlotte's favorite armchair upholstered in pale yellow silk, always placed next to the hearth.

Court Mansion—together with Court Industries and Charlotte Court—should have been *his*.

The first time he'd walked into the mansion, he'd felt it in his bones. The place was his, meant for *him*. This was exactly the home he'd dreamed of, worked so hard all his life for. And when he'd seen Philip's daughter, Charlotte, it had all fallen into place like the cherries in a slot machine, lining up for the jackpot.

His entire life had been an arrow, aimed straight at the heart of this. A company, a mansion, an heiress—they were all what he'd worked a lifetime to achieve.

He had a neat little background for himself all prepared, which he'd trotted out to Philip and then to an uncaring Charlotte. CPA father who died tragically young, wonderful stay-at-home mother with the law degree. He had the story down so pat in his mind he didn't even have to think of it. He could even summon up glossy eyes, bravely fighting back the tears, at the thought of his wonderful dad, tragically dead of a heart attack at forty-two.

As it happened, his old man had died last year in the drunk tank of some godforsaken hamlet in North Dakota, choking on his own vomit, lying in his own shit.

Haine would never have known the fucker had croaked if it hadn't been for the local cop down there in Bumfuck, ND, calling him up because the old man had had a newspaper clipping of him being appointed CEO of Court Industries in the back pocket of his jeans.

Haine had coldly denied knowing Stuart Haine and hung up. He'd kept his voice even, but his hands had trembled. The memory of the son of a bitch could still do that to him.

Haine shook his head. That was a long time ago. A lifetime ago. He was another person now. He wasn't an underweight boy struggling to study on a cracked Formica tabletop covered with his father's empty beer bottles and crushed roaches. No.

He'd gone as far as he could under his own steam, but now he could fulfill his destiny with this old, rich family, with the dying business he knew he could revive, with the old mansion just waiting for his modernizing touch. Gutted and refitted, it would be a showcase.

Charlotte, too, was meant to be his. The first time he saw her, he knew. Young, beautiful, classy. Exactly the woman he wanted for his wife.

How it grated that she wouldn't give him the time of day. Oh yeah, she was polite enough, but she was always cool, remote, faintly sarcastic.

And all the while he was working like a dog to save the Courts' asses.

His heart beat high and fast in his chest at the thought, at all that he'd almost held in his hands and that had been taken from him by that cold bitch.

Looking past Barrett's shoulder into the huge entrance hall, it was almost as if he could see her again.

At the beginning, he'd used every excuse to come to the Court Mansion, ostensibly to see Philip, but actually to see Charlotte.

Through the open hallway door he'd catch glimpses of her. She used to light the fire and curl up in that yellow armchair to read on dark stormy days. Warrenton had a lot of those during the winter.

None of this—*none* of it!—would have had to happen if only Charlotte had married him.

It was all her fault.

Stiff with rage, Haine stood in front of the ornate colonnaded front veranda of Court Mansion.

He was seeing red, literally. A doctor he'd met at one of the endless fund-raisers he'd attended while trying to court Charlotte had told him that seeing red wasn't a figure of speech. Extreme rage burst the blood vessels in the eyes, the doctor said. Robert wasn't surprised. He could feel waves of rage pulsing in every pore, every cell of his body.

He needed to destroy something of Charlotte's, something she'd cared about. He heard a soft noise in the bushes. Whirling, he caught sight of pearl white fur and a long, furry tail delicately picking its way over the broken earth, then disappearing into the laurel hedge. Federico, Charlotte's Persian cat. He'd spent many an awkward moment, seething with rage while she stroked the animal on her lap, long slow sensuous strokes, ignoring him completely while he tried to engage her attention. Stroking her cat, smiling softly into the yellow eyes, smile fading as she looked back up at Haine.

If she'd said it aloud, it couldn't have been more clear that she found that damned cat more interesting than him.

Haine pulled out a pocketknife and pulled the blade open.

With a lunge, Haine caught the fucking cat by the scruff

of the neck and held the animal dangling at the end of his fist. It fought him, hissing and spitting and growling. The edge of a claw caught him on the wrist. Two drops of blood welled from the shallow scratch. He shuddered at the sight of his own blood.

Haine plunged the long blade of the knife straight into the beast's throat, drowning the deep growls in blood. The cat twisted desperately in his left hand, but Robert held on firmly to the soft scruff. Pushing down with all his strength on the hilt of the knife, he widened the wound in the cat's throat. Blood spurted out, and Robert pulled back in distaste. He had on fifteen-hundred-dollar Ermenegildo Zegna gray silk twill trousers.

He pulled the knife out of the animal's throat, plunging it again into the abdomen, feeling the scrape of rib and backbone against the metal. The cat twisted in his grip as steaming red, blue, and white guts spilled out. It was struggling less now. Robert stabbed over and over again, in a frenzy, feeling the sharp knife plow through the vital organs like butter. Robert stopped when his arms hurt and stood there, chest heaving, holding the dead animal dripping blood onto the overturned dark earth. It was dead. It had died minutes ago.

With a sharp sound of revulsion, Robert opened his fist and let the disgusting creature drop to the ground. It was a mass of blood-matted fur and entrails, smelling of blood and piss and shit, hardly recognizable as a cat. He kicked loamy dirt over it. The earth made a pattering sound as it fell in clumps on the dead animal, disappearing into the gaping cavities in the belly, falling on dead, open eyes.

Robert's breathing slowed, and he straightened. He looked down at the butchered animal and smiled.

CHAPTER NINE

San Luis
April 26

Charlotte came up slowly out of sleep in soft, swooping stages, like smoke rising to heaven. She hadn't slept so soundly, or woken so gently, in what felt like forever. When she finally gained full consciousness, she was smiling.

There was bright sunlight streaming in, turning the inside of her eyelids a warm gold-tinted pink. Moira had probably already put the scones in the oven and was right now brewing the coffee. The scones would be wonderful, the coffee... not. No matter what kind of fancy imported Italian or French roast coffee beans Charlotte bought, Moira would burn the coffee, turning it into sludge tasting of old shoe leather. A family tradition, too, since Moira's aunt had burned coffee for the Courts before her.

Moira made up for it by brewing the best tea in the world in the afternoon. Well, after all, she was Irish. Good tea was in her DNA.

Dad would have been up by sunrise, Charlotte thought dreamily, feeling consciousness seeping in lightly. Working on that darned book of his, which had already eaten up seven years of his life—*Seventeenth Century Travel Writers: The New World*. Which maybe three people in the whole world would read. And she'd be one of them, Charlotte thought with a sigh as she opened her eyes.

The world slipped sideways. This wasn't her room. The bright light outside the window couldn't possibly be Warrenton light.

Instead of the pale yellow walls and teeming bookshelves of her room, the walls here were painted a dusky pink and were bare except for a few boldly designed earthenware plates hanging from brass chains.

Dad was dead. A bubble of grief welled up inside her, and instinct had her clamping her lips shut against it. The danger of the past months had taught her never to show her pain. The grief seemed to lie in wait for her, ready to pounce, taking her always by surprise. Her father had been so precious to her, so vital to what she was, that the thought of living without him was like a sharp knife to the heart, slicing deep, the wound forever fierce, forever fresh.

"Good morning," a deep voice rumbled at her back, and the world snapped into focus. She was lying on her left side, head pillowed on a massive biceps. Though it was like using a warm brick as a pillow, she was oddly comfortable. His other arm was around her, big hand on her belly. There was enormous warmth and—

Charlotte froze. She could feel every inch of Matt's big, heavily muscled body against her back. He was so long he completely mantled her. His breath ruffled the top of her head, and she could feel a hard shinbone against the soles of her feet.

She was naked, and so was he.

Not only was he naked, he was hugely aroused.

His chest hairs tickled her back. Her bare back. She could feel soft chest hair furred over hard muscles. She could feel it all, hard thighs tucked against hers, huge erect penis in the small of her back. His pubic hair was rough against her bare bottom.

"I—how—" she stammered. Matt didn't relinquish his hold. If anything, the big forearm around her waist tightened. Charlotte twisted her head to look at him over her shoulder, expecting smugness.

He didn't have the look of masculine satisfaction you'd expect in a man who'd gotten a woman naked in bed, something Charlotte had always found incredibly annoying. If anything, he looked grimmer than normal.

He didn't apologize, dark eyes watching her intently. "You started shivering and crying in the night," he said. "Shivering's good—it's the body's way of warming the muscles up, but I couldn't get you to stop, and you wouldn't wake up. Scared the fu—scared the hell out of me. I should have put you in a warm bath when I got you into the house, but I was scared of after drop." The deep grooves in his cheeks grew deeper as his mouth tightened. "Lost a swim buddy that way. I wasn't about to lose you." He drew in a deep breath. "The best way to warm someone up is contact with human skin. We were taught that in the Navy. Winter training involves placing us in just our swim trunks in subzero weather and making us survive in the waves rolling to shore. The only way to do that is to huddle together to generate heat. So we did, stacking up and sharing what body heat we could. You stopped shivering as soon as I stripped you and got into bed with you."

This was her first real look at him. Last night she'd

been too shocked, too numb to have the resources to think of him as anything other than the man she'd watched over, the man who'd rescued her and—later—a potential enemy who could uncover her secrets.

Now, in the full light of an early Mexican morning, she couldn't take her eyes off his face. He hadn't shaved. Dark stubble covered his face halfway up to his cheeks. His dark hair was too short for him to have bed head—the way she knew she had to have—and she could see now that he had a few threads of silver along his temples.

He had a scar along his temple that ran right into the hairline. A streak of white hair followed the course of the scar.

She had no idea what age he could be. He had the physique of a young man, but that was probably due to the intense exercises he put himself through. If she'd had to guess, she'd have said he was in his midthirties. Though he looked older, she could see now that it wasn't due to age but exposure to sun and wind. The skin around his eyes was weather-beaten, light-colored sun wrinkles fanning out from the corner of his eyes. His eyes were a lighter brown than she'd thought from observing him on the beach—from a distance they'd looked darker. He was looking at her narrow-eyed, thin nostrils slightly flared.

From the feel of his hot, hard penis, he was intensely aroused.

So was she. Charlotte was shocked to feel the warm flood of feeling between her thighs. Matt slowly spread open his big hand and it almost covered her entire stomach. As his hand moved against the skin of her belly, Charlotte could actually feel her vagina…*flutter*. The exact same feeling she had just before orgasm.

How did *that* happen? How had she become so turned on it was as if they'd already started making love? It must have happened in her sleep, feeling all that male warmth around her. Her subconscious mind must have just shut down the lobe dealing with danger, which had kept her awake and semialert most nights, and switched on the sex lobe.

This needed to be brought down a level—or three or four. Matt Sanders might be the sexiest man she'd ever seen, but an affair was unthinkable. Much too dangerous. Though her traitorous body felt a connection to him and was thrilling to his touch, she didn't dare trust anyone.

Sex was dangerous. She was feeling so weak and vulnerable that sex would just crack her wide open and let all sorts of monsters spill right out.

Charlotte grabbed at the first thought that crossed her mind, trying to tone down the sexual heat that had suddenly blossomed in her bed. "You Navy guys *cuddle* to keep warm?"

Matt shook his head slightly, eyes never leaving hers. He didn't smile. Not exactly. But there was a lightening of his features that would have been a smile if his mouth had moved. "Not cuddle. Huddle. Navy guys huddle. There's a difference." That big hand moved slowly up over her stomach and cupped her breast. He stroked the skin, running his thumb over her nipple. The skin of his fingers was calloused, rough on her supersensitized skin. The touch went straight to her loins in an electric line of heat. "*This*," he growled, "is cuddling."

It was more than cuddling, it was the next best thing to sex itself. The big hand cupped and stroked while he watched her so closely she felt as if he could simply reach inside her to pull all her thoughts out of her head.

As he stroked, heat rushed to her face. He noticed that. Of course he did, he was preternaturally observant. His hand with the rough skin stroked her breast lightly, the movements so delicate she almost wanted to thrust her breasts out to deepen his touch.

She was entirely in his embrace. Slowly, without seeming to use an ounce of his strength, he had turned her over onto her side, facing him.

She didn't feel manhandled—it was more like following a force of nature. A shift of those powerful muscles and there they were—lying face-to-face. As she turned over, her sensitized nipples scraped against his chest hair. Her belly brushed against his penis. Everywhere she touched him he was hot and hard. She'd never been naked with a man who was so... male before.

Charlotte was fastidious by nature—actually, *incredibly picky* was what her roommate at Middlebury had said. She hadn't had that many lovers. Not to mention the fact that her love life had been severely curtailed—or rather, abruptly cut off—by her father's illness.

The few men she'd been to bed with were all similar in nature. They shared her interests in art and literature— that was why she chose them. In retrospect, their bodies had been much like hers, just without breasts and with a penis. They'd been pale and slender and hairless and not much stronger than she was.

Matt was completely different from her in every way there was.

He'd thrown off the blankets, and she could see every inch of his beautiful body. Bulging, superbly defined muscles with raised veins, a heavy pelt of chest hair that narrowed only a little around the belly button, then grew into a dense dark thatch around his penis. His skin looked tougher than hers, as if it would take a lot to penetrate it, and it was several tones darker than hers.

About the only thing they had in common was bullet-wound scars—he'd taken a bullet to the shoulder, too, just like her. It had never occurred to her in her previous life that bullet scars might come under the heading of shared interests.

A large puckered bullet wound scar was on his right side, where the liver would be, with heavy surgical scars around it. She wondered if the bullet's trajectory had nicked the liver itself. Two more bullet wounds in the upper thighs, one dangerously close to the femoral artery. To round it all off, she could see a long, ugly scar along his right biceps.

A man who'd lived a dangerous life. She'd do well to remember that. She'd do well to remember that *he* was dangerous, down to his bones.

Matt was narrow-eyed, eyes watching hers, as if he could walk around in her mind and pull out her thoughts. His gaze dropped to her lips. Rolling over, her right hand had come to rest on his chest, just over his heart. She could actually feel his slow steady heart rate pick up as he looked at her mouth, then he raised his gaze once more. Mouth, eyes, mouth, eyes. And every time his gaze dropped, the heartbeat speeded up.

Eyes...mouth...eyes...mouth...

He moved forward, gaze frozen on her mouth. He was going to kiss her. Did she want it? Yes, no, yes, no...

Charlotte's hand on his chest pressed gently. She wasn't pushing back at him, she just kept her hand in place as he moved his chest forward. It had the effect of stopping him, though it wasn't a definite stop signal. It wasn't a go, either.

Matt's face descended toward her, closer, closer...only instead of kissing her mouth, he pressed his lips to the skin just behind her ear.

Oh, God, goose pimples broke out, and she shuddered when he lightly nipped the skin. As he drew in a long, shaky breath, the big hand along her back cupped her bottom and tightened its grip. Matt's hips moved forward at the same time, and she suddenly found herself riding his penis. The folds of her sex had just opened up of their own accord and there he was, against her sensitive skin.

He was huge, hot, so hard it seemed strange that this was human skin and not warm steel. It was irresistibly exciting. Charlotte's hand moved. Her palm slid over his pectorals, stopping for a moment over the hard male nipple. It was tiny compared to hers, surrounded by chest hair, but as sensitive as her own, judging by his jolt when her palm brushed softly against it.

What an amazing feeling of *power*. That this huge, immensely strong man could shudder and jolt at her touch. Tremble, too, as she discovered when she circled his nipple with the tip of her forefinger. His big hand tightened against her backside, pushing her hips more tightly against him. He ran his open mouth against her neck, licking the vein, nipping that spot where neck met shoulder. She had no idea it was so sensitive. When she shuddered again, she could feel the effect on his penis. It swelled even further against the tissues of her vagina, growing impossibly longer.

Her hand moved from his chest to slide under his arm, curling up over his shoulder. She could feel the play of those massive back and shoulder muscles as he moved his mouth along her neck. God, his entire body was an erogenous zone. Everything about him excited her—his size, his strength, his utter *maleness*.

Her eyes drifted closed. He was so delicious to the touch, the sight of him was almost distracting. His mouth was edging closer to hers, slowly, as if they had all the time in the world.

Maybe they did. Charlotte had never felt so out of the world as she did right now, in the tight embrace of this man. All thoughts fled from her head, all sense of time and space. Of past and future. The insides of her closed lids were flushed with a bright rosy glow, just like her entire body, responding to his touch.

Slowly, slowly Matt kissed his way to her mouth. When his mouth finally settled on hers, it shook her to her core. When his tongue touched hers, the jolt was electric. She felt it to her toes and felt him swell even more between the lips of her sex. For the first time in her life, she felt the connection between the lips of her mouth and the lips of her sex. Both highly sensitive, both opening wide to him. Her tongue tangled with his. She couldn't seem to draw in breath, except through him. Her sex was as wet as her mouth and seemed to slide as slickly and smoothly over his penis as her tongue against his.

This was so delicious. She'd never felt this sexy, this *alive* before. It seemed as if every part of her was touching him, mouth, breasts, vagina . . .

Another long, seamless kiss, and Matt rolled on top of her. He was incredibly heavy, but even this was delicious, his heavy weight something erotic in and of itself. He was so broad she had to open up to accommodate him, arms and thighs. In rolling over, somehow the folds of her sex no longer gripped his penis, and he was angling his hips to penetrate her. She could feel the large bulbous tip, right there, at her opening. It was so startling she opened her eyes...

And froze.

His face, only an inch above hers, was utterly transformed.

He'd changed color, from the deep biscuit tan to an even darker hue, with red flags riding the angular cheekbones. His lips were fuller, suffused with blood, wet from her mouth. Behind his narrowed lids, his eyes glittered almost black. The skin was drawn tightly over his cheekbones and deep grooves lined his cheeks. The tendons in his neck stood out like cords, and it seemed as if every muscle on his body was flexed and hard.

It was extreme arousal, but it was indistinguishable from extreme rage. He looked exactly like Martin Conklin when she'd defended herself, only much much more dangerous.

Charlotte's head knew she wasn't in danger but her body didn't. Matt looked feral, utterly and completely dangerous.

There was nothing she could do to defend herself. She was spread-eagled under him, her thighs wide open between his, arms caught between his arms and his sides. In lifting his hips to penetrate her, he pressed forward, his chest crushing hers. She had no breath to cry out.

That big penis was moving forward slowly, and Charlotte panicked. She couldn't run, and she couldn't hide. The only thing her body could do was close in on itself in total alarm.

He angled his hips and pressed forward but met resistance. He couldn't penetrate. She was closed up too tightly.

Frowning, Matt reared his head back and studied her face. She stared up at him, both frightened and aroused herself, shaking.

Matt tested himself against her, but there was no question of her body opening itself to him. She could feel her vaginal muscles clenching tightly and braced herself. She hadn't seen his penis clearly, but he felt enormous.

To her surprise, he pulled his hips back, withdrawing from where he'd barely begun to penetrate, and rolled to his side. Charlotte expanded her lungs for the first time in what felt like hours and drew in a long shuddering breath.

Their eyes met. She had no idea what to say to him. "I—" she began, then stopped. There were no words. There was nothing she could say that wouldn't put her at risk. She bit her lips, blinking back tears. "I *can't,*" she finally whispered.

"No?"

Charlotte's chest was so tight it hurt to breathe. She couldn't look away from him. She shook her head.

Matt was leaning on one strong forearm beside her head. He moved his hand and touched the scar on her shoulder. The touch was gentle, but he explored it thoroughly, the ugly puckered ridged scar tissue, the discolored skin, the deep indentation. Gently but firmly, with his other hand he lifted her shoulder and examined the exit wound. Charlotte rarely looked at it, the entry wound was bad enough.

She watched his face for clues to his mood as he examined her scars but it was impossible to know what he was thinking.

She was shaking so hard she thought she'd fall apart.

"Can't," she gasped. "Just . . . can't. Sorry."

He didn't blink, just watched her carefully. With a sound that might have been a sigh, he turned and lifted himself away.

Warrenton
April 26
Inside Court Mansion

Barrett pulled on latex gloves and slipped surgical booties over his shoes. Later, they would both go into a portable incinerator that would reduce them to their constituent molecules.

As far as he knew, he'd never left DNA or fingerprints anywhere, and he wanted to keep it that way. Before going to Haine's house, he'd put glue over his fingertips, so that even if he wanted to, Haine couldn't track him down. Surreptitiously, when Haine wasn't looking, he'd sprayed a small canister of bleach solution over the glass where he'd sipped the whiskey.

Barrett took his time once he was inside Court Mansion. There was no rush. The Court woman had disappeared two months ago. A few hours one way or another weren't going to make any difference. The more he learned here, the more he got into her head, the easier it would be to find her.

He had to do this right because he had a tight time line, which was unusual.

Most jobs were open-ended. Find my . . . *husband, wife, the bastard who sold me out*—and there usually wasn't any requirement other than proof of death.

This job required speed—Haine needed a dead body in five weeks' time.

Barrett had one important thing going for him. The Court woman had disappeared in a panic, with no outside help. The hardest people to find were those who'd prepared their disappearance for months, sometimes years, in advance and sometimes with the help of a professional. It was next to impossible to follow someone whose trail was erased by a pro. At times, it was as if they had simply stepped off the Earth. The only thing to do in that case was to wait for them to make a mistake.

Barrett had once waited three years to nail a woman running away from a rich, abusive husband. She'd planned her disappearance carefully, with professional help. There were three men in the continental US whose business it was to help people disappear. Barrett could recognize in an instant when they'd had a hand in the getaway. They could make people vanish into thin air. They couldn't, however, stop people from being too stupid to live.

Barrett knew the woman was a fanatical ballet aficionado and had subscribed to an obscure ballet magazine. He'd gotten hold of the subscriber list and had checked out all new subscribers. Luckily, the husband had given him almost unlimited funds to track his wife down. Subscriber number 2,127 turned out to be the runaway wife, and Barrett had—as per instructions—brought her head back to the husband.

This case was different. This was a woman who left in a panic without any preparation, without any planning, without the tools for a new life. A rich, pretty, young woman who'd lived a pampered life would be out of her depth as a fugitive. She'd need money and documents and would make endless mistakes along the way. Tracking her would be easy once he got to know her. He just had to make sure it was within the client's deadline.

Charlotte Court would have been incapable of doing out-of-character things to disappear. On top of it all, she'd been wounded. Shock, pain, blood loss would have all sapped her reasoning powers, her ability to plan. In her desperation and weakness, she would revert to her truest self.

When he knew that self, he'd know where to find her, as surely as day follows night.

Barrett knew of his reputation as a sniper, and he made sure potential clients thought of him as a sniper first, a tracker second. He made sure he carried his big Barrett around with him, to show when necessary. The Barrett's muzzle brake gave it a distinctive profile. The rifle was pure business, with no aesthetics to it whatsoever.

A Barrett's bullet was a small missile that could penetrate an armored vehicle at two thousand yards out. It was the most efficient killing machine possible. The rifle mesmerized clients.

The few times he'd had to use it, it had been to pull off a job that with any other weapon—and any other eye and any other hand at that weapon—would have been impossible.

Most times, he didn't need to use the Barrett. Too many assassinations using a .50-caliber sniper rifle, with its distinctive projectiles, would have raised a huge red flag for the FBI. Barrett preferred to rotate his working methods.

Keeping the Barrett to hand was more like a calling card.

Potential clients—most of them men, a few women—found the Barrett fascinating and snipers sexy—which was crazy, since snipers are essentially mechanics. Superb mechanics, but almost autistic in the narrowness of their talent, obsessed with the arcana of the hardware and the physics of projectiles. Though he kept his sniping skills well honed, Barrett was much more than a sniper.

There had been only a few jobs where his expertise with the Barrett made the difference. Three years ago, he'd taken a two-thousand-yard shot at a material witness being herded in the dead of night in a phalanx of guards up the courthouse steps of the old Pima County Courthouse in Tucson.

Twenty US Marshals in body armor and holding MP5s had jumped out of a bulletproof security van, hustling the witness toward the big white building at a dead run. Barrett, who had been waiting patiently for three days off a sandbag on a rooftop way beyond the Marshals' Worry Zone, eye glued to the scope, pissing into empty Coke bottles, had taken the shot in a two-second window of vulnerability.

He'd had an infrared sniperscope, seeing the world in the eerie underwater green light of night vision. Barrett had practiced with tens of thousands of rounds using night vision, and he didn't hesitate.

The witness's head had exploded under the impact of the Barrett's .50-caliber cartridge. The rifle was suppressed, and he could see the marshals drop, stunned, to a crouch, backs to the now-dead witness, scanning the horizon uselessly because Barrett was almost a mile out, in the dark. Until they laser-projected the shot the next day, they wouldn't even have an idea which direction it had come from.

While the marshals futilely barked into their cell phones, calling in a SWAT team and a totally useless ambulance, scurrying about like demented ants, Barrett had carefully wiped all traces of his presence, taking his time. He was good at policing his brass. The spent brass cartridge went into a vest pocket. The polyurethane sheet he'd lain on and the urine-filled Coke bottles into a carry bag, the Barrett and the Harris tripod broken down and seated into their foam beds.

He sprayed the area with a 10 percent bleach solution to destroy any traces of DNA he might have left. While the police dragged the dead witness into a doorway, leaving a black blood trail in his night-vision goggles, he quietly went down the fire stairs, exited, and drove away.

No one saw him come. No one saw him go.

That's when he started being known as Barrett. That's when his fee shot up into the six figures.

But sniping was the least of what he did. What he was truly superb at, what made him nearly unique, was his ability as a tracker. He could smoke out nearly anybody, no matter where he—or she—ran to ground.

He did what he had to do to get into his victims' heads and follow where their instincts took them. Under stress, humans, like animals, followed their instincts, their deepest natures. It was the closest thing to truth Barrett knew.

A rabbit in danger won't hide in a tree. A leopard won't dig a hole in the ground and burrow. A gambler will inevitably drift to Atlantic City or Vegas. A drunk won't end up in Amish country. A gangbanger won't end up on a ranch in Wyoming.

Each human being has a narrow range of behavior and reverts to it immediately when in danger.

So now he was going to learn everything there was to

know about Charlotte Court, and when he knew her, he'd know where she had gone into hiding.

Barrett walked from room to room, soaking up the atmosphere. He wasn't drawing conclusions, not yet. He had to get a general feel for the woman first.

Who was she? What made her what she was?

He looked around. There was wealth here, lots of wealth. Old money.

Okay, that was a start. She'd crave a reproduction in miniature of her old life. But she wouldn't go to ground in a luxury hotel—she wouldn't have the money for that, and even if she did, she wouldn't need or even enjoy ostentation.

There were no signs of conspicuous consumption in the big house. The kitchen was at least thirty years old, and the bathrooms didn't have the Jacuzzis and acres of marble now so necessary to the "new" rich.

That wasn't her style. Her style was classy understatement.

Good. That narrowed it down a little. Even without much money, she'd be incapable of settling down in an ugly slum, or a trailer park, or a ticky-tacky house in the suburbs.

The only kind of place a person like her could settle without much money was a place where other cash-poor but arty people congregated—an art colony. Places like Key West or Big Sur or Martha's Vineyard in winter.

The hunt was now on. He could feel the energy down to his fingertips.

There was an amazing amount of artwork on the walls—even he recognized some of the artists: a Renoir, a Picasso, three Winslow Homers. But most of what was on the walls was by one person, showing the same light, delicate, expert hand, whether oils or sketches or water-colors. Peering closely, Barrett could see that they were all signed with a small cc in the lower-right-hand corner. cc. Charlotte Court.

Charlotte Court was an artist. A good one. An obsessive one, too.

Obsession was good. Obsessions tripped people up like nothing else except sex.

Wandering toward the back of the big house, Barrett came across her studio—a big room that had been added onto the back wall, all windows and skylights, capable of catching as much sun as this frigid northern city could give.

There were easels everywhere—each with a work in progress. Unframed canvases were stacked against the walls, and another stack of thick notebooks—each completely filled with sketches—lay on a table. Charlotte Court had been under a lot of stress with a dying father. This was obviously where she came to calm herself down.

Barrett tucked this important information away.

When under stress, cc painted or drew. Obsessively. Barrett bent to look at a large, textured pad. Then another. And another. Interesting. All by the same manufacturer. Fabriano. An Italian company, it said on the back sheet. *Cartiere Miliani Fabriano S.p.A.* Made in Italy. He fingered the paper. Good thick stock.

He would have to find out if Fabriano was sold in the US or whether pretty cc ordered it specially from Italy.

Wherever she was now, she was sketching. On Fabriano paper. He would bet his left nut on it.

Barrett poked around in her bedroom and adjoining bathroom, discovering some interesting things about

Charlotte Court, though they were all negatives. She didn't do drugs. She had a relatively small collection of clothes, considering what she could afford and considering that she was a beautiful woman. That meant she didn't need to be close to trendy stores. She didn't have any modern jewelry. Everything in her jewelry box—kept right in plain sight in a big wooden box on her dresser, with a crappy little brass key that wouldn't keep the wind out, let alone a thief—was an antique, clearly family heirlooms. So she could stay away from jewelry stores.

Barrett had once capped a runaway wife—who'd run away with the chauffeur and a fortune in cash from her husband's safe—simply because she found it impossible to stay away from her favorite Bulgari store.

Charlotte read a lot, judging from the shelves of well-thumbed books. However, she didn't read anything she couldn't find in any well-stocked metropolitan bookstore. If she was where she couldn't readily find books, she probably used Amazon, and if she did, tough shit for him.

Barrett had long ago quit trying to hack Amazon. It couldn't be done. Amazon was more tightly defended than the Department of Defense, which Barrett had hacked into twice.

Barrett moved back toward the front of the house, walking slowly through all the rooms. He stopped for a moment in the middle of the enormous living room—as big as the ballroom he'd once seen in a drug lord's villa—and closed his eyes. He drew in a deep breath, trying to analyze what had been tickling at the edges of his subconscious, at a level deeper than words. He exhaled then inhaled again.

What *was* that smell? Citrusy, like . . . lemons.

Yeah, that was it. Lemon. Lemon . . . polish. He opened

his eyes again and the realization was there, full-blown, because his subconscious mind had been thinking it through.

Which was why he hadn't wanted Haine here, yapping away.

Someone was cleaning the house on a regular basis, a housekeeper or a cleaning service. Barrett again walked through the mansion. All the furniture was dusted, the windows sparkled, the rugs had been recently vacuumed. The house looked as if it was just waiting for the mistress to walk back in after a hard day's shopping.

Barrett looked harder, opening his senses wide. It wasn't a cleaning service. There were too many personal touches. The house was being cared for by someone who either loved the house itself or loved its owner.

There were freshly cut flowers in vases everywhere, presumably from the well-tended flower gardens outside. The gleaming surfaces were full of art objects, silver frames, silver knickknacks, Lalique statuettes. All objects that took time to dust. Time and attention.

Now that he knew what he was looking for, Barrett was quick. He rifled through notebooks, checked drawers, opened closets. Finally, he pulled open the top-right-hand drawer of a desk in the huge book-filled study, and there it was. The last two months, in black and white.

Barrett sat down in a big cracked-leather chair that was surprisingly comfortable and took his time slowly leafing through the papers. He would have liked to take the sheaves of papers with him, but the absence might at some point be noticed by the cops. He didn't think so—if the cops had been halfway competent they'd have caught

Charlotte Court in the first twenty-four hours—but he was careful by nature.

Someone—the housekeeper—had carefully kept Charlotte Court's mail for her, neatly stacked into three piles. Letters, bills, and junk mail. Barrett left the junk mail where it was and started reading the letters, slicing them open with the little silver letter opener on the desk.

He read them carefully. Once, twice, three times. Slowly, absorbing every word.

Interesting . . .

Most people communicated by e-mail these days, but it looked like the Court woman actually wrote letters. Three of the letters to her were in Italian, two in French.

So she was comfortable with foreign languages. He had enough Spanish to be able to decipher the Italian letter. Something about an art school in Florence. Barrett briefly toyed with the idea that she had escaped to Italy but discarded it. Her passport had been right where you'd expect a passport to be—in the upper-right-hand drawer of the dresser in her bedroom.

Barrett knew that the new security rules enacted by the State Department made passports almost impossible to fake. Certainly, someone like Charlotte Court wouldn't have access to the type of person who might have already figured out how to get around the security features, holograms and RFID chips.

If she had gone out of the country, it would be either to Canada or Mexico. Barrett thought about that for a moment, turning it over in his mind, letting the options unfold like flowers. Then he bent back to the letters.

The letters were all friendly in tone, enough to tell him what he already knew. Charlotte Court enjoyed art and literature and seemed to be well liked by everyone who knew her. It told him a lot about her as a person. She was friendly, cultured, and smart. Good-hearted, gave to charity.

Peach of a girl.

That didn't tell him where she'd gone into hiding, though.

When he felt he'd absorbed everything he could from the letters, Barrett moved on to the business correspondence.

This was more like it.

The bank statements were particularly interesting. Court had three bank accounts, two in Warrenton and one in Chicago. He bent forward, rapt. Money told you more about a person than anything else about their lives. Money talked to you, whispered secrets, opened souls. No friend, no lover was as close to you as your money. This was what would tell him what he needed to know about Charlotte Court.

The two Warrenton accounts were with the same bank. One account was her personal one, the other clearly was for household expenses. Barrett quickly ran down the items on her personal account, noting that she was neat and organized and paid all her bills on time.

This was stranger than one might think. A woman who'd inherited a bundle, who didn't have to work, did not necessarily have the life skills necessary to keep accounts neat and tidy.

But Charlotte did. She was organized and competent.

Barrett noted something else, as well. There *was* a housekeeper, just as he thought. He ran a practiced eye down the household account statements. *Follow the money* was his motto.

The housekeeper's name was Moira Charlotte Fitzgerald. She was paid $50,000 a year to look after the house, plus was given a budget of another $50,000 a year, presumably for food and household supplies. Generous but not wildly so, given the size of the house. There was a gardener, too, a Luis Mendoza, paid regularly from the household account.

Barrett finished looking at the rest of the business correspondence, most of which had slowed to a trickle after Charlotte Court had disappeared.

Barrett also noted that the insurance on Charlotte's car had been allowed to lapse. The car itself, a Prius, as Haine had said, was in the garage. He'd seen it himself. Whatever Charlotte Court was driving, it wasn't her own car. She'd either driven away in a borrowed car or had acquired one along the way. Or maybe . . . both.

Maybe she'd escaped in a friend's car she'd borrowed, then dumped it and bought another one. It might be a thread to pursue.

Barrett put the paperwork away and stood. He'd learned everything that he could here, and he now knew where to get more information.

Removing the gloves and the booties, he exited the house quietly. Robert Haine was nowhere to be seen. Barrett stood for a moment on the stoop, face lifted to the frigid morning air. There was a cold pearly cast to the sky, just enough to see a hundred yards. The dawn wouldn't come in a blaze of golden reds but as increasingly lighter shades of gray. Even dawn here sucked.

Embrace the suck. The Special Forces mantra.

When this job was over, he was going to take the 400K personally to the Caymans and stay for two weeks. He hated the cold. Most of his working life had been spent in the tropics and the desert.

Moving quietly was second nature for him, so when he rounded the corner and saw Haine butchering a cat, he was able to watch unobserved.

Interesting.

Haine was totally out of control, slashing again and again at the belly of a cat that was clearly already dead.

Fucking stupid. Never waste energy on a dead enemy.

So Haine was something more than a cool-headed businessman paying someone to remove obstacles for him, which was perfectly reasonable. Happened all the time. No, there was something more there, something that touched a deep chord in the man.

Maybe the delectable Ms. Court had rebuffed his advances? That made sense. The new CEO of the family company wooing one of the largest shareholders.

Oh yeah. Haine was the kind of man who'd have made a real effort. Clearly, it hadn't worked out, and Haine was reduced to digging up flower beds and killing cats. He was spattered with blood, hair wild, eyes showing their whites.

Barrett stepped back in disgust. Some men simply didn't know how to control themselves. *Good thing I have Haine by the short hairs—the guy is fucking crazy,* he thought.

CHAPTER TEN

Matt took a long, cold shower. He needed it. He couldn't remember when he'd wanted a woman more and when she'd stopped him, he'd nearly howled in frustration. But she wasn't being a tease. Her face had gone white, and she'd trembled.

So he'd focused hard on the bullet wound in Charlotte's shoulder and calmed himself down.

Charlotte was in trouble. That beautiful woman, who'd wanted to throw herself into the ocean to save him when she couldn't even swim, had an enemy out there somewhere. Someone who had tried to kill her once and maybe was planning to hurt her again.

His Angel was on the run here in San Luis.

Smart girl. This was a good place to go to ground. A lot of the foreigners were drifters, artists. Most refugees escaped from something, if only cold weather, a bad marriage, or a dead-end job. It was the kind of place where no one asked questions. So she'd instinctively chosen well.

Mexico had a 180-day tourist visa, and Matt was as sure

as sure could be that a lot of the foreigners here had run over the time limit of the permit, but as far as he knew, the local cops didn't enforce anything. She could stay here for almost forever if she didn't tangle with local law enforcement.

Matt rummaged in the neat kitchen, putting together a breakfast of tea, yogurt, and fresh fruit, fiercely missing the bacon and eggs he usually had at Lenny's. He worked slowly, making reassuring kitchen noises she was sure to hear, to give her time to put herself together.

That air of mystery was real. She was in trouble, probably a lot if someone was willing to shoot her. That didn't matter. He knew how to deal with trouble. Welcomed it, even.

Oh, yeah.

Suddenly, Matt felt an infusion of energy run through his body. He'd been drifting for way too long now, consumed with putting himself together, unable to see past the next set of push-ups. Living day to day, hour to hour. But now he had a mission again—protecting Charlotte— and it felt damned good.

To protect her, Matt needed a data dump, fast. You can't fight an enemy you don't know anything about. He hated going into a fight blind and never did unless he was forced to.

She was a woman alone, on the run, with no resources that he could see. Another woman would have angled for protection, probably through sex—God knows he thought about it enough—but not his Angel.

The hairs on the back of his neck stirred. She was here. He could feel her, he could *smell* her.

Turning slowly, he kept his expression bland, trying to look innocuous. Man in a kitchen, cooking. Nothing threatening about that. Too bad he hadn't thought to put on an apron.

She was watching him somberly, arms crossed tightly over her midriff, as if she were cold.

It wasn't cold. Yesterday's storm had given way to a glorious, warm morning. She wrapped her arms around herself in an instinctive gesture, meant both to provide comfort for herself—though he was more than willing to do it—and to protect the vital organs.

"Matt—" She stopped, as if uncertain of what to say. Her eyes searched his, as if uncertain of her welcome. Did she think he was the kind of guy who got angry, maybe violent, when he was rejected? Matt couldn't hurt her if he tried. He'd rather rip out his own throat. He needed for her to understand this.

Well, sometimes body language was better than words. He walked up to her, slowly, and bent to give her a warm kiss. He kept his hands by his sides and didn't touch her anywhere except with his mouth.

It took a moment, but she kissed him back, rising a little on her toes. Her tongue stroked his, and it felt like an electric jolt straight down to his groin.

Whoa. The point of this exercise was to reassure her, not for him to get all hot and bothered. He lifted his head.

"Good morning." Matt kept his voice low and even.

He turned back to the counter, where he had been slicing fruit. Turning his back to her was a signal that he wasn't tracking her, pushing her. "Sit down, and I'll feed you breakfast."

He heard her let out a pent-up breath in a long sigh as she decided she could handle breakfast with him. He almost let out a sigh himself when he heard the scraping of a chair as she settled at the kitchen table.

It could have gone either way. She could have told him to get lost. She could have thanked him for fishing her out of the water, then told him to get lost. Or she could accept his presence in her house. She'd opted for the latter. That first decision was over. She'd moved on to another decision branch.

Matt's prime priority now was to keep her safe, and to do that he needed to stay close to her. Brutally blunt with himself, always, he also knew that besides keeping her safe, he was eager to get into her pants—though that was Priority Number Two, which was way into the future because if he tried to get into her pants again, and she rejected him, he could more or less kiss Priority Number One good-bye.

To accomplish his goals—both his goals—he needed to stay as close to her as possible, and so he needed to keep it in his pants, for now.

Matt had been pretty much used to getting his way all the time in the Navy. Mainly it was because he was an officer, but the fact that he was a better shot than most and that he was damned good in CQC—Close Quarters Combat— didn't hurt, either.

None of that was going to help him now.

Charlotte definitely wasn't going to follow his lead because he shot straight and could wrestle most men to the ground. No, she was a lady, and ladies needed charm.

He was in deepest, deepest shit here, because he didn't have any charm that he knew of.

Charlotte sat gingerly at her small kitchen table, watching Matt's wide back as he fiddled over the stove. He was taking an amazingly long time to prepare what looked like coffee and sliced fruit.

She dreaded having him turn around. Pretty soon he was going to ask some questions she couldn't answer. So it was either lie or simply remain silent. She hated lying and wasn't good at it, so the only alternative was dead silence. Matt Sanders had saved her life, and however much she owed him the truth, she simply couldn't give it to him.

She'd love to, though.

For a brief, searing moment, Charlotte was fiercely tempted to simply let go of her burden. Sit down across from him, across from that calm, strong presence, and talk. Just go ahead and tip her problems into those broad, capable-looking hands. Once she did, though, there would be no taking it back. Once she confided in him, his reaction would determine her life.

Of course, his reaction might well be—*let me protect you while we figure out how to prove your innocence*. That's what would happen in a perfect world, but Charlotte hadn't been in a perfect world since her father had first been diagnosed with cancer. In no perfect world would Philip Court have been allowed to get cancer. This world was harsh, and bad things happened.

Because, of course, Matt's reaction might well be—*you've got to turn yourself in to the authorities*. Charlotte had no intention whatsoever of doing that until she was certain she could prove her innocence. Not as long as there was a chance of her being locked up while awaiting a trial for murder.

It would be nice to trust the system. Nice to feel that since she actually *was* innocent, that would make all the difference. Everything would be so simple then. All she'd have to do was go back to Warrenton, tell the chief of police what had happened and then go back home. But she knew better. Innocent people were locked up all the time.

Whenever Charlotte thought too deeply about the trouble she was in, it made her panicky and terrified. *She* knew she hadn't done anything wrong, but that wasn't enough. Anyone who didn't know her, didn't know how desperately she had loved her father, could probably easily believe a district attorney arguing that she was a spoiled heiress who'd grown tired of being a nursemaid, tired of putting her life on hold for a sick father. It was easy to imagine a jury of workingmen and -women wanting to slap down a young woman who'd never held a job in her life. Charlotte hadn't had time to find a job. She'd interrupted her studies to care for her father.

Charlotte had never thought of caring for her father as a sacrifice. She loved him. He was the most charming and adorable man she'd ever known. Dropping her life to spend time with him as he ended his had been a privilege, not a sacrifice. In this modern world, however, who would believe that? On paper, Charlotte became a very wealthy young woman upon her father's death, though she'd have gladly spent every penny to keep her father alive.

Robert had poisoned the chief's mind, too.

If the chief of police, who'd known her, at least superficially, all her life could believe her capable of murder, so could Matt.

"Coffee," he said, sliding the cup over to her. "Though judging by your supplies, you'd rather have tea."

"Um, yes. But coffee's fine." There was an awkward mix of embarrassment and shyness, emotions she rarely felt.

Matt sipped and watched her, his dark eyes keenly observant. She had no idea what he was thinking.

She put her cup down. "Matt," she said softly, "about before..."

He waved that away, crossing his forearms on the table and leaning forward. "You said he was alive."

"What?" The abrupt change of subject confused her. "Who—oh." The man who'd shot her. He'd asked whether he was alive. "Ahm, yes. I told you that last night."

"Okay, Charlotte." Matt's eyes never left hers. "Let me tell you what I know. You were shot about two months ago, and you didn't get proper medical care. Actually, from what I could see, you didn't get any medical care at all. I can't think it was because you didn't have the money, because any emergency ward would have taken you in and, frankly, you look and you talk like you come from money. So that leaves fear. For some reason you were afraid to seek medical care because you knew that bullet wounds have to be reported to the police. So one of two things. Either you were on the run from someone, or you were on the run from the police." His eyes gleamed in the morning light as he watched her. "And from your accent, I'd say that you are from the East Coast, New York State, maybe, so that means that you've traveled a long, long way to come here to San Luis. How am I doing so far?"

"Pretty good," she whispered.

He nodded. "The rest has to come from you. I've Googled every single Charlotte Fitzgerald on the Web, and you're nowhere. You might as well not exist for all the info I can find. Was he your husband?"

She couldn't stop the words tumbling out of her mouth. "God, no."

Matt nodded. "That's very good because I spent a couple of hours last night running through some scenarios of you running from an abusive husband." His lips tightened. "It wasn't fun. I'm really pleased you didn't marry the fucker."

"No, I couldn't."

His gaze sharpened. "But he wanted to? He wanted to marry you?"

"Yes." The word barely made it past the tightness in her throat.

"He's still looking for you, isn't he? You're not out of danger." It wasn't a question.

Charlotte's jaws clenched. The coffee roiled in her stomach, threatening to come up.

"Can he track you here, to San Luis?"

She bit her lips so hard she wondered whether she'd draw blood.

Matt sighed. "I need to know what's going on, honey. You're going to tell me eventually, might as well be now." He looked at her, waiting.

There was a huge boulder in her chest, weighing her down. Talking to him, telling him the truth would lift it. The temptation was enormous.

They sat in the silence of a sunny Mexican morning, listening to the faraway beach sounds coming in through the open window. It was warm, but Charlotte shivered. The silence was so deep it almost had weight and heft.

Finally, Matt closed his eyes and tipped his head back, letting his breath out in a long, controlled sigh. He got up, went into the kitchen, and came out with two plates.

"There you go." He slid a plate in front of her, slid another plate across from her, and sat down in front of it.

It wasn't a bad breakfast, considering. A wonderful brand of Mexican yogurt she'd discovered, fresh mango, and slices of whole wheat bread. Perfect. There was even too much food.

Then she saw his expression as he looked at what was on the table and nearly laughed when a grimace crossed his face.

He hadn't put on forty pounds of pure muscle in two months with yogurt and slices of fresh mango.

"I imagine you're used to a more...hearty breakfast," she said softly.

His hard mouth lifted in a half smile. "Yeah. Lenny goes on food runs to San Diego and comes down with enough bacon and link sausage to choke a horse. You should be eating more, too." He heaped sugar into his coffee, the teaspoon looking tiny in his huge hand. "But the rabbit food breakfast is okay," he said. "I'll eat something afterward. I should stay light anyway, because I'm going right into the water." He lifted his eyes, gaze hard and bright. "With you."

Charlotte froze. "I beg your pardon?" He had shifted to warrior in the blink of an eye. It wasn't so much a question of facial muscles tightening, it was more like steel suddenly flashing. She glanced out the window. It was a sunny day, but a brisk wind was blowing. "I don't want to go swimming. It's too chilly. The water will still be cold."

"Yes, it will be chilly but you'll warm up when you start swimming. It's not cold enough to harm you in any way, and you need to learn how to swim—starting right now."

"I know how to swim," she protested. This was ridiculous. "I took swimming lessons from the Red Cross when I was a kid."

Indignation masked her real feeling—fear. The ocean frightened her. It wasn't the tame Mediterranean or even the Atlantic, with its low breakers. The Pacific was huge, *felt* huge. She could well believe it covered half the world. The waves were often frighteningly high and unexpectedly powerful. She took a dip now and then because it was there, but that was it.

What Matt did every day—swimming way out to where he could never be rescued—was to her unfathomable and dangerous.

"You're frightened of the water," he said quietly, watching her carefully.

Charlotte put her spoon down and folded her hands in her lap to keep them from trembling. "Well," she said lightly, "of course. You can drown in the water, didn't you know that? I'm…cautious, that's all. I'm certainly not as strong a swimmer as you are. But then not many people are."

Matt nodded at this obvious truth. "You almost died yesterday. If you were a better swimmer, it wouldn't have been touch-and-go. I was scared to death I wouldn't get there in time." His mouth tightened.

The memory made her shiver. "I had a plank caught on my pants. That wasn't my fault. Anybody would have sunk."

He shook his head sharply. "Not good enough. I—" He looked away a moment, then back at her, dark gaze fierce. "I need to keep you safe. You're not giving me the information I need to do that. At least give me the satisfaction of knowing that you're not going to drown."

Charlotte's arms were wrapped around her middle as nightmarish images of yesterday bloomed in her mind. The dark, cold ocean. Watching the surface recede as she sank down, down . . . She shivered and shook her head. "I need—I need some time. I almost drowned yesterday."

"Which is precisely why you need to get back in the water today. If you put it off, you'll never get back in the water."

"Fine." Charlotte turned her head to look out the window. "I'll just be a nonswimmer. The world is full of them."

"Charlotte." Matt reached over to take her hand. She tried to resist, out of principle, but though he didn't use force, resisting him was impossible. "We need to drown-proof you. You live by the ocean, and you need to become a stronger swimmer. And another thing," he continued, when she opened her mouth to object. "You need to build up some shoulder muscle in your wounded shoulder. You need to build up muscle, period. You're too thin."

This was going too far. He was intruding into her private space. She wouldn't allow that even if what he was saying was true.

Charlotte tugged uselessly at her hand, looking him straight in the eyes.

"Listen, Matt, I really appreciate what you did yesterday—"

"Your shoulder hurts at night, and it hurts when the weather turns damp. You're losing strength in your left arm, and your left hand has lost some of its grip."

Her mouth closed with a snap.

Matt leaned forward, his face grim. "You were shot with a low-velocity gun; otherwise, you wouldn't be here today. You'd have bled out from the velocity shock. That's the good news. The bad news is that you didn't get medical care, and a low-velocity projectile carries debris into the wound—dirt, material, fragments—which probably wasn't debrided. Only a doctor can do that, and you didn't get medical care. Not only wasn't your wound debrided, you didn't have surgical drainage. You probably ran a high temperature for a week, ten days, then a low-grade fever for a few weeks after that."

Charlotte bit her lips and sat back in her seat, suddenly cold.

Matt nodded, once, then continued. "You're very lucky you were shot on the left-hand side and you're right-handed; otherwise, you could kiss your art good-bye forever, because you wouldn't have enough fine coordination left in your right hand. But if you want to avoid long-term trouble and muscle loss, you need to build muscle. You should have started rehabilitation right away, as a matter of fact. Right after the fever died down. Over and above muscle rehabilitation, you need to learn to swim for safety reasons. Right now. And you need to overcome your fear of the water. That's why we're going into the water today."

They stared at each other across the table, the bright Mexican sunshine streaming in, lighting a square on the dark wood. Charlotte could literally feel the strong waves of male power pushing at her. She should say no.

But last night her shoulder had ached with the damp weather, and she'd had problems gripping the blanket with her left hand while making the bed that morning.

She was proud and scared, but not stupid.

"I'll go change into my swimsuit," she said quietly.

CHAPTER ELEVEN

Excuse me."

Moira Fitzgerald turned around in surprise.

It was Friday morning, and Friday mornings were for shopping at Weegmans. Shopping for the Court household these past two months had been ... a *challenge* as the Yanks put it. *Bloody hard* was how she put it.

Moira was absolutely certain that Miss Charlotte would come back, her name fully cleared. The nightmare of the past two months would finally be over. It was monstrous that anyone could even think that Miss Charlotte would hurt a fly, let alone her da. Moira had never seen two people get on like Miss Charlotte and Mr. Philip. When this terrible, terrible mistake the local Garda had made was cleared up, Miss Charlotte would return. And when that day came, Moira was absolutely determined that Miss Charlotte would come back to a fully functioning household.

Oh, how she dreamed of that day! She could even picture it. Miss Charlotte, wearing one of her white linen suits, walking in through the big front door—the one that had been freshly painted last week, with the big brass doorknob Moira polished faithfully every ten days— smiling, asking for a cup of tea with a dash of milk.

And there would be tea, oh yes, all flavors. And milk and yogurt and bread and fruit. Moira kept the house fully stocked with Miss Charlotte's favorite foods, and then dutifully threw everything out on the expiration date. She faithfully cleaned five days a week, though there was no one to dirty the house.

Didn't matter. When Miss Charlotte came home, the mansion would be gleaming, fragrant, perfect.

Doing the Friday morning shopping presented enormous problems, because Moira wanted the house ready for Miss Charlotte whenever she showed up, day or night, but she also hated throwing money away. There was a household account available to her, and she was scrupulous. She could account for every penny of the household money she spent. But oh, how she agonized over her purchases.

She was holding two furniture polishes in her hands. One was on sale at half price, but it wasn't as good as the other, more expensive brand, made with beeswax. Ordinarily, Moira would always choose the better brand, but what if Miss Charlotte was still…away? Would buying the more expensive polish be justified—

Someone coughed behind her, and a man's voice said, "Excuse me?"

Turning, she saw a thin, pleasant-faced man with thick glasses, receding blond hair, and an apologetic smile.

"Hi," he said shyly. "I'm really really sorry to bother you, ma'am, but you look like you know what you're doing and I'm"—he shrugged his shoulders,—"well, frankly, I'm lost. I just moved to Warrenton, and I'm setting up a—household,

I guess you'd call it, and I have no idea what I need. I rented a studio apartment over the Internet, and the ad said 'ready to move in,' but it turns out that it doesn't have any household equipment or products." He looked helplessly at a sheet of paper in his hand, then held it out to her. "I made a list, see? But I don't know if it's a good list or not."

Men, Moira thought. Her own dear da, may God rest his soul, had never washed a dish in his life and wouldn't know which end of a broom to use. Moira looked at the list, read it twice, and barely refrained from snorting.

Men. It was a miracle they could tie their own shoelaces.

"Well," she said kindly, "you're going to need to add some dishwashing tabs—your new flat does have a dishwasher, doesn't it?"

At his nod, she looked back at the list. "All right, then. Hmmm. You'll also be needing laundry detergent, fabric softener, furniture polish, and bleach. Oh, and a broom and dust pan, even if you've got a vacuum cleaner."

The man had whipped out a pen and was frantically writing down her items as she mentioned them. He had at least five pens in his shirt pocket. Probably an engineer for that new software company on Madison. One of the pens had leaked, and an ugly blue splotch spread from the bottom of the shirt pocket.

The man blew out a breath of relief. "Okay." He blew out another breath, as if he'd been in a race. "Okay, now. If I get the things on my list and on your list, will I be all set?"

He looked so worried, she smiled reassuringly. He was thin and she wondered if she should write down a food list for him as well, then thought better of it. It wasn't her business if he wasn't eating enough.

Moira glanced at her watch and started in alarm.

She started work at ten o'clock. It was nine thirty, and she still had to pay, load the items in her new car, and drive to the Court Mansion. She'd never been late for work, not once, and had no intention of starting now.

"Oh yes, get everything on those lists and you'll be fine. Now, if you'll excuse me..."

He looked blank for a second, then realized he was blocking her shopping cart. He jumped guiltily out of her way. "Oh! Oh, of course. Sorry! Thank you so much, ma'am, I'm truly grateful for your help."

Moira nodded graciously and headed for the long row of cash registers, wondering if she should cheat and head for the line of ten items or less. She had eleven items. No, she finally decided, after a little mental tussle with herself. It wouldn't be fair to the others. But she was going to be late if she didn't do something.

Looking at the bank of checkout counters with long lines, she surreptitiously stashed the new set of kitchen sponges on a shelf in the wine section, hoping no one noticed. She'd buy new sponges next week.

Next week. Maybe next week Miss Charlotte would return.

Smiling at the thought, she headed for the Ten Items or Less line with only two people in front of her, happy and secure in the thought that at 10 A.M., on the dot, she'd be at work.

San Luis

It was too beautiful a day for resentment. Charlotte stepped out onto her terrace and felt the slight wisps of irritation at being ordered about dissipating in the warm sunshine.

People talked about perfect days, but actually they were few and far between—it was either too hot or too chilly or too damp or too dry. *This* was perfect. A combination of warm, buttery sun tempered by a gentle cool breeze that brought with it the smell of the ocean and the jasmine growing along her neighbor's terrace.

Yesterday's storm had done something to the air. It felt newborn—the first air of a new world. The air was diamond bright, and she felt as if she could see to the ends of the earth.

They walked down to the beach in silence, he adjusting his much longer stride to hers. He was dressed only in swim trunks and flip-flops. He'd probably had them in the big black bag she'd seen in her living room.

Charlotte was torn between putting distance between them and wanting to be as close as possible to all that male power. He was all but naked, and she was half-amused and half-appalled that the only way not to touch him was to bunch her hands into fists. He had a mouth-wateringly beautiful body. She'd seen gym-honed male bodies before, but never anything like this, a machine built for both speed and power.

He was in many ways unsettling, even frightening. She'd found a powerful paladin, if it turned out that Matt Sanders was placing his strength at her service. Or she might have stumbled across a devastating foe.

Her heart pumped high and wild in her chest, part excitement, part fear. He kept glancing at her, as if gauging her mood, and Charlotte kept her face an expressionless mask.

Charlotte stopped at the ocean's edge, the frothy waves curling over her toes. Matt stopped, too.

They stood in silence, looking out over the wide blue ocean.

The ocean was beautiful today, so totally unlike the roiling gray monster that had almost eaten her alive the day before. She could still remember the icy cold waves, the choking sensation, the long drop to the bottom...

She stepped back.

He looked at her. Charlotte hated it that he seemed to see everything, understand everything. His face was expressionless, but his gaze was warm and understanding.

"Just look at that," he said, nodding at the flat, brilliant blue expanse. "Makes up most of the Earth. A Martian from outer space would naturally assume that the dominant species on Earth was a fish. Without the oceans we would be dead."

Charlotte had never actually thought of it that way. She swished her sandals in the tide, washing away the sand of the beach.

He watched her feet, then lifted his eyes to hers. "Leonardo da Vinci thought that the seas were the lungs of the Earth, and that the tides were the Earth, breathing."

The lungs of the Earth. Charlotte blinked at the poetry of the image, and at the incongruity of the image coming out of Matt's mouth. "That's beautiful."

"Uh-huh." He turned his head to look out over the ocean, hard mouth lifted in a half smile. "As beautiful as the ocean itself. You must make friends with it. If it's not your friend, it's your enemy."

Well, someone who swam the way he did *would* think

that. "Easy for you to say," she said wryly, looking out to the horizon. "You swim like a dolphin."

"I have BUD/S to thank for that."

She looked up at him, surprised. "You have your bud to thank for that? Who's he?"

"Not bud. BUD/S. Basic Underwater Demolition. The Navy spent thirty months keeping us wet and sandy and wet and cold and wet and tired, and drownproofing us." His mouth quirked. "Among other things. It's our training course. BUD/S. That's what the Navy calls it. We called it Pain 101."

Charlotte lifted her face into the sun, contemplating the notion of being drownproofed. Sounded nice, really nice. "You said that before—that you wanted to drownproof me. How do you drownproof someone? It sounds great."

"I don't think you'd like our system much. Our hands are tied behind our backs, our feet are tied at the ankles, and we're tossed blindfolded into a nine-foot-deep tank. We're expected to bob for five minutes, then swim a hundred meters, then float, then bob, then we have to go to the bottom of the tank and retrieve our mask with our teeth. It's a little . . . intense."

Charlotte's eyes rounded in horror as she took an instinctive step backward.

Matt smiled down at her. "No need to worry, honey, I'm not going to do that to you."

"I should hope not," Charlotte replied heatedly. "That—that's tantamount to torture!" She tried to ignore the little leap her heart had taken when he called her "honey."

"Yep, that's what it was originally, torture. Or rather murder. The Viet Cong used to hog-tie American POWs and throw them into the Mekong, expecting them to drown. Only our guys survived and proved that you can swim even with your feet and hands tied if you have to. Since then it's become part of training. You'd basically have to tie a weight, a heavy weight, to a SEAL or shoot him in the water to drown him. But don't worry. You don't need to learn that kind of swimming. All I want is for you to feel comfortable in the water and learn to do the crawl and maybe a backstroke, so you can exercise your shoulder muscles."

She didn't answer, intensely aware of the big big ocean and the big big man by her side.

He looked down at her and silently held out his hand, exactly as he had last night. He didn't coax, he didn't cajole. He just stood there, his hand brown and broad and steady.

Without even thinking about it, Charlotte found herself with her hand in his.

It was as if someone had thrown a switch and turned her on.

She was suddenly intensely, keenly aware of everything. The feel of her hand in his, immensely safe. The bright sunlight, the tang of the ocean, the wavelets lapping at her toes, the soft plashing of the water. The clear air, bringing both warmth and coolness that she could feel in every cell of her body. She felt awake and aware and *alive*. She felt good for the first time in two months. Two years.

"Come on," he said softly, tugging at her hand. "You'll enjoy yourself more in the sea if you can swim."

That remained to be seen. Still, Charlotte shucked off her sandals and, letting go of Matt's hand, reached down to whip off her beach cover-up.

Matt's sharp, dark eyes went immediately to her

shoulder. She'd bought three one-piece swimsuits in
Cabo, all with broad shoulder straps. If you didn't know
the scar was there, you wouldn't notice anything, and,
anyway, Charlotte had taken to going into the water only
when there were very few people around.

But Matt knew. He noticed the white scar tissue edging out from under the straps. His mouth tightened but he
didn't say anything. He started walking slowly backward
in the water, coaxing her forward. Charlotte stepped gingerly forward, until the water was up to her knees, and
sucked in a breath.

"It's *cold!*" she said indignantly. This wasn't going to
work. Only dummies went into the water when it was cold.

"Not if you move. Shuffle your feet, get your circula-
tion going." He turned and, executing a neat dive, swam
underwater for so long she started to get worried. At the
last possible instant, when Charlotte would have already
drowned three times over, his head popped up, farther
away than she would have imagined anyone could go
on one breath. Before she could call out to him, he dove
again, and she watched the large, dark shape moving
underwater fast, coming closer.

He surfaced a foot away from her. "Don't you dare shake
yourself and get me all wet!" she warned, palms up and out.
Matt grinned at her, the mischievous look in his dark eyes
telling her he had, indeed, been about to shake himself.

His face was utterly transformed when he smiled. He
dropped years and looked almost—almost handsome.

He *was* handsome, Charlotte realized suddenly.

She hadn't really noticed it before.

Most handsome men carried themselves with vanity,
and were intensely self-aware, their words and actions

gauged for maximum effect. Matt had such a serious, somber—almost grim—air about him, his looks were the last thing you noticed. Mainly you noticed his size and watchful eyes.

"Wouldn't think of it," he said piously, that damned grin plastered on his face. "Come on," he coaxed. "Move in the water, warm yourself up. Just dunk yourself. I promise you it's worse when you go in slowly. Like ripping off a Band-Aid slowly. Now just follow me."

Matt walked backward while he talked. He was walking directly toward where the bottom suddenly dropped.

"Hey," Charlotte called, alarmed. "Come back here! I can't touch where you're going."

The water lapped his shoulders. "Don't worry, I can touch. Come on, Charlotte, trust me. Nothing will happen to you, guaranteed."

Charlotte didn't know where her fear of water, her terror of drowning, came from. She'd never learned to swim well, so she was naturally very cautious in the water, but she'd never had a bad experience while swimming. Still, when she had nightmares, they were often of drowning, of water closing in over her head while she sank deeper and deeper. These past two months, she'd woken often choking and gasping, having dreamed of drowning.

Her near death in the water had been her worst nightmare come true.

He watched her eyes. "Fall forward, honey," he said softly. "I'll catch you."

There wasn't another human being on Earth she'd do this for. But at some level of her being, deeper than thought, deeper than emotions, she trusted Matt utterly. In the water, anyway.

Taking a deep breath, Charlotte toppled forward into the water. Before the awful truth—*she couldn't touch!*—had time to make it to her brain, before she even had time to start flailing, two strong hands gripped her under her arms, and she was steady in the water, facing Matt.

They were so close she could feel his breath wash over her face. So close her breasts brushed his chest. Though she was held as steady as a rock, her legs automatically churned frantically, the reptilian part of her brain telling her she was in free fall.

Her toes kicked his shins and, with difficulty, she forced herself to stop. She wasn't having to work to keep herself afloat. He was holding her up.

Her heart rate, which had started trip-hammering when her toes couldn't reach the sandy bottom, started calming down. Matt's hands were still holding her, but his grip had loosened even farther. All of a sudden she realized he'd let her go completely.

She slipped, the water covering her chin.

"Don't panic," Matt said quietly. "Breathe normally. In and out, deep breaths, that's great. Perfect. My hands are an inch away. Move your arms and your legs gently, you'll stay afloat."

Matt's low, deep voice was calm, reassuring. It set up a little hum in her diaphragm underwater. Just listening to him made her feel better. Her movements in the water slowed, became more rhythmic.

"You're doing fine."

She was. Sort of. Maybe.

Charlotte was taking it on faith. If Matt said it, and it had to do with water, it was probably true, though she slipped a little farther down. Still, to be polite, she nodded.

This close up, Matt's face was so fascinating. He'd shaved closely this morning—when had he done that?— but she could still clearly see the line of demarcation where the beard started. He had a scar running through his right eyebrow, lifting it, giving him a slightly devilish cast to his face. The silver threads at his temples were echoed by even more silver hairs in his chest hair.

She watched his eyes for clues to what he was thinking. They were the only eyes she'd ever seen with no striations of color at all—just an even monotone chocolate brown.

"Better?" he asked quietly, as she quietly trod water.

"Um." It was, sort of. If she didn't actually *think* about the fact that she couldn't touch, that if she dropped in the water, it would close in over her head...

She slipped, but before the water could cover her mouth, and she could panic, Matt caught her.

"I'll just bet you were thinking about the water just now instead of letting your mind go blank."

"You didn't tell me I had to let my mind go blank," Charlotte complained. "You have to say these things. And I don't like having my mind go blank, not unless I'm at a yoga lesson. It doesn't go blank naturally; it tends to think of things all on its own."

"Okay, then, think about this." He nodded his head gravely. "I never thanked you for my watercolor and that incredibly beautiful painting of the conch shell. I've never owned any art before, and here I start my brand-new collection with a couple of masterpieces."

Charlotte smiled. "They're not masterpieces," she protested. "Though it's nice of you to say so. And I guess I can forgive you for not thanking me yesterday, considering you were busy saving my life."

"Do you think two thanks cancel each other out?"

"No. I'd like to think that they are mutually rein-
forcing."

"Okay, that's a nice way of looking at it." Matt watched
her eyes. "By the way, this might be a good time to tell
you that I poked around your artwork this morning. I
won't apologize because most of it was out there for me
to see. I have to tell you that I've never seen stuff like that
in my life outside of museums, not that I've ever been to
that many."

Charlotte was instantly distracted. He hadn't seen many
museums? "I thought Navy people traveled the world?
Isn't that what the posters say? Join and travel the world?"

"That's the Army recruitment slogan, but we travel
a lot in the Navy, too. Only we travel mainly to places
where there aren't that many museums. Lots of armed
fu—scumbags itching to cause trouble, oh yeah, plenty of
those, but not much artwork. My last posting was Afghanistan. Any artwork there was blown up by the Taliban."

"How much time did you spend in Afghanistan?"

"Six months, before—before I was shot. My Team
is still deployed there." Something—some expression
crossed his usually expressionless face.

"You miss them," Charlotte said, on a sudden insight.
"You miss being with them, and you miss Afghanistan."

"Miss sleeping in the desert with a bazillion scorpions?
Miss carrying my water on my back because there isn't an
oasis or a water hole within a hundred miles? Miss hik-
ing sixteen miles a day in hundred-degree heat, hoping
not to step on a Soviet-era land mine, dodging snipers
in the hills while carrying a hundred-pound pack? Miss
Mylowski who snores, and Gardner who smells, Her-

nandez who fa—who has flatulence, major *major* flatulence, and Lopez who never remembers the punch lines to his rotten jokes?" Matt's mouth twisted in a bittersweet smile. His pain was visible. "Yeah," he said softly, "I miss it, miss them. What's not to miss?"

"I'm sorry," she said softly.

Oh *God,* Charlotte knew all about missing someone you cared for. How many times she'd stopped to watch something interesting or thought of something amusing and thought—*I must tell Dad.* And right on the heels of that thought, a sharp searing pain, as fresh as if she were back in the hospital room, watching his life being snuffed out. Her father wasn't there. Would never be there again.

"Now you're thinking about something sad." Matt's deep voice interrupted her thoughts, and she was reminded all over again how observant he was.

In a dinner date, that was a good quality to have. In a man who would probably turn her in to the police if he knew the truth about her, it was a highly dangerous quality.

"Not at all." She paddled gently in the water, looking away from those too-perspicacious eyes. She studied the horizon, water as far as the eye could see, all of it deep...

A current of cold water caught her, and she shivered.

"You're tired and getting cold," Matt decided. "Time to get out."

Somehow, without appearing to have helped her, she was back where she could touch. A moment later, they were on the shore, and Charlotte was drying her hair with a towel. She *was* a little tired and was looking forward to relaxing with the new Faber-Castell pastels, which had just arrived.

Matt looked back toward the cheerful line of brightly

painted shops and houses past the *ramblas*. "We'll have lunch at the cantina. And then when we've digested, we'll have another swimming lesson."

Charlotte stopped drying her hair and looked up. Had she heard him correctly? He was telling her what to do? The bright Mexican morning cooled several degrees. "I beg your pardon?"

"I'm sorry." Matt was a smart man, too smart to smile, but his eyes crinkled. "That sounded like an order, and I didn't mean it to. So let me see if I can put it another way. I really need to eat because I had a lighter breakfast than I'm used to, and there's no food in your house, and you need to eat, too, after falling into the ocean and almost dying yesterday. So it would be a really good idea if we went to the cantina where Mama Pilar will feed us some fabulous, warm food and lots of it. And afterward, in the early afternoon, when we've digested, it would be a really good idea for us to have another swimming lesson. Swimming is a physical skill and, like all physical skills, it can only be learned through repetition. The more you do, the better you are at it. You have to do enough of it so that your muscles retain the memory. You're an artist, so that's something you can understand. I'm sure you've done thousands and thousands of sketches to be able to draw as well as you do. So, given that, I think it would be a good idea for you to get back into the water this afternoon."

Put like that, it sounded . . . well, reasonable. It would be churlish of her to refuse. That first rise of temper at being told what to do subsided. "Well . . . okay," she murmured.

"So, let's say the swimming lesson around four," Matt continued in his reasonable, matter-of-fact voice. "And tomorrow we start with the shooting lessons."

CHAPTER TWELVE

Warrenton
April 26

Friday was live music night at the Ceili, Warrenton's biggest Irish pub. The Ceili was a notorious pickup bar, but that wasn't why Moira went every Friday after work, regular as clockwork. One-night stands didn't tempt her. No, indeed. She'd been raised better than that.

No, she went for the bands, she did. It was her own little weekly nostalgia trip, nursing a single Guinness all evening, tapping her foot to the wild Irish music that cracked her heart open just a little, just enough to remind her of home, every time.

She was happy in America, she was. A trip back to the old country once every two years was all she needed to keep on an even keel. A few weeks in Doro in County Donegal always reminded her all over again why she'd followed Aunt Meg to America. After a short time, she felt cramped by how small her hometown was, how far from Dublin, how narrow her old schoolmates' lives seemed.

No, she wasn't homesick. She'd made a good life for herself in America, and there was no turning back.

But, oh, how the music misted her up. It was just like being home of a warm, rainy summer evening at Aunt Aideen's house, all the Fitzgerald cousins having a couple too many under their belts, which God knows never stopped them from singing in perfect harmony.

The music at the Ceili was always good, and tonight was no exception. The group was great, the female fiddler with wild corkscrew black hair flying around her face as she fiddled up a storm.

The group—the Stone of Turoe—had the audience stomping their feet and swaying drunkenly in their seats. Moira marveled at how the nimble waitresses managed not to slip on the beer suds that slopped onto the floor.

The first set wasn't over until almost midnight. Moira stifled a yawn. Much as she'd love to hear the second set, it was time to go home. Since the group was breaking now, the second set wouldn't be over until after one, which was way past her bedtime. Moira was moving to gather her purse when her arm was jostled and what felt like a whole keg of cold beer was splashed all over her cream silk blouse. What was left of her pint of Guinness was dumped into her lap, where it made a dark stain on her brand-new white wool trousers. They'd cost her half a week's wages and were ruined forever.

"Oh…my…*God*," a male voice breathed, and Moira looked up from the disaster of her blouse and pants. The man was skinny, with short receding blond hair, big black ugly square glasses and a polyester short-sleeved shirt. Total nerd, as they said here.

Moira slid to the end of the bench, and his beer—one of those pale, wishy-washy American brews that smelled of piss—cascaded from her shirt onto her trousers. Wonderful. American beer drenching her shirt, Guinness on her trousers. And like all the bloody drinks served in this country, they were both ice-cold.

He was bent over her, trying to wipe her blouse and pants with the tiny little single-ply napkins he'd ripped from the table dispenser. The napkins disintegrated immediately, leaving white blobs all over, making her look even more like a mess.

"Oh, damn, I'm so sorry, I'm such a clumsy fool, I'm so very sorry, what an idiot I am," he kept repeating, over and over.

Well, yes he was. He was a sorry, clumsy fool. Still, Moira's mom had drilled manners into her, with the flat of her hand when necessary, may God rest her soul, so instead of taking a strip off the man's hide, Moira counted to ten, and said, "It's okay. It was an accident."

Moira raised her eyes from her sodden blouse and as he saw her face, the man took in a shocked breath, loud even over the background noise of happy drinkers. "Oh. My. God."

Honestly. His vocabulary appeared to have departed to the same place his manners had.

He was looking at her in horror as if she'd sprouted two heads, staring at her openmouthed, like an idiot. He didn't move, didn't even seem to breathe. He just stood there, wide-eyed and slack-jawed. Was he going to stand there forever, the ninny? She suppressed a sigh. So much for a pleasant evening relaxing to music.

Moira rose, grimacing with distaste. The Guinness had soaked through her trousers to dampen her stockings. It was freezing cold outside, and it was going to be unpleasant, to put it mildly, facing the chilly night with cold, wet stockings. When she gathered her gloves and hat, it was as if the man had been set free from some spell.

"No, no!" He sprang forward, made to touch her, then withdrew his hands, wringing them in distress. "My God, I can't believe I spilled my drink on *you*. A hundred thousand people to choose from—" He blinked, eyelashes so pale his eyes looked naked. "Actually, Warrenton has 97,314 people, according to the last census. And out of 97,314—though now it's probably more like 96,500 factoring in attrition and the—" He blinked again. "Sorry. I'm a mathematician. Anyway, of all the people in Warrenton to spill my beer on..."

Of all people? Moira peered more closely at him. Medium height, balding, light blue eyes behind thick overlarge glasses—he did look familiar.

"You don't remember me, do you?" His voice was wry. "I get that a lot. You were extremely kind to me this morning with my shopping list."

Shopping list?

"At the supermarket? Remember?" He stared at her hopefully. "Brooms, and detergent and...and things?"

Brooms and detergent...The penny dropped. The clueless new guy, trying to set up a household with zero experience. She'd almost been late to work, thanks to him. How could she forget?

"Oh! Oh, yes. Of course I remember you."

Still, it wasn't the man's fault he'd needed help. Pity kicked in. Her ma hadn't raised her to be unkind. The guy was a total loser, as the Yanks said, but he was also new in town and—from the looks of him—desperately lonely. "Did you find everything you need?"

"Yes, thanks to you. You were so incredibly kind."

He stopped wringing his hands and touched her elbow, gently turning her back to her seat. "You *must* let me buy you another drink. Oh, please, I *insist*," he said, when she shook her head. He bit his lips, and Moira was afraid he'd actually break down and cry. "I feel terrible about ruining your pretty blouse and your pants. You must let me buy you another drink, I simply won't take no for an answer. It's the very least I can do. Please sit back down, that's right." He beamed, light gleaming off his ugly glasses. "What kind of drink were you having?" He peered at her once-white trousers, now stained dark brown by the Guinness, and at the small amount of dark liquid left in the bottom of her pint glass and winced. "I'm sorry, I don't know anything about beers. I'm not much of a drinker," he apologized, lifting his own empty glass, the contents of which were still soaking through her shirt. "I just order a beer and drink what they give me. But I'd love to buy you another glass of whatever it is you were having." He looked like a lost puppy. If he'd had a tail, it would have been wagging. "Please."

"All right." With an inward roll of her eyes, Moira sat back down, wincing at the sodden feeling of wet wool against her thighs. "But not anything alcoholic. A Coke will be fine." No more alcohol for her, not with the ice-slick roads.

"Great. Great. That's really, really great. In just a second you'll have your drink." He looked around, trying to catch the attention of one of the wait staff, but it was as if he had suddenly become invisible. He sighed, and muttered, "Story of my life." Putting his hands on the table, he leaned forward. "Listen, it would be quicker if I just went to the bar and came back with your Coke. So—you'll wait here?" He stood there for a moment, blinking uncertainly at her. "You—you won't leave, will you?"

The thought *was* tempting—just slip out while he was at the bar, but— "No." Moira drummed up a smile. "No, I'll wait here."

"Great," he said again, and disappeared into the rush around the bar. Moira barely had time to register with distaste that the backs of her thighs were wet, too, when he was back with two big Cokes. He sat down across from her and lifted his glass. "Well, here's hoping you can forgive me my clumsiness and to the start of a friendship."

Moira lifted her own glass reluctantly. It was half ice, of course. She could never get used to the Yank habit of serving all drinks teeth-clenchingly cold, including when the temperature outside was below freezing. Even the beer was served so cold you couldn't taste it. Moira sipped slowly, trying to warm up the drink in her mouth.

The man was staring at her, hand holding up his Coke, looking ridiculous. He wasn't going to leave her in peace until she'd downed the freezing-cold drink. This was one of those rare moments when she positively yearned for the old country.

With a heroic effort, she finished the Coke in a few gulps, hoping that it would earn her points so she could go home.

"You're Irish, aren't you?" His voice was light and friendly. He was leaning forward on the table as he talked so she could hear him better. "Going to Ireland someday has always been my dream. How long have you lived in the States?"

He seemed genuinely interested. It hurt, just a little, to

think that it had been a long time since a man had showed personal interest in her. He completely focused on her, and it felt good to have all that male attention, even if it was only from a lonely mathematician.

He wasn't *that* bad-looking, either. Take away the nerdy paraphernalia like the thick glasses and cheap plasticky shirt with the polyester sheen, and he'd be almost presentable.

He was such a good listener, too, unlike most men. Moira found herself talking about the decision to leave Ireland against her parents' wishes, God rest their souls. They were gone, now. She found herself telling him how lonely she'd been at first and how she missed her sisters and brothers. She must have talked for a long time, because she was out of breath. She had to stiffen her backbone not to sway in her seat. How late was it? Bringing her wrist up to her face took an enormous effort.

It was past one. When had that happened? It was way past time to get home. Moira tried to slip out from the bench, but her muscles had turned to water. Her newest best friend was talking, but somehow she couldn't focus on what he was saying.

"What?" It came out as *wha?*

"I said—do you need any help getting home?"

Of course not. She'd never needed help before. She was an independent young lady, thank you very much. It was just that her legs felt rubbery and she was finding it hard to stay awake. "No, thanks, ah—" A blank. "Um, what's your name again?"

"John." His shy smile was sweet. "But my friends call me Barrett."

San Luis
April 26

They argued all the way to the cantina.

Charlotte gathered up her things in a cold, shaking rage and started walking back to her apartment. Matt grabbed her by the elbow. His grip was gentle, but unbreakable. Charlotte looked pointedly at her arm, then up at him. That usually worked with a man's unwanted touch. To her surprise, he didn't let go.

"I'll thank you to let go of my arm." Charlotte's voice was icy.

"No."

She blinked. "I beg your pardon?" That tone usually brought results, but Matt didn't relent. He actually looked as if he were biting back a smile, the bastard.

"Charlotte, listen to me."

"No, you listen to me," she began heatedly. The icy chill she'd felt had melted into a fiery upswelling of rage. "You seem to think you've acquired some kind of rights over me. It's true, I'm grateful, you saved my life yesterday, but—"

"You were shot," he said simply.

Charlotte's back teeth ground together, hard. It was a surprise that shards of enamel weren't flying out her ears. "I'm well aware of that. It doesn't mean—"

"The guy who shot you isn't in jail, and he isn't dead. You told me that yourself."

Her jaws were aching. "I fail to see—"

"He's still after you. You can't stay hidden here forever."

Yes, she could. No, she couldn't. Charlotte stared angrily at him.

His grip on her elbow finally loosened. He hadn't hurt her in any way, but she massaged her arm, out of principle.

"You don't want to think about this. You'd like it all to disappear. None of this is part of your world, and you'd love for it to be some kind of nightmare that will just...go away."

Charlotte shuddered. He'd just spoken her deepest desire out loud.

"The nature of guys with guns is that they don't go away, honey," he said in the gentlest voice possible. "They don't disappear because you find them distasteful. I know because I'm one of them, only I'm one of the good guys. You won't tell me anything about what happened, but if your troubles were over, you wouldn't be here in San Luis, hiding out. You'd be back in the States, wherever it is you come from, happily painting your heart out. Instead you're here, in a place where broken soldiers and people on the run come. This isn't where you belong," he continued, his voice even more gentle than before. "You belong somewhere else, surrounded by friends and family, with no cares other than to paint and draw."

Charlotte stared at him, muscles tense. Tears pricked behind her eyes. *Surrounded by friends and family.* Her father, her family, was gone. She couldn't contact her friends without embroiling them in the danger that had reached out to snare her. She was alone.

A sudden, fierce, deep longing for her old life swamped her. What she wouldn't give to turn the clock back to two—no, three years ago. Before her father's illness. Back to when her greatest worries had been chiaroscuro and perspective.

"Ah, honey," Matt said, and stepped forward to fold

her in his arms. "I can't even say it'll all be okay, because that's not the nature of the beast."

Charlotte wanted to resist. This man was taking over her life and pushing her in directions she didn't want to go. But for just one second it felt so *good* to lean against him. Her head fit neatly against his shoulder. His hand came up to cradle her head against him. She rested against him for one heartbeat, two. This was when she was supposed to pull away, but it was as if his shoulder was a magnet, and her head was full of iron filings.

"I hate guns," she said into his tee shirt. The words were fervent, and came from the deepest reaches of her heart. She belonged to every antigun organization there was and had marched and campaigned for gun control. She'd collected petitions and written letters to the editor and her senator and consistently voted for the gun control candidate.

"I know, honey. I hate guns, too."

Charlotte pulled away at that, looking up at him, sure to find him grinning at her inanely. A soldier hating guns. Yeah, right.

Instead, what she found was Matt looking grimmer than ever. Sober and deadly serious. "You don't believe me."

"N-no, I don't."

"Trust me, we hate violence the way only someone who goes in harm's way can."

With an electric shock, Charlotte remembered the bullet scars on Matt's body. The fact that he'd spent months in a coma. He'd been shot, too. And more times than she had. She'd completely forgotten.

"If this were a perfect world, and no one meant me or my country any harm, I'd have been a math teacher or a high-school football coach. But the world's not like that. We need weapons because the bad guys have them."

It was an age-old argument, and Charlotte had heard it more than once. But never from a soldier who bore bullet wounds on his body.

He reached down and ran the back of his index finger down her cheek. "You're scared," he said gently. "You're right to be scared. You're in trouble, and you need help. Listen to me, honey. No, listen," he insisted, as she tried, uselessly, to pull away from him.

"I can't protect you against a danger I can't see. You won't talk to me about your troubles, which means no one can protect you other than yourself. So either you talk to me, right now, and tell me what trouble you're in, and I take precautions, or you learn at least the basics about handling guns. I want you to be able to defend yourself."

She stared up at him numbly.

"I want that for you," he said softly. "I don't want anything else to happen to you. I want you to be safe and happy and spend your days drawing and painting. Usually the bad guys get their way in this world, did you know that?" His eyes were dark, intense pools. "I hate that. It makes me angry. Doesn't it make you angry? They never stop, Charlotte. They just keep on coming until someone stops them."

This was so *true*. For the first time, Charlotte allowed herself to feel anger instead of fear and panic and grief.

She had an idea what had happened. Robert had gotten greedy. His huge salary at Court Industries hadn't been enough. Deep down, she realized that for someone like Robert, nothing would ever be enough. For some reason, he had felt that the Courts were in the way of something he wanted. And so he hadn't hesitated to murder her father.

Charlotte stiffened. An electric surge of knowledge coursed through her. Robert had wanted to kill *her,* too! Whatever it was that required Philip's death would have required hers, too. The plan hadn't been to kill Philip and frame her. The plan had been to get rid of the Court family. Framing her had been Plan B when Plan A—putting them both underground—hadn't worked.

She'd escaped by a miracle.

Matt was too attentive not to notice something. "What?" he murmured, pulling away and angling his head to look her full in the face. "You just thought of something. Something that scared you or shocked you. What?"

Charlotte wasn't used to this. She didn't know how to mask her feelings from someone as perceptive as Matt. But burrowing her head more deeply against his shoulder didn't work. Matt gently gripped her jaw and pulled her face away.

"Don't hide from me. What's wrong now?"

Charlotte bit her lips and shook her head.

Matt sighed. "Okay, we're having lunch at the cantina, then another swimming lesson. And tomorrow a shooting lesson and a few pointers on self-defense. I'm not taking any chances with you."

"Okay," Charlotte said sweetly. "And then tomorrow evening you can accompany me to a concert at the old mission." She nearly laughed at Matt's panicked expression. "You'll love it."

Warrenton
April 27

Moira Fitzgerald weighed about 140 pounds. *On the plump side, aren't we darling?* Barrett thought as he carried her easily to his van. He'd gotten her out of the Irish pub while she was still able to walk, though her head was lolling on his shoulder, and her eyes were closed. Nobody gave them a second glance. Lots of drunken second-generation Irish girls were staggering out of the pub, helped along by their equally drunk boyfriends.

Once in the parking lot out back, Barrett simply picked her up and carried her in his arms. There was no one to see. He'd parked in the northwest corner, where the light of the big halogen streetlamps didn't carry. Barrett never left anything to chance.

Three-quarters of an hour later, they were in a warehouse in the industrial district he'd rented by e-mail, using a perfectly legitimate credit card stolen off a man in Times Square. The two magnetic passcards to enter the gates and open his individual unit had been couriered to the Hotel Plaza, care of Mr. Vincent Bender, who had checked in that morning. Barrett had even gone into the room, mussed up the bed, and run the shower, making sure not to leave fingerprints or DNA.

The industrial area was perfect. There was no one around as he used his passcard to enter the big, empty space. Within a couple of minutes, he had Moira in a chair and the metal door shut.

Perfect. There were no windows, and though it wasn't soundproofed, the walls were cement, and he was certain sound wouldn't carry.

Not that he intended making Moira scream. It wouldn't be necessary.

Everything was prepared for her. A big tarpaulin was spread in the center of the empty concrete floor and on it was a metal chair. The only other item in the room was a big bottle of industrial-strength bleach.

Barrett stripped Moira, folded her clothes neatly, and put them in a big condominium-sized black garbage bag, poured bleach in, and used twist ties to seal the bag off. The bag would be tossed into the big landfill he'd seen twelve miles north of town.

Barrett placed Moira's naked, unconscious body on the chair placed in the center of the tarpaulin. He had a roll of duct tape and made three circuits around her breasts, tying her to the chair. Plastic flexicuffs went around her wrists and ankles, rendering her completely immobilized.

Barrett wore latex gloves on his hands, and his feet were encased in sterile booties. Tomorrow, he would douse the clothes he was wearing with gasoline and burn them. He knew all about Locard's theory of transference. Nothing was perfect, but he intended to leave behind as little of himself as possible.

As he wrapped the maid in duct tape and tugged the snap-ties closed, Barrett handled her naked body as impersonally as he would a side of beef.

Rohypnol was a date-rape drug, but rape never even entered his thoughts. He'd once shot a soldier under his command for breaking opsec in order to have sex with a prostitute. Sex messed with men's heads, not just their dicks. Barrett bought clean, energetic sex a couple of times a month from a reliable supplier and never thought about it outside those pleasant interludes.

Moira was rapidly metabolizing the Rohypnol he'd administered in her Coke. An hour had elapsed. She should be coming out of her drug-induced stupor any moment now.

Barrett sat on his haunches and waited, patient and

attentive. He was prepared to wait all night, if necessary, but it wasn't necessary.

After thirteen minutes, she moaned. Four minutes later, her eyelids flickered. She mumbled something. Barrett waited patiently. She wasn't yet in a position to tell him anything useful. He knew there'd be some nonsense to get through. "Cold," she muttered, licked her lips. Yes, she was cold. She was naked in an unheated warehouse unit in the dead of night.

Barrett had contemplated and then discarded torture. As a professional soldier, he knew that torture seldom worked. A soldier who'd trained properly—or a terrorist whose fanaticism created a mental shield—could seldom be broken. Their hearts gave out first.

For civilians, using torture as a tool to obtain information was stupid. It worked just fine as an instrument of oppression, as a warning to others. Having a tortured body dumped into the central square of a village softened the villagers up nicely.

But in this case, Moira Fitzgerald wasn't going to cough up info on the Court woman because he hurt her. Fear and pain would overwhelm her mind with catecholamines and cortisol, rendering her incapable of coherent thought. She'd be willing to say anything to make the pain stop, and any information she gave him would be suspect. He could spend weeks chasing down her intel and end up with nothing. He didn't have weeks. He needed a reliable info dump from her and he needed it now.

She moaned again, and her eyes opened. They were unfocused, pupils dilated.

"Hi, Moira," Barrett said softly.

"Cold," she mumbled again.

"Yes, honey," he said, his voice gentle. "We'll get you warm in just a minute. But first you need to tell me a few things."

Her eyes were a little more focused now. Her head turned slowly as she took in her surroundings, not that she could see much. Most of the unit was lost in darkness, the only light a two hundred-watt spotlight focused on her, blinding her. She closed her eyes and turned her head away.

She struggled briefly against the tape and the flexi-cuffs, then subsided. Good. The drug made most people compliant, robbing them of the will to resist. Moira didn't appear to be the rebellious sort, and anyway, Barrett supposed that obedience would be part of a maid's mental makeup. After a brief tussle with the restraints, she simply accepted that she was tied up.

"Where—where am I?" The words were slurred. Her mouth would be dry, her tongue would feel swollen.

"You're with friends, Moira. And pretty soon you'll be with Charlotte. Won't you like that, when you can see Charlotte again?"

She smiled, her head wobbling gently on her neck. "Miss Charlotte. She's coming back."

"That's right, Miss Charlotte's coming back. She wants to come back. But she needs for us to go get her and bring her back, Moira. So you need to tell me where she is. Where is she? Where is Miss Charlotte?"

A pucker appeared between her eyebrows. "Sure an' I don't know. Gone. Accused her of murder, they have." She scowled. "Nasty buggers. Idiots, the lot of them."

A woman who faithfully cleaned an empty house obviously valued duty. And it sounded like there was affection there. Barrett tried a different tack. He put some sharpness in his voice.

"Miss Charlotte's in trouble, Moira. Terrible trouble. We have to get to her. Where is she?"

She blinked. "Don't—don't know."

"How did she get away, Moira? Miss Charlotte's car is still in her garage. Is she driving your car?"

She blinked rapidly and nodded. "Yes. That day—it was snowing so hard. Miss Charlotte's car wouldn't start. She borrowed my Tahoe." A look of grief crossed her face, and a single tear trickled down her cheek. "Never came back." She began to cry quietly.

Barrett had done his homework. He'd spent the day holed up in a motel, logged onto the Internet via an encrypted line. He probably knew more about Moira Charlotte Fitzgerald than her own mother did. After a day spent digging into the maid's life, he'd found a number of facts that intrigued him.

One: Though a secondhand Tahoe bought for eighteen thousand dollars seven months before was registered in Moira's name, she had bought a new Escape on the first of March. Why would a single woman need two vehicles? Then a week later, she reported the Tahoe as stolen.

Two: Eighteen thousand dollars had showed up in Moira's personal account on February 26 and two days after that, Moira received a telephone call from a public phone in San Diego, California.

Moira Fitzgerald was not a chatty woman. She received a phone call every two weeks from a number in Ireland, she received about four phone calls a week from a number that corresponded to a certain Maureen Dougherty, a twenty-seven-year-old shop assistant from Ireland in the US on a green card. The other phone calls were traceable to phone vendors, a plumber, and a clothing store. Except for one phone call from San Diego, Barrett could trace the origin of every call she'd had since the beginning of the year.

Three: Moira Fitzgerald had recently reported her passport as stolen. Someone who looked a little like Moira was traveling on the stolen passport. Moira had light blonde hair, blue eyes, even features. She was about twenty pounds heavier than Charlotte Court and not anywhere near as beautiful, but the ID could pass with an inattentive cop.

It was all pretty clear what he had to do next. But first he had to get Moira to stop sniveling and start talking. He put command in his voice. "Listen, Moira, Miss Charlotte needs your help. She needs it now."

The tears dried up and Moira sat, wet-cheeked and patient, placid as a cow.

"Charlotte sent you the money to repay you for the Tahoe she took that night. She called you from California to make sure you received the money. She said to wait for a few days to report it stolen."

They were statements, not questions, and Moira nodded. "'T'was so *good* to hear from Miss Charlotte. The Garda was saying such terrible things about her. Miss Charlotte wouldn't hurt a fly."

"That's right," Barrett said, making his voice soft and soothing. "Miss Charlotte is innocent. She's hurt and she's alone. We have to help her."

Moira nodded tearfully.

"What did she say when she called from California, Moira? Was she okay?"

She nodded again.

"Tell me," Barrett invited. "Tell me how she was. What

did she say? Where was she going? We need to know where she is. How can we help her if we don't know where she is?"

She didn't answer, breathing with her mouth open in the deep, slow cadence of the drugged.

"Miss Charlotte needs help," Barrett said sharply. "Only you can help her. Only you can save her."

Tears rolled down her face and dripped down to her breasts, sliding off the duct tape.

"You want to help Miss Charlotte, don't you?" Barrett made his voice low and sorrowful. "I know you do. Of course you do. Let's help her together. Let's bring her home."

"Home," she whispered, tears and snot running down her face. "Miss Charlotte home."

"What did she say when she called you from California, Moira?" Barrett wasn't an impatient man. If necessary, he could have stayed here for days, squatting on cold concrete, patiently interrogating. But he had time constraints, he knew most of what she was going to tell him, and this had an end point. He glanced at his watch: 0200. He'd give it another hour, then he had some work to do on Moira's dead body, he had to clean up here, dump the body in Morrison Park, and head out to San Diego, the subject's LKA—last-known address.

He started in again, patiently. "What did Miss Charlotte say to you when she called? Was she well? Was she recovering from her wound?"

Moira stopped sniveling for a moment and looked blank. "Was she *wounded*, then, me miss?"

Barrett changed tack. "Did she say where she was going?"

She shook her head, eyes unfocused. Direct questions weren't working well. It was impossible to tell whether she meant—*Miss Charlotte didn't say where she was going* or *I can't remember.*

"What did she say?" Patience was the hallmark of a professional, but Barrett couldn't help checking his watch again. This was tedious work.

"Say?" Her eyes were unfocused, mouth open. At least the tears had dried up.

"In the phone call. From Miss Charlotte. From California." He kept his breathing low and even. She would be hearing no human sound beyond that of his voice in the darkness. "You spoke for ten minutes. What did she say?"

Silence. It wasn't resistance, he knew. She was having problems marshaling her thoughts, recalling something that had happened over two months ago.

"Moira, me lass," he said softly, in perfect imitation of an Irish-born SAS member he'd cross-trained with in Cheltenham, "we can't be after helpin' Miss Charlotte if we don't know where she is, now, can we?"

She shook her head slowly, dilated eyes moving with the head.

"Now what did she say when she called?"

"She said—" Moira's eyes screwed shut with concentration. "She said that she was all right, that she would come home as soon as she could. She said not to pay attention to what I was reading in the newspapers." Tears started flowing again. "As if I would. As if I could believe she'd kill her da. As if I could believe Miss Charlotte could kill *anyone*..."

This wasn't going anywhere. Barrett put more Ireland into his voice. "What else? Think, me girl. What else did

she say? We have to help her now, don't we?" Time to go.
He was going to have to end this—and her—in another
five minutes. "Don't you want to help Miss Charlotte?"

Moira nodded solemnly, cheeks wet. "She said to stay
on at the Court Mansion, to use the housekeeping money
from the account. She said the account would keep for a
long time. There's a standing order from the account to
pay my salary. She said that the money she sent would
cover the loss of the Tahoe but that I could report it as
stolen and collect on the insurance. She said that would
be my yearly bonus if—if she couldn't make it back by
Christmas. Miss Charlotte always gives me a yearly
bonus come Christmastime, bless her soul. And she said
to report my passport as stolen, too."

The tingling sensation he always got when he crossed
the prey's trail coursed through Barrett's lean body. People were always true to themselves, *especially* on the run.
Charlotte Court saw herself as Lady of the Manor, kind
to the lower orders, good to the servants. She'd taken the
extra time in Chicago to send her maid money for the SUV
she'd disappeared with. Then from California she called
the maid to say that she could report the van as stolen and
collect on the insurance money. That was insane. She'd
put herself unnecessarily at risk to do right by her maid.

Allowing the vehicle she was traveling in to be reported
as stolen meant one of two things—either she was going
to buy or steal another vehicle, or she was going to travel
out of the country with it, where it wouldn't be in a stolen
vehicles database.

Barrett ruled out stealing another car. Charlotte Court
wouldn't know how to do it, and she wouldn't know how
to find the kind of person who could. And as for buying

another one—she wouldn't know how to get around the paperwork involved.

No. She hadn't acquired another vehicle. Every instinct he had, honed from years of tracking people, said that Charlotte Court had headed out of the country. The woman who loved France and Italy, who had trekked across the States to San Diego, had headed south, into Mexico. He'd bet his rifle on it.

CHAPTER THIRTEEN

San Luis
April 27

The bullet sliced the top off the cactus, which would have been good if Charlotte had been aiming at it. The Corona bottle on the boulder was, however, unfortunately still intact.

They were five miles out of San Luis, on a long flat stretch of desert both Matt and Lenny used for target practice. The ground in a ten-yard radius was littered with shell casings.

Charlotte was holding her weapon as if it were a rattlesnake and while pulling the trigger, she'd definitely closed both eyes. Matt was really grateful the weapon was pointed away from him. "Have to keep your eyes open to hit anything, honey," Matt said mildly. "Let's try it again, okay?"

So far, she'd hit air, a couple of rocks, air, a cactus, and air, but no bottle. They'd been shooting for an hour.

She shot him a haughty look and lifted once more the Tomcat Matt had borrowed from Lenny.

"Remember what I said about sighting. Now, take a

deep breath and pull the trigger halfway through exhaling." Matt had talked shooting theory all through breakfast, and on the way out, even though he knew he was boring her. No matter, something would stick.

"Sounds like you're correcting my golf swing," she grumbled.

"It's a little more serious than that." Matt looked down at her, into that beautiful face, and felt it all over again—rage that someone would want to harm her and fear that he could lose her. What would motivate her to do better? "Listen, honey. I want you to imagine that you're back wherever you came from. And when this guy comes after you, you've got this gun in your hand. He knows he's going to win because he's armed, and you're not. However unfair it is, he can do what he wants and get away with it. What he wants is to kill you. He's moving toward you, he's raising his gun, and so you—"

Matt didn't finish the sentence. He was interrupted by the sharp report of the Tomcat, immediately followed by the high *ping!* of a bullet smashing a long-neck. "Take that, you son of a bitch," Charlotte whispered.

Well, *that* worked. Matt touched her lightly on the shoulder. Her muscles were tense. "Great shot, honey. Now remember the feel of that in your hands. Remember it carefully, because right then, you shot what you were aiming at. Your hand and your eyes were working together, and that's the only way you're going to learn how to shoot."

Inside, he was exulting. It might have been a fluke, and it might not. Charlotte was an artist, a good one. She had superb hand-eye coordination, and if she wanted to, she could probably become a good shooter.

He'd found the key to motivating Charlotte, and it was

an important part of a warrior's emotional arsenal, too. The thirst for revenge.

Couldn't beat it.

Warrenton
April 27

It was time—0300.

Barrett uncoiled from his crouch and went to collect his tools. Moira was still babbling, but she was saying the same things, over and over. She'd told him everything she could. Now it was time for her body to tell another story.

Wherever she was, Barrett was betting that Charlotte Court was keeping in touch with events in Warrenton, either from a connection in her new home or via an Internet café. The *Warrenton Courier* was published daily online. Court would be following what was going on back home.

Since nothing was going on, she was starting to feel safe, wherever she was. Charlotte Court and the murder of Philip Court and Imelda Delgado was old news, seventy news cycles ago. He'd Googled it, and there'd been no mention of Charlotte Court in the press for two weeks, and then only in an article on the historic homes of upstate New York. She'd be feeling complacent and secure, the heat off.

Barrett needed the heat back on. He wanted Charlotte rattled and scared, jolted out of her complacency. He knew exactly what would make her panic.

Each job needed a different tool kit. This one consisted of a preloaded syringe, a brand-new ball-peen hammer, a brand-new KA-BAR, a pack of cigarettes, and a lighter. Except for the syringe, it was exactly what he imagined some brutal thug in a Soviet prison using. Barrett was no brutal thug, and he took no enjoyment from what he was about to do. It was simply necessary, and that was that.

He walked slowly out of the darkness and into the spotlight. Moira stared up at him numbly, finally able to see his face. It didn't matter. She'd never be able to talk again.

Barrett held up the syringe, pushing the plunger until a drop of clear liquid gleamed at the tip of the needle. There were things he had to do to her body that would have given a sadistic man pleasure. Moira's body had to show signs of torture. Barrett was fully capable of inflicting wounds efficiently and emotionlessly, but he didn't get his rocks off on it, as others did. For this job, he preferred for Moira to be out. A conscious woman feeling brutal pain would flinch and wriggle and make annoying sounds under torture. He'd waste time trying to get her to hold still.

Barrett had contemplated killing her and inflicting damage on the body, but the body would definitely be autopsied and postmortem wounds are easy to detect.

"Open your mouth and say ah, Moira," he commanded softly.

She blinked and obeyed, opening her mouth wide. Gripping her jaw tightly at the hinges so she couldn't close her mouth, he lifted her tongue with his left index finger and plunged the needle full of anesthetic into the lingual vein, one of the few places a pathologist wouldn't think to look for a needle mark. She struggled ineffectually, making shocked, mewling noises, eyes wide open and fixed on his face. He easily held her jaw open until the syringe emptied, then stepped back and waited.

She was crying again, in great gulping sobs, tears streaming down her face. The tears would leave a salt residue on her cheeks, which the pathologist would pick up on. Great. Barrett watched as her breathing slowed, the sobs dying down, right on schedule. In ten minutes, she was breathing deeply, head lolling forward, blonde hair falling over her face. She was unconscious.

Barrett got to work. He wanted to get the body in the park before first light. He reckoned it would be found by midmorning. An unidentified body would take up the first news cycle. He'd make it just a little difficult to identify the body, which would throw the media into a frenzy. Then they'd figure out who she was and the tortured and mutilated body of Charlotte Court's maid would make for at least a week's worth of news. Charlotte Court, fugitive heiress, would be front-page news all over again.

Working quietly, efficiently, he sliced off the first phalange of each of her fingers with the KA-BAR. The big combat knife, together with the ball-peen hammer, was going to go into a weighted sack he'd throw into the Soren River on his way to the airport. The FBI Toolmarks office was good enough for him to take extra precautions.

The tips went into a sealed container half-filled with acid. He dropped the tips in and sealed the container again as the acid began to froth. In an hour's time, only the lozenge-shaped bones would be left. They would be buried.

Blood from the severed fingertips dripped onto the tarpaulin sheeting. Barrett took great care that not a drop touched him. Taking the hammer, he methodically broke all the bones of her fingers, then carefully, with the precision of a doctor tapping the knee for reflexes, shattered both elbows and knees, then stood back, thinking.

Was this enough?

Run through the scenario, he told himself. Moira Fitzgerald was abducted, taken somewhere—he was certain the police would never find exactly where—and tortured. The only reason for that would be for information regarding Charlotte Court's whereabouts.

Barrett contemplated her, unconscious in the metal chair, blood from her shattered hands dripping to the tarpaulin. It was the only sound in the warehouse as Barrett considered the situation.

She was soft, a woman, a *maid.* She'd have no clue how to hold out against pain. If she'd been conscious, by this point she'd have been screaming and babbling and would long ago have given up whatever intel she had. By this point, her notional torturers would have what they needed if she had it, or would be empty-handed, at which point she was of no further use.

And for Barrett, she was of no further use.

Putting one gloved hand palm flat against her ear, the other flat against her jaw, he neatly broke her neck.

In a few minutes the bleeding would stop, the heart no longer able to pump blood uselessly to her fingertips. Waiting for that to happen, Barrett carefully went about eliminating all traces of his presence.

Barrett opened the unit's metal doors a crack and looked carefully left and right, but as he expected, there was no one. It was 4 o'clock, an hour before first light. The hour in which the human body's energies are at their lowest. It was the hour soldiers struck.

He wrapped Moira's limp body in the tarpaulin, doused the chair and the floor with bleach, and loaded the tarpaulin-wrapped body into the back of his rental car.

He drove slowly out through the gates, using the electronic pass. There had been one security camera going in. A single bullet with a throwaway cold gun had taken care of that. To be double safe, Barrett had clipped the wires.

It was the one thing that made life hard for people in his profession—the prevalence of security cameras since 9/11. Thirty million cameras in America. Four billion hours of footage a week. They were everywhere, like flies on the wall, and most of them had been upgraded. Instead of providing grainy, jerky footage that was recorded over every twenty-four hours, digital technology made it possible to have clear images stored forever on a hard disk.

Not all security cameras were as visible as the one he'd shot out. Some were hidden, feeding back to an off-site analysis center via optic fiber. There was not much he could do about that. It was a constant worry. It meant that the odds were against him—one of these days there would be a camera with footage of him, and there was nothing he could do about it.

Barrett had heard of a rogue computer specialist who was working on a device that would fry all security camera circuits within a two-mile radius. The man who did that would become rich. When this job was over, Barrett was going to track him down and buy a prototype, no matter what the cost.

He drove out of the warehouse district and took a circuitous route to the park. Morning rush-hour traffic was two and a half hours away. If he was being tailed, he'd know about it.

Morrison Park was on the road running east. Barrett intended to drive to Buffalo and fly to San Diego from there. When the body was discovered, the police would check all outgoing flights from Warrenton within a twenty-four-hour time frame, but they probably wouldn't check Buffalo.

He parked in a small circular lot surrounded by hedges. An owl hooted in the center of the park, and Barrett stopped, the tarpaulin-wrapped body in his arms. When there were no further noises, he continued.

Disposing of dead bodies was a science and an art, and though he respected those who were masters at it, Barrett wasn't. He usually left his bodies where they were. At least he didn't have to hide Moira Fitzgerald. If anything, he had to display her, like a storefront dummy. Advertising, as it were.

He laid Moira's naked, mangled, blood-smeared body down in the grassless circle under a big sycamore, about ten feet from a jogging path and twenty feet from a bridle path on the other side of the tree. Barrett spread the tarpaulin on the grass and gently rolled the body out. He stood looking down at Moira Fitzgerald, at the jogging path and bridle path, assessed the lines of sight carefully, then tugged her limbs apart, shifting her, arranging her just so, until she was spread-eagled out, a pale body on the dark earth, visible from the four cardinal points of the compass. She'd be seen by the first jogger or rider in the park. It didn't much matter when. Barrett would be in the air by the time the 911 call came, and he'd be halfway across the country by the time the forensics teams rolled up. He folded up the tarpaulin and tucked it under his arm, satisfied. Anyone within forty feet couldn't help but see her—a white human X on the ground.

The park had restrooms in a square concrete building about two hundred yards from the entrance. Barrett retrieved a suitcase from the trunk of the car and went into the men's room. He wrinkled his nose at the smell of urine, bleach, and sweat.

Slipping a bicycle lock through the pull handles to make sure he wouldn't be interrupted, Barrett quickly stripped, washed, shaved, and dressed from the skin out. Silk boxers, silk tee shirt, Egyptian cotton shirt, four-thousand-dollar Hugo Boss suit, three-hundred-dollar English shoes. He looked at himself carefully in the cracked and stained mirror, turning this way and that. One final touch—a pair of small Luxottica platinum-framed clear glasses. He had perfect twenty-twenty vision, but glasses always made a man look trustworthy. Glasses meant you spent hours and hours poring over boring paperwork, which made you essentially harmless.

A splash of Armani for Men and he was ready. He was Frank Donaldson, of Donaldson Securities. It said so right on his visiting card. A busy, successful broker. In the car, he had matching Louis Vuitton luggage—a suitcase and briefcase. The briefcase held his Barrett, broken down and embedded in its foam compartments. The suitcase held travel clothes, two separate sets of documents, $10,000 cash, ammo, his combat knife, and a Beretta Cougar with four magazines.

Bending, he strapped on the ankle holster and slid in the Kahr 9 mm, specially designed to be small and deadly. He let the fine virgin wool of his pants fall lightly over the holster. Nothing was visible. Perfect. It confirmed his belief that money spent on quality goods was well spent.

The entire process took him a little under twenty minutes, and when he unlocked the doors to the men's room, an entirely different man stepped out from the cinderblock structure. A successful businessman, pillar of the community and, above all, wealthy. Nobody gives a second glance to rich people, unless it is an envious glance at their possessions. They slide through the world on the skids of money. Certainly, no one could possibly suspect Frank Donaldson, of Donaldson Securities, in his gray Boss suit, of being responsible for the white, tortured body of Moira Charlotte Fitzgerald not fifty yards away.

The sun was rising now, a huge shimmering white ball on the horizon, the cloudless sky slowly turning indigo, then cobalt blue, then light blue as it rose. It was a beautiful spring morning, perfect for flying.

Barrett drove to the Buffalo Niagara International Airport, very satisfied with the way things were going so far.

Warrenton
April 27

It's done.

Haine sat and watched the sky turn light gray. Sleep was impossible. He was wired with adrenaline, could feel it coursing through his veins. The Pentagon contract was open on his desk, though he knew every word by heart.

But there was another contract, now, unwritten but as binding as a compact in blood. He'd loosed Barrett, and there was no calling him back. Barrett had been clear on that. Once he started the hunt he couldn't be called off. It was the biggest gamble of Haine's life. His entire future was in the hands of a stone killer. But what choice did he have?

He looked around his opulent home study. He'd worked so fucking *hard* for what he had. Every second of every day, step by step, he'd created his life. His study was part of it, a big part. So was the penthouse apartment, the 180,000-dollar Lamborghini, the Ermenegildo Zegna suits, the art collection carefully put together, the perfect, ancient, faded Bijar carpets, the staff who kept everything running smoothly. Not to mention the $50,000 in yearly donations to the policeman's fund and the Premier membership in the Clearview Golf Club. He hated golf, though he made sure he kept a decent handicap. Season tickets to the theater, the holidays on St. Mustique, the condo in Aspen—they were all what he'd worked a lifetime to achieve.

With Proteus, he could go even farther.

He tilted his head back and closed his eyes.

His entire life was in Barrett's hands.

Buffalo Niagara International Airport
Buffalo, New York

"Welcome aboard, Mr. Donaldson. Can I take that for you, sir?" At the top of the steps, the pilot of the Cessna Mustang stretched out a friendly hand to take Barrett's onboard case. The early-morning sun glinted off his shiny brass badge with engraved wings on his lapel that said—F. ROBB.

Robb was exactly the way Barrett liked his pilots—freshly shaved, showered, and barbered. Smelling of expensive cologne. Relaxed and rested. Confident. Dressed in an immaculate uniform, manicured hand out to help at the top of the steps.

Barrett had had the limousine come directly to the bottom of the steps of the Mustang and he had sprinted up to the top. He turned for a moment to look out over the airfield. The Mustang was the only plane in the general aviation section. The faint smell of diesel came from the 727 taking off a mile away.

"No, I'm fine, thanks." Barrett carried the briefcase as if it held nothing more dangerous or weighty than contracts and the morning edition of the newspaper, though actually it weighed over forty pounds. Inside was his Barrett and tripod, broken down, the pieces embedded in cutout foam compartments, sixty rounds of ammo, including incendiaries, his Glock, a Cougar, three clips for each gun, his combat knife and four pounds of Semtex. He could probably start a small war with what he had in the expensive leather case.

He easily shifted the heavy case to his left hand, and extended his right. "I'm hoping to get some work done on the flight."

"I understand, sir. Well, we're expecting a very smooth flight, so you should get a lot of work done." The pilot opened his palm and waved Barrett into the cabin. "Welcome aboard, sir. We're cleared for takeoff just as soon as you're ready."

"Great, great," Barrett said heartily. "I'm looking forward to the trip."

"Yes, sir," Robb said, as he led Barrett into the cabin. It was a small, luxuriously appointed space, smelling of new leather and brass polish, with eight white leather ergonomic seats that tilted back to become beds, a five hundred-channel entertainment system, broadband access, and a wet bar with a selection of over two hundred drinks. It said so right in the pamphlet. The pilot pulled the steps up and swung the door closed with the muffled *whump* of expensive equipment.

Barrett sat down in one of the comfortable chairs, the smell of new leather wafting up as he took his seat and tucked his briefcase under the seat. He'd barely had time to buckle up when the pilot returned with a steaming cup of fragrant coffee and a hot croissant on a silver tray covered by a lace doily. Barrett could hear the crackle of voices as the copilot in the cockpit communicated with the control tower. *"Prepare for takeoff,"* he heard a staticky voice say.

"There you go, sir. By the time you've finished that, we'll be in the air. If you need anything at all, just press the red button in the armrest. There are gourmet sandwiches and fruit in the fridge over there and a broad selection of beverages in the bar. Coffee and tea in those thermoses. We plan on arriving in San Diego on schedule, and the indications are that we'll have good weather all across the continent, with no turbulence. We'll be giving updates on the flight throughout the morning. Enjoy your flight, sir."

"Great." Barrett smiled, showing teeth.

The engines revved and the small, sleek plane started taxiing immediately to the runway. The heels of his three-hundred-dollar shoes bumped reassuringly against his briefcase. There had been no security inspection whatsoever. He'd been picked up by the company limo at 10 A.M. as arranged, and had been driven directly to the steps of the plane. No one had inspected his luggage or his documents or his person.

The gun resting in the foam compartments in the briefcase under his seat was one of the most powerful weapons on Earth. At a distance of two miles, it carried more firing power than Dirty Harry's .44 magnum at point-blank range. On this gig, Barrett didn't think he'd need the incendiary .50-caliber bullets, but he packed them all the same. You never knew. But even the standard .50-caliber bullets could pierce the armor on a tank. They could puncture the hull of an aircraft or a helicopter and bring it down. With incendiary bullets, he could penetrate a rail tank car or an LPG facility and take out an entire port. Or, the biggie, penetrate the cooling towers of a nuclear power plant.

It was a good thing all Barrett was after was one lone woman. And it was a damned good thing he was a true-blue, red-blooded American patriot.

The light, sleek plane lifted cleanly into the clear sunny morning and veered westward.

The landing was as smooth as the takeoff. The pilot's soothing voice with its hint of a Southern twang had made announcements all across the continent about the progress of their flight, geographical landmarks they were passing over, and weather conditions. Fifteen minutes ago, he'd come back personally to advise Barrett that the plane would land in a quarter of an hour and it did, to the second.

When the small plane wheeled to a stop, the pilot and copilot emerged from the cockpit to escort him out. Robb carried his suitcase down the stairs, but Barrett kept the briefcase in his own hands. At the bottom of the steps, the pilot shook his hand, a good tight, dry grip.

"It was a pleasure to have you, Mr. Donaldson."

Barrett smiled. "The pleasure was all mine." He meant every word.

The jet charter company had sent a limo to pick him up on the tarmac. The driver stowed his suitcase in the trunk, made sure Barrett was comfortably settled, and drove off. Barrett had told the company his destination—the Coronado.

Forty minutes after landing, Barrett was being shown into his suite, the most expensive room in San Diego. He tipped the bellboy, had a lavish late lunch sent up and ate leisurely, then showered, pulled the heavy drapes closed, and fell into the comfortable bed. He'd been up for forty-eight hours straight and needed sleep.

Barrett could go—and had gone—for days without sleep. In an endgame, in the thick of battle, the body is flooded with adrenaline and doesn't need sleep. But a man would be crazy to forgo sleep when it wasn't necessary. It was the kind of mistake a businessman paid for in lost sales. A soldier paid with his life. It was a lesson Barrett had learned well.

He was closing in on Charlotte Court, he could feel it in his bones. The urge to press forward was strong. But he was also a highly disciplined man and knew that he needed to recoup the hours of sleep he'd lost when inspecting Charlotte Court's home and dealing with Moira Fitzgerald.

He set the alarm in his head for seven the next morning, and fell into a deep sleep. The next morning, refreshed, Frank Donaldson shed his expensive outer layers and disappeared.

CHAPTER FOURTEEN

San Luis
April 28

Charlotte finally gave up trying to log on, in the small, brightly colored Café Flora, one of San Luis's many Internet cafés. The connection was down. It surprised her that Matt let her spend time there without dogging her every footstep, maybe sitting right next to her as she surfed, but he did. Maybe he had things of his own to see to. He had, however, told her very sternly that she was to stay put until he could pick her up at noon.

He'd be here at noon, or he'd be dead. The one thing she was absolutely certain about was that Matt was a man who would do what he said he'd do. He said he'd pick her up at noon at the Café Flora and when she walked out at noon from the pleasant, air-conditioned café, he'd be there.

He seemed to have appointed himself her bodyguard, and, soldier that he was, he took his duties seriously. Not only that, he'd somehow got it into his head to turn her into this...this warrior. Warrioress? Somehow, in one day, he'd managed to drum enough gun information into her head for her to get off a couple of accurate shots. If you'd said to her six months ago that she'd have started learning how to shoot a gun, she'd have called the nearest psychiatrist. Even more astonishing, Matt had managed to inspire her.

How had he done it? He'd somehow reached inside her head and pulled out exactly the image she needed to motivate her. It was an image burned into her soul. She saw it nightly. One of Haine's minions, a member of the little personal army he'd assembled right under their noses, lifting a pillow from her father's face. Charlotte hadn't needed the steady whine of the EKG to tell her that her father was dead. One look at his white, still face was enough.

She revisited the next five seconds endlessly—Conklin turning, mouth gaping with surprise when he saw her, hand reaching into his sheepskin jacket and coming out with a big black gun, taking aim and firing as she instinctively ran toward him, grabbing the IV tree, the pain blooming in her left shoulder just as she swung.

Every time she thought of that scene, rage filled her at the thought of Conklin, who'd snuffed out her father's life like that of a molesting insect. She'd seen the truth in his eyes—he'd killed Philip because he could. Because Philip somehow stood between him and what he—or rather Haine—wanted. And she would never, ever forget the smirk on his face as he pulled a gun on her.

Philip Court had been a wonderful man, a fabulous father, and a loyal friend.

The whole city of Warrenton was a better place because of Philip. He'd donated heavily to the local library, the Historical Society, to the Warrenton Philharmonic, to summer camps for underprivileged kids.

Her father had been dying, yes, but he might have had

another couple of months left, and Charlotte had meant to spend every second she could with him. He'd been a remarkable man, and she'd loved him with all her heart. And Robert Haine had snuffed his life out as if it had been worthless.

Somehow Matt had tapped into that rage, into the feelings of helplessness and raw injustice that had swamped her, and channeled it into... guns.

Charlotte Court, warrior princess. Talk about surprises.

She was shaking her head ruefully as she walked out of the dim café into the bright light of a Mexican morning.

"What?" Matt came away from the low wall where he'd been waiting for her. She almost laughed out loud at his wary expression, as if he expected her to explode at any moment.

Her reaction to Matt was another huge surprise. Charlotte prized her freedom, hated feeling controlled or told what to do. By all rights, having someone like him stuck to her side, checking her every movement, should have driven her insane. Instead, she felt... safe.

Last night he'd insisted on rolling out a sleeping bag on the floor of her living room and it had been—been like having a loyal knight guarding her sleep. And she'd slept deeply and well.

"I was thinking that maybe I'd been a warrior princess in another life."

"Maybe you were." He smiled. "I've got something for you. I ordered it yesterday, and Lenny said that a friend dropped it off this morning."

"Something." Charlotte frowned up at him as they walked down the Calle Cinco de Mayo. "Something like a... present?"

"Mm," was all he said until they got to Lenny's dive shop. Lenny was out with two Frenchmen who'd hired him as a skipper. Matt unlocked the bright blue front door and walked around behind the cash register, pulling out a large box wrapped in plain brown wrapping paper and tucking it under his arm. "Let's open it at your place."

"Okay," she agreed, puzzled. What on earth had he got her that was large and bulky? It might even be heavy, but with Matt carrying it, who could tell?

San Luis was changing daily, she reflected on the walk back. Each day, it seemed, there were more people about. Most were tourists, easy to spot because of their garish holiday clothes and beet red complexions. The Mexicans were always perfectly dressed for the weather and had the sense to stay out of the sun. There seemed to be more of them, too, more of everyone. Several shops that had been closed when she'd arrived were open now, most of them catering to the tourist trade.

She wasn't unhappy about this. It was easier to hide with more people to hide around, sort of like a human purloined letter. Instinctively, she knew that fate had handed her a good bolt-hole.

And then, of course, there was Matt, walking along beside her, matching his long stride to hers. He often held her by the elbow, like now, but he rarely looked at her when they were outside. Sure that he knew where she was because he was touching her, he dedicated the rest of his attention to the dangers of the outside world. He was intensely aware of everything, dark eyes checking every corner, scanning every person they passed for possible danger.

It didn't make for good conversation while they were

outdoors, but it did have the astonishing effect of making her feel remarkably safe.

That and the gun in her purse.

Amazing.

She, Charlotte Court, *Ms. I-hate-guns* in person, felt safer because she had a pound of machined metal in her purse. With *bullets* yet. And she knew how to use it. Sort of. If Conklin or Haine had been a beer bottle, she'd have nailed him right between the eyes.

That was another amazing surprise about herself—these primitive feelings of rage, this thirst for revenge. Not only was she now capable of defending herself—well, in theory anyway—but she also harbored deep, raw, primitive feelings of hatred for the men who'd killed her father and shot her. She was a fugitive, her life in smoking ruins, and she hated the men who'd done this to her.

Charlotte had never hated another human being before in her life, had never even thought she was capable of such barbaric feelings, but there it was. She shook with rage every time she thought of Haine or his minions.

"You've got some complicated thoughts running around in that beautiful head of yours," Matt said idly. He'd barely glanced at her since they'd left the dive shop, yet here he was, more perceptive than a dinner date. He looked down at her. "Care to share?"

"Um…" To her surprise, she did. She took a deep breath. "It's really hard for me to say this, because it goes against everything I've always believed in my whole life."

"Go on," he said softly.

"When I said I hated guns, I—I really meant it. I always thought that was an integral part of my being. And yet…" she blinked and looked down toward her purse, feeling like a traitor to everything she'd ever believed in. "And yet—I feel safer because of what's in my purse." She glanced up at him. He was listening intently. "And I hate that. I *hate* it that I feel better because I've got the means to kill someone close to hand."

It was like taking a step into a new world. A dark and fierce one, violent and full of traps. "It's all new to me, these feelings. I don't know how to deal with them."

His voice softened. "I know, honey. It's hard. And probably I'm doing humanity a disservice teaching you how to shoot, because you're naturally good at it. You'll become a menace. Who knows whether you'll turn into some female gangster, like Bonnie, or a killer like Nikita."

Charlotte elbowed him, encountering rock-hard muscle. He probably barely felt it, though he did grimace and say ouch, just to salvage her pride.

When they reached her house, Matt took the keys out of her hand, opened her door, and went in before her. "Wait here." A massive arm like iron barred her entry. She stared up at him, and he smiled briefly. "Please."

Well, maybe he was learning. She stepped back and let him do his thing.

His thing was quick and thorough. In a few moments, he was back at the front door, holding it open for her. When she stepped into her own apartment, she could be certain that there was nothing there that could harm her.

The big brown package was on the dining table, mysterious and large. Charlotte looked up into Matt's impassive face then back at the package. "Don't tell me," she said. "Let me guess." She circled the table, inspecting it without touching it. It was about fourteen by twelve inches, about six inches high, wrapped in the plainest brown paper imaginable. Not trendy, elegant uncut stock but normal kraft wrapping paper.

Finally, she picked it up. It wasn't heavy, wasn't light. She shook it. Silence.

Matt was watching her, no expression on his face.

"Okay, I give up," Charlotte said and started carefully picking at the Scotch Tape at one end. She'd always done this, even as a child. She'd been able to unwrap her gifts so neatly that the wrapping paper could be used again. And was used again—for years she made collages out of wrapping paper.

Inside was a box. A black plastic box. Not empty, but not filled with something loose. She shook it, holding it up to her ear. Nothing rattled.

It looked expensive, well and carefully made, whatever it was. An expensive, black plastic box.

"Okay," she said, putting it down on the dining table. It sat there, dark and gleaming, with little steel...doodads running around the sides. "I give up."

Matt lifted a layer of Styrofoam and lifted out a thick instruction booklet, a series of cables, some black plastic...thingies and—what looked very much like a series of guns. No, not guns, plastic replicas of guns.

Without reading the instructions booklet, he hooked up the cables to the small TV set on the sideboard, snapped the black plastic cubes onto the box, then attached one of the plastic guns. He didn't fumble, and he didn't hesitate. The whole process took less than five minutes.

"Voilà," Matt said.

"Voilà what?" Charlotte looked at the contraption linked to her TV. "What is it supposed to be?"

"Can sure tell you're not a teenage boy," Matt said, and

pressed a button. The machine beeped then glowed into life. *Drug Lords from Hell—Combat Action,* glaring red letters stated. Two huge soldiers loaded with enough fire-power to bring down a small country glowered at her.

Charlotte was more puzzled than ever. "You bought me a video-game console? Why?"

"You're clearly not into video games," Matt said dryly as he pushed a button on the black box and something inside whirred to life. "Particularly shooter games."

"No," Charlotte said, eyes wide, appalled. "I'm—"

"—against violent video games," he finished for her. "Yes, I know. Or rather, I can imagine." He turned on the TV set, fiddled with a remote control, and all of a sudden a garish cartoony scene appeared on the screen—a desert with four Mad Max-like creatures, led by a huge, hulking tattooed bald creature with lats so wide he had to hold his hands away from his body. In the foreground was the bar-rel of a gun.

The whole system hummed gently, waiting for her to pick up and start shooting.

"Oh, no," Charlotte said. She put her hands behind her back. "No way."

"Okay, this is how it is." Matt pulled out two dining-room chairs and set them down on the flagstones, facing each other. With a gentle pull, he urged her to sit down. He sat down across from her, pulled her hands from behind her back, and held them. His large hands were warm, the skin slightly rough. His hold was gentle but unbreakable. Charlotte tugged once, then gave up.

"There are ways to deal with someone gunning for you, but none of them apply to you. If you've run away here to San Luis, it would be pointless to run some more, because whatever it was that could lead him to you here could lead him to you somewhere else. It takes a lot of street smarts to disappear entirely, and sweetheart, intelligent as you are, I just don't think you're savvy enough to erase your tracks entirely. Not to mention the fact that you've got someone watching your six, now. Me."

Eyes wide, Charlotte whispered, "Watching my what?"

"Six. Your back. I'm here, and I have no intention of going away."

"I could—" Charlotte licked dry lips. "I could run away." *Again,* she thought.

"You could." The big hands tightened briefly. "But I'd find you. Make no mistake. And it would be stupid to run away from me. I don't know you well, but I do know you're not stupid."

"No." The word came out a whisper.

"If I'm alive, I'll be there, and I'll stand for you." Matt's voice had turned harsh. "But I can't guarantee that I can be there forever, it's beyond my power. So you need to know you can defend yourself. *I* need to know you can defend yourself, in some way at least."

"Kung fu and judo. Not my style."

"No." Matt shook his head without taking his eyes from hers. "There's no way on this earth you could defend yourself in a physical fight against a man. You simply don't have the heft or the muscle, and there's no way I can give it to you. That's why you need to learn to shoot. Guns are many things, most of them bad, but above all they are *equalizers.* The biggest toughest man will go down with a bullet to the head.

"But to be able to use a gun," Matt continued, "it needs to become second nature. Part of the indoctrination process is having soldiers fire thousands of rounds, until it's second nature. Special Forces soldiers even more so. My team of twelve men fired more rounds than the entire Marine Corps during training." Charlotte's eyes rounded. "That's extreme," he conceded, "and that's not what I'm aiming for. What I want for you is to have conditioning and muscle memory, and going out in the desert and popping a few beer bottles isn't going to do it. That"—he indicated the black box cabled up to the TV with his chin—"that's what will do it."

Matt was so close that she could feel his body heat. He was pumping heat out like a human furnace, waves of it, warmer than the spring air outside the open window. Her hands felt as if they were encased in heated gloves.

Charlotte had never been this close to an attractive single male, certainly had never sat touching an attractive male, without there being some form of flirtation going on.

Matt wasn't flirting, not in any way. He was deadly serious. The skin over his cheekbones was tight, eyes narrowed, lips thinned with tension. This was his essence, she understood. The seriousness, the ability to think about violence and killing without shirking, facing it head-on.

"A video game is going to help me learn how to shoot?" Charlotte tugged once again at her hands, and this time his fingers opened and released them. It felt like a mild electric current had been switched off inside her.

"A personal shooter video game is basically conditioning, pure simulation of battle conditions. It gives muscle memory—"

Charlotte zoned out a little as Matt started talking about combat simulation and sight picture and trigger pull and simply watched him, fascinated.

He was sitting in classic male mode—big hands dangling over his spread knees, broad shoulders leaning forward to make his point better, totally focused and intent.

She would draw him like this—no, no she'd *paint* him like this. An oil, in earth tones, the bright red tee shirt covering his broad chest the focus of the painting. Around him, as frames, the bookcase in shadows and the tall saguaro in the big ceramic vase of swirling greens and yellows. The window at his back, the sea a thin bright line on the horizon just over the sill. Any portrait of Matt should have the sea, anyway. Right now the structure of the painting was perfect, with Matt sitting slightly off center, his forward pose bringing him to the center. Darkness and shadows on his right, to mirror the darkness and shadows in him. Light at his back, lighting only part of his face, the other half lying in the penumbra.

Her fingers itched to sketch him, to capture the coiled energy and strength just behind the relaxed façade. He looked so compelling, sitting in the carved wooden chair, serious and sober, still and concentrated. All his coiled power and energy was visible in the thickly corded forearms, the broad shoulders straining the tee shirt, the long, strong lines of his thighs visible underneath the faded jeans.

It would be a study in contrasts, which was what *he* was, his essence, a contrast of lights and shadows, and it would all appear just underneath the surface of the painting, the layer upon layers, drawing the eye closer.

"Mmm?" He had finished talking, and there had been an upward tone to his voice at the end. A question. She rewound the tape in her head to a few seconds ago. *Don't you think?* Matt had said.

"Absolutely." Charlotte didn't blink, just put certainty into her voice. Over the years she'd learned how to cope with social situations when she zoned out planning a drawing or a painting in her head. People did not find it amusing when they discovered that she was often much more interested in the planes of their face or contrasts in coloring than she was in what they were saying.

"That's reassuring," Matt said dryly as he uncoiled himself from the chair. "Since after I explained to you all the reasons why it was important for you to practice as much as you could on the first-shooter game, including statistics, I started reciting the multiplication tables. Good to know you were paying attention in math class."

Oops. Caught out. "Sorry." She tried to look repentant, though she'd had very little practice at it.

Matt caught her hand with his and brought it to his mouth, kissed the back of it. His breath was like steam. She could feel the touch of his lips to her skin all the way up her arm. Heat tingled in her veins. For a moment, her hand trembled in his. His dark eyes watched her face carefully. "Charlotte. Promise me you'll practice as often as you can on the game. I want to keep you safe. Considering I just spent ten minutes in which you weren't listening explaining why, I think you owe it to me."

Charlotte nodded. He smiled and put a big hand to her back. "Let's go eat. I'm starving."

CHAPTER FIFTEEN

There was something to be said for dining out with an artist, Matt thought as he walked into the dark cantina, blinking a little as his eyes adjusted from the glare of the bright Baja sun outside. The entire Garcia family had come out to welcome them, including the ancient, stooped geezer in the kitchen whose gnarled, horny hands could somehow build a burrito in five seconds flat.

Charlotte's watercolors and drawings were everywhere.

This time Charlotte had brought a watercolor of the cantina's façade at sunset, and even Matt, who knew exactly zero about art, could see that it was a small masterpiece.

She'd caught it perfectly—that breathless moment just before the sun disappeared into the ocean, when everything was calm, the whitewashed adobe beachfront stores tinged bright pink by the setting sun. The cantina beckoned, door open in welcome, sweet jasmine framing the windows, peaceful and friendly.

"*Para ti,*" Charlotte said gently to Mama Pilar, placing the watercolor into those rough, brown, workingwoman's hands. Though Charlotte was an American, a *gringa,* at least thirty years younger than Pilar and a world away in terms of interests and education, the two women had somehow forged an intense bond in the time Charlotte had been in San Luis. Matt could almost see the ties linking them as they huddled together, a beautiful blonde *gringa* and a short, squat Mexican cook, in perfect harmony.

Charlotte had also soaked up a good working knowledge of Spanish. Matt couldn't hear what they were saying, but he could tell they were speaking in Spanish and that Charlotte was making herself perfectly understood.

Lots of guys in the Teams were excellent linguists, though not Matt. Being able to pick up languages easily was almost a precondition for becoming a SpecOp warrior, and Matt had had to work doubly hard to make up for the fact that he had absolutely zero linguistic abilities, which together with his zero musical and artistic talent made for a little trifecta of talentlessness.

Though they'd sent him to the Monterey Institute, where he'd had full immersion courses in Arabic and Farsi, and what were supposed to be introductory courses in Spanish and Russian, he was never able to get much beyond *where's the bathroom* and *freeze motherfucker* in any language.

It had been a real handicap and it was only because he was so damned good at mission planning and strategizing that he hadn't been tossed out on his ear. His tin ear.

But Charlotte seemed to just pick up Spanish out of the air. It floated into her head and out of her mouth, easy as you please. Who was she?

Matt had Googled her, of course, on Lenny's laptop. Endlessly. Charlotte Fitzgerald, Charlotte Fitzgerald, Charlotte Fitzgerald, over and over again. He didn't even have to fill in the name in the blank field. All he had to do was type in *Cha* and the machine knew what he was doing. Following his obsession. It helpfully filled in the rest of the name for him, and waited, humming, cursor blinking, for him to strike out, fall flat on his face once more. Matt was sure that the damned machine was laughing at him.

For all his forays into the Internet, she might have come from the moon. It wasn't that he hadn't found plenty of Charlotte Fitzgeralds. Jesus, there must have been three thousand Charlotte Fitzgeralds in the US alone, not to mention England and Ireland, where the name was about as common as Jane Smith. They ranged from Charlotte Fitzgerald, aged two months, born in Roanoake, Virginia, to Charlotte Fitzgerald, aged ninety-eight, from Anchorage, Alaska, and everything in between. He checked all the photos on the Net he could find, flipping through them as fast as he could. He didn't worry about missing a photograph of her—he'd recognize her face in an instant, her features were burned into his brain. There was no way he could miss even a fraction of a second in which her face was up on a screen. He could see her face at night on the inside of his eyelids.

She was such an unusually beautiful woman, you'd think there'd be a picture of her *somewhere*—as Homecoming Queen, maybe, or Best-looking Woman in Town. Or—shit—Divorcée of the Month. But no, he came up blank, time and again. He'd started looking that first day, the day he'd seen her on the terrace, as soon as he knew her name. He'd spent a couple of hours a day at it, day after day, with the regularity and dedication he put into PT, except he'd come up with zilch. At least when he exercised, he got conditioned.

He'd searched for an ID—for her passport and driver's license. She couldn't have made it down here without at least one of them. A driver's license or a passport would give him an address, a state. *Something,* dammit, to narrow the search down. If he had an address and a photo, he knew where to go to get more intel. With an address, he could start getting somewhere—her DOB, SSN.

He should have felt guilty about searching through her purse and her things, but he hadn't. Not a bit. It took him two days to realize that she'd hidden her documents, and another day to figure out that she'd hidden them for a reason.

What could the reason be? What was it about her ID that she didn't want anyone to see? Where she came from? Was there a document that testified as to her marital status, and she didn't want anyone to know? Did she have an unusual profession she didn't want him or anyone else to know about? He needed to know it all. The more info he had, the more he could figure out who or what she was running from.

An insanely abusive husband was his first guess. If that was it, Matt itched for a showdown. *Come on, tough guy,* he thought, fists clenching. *Let's see if you're so brave when you have me to deal with and not a 115-pound woman.*

He watched Charlotte speaking gently with Mama Pilar, who was oohing and aahing over the watercolor of the cantina, delight on her weather-beaten features.

Charlotte was standing next to Pilar. Her delicate frame was emphasized standing next to the fireplug build of the older woman. Everything about Charlotte was delicate, fragile. Her hands were smooth, long-fingered, fine-boned, wrists narrow, the tendons clearly visible. Everything about her was small and fine. She was a delight to look at; that stunning femininity drew males' eyes wherever she went. Any normal guy would desire her instantly, while wanting to protect her. But fragile and delicate, with the wrong guy, with the sick fucks of the world, meant vulnerable.

At the thought that Charlotte had somehow hooked up with a violent and vindictive man—his hand flexed once, hard. The left hand. He wanted to keep the right one free.

Something of what he was feeling must have somehow manifested itself, because Charlotte looked at him quizzically, then walked over to him, placing a small hand on his arm.

"Matt? Are you okay?"

No, he wasn't okay. He was breathing in spurts through his nostrils, like a bull just before charging, at the image in his head of a wounded, beaten Charlotte.

Get yourself under control. He looked down at Charlotte, at the beautiful gray eyes, now full of worry for him, at the delicate artist's hand on his arm, and felt ashamed of himself.

He shook himself and placed his hand over hers. "Feeling hungry," he lied, hoping she'd take it at face value. "Makes me a little grumpy. Let's eat." He drummed up a smile and even showed some teeth.

"Men and their stomachs." Charlotte said it amiably enough. "Okay, let's find a table."

"Over there." Matt pointed to a corner table where he could see the whole room, and put a hand to Charlotte's back, nudging her in the right direction. While walking to the table, Matt was mentally kicking himself in the ass every step of the way.

He was a trained bodyguard. His training had cost the US government something like $3 million and a lot of it had gone into teaching him close protection work. He'd been on three bodyguarding details in his life, and he'd never lowered his guard, not once, never done the job in anything less than a professional manner.

He'd just zoned out, wasting time and attention wondering about who Charlotte was running from when it didn't matter in the slightest who she was running from. The important thing was that Matt had to be ready for him, every second of every day. Getting lost in his own head could get them both killed.

It was at that moment that he realized how much she was messing with his head.

Every time she moved, or spoke, or even breathed, he wanted her. Sometimes he couldn't even hear what she was saying because he was watching her delectable mouth, wanting to kiss it. It was a miracle he wasn't tripping over his own boots when she was around. This was definitely not the way you protected someone.

Wanting to go to bed with the person you were protecting was way off the charts, a recipe for disaster, but Matt could no more have switched off his desire than he could have turned his back on Charlotte.

How much easier it was to protect visiting dignitaries in war zones. Matt had had no emotions about them other than a strong desire to get the job done without anyone's head being blown off.

If his own head had been as much up his ass as it was now, half the time thinking about logistics and fields of fire and half the time obsessed with getting Charlotte into bed, he'd have been in deepest shit.

They sat down, and Mama Pilar slid a handwritten piece of paper on the table, with today's menu, the *comidas corridas*. The special today was tortilla soup and quesadillas.

Matt didn't even look. Whatever the special was, that's what he was having. It didn't really make much of a difference to him, as long as it was warm and abundant. He'd never eaten badly at the cantina, so he was good. Whoever the old geezer at the back was, he knew what he was doing.

After they'd ordered, Matt took his eyes off the people in the room—none of whom seemed to pose a danger after he'd given each one a hard, close scrutiny—and noticed that there was something new on the wall next to the entrance. A set of four drawings and a watercolor, neatly framed and hung so they caught the light from the side window. The cantina's walls were hung with tons of stuff. Mostly junk, from what Matt could see. Faded photographs, a messy collection of postcards from all over the world, clearly from loyal customers, a fishing net, odd sketches Scotch-Taped to the wall, and a creepy collection of Day of the Dead masks.

The four drawings and the watercolor stood out starkly against the jumbled collections of junk that had been thrown up on the walls. They stood alone, separate and perfect, a little four-cornered island of beauty. They were unmistakably the work of a true artist and just as unmistakably Charlotte's.

The food came immediately, and Charlotte smiled up at the waitress. Matt had seen her around before, one of the endless line of Garcias working at the Cantina. "*Gracias, Rosario. ¿Y cómo está Carlitos?*"

The woman beamed. "*Mucho mejor, gracias. Buen provecho.*" She stood back for a moment, hands folded over the big white apron, and watched to make sure the first bite was acceptable. Matt took a big bite and smiled. "Yum," he said, and licked his lips, just to make sure he got the message across.

He might as well have been invisible. Rosario didn't

even look at him, but watched Charlotte carefully as she cut off a tiny bit of her taco salad and delicately sampled about a tenth of what Matt had put into his mouth. She smiled and chewed. "*Es muy sabroso.*"

Matt didn't know what Charlotte said, but it sure pleased Rosario. She backed away with a huge smile on her face.

Charlotte didn't comment or show in any way that she was receiving special treatment. Matt filed that away, adding to the small store of data he had on her. Wherever it was she came from, she was used to being treated like a princess.

Charlotte put her fork down and leaned forward to talk to him. The cantina was full of people—tourists and locals—and the noise level was high. Lenny had said that the town tripled in size over the summer months.

"'I need to ask you a favor." She tilted her head, studying him, a faint smile on her face. "I don't think you'll like it, but I'm hoping you'll say yes."

Matt couldn't even imagine him saying no to her. Did she want a pint of blood? Gladly. He had tons of the stuff and had spilled half of it in his lifetime, anyway. Giving some to her would be a big improvement over splattering it all over the Afghan desert.

"Yeah, whatever it is, the answer is yes." He frowned and pointed at her with his fork. "Eat."

"What?"

"Eat. Whatever it is you want from me, you're going to have to eat something first; otherwise, you're not going to get it. You don't eat enough. Dig in. It's great stuff." He watched pointedly until she put another micron-sized bite of food in her mouth. "More. What are these guys cooking for if you're not going to eat?"

"Yes, momma." Charlotte rolled her eyes and put another tiny forkful in her mouth.

Matt didn't let her talk until she'd finished half of what was on her plate, the most he'd ever seen her eat. He didn't imagine he could coax her to eat any more, so he relented. "Okay, now you can ask whatever it was you were going to ask, and the answer is yes, whatever it is. Just so you know."

Ash brown eyebrows rose over her beautiful gray eyes. "Well, that's useful to know. Though perhaps it isn't too smart to give someone a blank check like that. You should wait to find out what it is, before saying yes. Suppose I asked for a million dollars?" She smiled to show how utterly absurd that would be.

Matt answered, voice and eyes sober. "If I had a million dollars, I'd give it to you. I don't have a million dollars. I don't have anything even approaching a million dollars. I've got some savings in the bank, not much, and a small government pension. But whatever I have, you're welcome to it." He could tell by her eyes that she believed him. She should because he meant every single word. Her face had turned lightly pink, a beautiful blush of embarrassment. She looked down at her hands, then back up at him.

"I—I don't know what to say. What I was going to ask is much less than that. I want you to pose for me. I'd love to paint your portrait, and I have just the pose and setting in mind."

Matt froze. "Pose?" She wanted him to *pose*? God. "Not—not *naked*?" he asked, horrified.

"No, heavens no!" She let out a peal of laughter and sat back, amused. Then she narrowed her eyes at him. "Though, I must say, you'd be absolutely—no...never mind," she said primly, with a shake of her head, as if getting rid of a way-ward but tempting thought. "Not naked. Don't worry. In fact, I want you wearing that red tee shirt you've got on right now. The red will anchor the painting. I have it all blocked out in my head."

He'd rather have given her the million dollars he didn't have. She must have seen his thoughts on his face because she said softly, "You promised."

God, that's right, he did. He gritted his teeth. He opened his mouth, closed it, then asked, "How long will it take?" Maybe it was like a half hour thing.

"I don't know..." Charlotte tipped her head, studying him. "A couple of weeks, maybe."

"*A couple of*—" She was smiling. "That was a joke, wasn't it? Please tell me you were joking." A couple of weeks sitting still, hour after hour... As a soldier, Matt had infinite patience. He could lie in wait for days, and had. As a model... gah.

"Ms. Fitzgerald?"

Charlotte whipped her head around to the man who'd come up to the table. Matt had noted him in his first scan of the cantina and its patrons, the instant he'd walked into the door. This guy had flown right under his radar.

Tall, thin, a *gringo*. Dressed casual-expensive. Soft hands. Long gray-blond hair tied in a ponytail. Necklace and rings. Talking intently to an elegant Hispanic couple at the same table. One of about thirty people in the cantina, eating and enjoying themselves.

He hadn't registered on Matt's highly refined Danger-o-meter at all. Not even when he'd stood up and walked toward them. Matt simply assumed he was heading for the john. But then he swerved and stopped at the table and Matt went instantly to Defcon 4.

"Yes?" Charlotte's face had gone blank, a polite mask. But her hands were shaking. Fucker'd scared her.

The tall thin guy moved his right hand, and Matt reached out fast and closed his fist around the guy's hand. A move he didn't like, and he'd break the guy's fingers.

The guy was simply holding his hand out with a visiting card between the index finger and thumb.

There was utter silence. The corner of the visiting card stuck out like a little beige flag. Matt opened his fist and released the man's hand and sat back, not apologizing, openly staring at the man with suspicion. The man ignored him and addressed Charlotte directly.

"Ms. Fitzgerald, name's Perry Ensler, I'm Canadian and an art dealer—I run three galleries—two in Canada, Montreal and Toronto, and one here in Baja Sur, in La Paz, the one in La Paz I keep open from May through October, and I'm always on the lookout for talent—stopped by last week and saw your portraits here in the Cantina Fortuna and just now I saw the four sketches and the watercolor, you have a fantastic style, I'd love a couple of works for the season's opening collection if you're selling, I imagine you're a pro, can I sit down?" He had a staccato way of talking, the sentences running into each other. Without waiting for an answer, he sat down across from Charlotte, next to Matt, who'd let go of his hand but was ready for anything.

He flicked a glance at Matt, then sighed, focusing again on Charlotte. "You can tell your very large friend here he can stand down, there's no reason to worry. I'm not coming on to you, I'm gay, wouldn't know what to do with you, except as an artist, and maybe a friend."

Charlotte stirred at that, looked at Matt, and winced at his expression.

"Matt," she murmured and laid her hand over his. "It's okay." Matt looked down, mesmerized. He had big, strong hands but her hand over his stopped his as effectively as if she'd nailed his palm to the tabletop. He gave an inward sigh as he reined in his urge to tell this guy to fuck off. Charlotte could feel his struggle in his hands, and felt it when he decided to hold off on tossing the guy out on his ear. When she felt him relax, she slid her hand away from his and picked up Ensler's card. She looked down at the card, then up at Ensler.

It was all the encouragement he needed. "Could I have a list of your showings and look at your portfolio? Please tell me you don't already have an exclusive with a gallery around here because then I'll simply shoot myself, which would be bad for the art world because my partner has a good eye, but he'd send our galleries into bankruptcy in a year."

"I'm actually not a pro, Mr.—" Charlotte looked down at the card again. "Mr. Ensler. I don't have a portfolio and I've never had a show. My art is strictly amateur."

There was pink color in Charlotte's face. Matt knew it wasn't necessarily ego-driven—she didn't seem to have a vain bone in her body—but was probably the sheer pleasure of meeting someone else as obsessed as she was about art and who appreciated what she did. Sort of like meeting a fellow soldier at a gun show, Matt thought.

Ensler sat back, head shaking. "Americans," he said. "Wouldn't know quality if it bit them on the ass, eh? Though I can't believe you haven't shown, just doesn't seem possible, there's an assurance there, such a fine hand, such a feeling for structure and balance, I just assumed you were a pro. Well—" He rapped his knuckles on the wooden surface of the table. "That's going to change, I hope. Listen, Ms. Fitzgerald, my partner and I specialize in portraiture, neorealism, some hyper, and some thinkism lately, not much—" He grimaced, peered at her, and grinned when she grimaced back. "It sells, and it's what's hot now, what can I say, eh? If you know anything about Canadian art, I've got Simone Fast, Randy Hirsch, and Peter Perricone.

"The show, this is how it'd work. We take care of matting, framing, and transport, insurance included, and we take 35 percent. It's a really good deal, most US galleries take 40–50 percent and charge you for matting and framing. Starting asking price for watercolors is $800. Three thousand for an oil."

Matt could see Charlotte turning it over in her mind. "It *is* a good deal," she said, finally, sounding surprised.

Jesus, she isn't a bargainer. Matt would have doubled that, on principle, then let the guy negotiate the price down a bit.

"Good." Ensler slapped the flat of his hand on the tabletop and stood up. "So let me know when I can stop by to see what you've got, I'm really looking forward to it, don't see this quality often, and in an unknown—great. I'll need your address, how about later this afternoon, I'm here until Sunday, what do you say?"

"Okay," Charlotte said. "You can stop by after lunch—"

"At six," Matt interrupted. "And come alone." Ensler didn't know how to react to that. He looked to Charlotte for guidance. To her credit, she watched Matt's eyes a moment, face somber, then nodded. Good girl. Whatever it was she saw in his face was enough for her to trust him.

Charlotte turned to Ensler. "Yes, you can stop by today at six, and I'll show you a selection of works. We can discuss what you want in the permanent collection and for the show."

"Okay." Ensler stood up, tapping the card on the table. "Cell-phone number's there, if you need to contact me, it was a pleasure, eh? See you later." With a nod to Charlotte and a half nod to Matt, he walked back to his table.

Charlotte waited until he was out of earshot, pushed her plate away, folded her arms on the table, and glared at Matt. She kept her voice low but there was anger in it. "What was that about? Why on earth do I have to wait until six? Why—"

Matt held up a hand to stop the flow of grievances and steeled himself. This next bit was not going to be pleasant. He was going to have to give her a crash course in opsec, which most people took for paranoia.

"The extra hours are going to give me time to check this Ensler guy out. Make a few calls—I have friends in Canada who can check—do some Internet research." Matt hated that look on her face, as if she'd been sucker punched in the stomach. He hated even more that he'd been the one to put it there. "It just so happens that I think the guy's on the up and up. I think he has a gallery, and I think he wants to buy your stuff. You're getting a free one this time. But it could have been a disaster." Matt leaned forward and lowered his voice. "So I guess that, all things considered, it's a good thing that Charlotte Fitzgerald isn't your real name, isn't it?"

CHAPTER SIXTEEN

San Luis
April 28

Charlotte's first instinct was to run. But Matt was quicker than she was. Before the thought even materialized, before she could even take a breath to move, he'd caught her hands in a gentle but unbreakable grip.

She hadn't even seen him move. One second she'd blanked on what he'd said, and the next second, her hands were in his.

Charlotte couldn't seem to catch her breath. Great bands of panic tightened around her chest, and her heart thudded so hard, she was certain Matt could hear it. His gaze flicked down, then back up to her face. He didn't need to hear her heart beating, he could see the echoes of her heart in the frantic pulse beating in her neck. He could feel the wild pulse in her wrists, beating a violent tattoo.

"Ah—" Charlotte blanked. Utterly and totally. She was usually a quick thinker, able to get out of awkward situations with grace, but this threw her. There was no possible answer to give, no way out. She looked left and right in little darting glances, but the thought of escape was ridiculous with Matt Sanders holding her hands in his, watching her carefully. His gaze was steady, completely neutral. She had no idea what he was thinking. It was so unfair because she knew her own face mirrored her emotions—shock, then fear, then a longing to get away.

The time to deny his words was long gone. She'd betrayed herself unwittingly, a second after he'd spoken, by not denying it immediately. Her paralysis and panic spoke for themselves.

He'd figured it out, though she couldn't understand how he'd done it. The only good thing in this whole mess was that he didn't know her real name. Thank God for that. Moira's passport was hidden in a pocket she'd created in the canvas backing of her father's portrait.

Once he'd seen the passport, he'd have a city to check—Warrenton. Two seconds on a computer with an Internet connection, and he'd have known all about her. The Charlotte Court case still hadn't died down. Any checks on Moira Charlotte Fitzgerald would come up with Charlotte's photograph in all the papers. Matt would recognize her and instantly know the truth. And if she was unlucky, if Matt did his duty as a citizen as he was probably hardwired to do, half an hour after that she could be in a Mexican holding pen, awaiting the FBI agents flying in to take her back to the States.

"That—that's ridiculous," she gasped, finally. Too little, too late. Oh God, she sounded so lame, even to her own ears. "Of course my name is Charlotte Fitzgerald."

"No, it's not." His hands tightened briefly. "Don't take me for a fool, honey." His deep voice was low and soft. No one else could hear him. From a distance, they probably looked like lovers, holding hands over a tabletop. "I want you to know that I'm on your side, whatever kind of trouble you're in. Whatever it is that's wrong, I want to help. But don't lie to me. That won't help me, and, above all, it won't help you."

She couldn't lie to him, and she couldn't tell the truth. Charlotte watched his dark brown eyes, searching for a way out. He wasn't giving her one. His gaze was calm and steady. Then he did something totally unexpected—he lifted her hands, turned them upward and raised them to his mouth, pressing a soft kiss in each palm. Her hands were icy-cold with shock, and his warm lips and breath felt like steam against her cold skin. The gesture was tender and unnerving. He kept his lips against her right palm, his gaze calm and direct.

"Let me help you," he whispered, the words a hot breath against her skin. He no longer looked impassive, expressionless. There was heat and yearning and tenderness in his face and oh, how she wanted to reach out to him. He was fire on a gelid night, and she would give anything to be able to warm her hands by it. All the fear and loneliness and despair of the past months rose up and seized her by the throat.

Let me help you, he'd said. *Oh God, if only he could. If only it was that simple*. Everything about him called to her—that steadfast gaze, those capable hands, that amazingly strong body, the look of tenderness on his rough features. A few words, and she wouldn't be alone anymore. It was almost too strong a temptation to resist.

Charlotte's hands trembled in his. She shook all over, a trembling that started deep in the core of her. Her throat ached with unspoken words and unshed tears.

This was too much. The tenderness, the patience in his

gaze, the soft caress against her hands, the gentle grip—it was too much. A single tear slipped out of her eye, slid down her cheek, and plopped onto the wooden tabletop. "I can't talk," she whispered. It was hard to get the words out against the rock weighing down her chest.

Matt's eyes dropped as he followed the path of the tear, as if that one teardrop could contain all her secrets, and all he had to do was study it to learn everything about her. When his eyes rose again, his face was impassive again. Not cold, not warm. It was as if the look of tenderness she'd seen before had never existed, as if she'd dreamed it.

"Let's go outside," he said softly, and rose. "We need to talk."

Charlotte waited while Matt tried, uselessly, to pay for lunch, then followed him outside. She stood for a moment, blinking in the bright early-afternoon sunlight. Matt took her hand in his and tugged. "Let's go for a walk. I need to stretch my legs."

He adjusted his stride to hers as they walked across the brightly tiled *ramblas* down to the beach.

"Some new yachts in," he observed casually, looking across the azure bay at the long quay jutting out into the water. There had only been a few fishing boats moored there the day she'd arrived in San Luis. Now a dozen sleek white yachts were anchored, gently rising and falling with the tide, brass gleaming in the sunshine. "It's the season. Lenny says the marina will be full by midsummer. He does about 80 percent of his business from May to September."

"Mmm." They were walking along the hard-packed sand toward the northern end of the bay. He was making general conversation to calm her down.

He didn't have to. She was already calm. That pinwheel

moment of bright panic was gone, and in its place was a determination to play the hand life had dealt her.

They slowly walked along the beachfront. The sun had started sinking westwards and lit the buildings along the waterfront until they glowed, picking out the bright colors of the doors and windows. The light—that radiant light any artist would kill for—shone like diamonds. It was siesta time, so there weren't many people walking along the waterfront, but the few who did nodded at them. Charlotte had yet to meet an unfriendly San Luiseño.

Charlotte loved it here. She loved the people, the colors, the light, the very air. She loved the feeling of creating a life for herself here, with every day that passed. She wanted to protect that life with every cell in her body. She wasn't going back until she'd found a way to prove her innocence. And if she never managed—so be it.

If she kept out of trouble, she could live here forever, if need be. Mama Pilar had discreetly let her know that Janet, the tenant before her, had lived in San Luis for twelve years without a *permiso*. She just came and stayed. Not all the foreign artists in San Luis had their papers in order. The police turned a blind eye. Everyone was cool with it.

She'd been worried about money, something she'd have once thought impossible. Charlotte Court, of the Warrenton Courts, with a dwindling supply of money. If she was careful, she could last out the year, maybe until next summer with her Chicago money, if she was incredibly frugal. A job was impossible. She had no papers and no work permit, she had to stay under the radar of the authorities.

Perry Ensler was a godsend. If she could sell her paintings and make a living, her money problems were solved.

And the big man walking beside her, he was a huge

problem, too. He'd made it clear he was sticking close, and Charlotte didn't even try to kid herself she could drive him away or shake him off. What made things worse was that she didn't want to drive him away.

He'd stopped walking, and she did, too. They'd reached the low stone wall that ran from the marina halfway up the beach.

"Here, let's stop a while." Without any effort whatsoever, Matt picked her up and sat her on the wall, stepping right in front of her. Her legs opened automatically, and he moved between them until her thighs were hugging his legs. He leaned forward a little, resting his hands beside her hips. She was caged in by his big body. Sitting on the wall, her face was level with his, and she was able to study him openly. The afternoon sun shone straight on him, turning his tanned skin bronze, casting deep bronze highlights in his dark brown hair, emphasizing the high, broad cheekbones.

It was a fascinating face, in so many ways. The shape and structure of it, so strong and so intensely male. His face had her hands itching for a pencil. The intelligence of those chocolate brown eyes that missed nothing. This close, she could see another faint scar beside his right eye, hidden in the sun wrinkles fanning out from it. Any closer, and he'd have lost the eye.

He had scars all over his torso and legs, some white, some red, all of them ghastly.

He'd led a dangerous life. He was a dangerous man. She had to remember that.

Right now, he didn't present a danger to her. He was looking at her with heat in his eyes, gaze dipping down to her mouth, then up again. Charlotte held her breath.

What she saw in his eyes made her heart lurch. Strength, tenderness, toughness. And a scary kind of pitilessness that reminded her all over again that this was a man who had killed and was perfectly willing to kill again. He'd killed in the service of his country, it was true, but he had blood on his hands. It hadn't crushed him, it had only made him harder.

He moved his head the few inches necessary to cover her mouth with his, lips settling gently over hers. He didn't fumble, angling for the right fit. He found it right away, tongue slowly entering her mouth in a kiss so warm and coaxing that all the thoughts that had been circling round and round her head, in an endless loop of worry and fear, disappeared. Simply went up in smoke. His mouth was so warm over hers, so soft, she drifted dreamily, forgetting where she was and who she was.

His lips slid over hers, coaxing hers apart to allow his tongue to slide against hers once more. Oh God, he tasted so good! He tasted of the mole and the Corona he'd had at lunch. He tasted of musk and man. When her tongue shyly met his, he groaned in her mouth and shook. She felt the moan throughout her body. They were so close the noise echoed in her mouth, she could feel the vibration in his hard chest pressed against hers. His hand at her back pressed her forward against him, against his aroused penis, until the lips of her sex opened. A shift of his hips, and she was riding him. She licked his tongue again and felt his penis surge against her, becoming thicker and longer.

Amazing. She could feel in another part of her body what her mouth was doing to his. It was so intriguing, she tried again, lifting her head slightly, licking his lips.

Immediately, she could feel the ripples against her sensitive flesh. A blast of heat rose from her groin as he moved slowly against her, letting her feel the full length and breadth of him.

He was holding her tightly now. If she'd wanted to breathe, she'd have found it difficult, so it was a good thing she didn't care. All she needed, she got from his mouth, the source of all pleasure in the world. He bit at her lips, lightly, then harder, lifting his mouth just long enough to find a better, deeper fit.

Charlotte's heart thundered, pounding painfully hard in her chest. It was a miracle he didn't shake with it, too, they were so tightly wound together. She could feel everything he was feeling. His heartbeat, as strong and fast as hers. The panting breaths he took between biting kisses. Every time he fit his mouth to hers, every time his tongue touched hers, she could feel the effect she had on him in the heavy shaft pulsing between her legs. His arms tightened, and he pressed himself even more tightly against her, this time moving his hips explicitly. If they hadn't been separated by their clothes, he'd have been inside her, moving.

Charlotte had a sudden vision of them in bed, Matt moving heavily over her, thrusting, her legs entwined with his...

The vision filled her with heat, with an almost burning desire to feel his skin against hers, without any layers of cloth between them. Without *anything* between them—no lies and no secrets. Just the two of them naked, his body in hers, and no barriers between them at all.

He tugged at her hair until her head fell back, then moved his mouth to her throat, delicately nipping at the sensitive cords of her throat, making her shiver. The hand that had been holding her tightly against him slid up under the loose cotton sweater she wore, his big rough hand making her skin come alive where he touched her. His mouth covered hers again in the same instant his palm covered her breast, sending sparks of sensation through her. When his thumb swirled gently over her nipple, she gave a wild high cry in his mouth, felt him swell even more against her at the sound, and then she exploded. Her entire body stiffened with pleasure as her vagina convulsed in sharp contractions, which he followed, pulsing against her rhythmically, in time with her climax. Charlotte was clinging to him, helpless, as her body took over, prey to its own pleasure.

He lifted his mouth from hers and thrust her head into his shoulder, holding her as tightly as she was holding him. Charlotte's entire body shook as she hid her face against his shoulder, breathing in the smell of his skin, the sea, her own arousal.

Her body finally settled, calmed. Her breathing slowed, and she couldn't feel her heartbeat any more. Tears had somehow leaked out of her eyes, but they were drying, and no more came to replace them. Her hands were clenched around Matt's neck so tightly, she didn't know how to let go. It took an effort as she lifted her fingers from him, one by one.

His skin against hers was so hot, at points it felt as if she was melting into him.

It had been so *long* since she'd felt another human being's skin, felt a heart beating next to hers. It was exactly as if she'd been in the desert without water for months, for years, and she'd been offered a pitcher of clean, clear water from a cool well.

Charlotte rested with her cheek against his hard shoulder, too weak to lift her head. She sighed and breathed in his scent. He seemed content to let her lie against him. The hand under her sweater was no longer rubbing her breasts in an attempt to arouse her. Rather, he ran his hand up and down her back in a comforting gesture.

Charlotte opened her eyes, taking in the beach, the long row of stucco buildings along the waterfront, the soft little waves splashing against the sand. Everything was the same. Everything was different.

She pushed against his shoulder and eased back to look him in the face. He was aroused, there was no question. She could still feel him, hard and thick against her. He was flushed under his dark tan, his lips wet and slightly swollen from their kisses.

It wasn't enough that her life lay in tatters around her. She'd just tossed sex into the pot.

She leaned forward to kiss him again.

San Diego
April 28

Barrett dressed in a cheap black polyester suit and short-sleeved white shirt, with a narrow black tie that didn't reach past the fourth button. The pant legs were about an inch too short, showing off white socks and spit-shined black oxfords. The trendy small metal-rimmed Luxottica glasses gave way to unfashionably large black horn-rims. The expensive Louis Vuitton suitcase was ditched. A very very authentic-looking FBI badge, which had cost him $5,000, was in its leather holder, completing the transition.

Barrett ate, dressed, and looked at himself in the mirror, satisfied. The spitting image of a government employee, a stolid, unimaginative, government clerk.

He'd made arrangements with a car rental agency the day before and, sure enough, a Ford Fairlane with its keys was waiting for him. He got into the car, a nondescript man in a nondescript vehicle.

Frank Donaldson, NY stockbroker, had checked into the hotel the evening before. FBI Special Agent Samuel Hunt of the Oklahoma City bureau walked out.

The call Charlotte Court had placed on February 28 had originated from a pay phone near the outskirts of town, a flat, depressing, sun-baked landscape of failing businesses and used-car dealerships. After half an hour on the Internet, with a detailed city map next to the keyboard, he'd made a list of possible hotels and motels in concentric circles around the pay phone. Barrett patiently made the rounds, and by four o'clock he'd nailed her.

It was one of the most forlorn motels he'd ever seen, and he winced at the thought of sleeping there. He'd slept rough thousands of times in the field, but this was worse. MO EL—ACANCIES, the broken neon sign said outside. The big plate-glass windows were smudged, and a crack like a dried riverbed in the lower-right-hand side had been repaired with duct tape.

Inside it wasn't any more savory. The dull brown carpeting was stained and worn through in places. Barrett didn't even want to think about the beds.

A tiny Southeast Asian was manning the front desk—Pakistani maybe. Barrett had more than a smattering of

Punjabi, but Sam Hunt, FBI agent, sure wouldn't. The FBI didn't do foreign.

Barrett walked into the hotel lobby with that FBI Master of the Universe swagger, badge out, flap open at chest height. By the way the man's eyes shot to the badge and widened, Barrett knew that the Pakistani would never be able to give a coherent description of him—he was too blinded by the badge. It was altogether possible that his papers weren't in order, judging from the sudden trembling of his small, brown hands.

"I'm not the INS, sir, don't worry. I just have a few questions to ask about a possible client of this—" He stopped and took a long, deliberate look around the shabby lobby—"this establishment on the night of February 28."

Barrett was good at accents, and this one was perfect. Deep Southern cracker with an overlay of college and some time in the East. Actually, Sam Hunt's accent was wasted on this guy, but it was still good practice. Barrett believed in redundancy when it came to covers.

Barrett pulled out several glossies of Charlotte Court from his briefcase and spread them over the spotted, cracked Formica desk counter. "Do you recognize this woman? Did she stay here?"

The Pakistani's eyes showed white all around the dark brown irises. He reached out a trembling finger to touch the photos, as if he needed to remember through his hands.

"No, no," he said in a singsong voice, "I don't—" Then he frowned, looking more carefully. The photos were all taken in formal settings. In two of them, Charlotte Court was wearing an evening gown. In all of them, she'd clearly just been to the hairdresser and in all of them she was wearing jewelry and her makeup was perfect.

Barrett nudged the photos closer to the guy with his forefinger. He tapped them, one by one. "These were taken under...different circumstances. She's on the road and wouldn't be dressed like this. And her hair, it wouldn't look this perfect."

"No," the man said slowly. "No, it didn't. And she looked thinner, very very pale. But she did stay here. I remember." He looked up at Barrett, a small frown between his brows. "Is the lady a criminal? I remember her very well, and she didn't look like a criminal."

"I'm not at liberty to give any information. Let's just say that she's wanted for questioning. What name did she sign in with? Can you check your records?"

The man drew himself up to his full height of maybe five-three, visibly gathering his dignity around himself like a cloak. "In this country, I think it is necessary to have permission for something like that—what do you call it?" He snapped his fingers, face scrunched, and remembered something he'd probably heard a thousand times on Fox Crime. "Warrant? Yes, a warrant!" He scowled, trying to look tough. "You will need a warrant, sir," he said triumphantly.

Barrett leaned forward, leaving the open FBI badge on the dirty countertop. He knew the Pakistani—or whatever he was—would be aware of the fact that the entire weight of the most powerful government on Earth stood behind that badge. It was what made FBI agents so pissy. The badge was fake, but the power was very real.

"Okay. Let's get a few things straight here, sir. You might have heard of a law called the Patriot Act?" The man swallowed. "Well, what the Patriot Act does is give me a perfect right to ask for your hotel registers and to arrest you for obstruction of justice if you don't give them to me, right now. And all sorts of unfortunate things can happen to people under suspicion of providing aid and comfort to suspected terrorists while they are in custody." Barrett laid it on thick because he was in a hurry. He didn't want to get into a pissing contest with this guy, who was just some poor fucker in the wrong place at the wrong time and who happened to have a bit of info Barrett needed.

Poor guy was busy weighing his status in this country—which was lower than dog shit—and loyalty to an unknown woman he'd taken a liking to. Fear trumped loyalty, just like it always did.

The man pressed his lips together so tightly they turned white and reached underneath the counter to dig out a big, tattered ledger. He flipped through the pages silently until he came to the right page. Without lifting his eyes, he turned the ledger around and tapped his finger next to a name.

Georgia O'Keeffe Charlotte Court had written, in neat italic script.

Barrett read it and added one more item to the things he'd learned about his prey.

She had a sense of humor.

CHAPTER SEVENTEEN

San Luis
April 28

Are you done yet?" Matt whined, well into his third hour of posing, wanting to rub the kink out of his shoulder muscles but not being able to.

Posing sucked. Big-time.

He winced. He hadn't meant to whine, it just sort of came out that way. It was just that on his own personal list of things he didn't want to do, posing for a portrait pretty much topped it.

He'd blindsided Charlotte—or whatever her name was—when he asked what her real name was. If he had any doubt about what kind of person Charlotte was, watching her fumble for an answer had wiped it out. Charlotte couldn't lie her way out of a paper bag.

Now if Matt had been under cover, he could have said his name was Engelbert Humperdinck or George W. Bush or Ella Fitzgerald and never even blink. Charlotte had turned white and floundered around until she just pressed those pretty lips together and silently took the Fifth.

When he'd lifted her up on the wall, his intention had

been to get her to drop her defenses and talk to him. Tell him her secrets. That was the mission—get Charlotte to open up. Man, he'd gone down in smoking flames.

With her face so close to his, at the same level, he'd immediately started drowning in her gorgeous eyes, the color of a mountain lake at dawn, with lashes so long it was a wonder she could keep her eyes open. Even close up, she was flawless. No woman should look like that—particularly without makeup. It wasn't good for a man's heart. Instead of trying to pry her secrets open, all Matt could think of was touching her, kissing her, putting his arms around her, taking her to bed. She was probably the only woman in the world who would look perfect the morning after.

She'd opened her mouth, and he didn't want to hear words come out. All he wanted was his mouth on hers, his tongue touching hers. Damn, but she'd felt like silk fire in his arms…

He moved uneasily, feeling the heat in his loins, a pale echo of what he'd felt pressed up against her. *Shit, this is not the time to get a hard-on. Think of something else.*

"Is that your dad?" Matt inclined his head slightly toward the corner containing the portrait of the old gent stood on its easel, where the afternoon light caught it. He didn't dare point because *not moving* had been forcefully impressed on him. Charlotte had spent a good ten minutes before he starting *posing,* lecturing him on the evils of moving even a finger while she was immortalizing him.

God help him.

"What?" The sound was muffled as she stuck that pretty nose closer to the canvas. Finally, she stood back, finger on chin. She seemed to shake herself out of her reverie and took a glance at the corner. "Oh, yes." The thought brought a smile to her face.

"Is he alive?" It seemed impossible to Matt that she could be so close to her father, love him so much, yet be on the run. The man in the portrait didn't look tough. He looked amiable, good-natured, and cultivated, definitely not an operator, but still. His daughter was in trouble, and serious trouble at that, if someone was willing to shoot a hole through her, and she had to hide out from him here in San Luis. So where was good old Dad in all this?

If she loved her father so much, why wasn't he doing his best to protect her? Matt tried to imagine having a daughter in trouble who couldn't run to him for protection. There was no question in his mind what he'd do if his daughter was in danger. Defend her to the death.

Charlotte froze, her eyes suddenly bright with a sheen of tears. With a visible effort she controlled herself, an impassive expression falling over her like a veil, her face becoming as smooth and as expressionless as a porcelain doll's.

"No," she said, seeming to choose her words with care. "No, he passed away. A . . . little while ago."

"When—"

"Okay," she interrupted. "That's it for today. I'm done." She laid down her brush, and it was as if that gesture pulled a curtain closed. No more portrait painting and clearly no more questions.

Frustrated again.

Matt was beginning to associate frustration with the woman. She was shutting him out. Him. *Him*.

He'd never met a more impossible woman in his entire life. Matt had never had woman troubles. Not that he'd had to beat them off with a stick, but whenever he'd been attracted, it had just turned out that the attraction was mutual, which made things easy all around. He'd never had to exert himself with women, try to figure them out. In fact, half the time, he'd had to endure what felt like hours of monologues as his date du jour explained herself to him, in excruciating detail.

In Matt's experience, women became high-maintenance very fast, and when they did, he was out the door.

Charlotte was the least high-maintenance woman he'd ever met. He had to pry information out of her with a crowbar, and even then he got the bare minimum. He knew she was human, female, American. She'd studied art. That was about it except for the fact that she was beautiful, fascinating, and messed with his head in a major way. After two months of being concentrated almost exclusively on her, he basically knew zip about her. Direct questions were avoided, indirect questions sidestepped. Asking her things point blank got him a cool brush-off.

Well, there was always that old standby, sex.

Matt rose and crossed the room in two easy strides. Charlotte was busy putting her painting stuff away, or she would have seen him, clearly seen what he wanted from his face. She had her back to him, fussing with things on a table. Matt knew how to move quietly. When he stood at her back and put his arms around her, she jumped, then stilled in his arms.

He was a full head taller than she was and could rest his chin on the top of her head if he wanted to, but he didn't. His height could be intimidating, and he didn't want her intimidated. He wanted her relaxed and trusting. His arms went around her waist, and he pulled her tightly against him, until he could feel her all along the front of his body, soft and warm.

Having her in his arms somehow calmed something deep and inflamed inside him. Just holding her tightly against him, her arms clasped over his, made him feel better. He was all tangled inside with feelings he didn't know how to analyze because he'd never had them before. His head wasn't giving him many clues about what was going on, but his body sure was. He felt better when Charlotte Fitzgerald was in touching distance. He felt even better when he was touching her.

She didn't fight being in his arms. If anything, she relaxed back into him, as if grateful for the support. Fine. He'd be at her back forever if she'd let him.

They stood there, in the quiet, colorful room, the sinking sun streaming directly in through the big windows, bathing the room in intense pink light.

The front windows were open to the sea breezes. Over Charlotte's head, Matt could see the light wind ruffle the ocean surface, raising little waves. A panga came in early, unloading its catch, the silvery fish catching the light in gleaming flashes. He could hear the distant shouts of jubilation at the fine catch. A dog scampered eagerly among the fishermen, the sound of the barks distant.

The wind blew back a fine pale champagne tendril that fluttered against his neck.

Charlotte seemed content just to lean against him, looking out the window as he was at the peaceful beach scene. She felt perfect in his arms. He leaned down to nuzzle the soft skin of her temple, the fine hairs tickling his nose. She smelled so wonderful he was nearly dizzy with it. It wasn't perfume, it was more subtle than that. Some mixture of soap and shampoo and warm woman, blending into an unmistakable mix. The smell of Charlotte.

His hands tightened as she tilted her head to one side. It was an invitation he couldn't resist. He bent his head and kissed her long, pale throat, running his lips along the velvety skin of her neck from the jawline to the small, intriguing hollow at the base of her throat, where that special smell was particularly intense. He wanted to rub his nose in her like a dog, and snuffle. She was relaxing against him, more like melting, hands tightening over his. He lifted one of his hands from her waist to rub her stomach, then higher, the palm of his hand fitting itself over her breast. She fit utterly perfectly in the palm of his hand. His arms were around her so he could not only hear, he could feel her breath speeding up. Her heart beat frantically against his hand, like that of a wild bird that had been captured.

Everything about this was such a delight. Every touch, every breath. He wanted to turn her in his arms and start kissing her, but that would require that she be out of his arms for a nanosecond and he couldn't bear the thought. He bent down and nipped the lobe of her ear and felt her shudder. "Charlotte." The word was a whisper because his throat was tight.

Her answer was a sigh, back arching against him.

Oh God, every move she made heated his blood, until it felt like hot liquid was scalding his veins from the inside out. He resented the clothes that separated her from him—the long-sleeved paint-stained white shirt with the sleeves rolled up to her elbows, the jeans, his red tee shirt and jeans. He wanted them away, right now. He wanted to feel her skin against his, soft and yielding.

A sudden mental image of a naked Charlotte filled his head with such heat and light he couldn't think straight. He imagined her on the big bed he could see through the open bedroom door, with the wrought-iron bedstead, on the vivid green blanket. He could see her, all that pale, soft skin—the narrow rib cage arrowing inwards, the long, slender legs...

The thing vibrating in his pants wasn't just his dick, though it took him a second to realize it. For just a second, eyes closed against the pleasure of nuzzling Charlotte's neck, it seemed entirely appropriate that his dick would buzz and leap in its pleasure.

"Your cell phone," Charlotte murmured.

He could ignore it. He *should* ignore it. What on earth could anyone tell him that was more important than knowing what Charlotte's collarbone smelled like, what the underside of her breast felt like? Nothing.

The buzzing continued, like an enormously annoying gnat.

She twisted her head to look up at him. "Aren't you going to answer that?"

No.

The word was on the tip of his tongue, but he swallowed it and dragged his cell phone out of his pocket. The display showed a number he didn't recognize. He flipped the cell open and barked—"Hello?"

"Hey, big guy," a deep voice from his past said, and, instinctively, Matt straightened. Tom Reich, his old XO from back when the world was young. Reich had retired six years ago to found a security company in San Diego and had made his first gazillion in two years. Since 9/11, security work had been low-hanging fruit. "Hozzit hangin'?"

It was their old greeting, and the answer couldn't be said in front of a lady.

"Straight down," Matt said, instead. It was even partly true. Charlotte had parted his arms with her hands and moved back toward her easel, and it felt like a heat source had been suddenly snatched away. It was a warm day, but the entire front of his body felt cold and bereft. There was a hollow empty ache in his stomach and between his thighs.

"I don't know if I'm glad to hear that. Time was when the answer would have been different." Reich's voice held a faint undertone of irony. "Listen, I need to talk to you about something. When can you make it up to San Diego? Yesterday would have been good. It'd be on my dime."

Matt didn't even bother to ask what it was about. Whatever it was, it wouldn't be discussed over an unsecured phone line. *Cell phone* line at that. Just about any kid with a tin can and a string or even a smattering of electronics could listen in on cell phone conversations. Opsec had been drilled into their hard heads by equally hardheaded men using hammers, and it was by now second nature. Reich wasn't going to give anything away over the phone, and Matt knew that.

If Matt wanted to know what Reich wanted, he'd have to see him, face-to-face.

Matt's gaze shot to Charlotte, calmly putting away her painting stuff. She did it the way she did everything—methodically and neatly. She was absorbed in her task, looking like a student, barefoot, dressed in ancient jeans and a white shirt with streaks of paint on it. She wasn't in his arms anymore, but there was still a telltale wash of pink on her high cheekbones.

She'd been gone from his arms for maybe a minute and a half, and he already missed her ferociously.

Matt watched her for a couple of seconds, so beautiful, so precious. Because he had a hard-headed cynical view of the world, Matt didn't find it hard to imagine that there was a scumbag out there waiting to take her out of that world. There were fuckers out there who'd kill something beautiful for the sheer pleasure of it, and he'd met more than his share of them. The world was a harsh, dangerous place with precious little room in it for beauty, of whatever kind. Lots of people planned day and night to wipe out anything beautiful or graceful because what was in them couldn't stand the thought of beauty or grace. But they couldn't have Charlotte. Charlotte was his, and he was going to keep her safe and out of harm's way.

She looked up suddenly, as if aware that he'd been staring, and gave him a small smile. His heart leaped in his chest like a landed trout.

No way was he leaving her.

"Can't do it, buddy," he said, turning back to Reich on the phone. "I've got . . . commitments here."

His commitment was watching him out of huge, gray eyes, suddenly still.

That didn't throw Reich. Reich stayed cool under fire, let alone when a minor spanner was thrown into his works. "Okay," he said calmly. "If you can't, you can't. That means that I'll come down to you. I'll fly down to La Paz tomorrow morning and have a car waiting for me. I can make it to San Luis by noon. Where can we meet?"

Well, Reich was persistent, if nothing else. Matt knew that. He was the same way himself, like a dog that wouldn't let go of a bone. Would *never* let go of a bone he wanted.

Okay, so there was going to be a meet.

They could meet at Lenny's shop, except for the fact that the tourists were starting to swell from the small, steady trickle in winter to great gushing geysers of them. Half the time the shop was so full of bloated, sunburned Americans it was like wading through a sea of pink foam rubber just to get to his room at the back. And his room wouldn't work—it was increasingly full of snorkels, masks, tanks.

There was another reason Matt didn't want Reich out back. He didn't want him to see what Matt had sunk to—camping out in the back of a dive shop. Technically, Matt was now camping out on Charlotte's living room floor, but still. It was a hell of a comedown from someone who'd commanded the finest soldiers on the face of the Earth. Back in the day, Matt's team had had a budget of $25 million and he'd been an integral component of the shield protecting America.

Tom Reich had been all of that and more, and now he ran what was said to be one of the finest security companies in the States. He was worth millions.

Matt had exactly $13,000 to his name, a small state pension that carried him through to the end of the month in Baja but would carry him to the twelfth of the month up north. All his worldly possessions could fit into two duffel bags. In all the ways that mattered, he was no better off than a student crashing in a friend's pad.

Having Reich see exactly what his living conditions were like was too much of a humiliation.

Matt would rise again. He'd been brought low, but he'd come back, he knew that. He'd already come back physically. His life plan had been to stay in the Navy and rise as far as he could, but dying had messed with that plan, and so now the rest of his life was up for grabs. He'd rise again, but right now, keeping Charlotte safe was his main priority.

In the meantime, Reich was waiting for an answer.

"There's a pretty good restaurant here called La Cantina Fortuna. Great food. It's on the waterfront, you can't miss it. Let's meet there. I'll be there from, say, twelve thirty on."

"Okay, see you then." Reich wasn't one to waste words. Matt was listening to an empty line. He flipped his cell phone closed with a flick of his wrist and turned to Charlotte. He wanted to get back to where they were before the interruption, but her body language had changed. Arms crossed, expression wary and troubled. "Matt," she murmured, taking a slight step back. "I don't want you to—"

They both turned at the loud knock. Charlotte jumped a little, then looked at her watch. "Oh! It's already six. That must be Mr. Ensler." A glance down, and she grimaced. "Heavens, I can't present myself like this! Matt, please open the door and keep him entertained while I go change." She disappeared into the bedroom.

Another rap on the door, this one impatient.

Well, looked like he was the designated entertainer.

Matt opened the door and yup—there he was. Mr. Art Gallery himself.

Matt didn't shoot him on sight because Ensler had checked out. Not only had Matt's Canadian friend vouched for there being a Perry Ensler—he'd actually *heard* of him! It had taken Matt a good ten minutes to get over the shock of a former soldier recognizing the name of an art gallery owner. But then how many Canadians were there, anyway? Maybe they all knew each other.

Plus the Internet was full of photographs of the guy, usually holding a glass of something, in a tux, at some show opening. The only thing Matt had ever opened was cans of beer, doors, and envelopes.

To his credit, Ensler tried to hide his disappointment at seeing Matt instead of Charlotte. He nodded, entered, and immediately started studying her paintings and sketches, without a word. He did it methodically, studying each work—whether an oil painting or a quick line drawing—with the same intense regard, sometimes sticking his nose so close to the canvas he could probably smell it, sometimes standing back, head tilted, but always with an intent, interested gaze, totally focused on the piece. Matt watched him make the rounds, praying for Charlotte to come back out. He was in a sweat at the thought that the guy would ask him questions. Matt knew shit about art, and in his fumbling, maybe he could harm her prospects.

Eventually she came out. She'd changed, combed her hair, put on some lipstick, and looked wonderful. Ensler finally showed signs of animation as she stepped into the room.

"Ah, Ms. Fitzgerald! How delightful to see you again." Ensler and Charlotte went into this graceful little dance, kissing the air on both sides of their heads. She held out her hand, he kissed the back of it and smiled into her eyes, while Matt's back teeth ground.

"Mr. Ensler, thank you for coming."

He looked pained. "Perry, please, good Lord, calling me Mr. Ensler makes me feel like I'm a thousand years old and actually I'm only five hundred years old, or at least that's what it feels like at the end of the winter season, which is why I love coming down to Baja so much, it's just so relaxing, and yet I get so much work done, don't you just love it?" He stopped, but only because he ran out of breath.

"Perry." Charlotte smiled up at him as he finally let go of her hand. "And please call me Charlotte."

It was as if Matt weren't even there.

Ensler looked around the room. "I admired your work at the cantina, what I saw of it, but this is magnificent. You've got an amazing number of pieces here. How many years have you lived here?"

It wasn't a question she was expecting. And after Matt's little lecture, it all of a sudden occurred to her that too much personal info was a no-no. "Ahm...about...six months," she finally said, her voice a little strangled as she tried to fudge her time line.

Ensler had continued looking around the room but turned his head at that, eyes wide. "Really? Wow. All this work done in only six months, you're incredibly prolific, I'm amazed, I might have room for you in the Montreal gallery as well, we're always on the lookout for good representational art, and this is really good. And your portraits—such interesting studies. We do a great trade in portraits. For example, the old gentleman over there"— he pointed to the portrait of Charlotte's father—"I could probably get about eight or nine thousand dollars for that, minus our commission—Canadian dollars of course, though lately Americans aren't sneering so much at the Canadian dollar, such a pleasure for those of us north of the border, it makes you feel that there really is a god, eh?" Ensler watched her carefully. The man clearly loved art, but he was also clearly a businessman. If he was offering eight thousand dollars for the portrait, it was probably worth at least fifteen. Matt opened his mouth to say something when Charlotte spoke.

"The portrait of . . . the old man isn't for sale." Her hand caressed the frame of the picture, lingered as if for reassurance. "But I have several others you might want to look at." She handed him a sketchbook. Matt had leafed through it himself. Sketches of San Luiseños—the guy who sold *leche dulce* from a cart on the beach, the fisherman who always seemed to come back with a full catch, the one-eyed postman. They were all there, brought to startling life on the page.

Ensler flipped the pages, looking quickly but carefully through the drawn portraits. He set a number of them aside. "Good," he said finally, looking up, pinning her with an intense pale blue gaze, "I'll take fourteen of those, but the portraits we sell best are oils, do you have any besides that one, that you're not selling? Ah, what about these?" He walked toward the west wall, where Charlotte stacked her finished oils. Without asking permission, he looked at them, pulling them out from the wall one by one, head tilted, like flipping through cards. Matt knew what was there. Landscapes, a couple of still lifes, and a portrait of a blond woman. It was third from the back.

Sure enough, Ensler's long fingers stopped at the canvas. He shunted the others to one side, carefully, and set the portrait up on a side table, leaning it against the wall where it could catch the light.

It was a young blonde woman, in casual dress. She was pretty enough, though not remarkably so. What set her apart was a feeling of energy crackling through her.

Everything about the woman suggested movement, as if she could scarcely stay still for more than a minute or two. The woman was sharply painted, so true to life the oil could have been a photograph, but the background was slightly blurred, as if in motion.

Even Matt—art bonehead that he was—could see that it was stunning.

"I'll take it," Ensler said, not lifting his eyes from the portrait for long minutes. Silence. Finally he looked up, eyebrows raised. "This isn't for sale, either?"

Charlotte was fairly quivering with some unnamed emotion. She took a sharp breath, two, realizing that she had to make something available to the guy. "No," she said on a sigh. "No...that can be sold."

"Done," Ensler said promptly. "Six thousand five. This will go into our permanent collection." He stuck his nose close to the painting again, then pulled back. "Wonderful luminosity, masterful brushstrokes...superb flicker, direction and tone—perfect balance of volume."

Ensler walked around to look at the canvas Charlotte had been working on. Matt's portrait.

"Whoa." Ensler's head reared back. For the first time, he seemed to be at a loss for words. Though Matt had had strict instructions from Charlotte not to look until it was done—*don't look* and *don't move* had been repeated until his ears rang—he couldn't resist. Ignoring her glare, he rounded the easel and stared. And stared.

It was...magnificent.

He was a former soldier, in a red tee shirt, sitting on a plain wooden chair, hands on knees, slightly bent forward. As ordinary as they come. And she'd turned him into this...this *king*, sitting on the wooden chair that she'd somehow made look like a throne. Matt was look-ing straight ahead, gaze intense, as if looking directly into the eyes of the viewer. He didn't realize how grim he usually looked until he saw himself through Charlotte's eyes. Though the objects in the picture were all modern, they were also timeless—a bright green bowl on a nearby table, a tapestry hanging from the wall behind him in bold, bright colors, a slice of intensely blue ocean visible in the window behind him.

Ensler broke the silence. "I'll offer you ten thousand dollars for this, and I can tell you right now, it's being shipped straight to Canada."

"No," Matt said softly, suddenly. "It's not for sale." Buying it himself would nearly wipe out his savings, but there was no question in his mind that the painting was *his*. He'd go into debt to have it, if necessary. "It's mine."

For once, Ensler had nothing to say. He looked at Charlotte.

"That's right," she said softly, with a nod. "I'm afraid it's not for sale, Mr.—Perry. It's my gift to Matt. But we've already agreed to the purchase of four oils and fif-teen drawings, so you should have enough material for the show. When will you be picking them up?"

Ensler touched the unpainted side of the canvas gently, with lingering regret. "I'm really really sorry this isn't for sale, the composition is stunning and the colors, wow— you're absorbing subconsciously the Mexican palette, it's amazing to see, I just love it when artists absorb, process, refine, move on, if you squint your eyes, this could be part of a Rivera mural, where on earth did you get that red?"

Charlotte reached over behind him and held up a tube. "Cochineal, the real thing."

Matt heard something like cochy-kneel. Was that a *color*?

"Well, that's not something you see every day. It's fairly rare nowadays," Ensler said, taking the tube from her. "Hard to find and not used much anymore, such a pity, it's really effective, so bold, so clean, so bright—" This with a last, lingering glance at Matt's portrait. He gave a gusty sigh of regret and stuck out his hand. "Well, it's been a real pleasure doing business, these won't be the last things I buy from you, but it's a good start, particularly if you're moving into these intense colors, I can tell you right now they're going to sell, my partner and I will stop by tomorrow to pick them up, see you tonight, eh?"

"Yes, we'll be there." Charlotte put a cloth over her portrait of Matt that reminded him of a shroud. Gave him the creeps. It took him a second to run over what they'd said in his mind.

"We'll be where?" he asked Charlotte.

She turned, surprised. "Why, the concert," she said, just as Ensler said, "The concert."

Concert? Oh sweet Jesus, he'd completely forgotten about it. Matt wasn't real big on concerts. Sitting around listening to music in a crowd when you'd had to get dressed up to do it seemed insane to him when you could slip a CD into the player and listen in shorts and a tee shirt, with a beer in your hand. "What kind of music?" he asked suspiciously. *Please don't let it be long-hair music.*

"Classical," Charlotte said, with a smile. "Mozart."

CHAPTER EIGHTEEN

San Diego, California
April 28

Barrett pulled to the side of the road and braked to a stop. He kept his hands on the wheel, looking straight ahead, thinking ahead.

This was the point where he couldn't make a mistake, the point of no return. This was where the decision tree branched out into speculation. If he chose the wrong branch, he could find himself chasing his own ass forever and he could kiss two hundred thou good-bye.

That was why he'd pulled off the road that led out of San Diego to Tijuana, to reason it through. A mistake now was unthinkable. He couldn't afford it.

The motel in San Diego was the last place he could be certain Charlotte Court had been. He'd walked the ground she'd walked two months before. Seen what she'd seen, heard what she'd heard.

Court had made herself an arrow and had shot herself across a continent because she was aiming at something specific. Somewhere specific.

And that could only be Mexico.

Mexico, where bored Mexican customs officials barely looked at the ID bored drivers held out from their car windows, a hundred of them an hour. Totally unlike the hard-eyed scrutiny passports now received in airports. If she had a fake passport, security in an airport would pick it up. A Charlotte Court trying to get into Mexico would in all likelihood have been waved through after a cursory glance at a passport held open, the bright sunlight glinting off the new plastic-coated pages.

Definitely Mexico.

He let that thought settle in his mind, picturing her in some artists' colony, adobe houses, bright colors, brilliant sunshine.

Barrett was proud of the way his mind worked. He had a neat, logical mind that could think things through carefully and rationally. But the rational part of his mind was only one weapon in his armamentarium. Underneath the rational, superbly logical mind was a subconscious that was constantly churning, taking bits of data and analyzing them, twisting them this way and that, seeing what fit and what didn't, and when something fit, the message was sent to his conscious mind in the form of a hunch. Barrett trusted his hunches. He trusted his instincts because invariably they were backed up by logic, only not always immediately accessible.

Everything told him she was aiming at exiting the country and that the point of exit would be San Diego. His mind and his instincts were on the same page.

Okay, he'd taken his decision and committed himself to the new course. He put the car in motion and eased into the traffic, heading south.

Convent of San Agustìn
San Luis
April 28

"Turn here," Charlotte said suddenly.

She didn't have to say it.

Though the road in the desert wasn't lit, and there were
no signposts, Matt could have figured the turnoff himself,
seeing as how there was a long line of cars—almost a pro-
cession—all going in the same direction in the twilight,
all peeling off to the right, turning off the two-lane black-
top angling eastward out of town, and onto a narrow dirt-
packed road.

Matt was going to a concert. A *classical* concert no
less, and he wouldn't have done it for anyone on this Earth
but Charlotte. To make her happy and to guard her six. He
was even dressed up—in black slacks and a white shirt,
which was just about his own personal limits of formal-
ity. Charlotte herself was all dressed up in a simple turquoise...thing—frock? gown? whatever the fuck it was
called—and strappy black sandals that showed off her neat
little ankles and pretty feet. She was made up in some unob-
trusive, classy way that nonetheless made her a wet dream.
She'd done something that made her eyes mysterious, her
lips dark—some female alchemy that somehow made her
even more beautiful than before. When she'd come out of
the bedroom, Matt had nearly swallowed his tongue, and
instead of "Wow, you look great," a sophisticated "Gah"
had come out of his drooling mouth.

She'd smiled and taken his arm. Which he'd extended
without even thinking about it. The gesture came out of

some primordial male DNA he hadn't even been aware of. He hadn't grabbed her hand, which he would have done normally. No, he'd offered his arm, just as if he were Count Matthew of Sanders. The crazy thing was, Charlotte had taken it completely naturally, as if men had been offering their arms to her forever.

Maybe they had.

Maybe she was Princess Charlotte of Fitzgerald in disguise. Jesus, what did he know? He'd seen her emerge from the bedroom, so beautiful and so regal, and every cell in his body had snapped to attention, as if escorting POTUS himself. Only gorgeous and female, and not some middle-aged politico. He'd offered his arm, she'd taken it, and they'd walked to Lenny's scruffy Jeep as if to a limo.

"What was that thing you were talking about with Ensler—koochy-koo? Something about the paint."

"Koochy..." Her brow furrowed, then she shook her head, smiling. "Oh, I see. We were talking about a pigment. Cochineal. Red. That was the color I was using to paint your tee shirt. Which was gorgeous by the way."

That was nice of her to say so, but it was just a plain, ordinary, red tee shirt, which he'd bought in a packet of three for five bucks at the local market. Matt never spent much on clothes.

"Glad you liked the tee shirt. What's cochineal? Why is it so special?"

"Well, first of all, it's got a long and glorious history in Mexico. It was Mexico's second most important export after silver. It was a dye, used for the robes of kings and cardinals, as precious as silver or gold. Before it was discovered, red—or better yet, scarlet or carmine—was the rarest dye of all, exclusively limited to royalty and the Princes of the

Church. After the discovery of cochineal, even the aristocracy could use red cloth. And then upper-class women all over Europe went crazy because they could paint their lips and cheeks red. It was called Spanish Red, and it earned Spain millions and millions of pounds. How Spanish Red was produced was one of the greatest industrial secrets of all time—sort of like the secret to nuclear fission in the fifties—and it was fiercely protected. Men died trying to crack the secret of cochineal. Most people thought it was a rare berry, some thought it was a nut."

"So?" Matt glanced over at her, lips curved upward as she told the story. "It wasn't a berry, it wasn't a nut. What was it?"

"Insects," Charlotte said crisply. "The blood of insects. Trillions of them. Growing on the prickly pear native to Mexico. You scrape them off and boil them and—voilà! Crimson. There were probably 10 million insects in that tube I used to paint your tee. It's still used in lipsticks and it's one of the few substances allowed in eye shadow. And you've probably consumed millions yourself."

A sharper rut than most rattled their bones as the Jeep dipped violently in and out of the hole. Matt handled the Jeep with ease. This was a smooth stretch of interstate compared to some of the roads he'd driven on in Afghanistan. He wrestled the steering wheel instinctively and turned over what she'd said in his head. Lipstick and eye shadow? *I don't think so.*

"Honey," he said, "I don't want to disappoint you, but I think I can safely say I've been cochineal-free all my life. I can guarantee you that I have never worn lipstick or eye shadow. Ever. Not even at Halloween. Not even when drunk."

"No, but you've probably downed Cherry Coke or eaten junk food. The insects are otherwise known as coloring additive E120."

Bingo.

"Damned if you're not right." Matt laughed. "I've probably consumed trillions of insects, then. Well, I've eaten worse in the field, and I'm still alive."

He was glad the talk had come round to the painting. He'd been waiting for a way to introduce the topic, and this was perfect.

Matt wasn't greedy. He never had been. When the other guys went on and on about some car they wanted— *needed* somehow—to make their lives complete, or some watch or expensive gun, he just shut up. The Navy provided everything he needed, and more.

He had been part of the greatest military machine in the history of the world and it provided just fine. He lived first in barracks, then in BOQ, he had three square meals a day—ten hot squares during Hell Week when they were burning ten thousand calories a day—and the best weapons on Earth.

How could an Armani suit or a jacket by those other Italian guys with the initials compare to his dress whites? Any jerk with five thousand bucks could buy a suit. You had to *earn* the right to wear the dress whites of the US Navy—especially with the chestful of medals he had. He'd paid for them with about a million drops of sweat and pints of blood.

No car he could buy could compare to the 130,000-dollar Humvees he drove in Afghanistan. No expensive flat watch could compare to the sophisticated diver's watch the Navy had provided. So the greed gene had just passed him by.

Or so he thought. But as he was staring at his half-finished portrait and he heard that Ensler wanted to buy it, a tsunami of possessiveness roared through him. When he heard Ensler make the offer, a voice in his head roared—*No! No way! That painting is mine!* He wanted that portrait with a ferocity that astonished him. No one else could have it.

It only occurred to him later—much later, when the flash heat of possessiveness as intense as that of a dog with the last bone on Earth had faded—that he might in some way have done harm to Charlotte. She needed the money, she was just starting out her business relationship with this guy Ensler, and Matt had stepped right in the middle, maybe wrecking her chances by laying claim to a painting her new client wanted.

Though Matt had no intention of giving up the painting, he did owe Charlotte an apology.

"Honey..."

Charlotte turned her head sharply at the suddenly serious tone of his voice. "Yes?"

"I'm not too sure how to say this, so I'll just come out with it. I want you to know I'm good for the painting." He was, too. Even if he had to use every last cent he had stashed in the bank. Matt was very conscious of the fact that he'd deprived Charlotte of a good sum of money. Though Charlotte looked like a princess, she lived very frugally. Her delight at being able to sell her works had been impossible to hide—she needed the money. But that painting of his couldn't go to anyone else but him.

"I'm sorry, I don't understand." Her hand touched his forearm briefly. "You're...good for it? Good for what?"

"The money. For the painting." She continued looking

at him out of huge eyes, as if he were talking Sanskrit. "My portrait. You know—the one with the red—"

"Oh!" She blinked and gave a half laugh. "This is crazy. Good Lord, I'm not going to take your money. That portrait was for you, anyway. I was flattered that Perry wanted it, but I wouldn't have sold it to him. I might sell him another one I was thinking of painting, though"—she glanced at him with a sly smile—"just you in your swim trunks and nothing else, pure beefcake. Women will go wild. I'll make double the price of the other one. Sort of like a *Playgirl* centerfold only classier." She made a little cluck of false sympathy. "Of course you'd have to pose for hours and hours and *hours*. And you will because I'm going to give you your portrait, and you'll owe me, big-time."

Matt's hands tightened on the steering wheel until he saw her face. She was laughing at him, the little witch.

The rutted track was straightening out, and candles in low bowls appeared, lining both sides of the road.

Matt could see straight ahead to a large, torchlit structure, the uncertain light reaching only about twenty feet high up the walls. It was a massive shape in the darkness limned by the flickering light of the torches and the last embers of the sun. Cars a mile ahead were turning off the track and parking.

Matt wished he could drive at a mile an hour and that the concert would be over by the time they made it. "I guess we're almost there."

Charlotte looked at him and smiled knowingly. "You look like you're about to go to the gallows. It's only a concert, you know. You might even enjoy it."

Yeah, sure. "Do we have to sit next to what's-his-name—Ensler?"

The road took a sudden, steep dip, and Matt shot his arm out to steady Charlotte.

"No," she said, softly. "We can sit by ourselves."

Thank God for small favors, he thought sourly.

They were there. Two young men in black pants and formal white shirts with ruffled fronts were stationed between two tall torches, pointing the cars to the right, to a huge empty lot, which was filling up fast with cars, trucks, and pickups.

Matt parked and walked around the Jeep to open Charlotte's door. Her long skirt was tight, and she had to swivel both legs to the side. Matt reached inside the cabin, grasped her narrow waist, and lowered her to the ground. Her feet touched the ground, but he didn't let go.

Her arms were curled over his, and they stood there on the gravel, car doors opening and slamming shut, voices calling out in Spanish and English from across the parking lot. The wind brought in the smells of the desert, and Charlotte's perfume rose in his nostrils. Her mouth was open, delectable and wet, her gray eyes wide, eerily pale in the torchlit darkness. They were surrounded by people. Cars kept driving in, the passengers pouring out, streaming into the big building. Several hundred feet crunched over gravel, and women's laughing voices rose in the night air.

Matt barely noticed. They could all have been on the moon as far as he was concerned. All he saw was Charlotte's lovely face looking up at him, and his entire world narrowed down to that pale oval.

Matt bent his head, pressed his mouth to hers, and felt her mouth open to him with a sigh. Oh God, she tasted like heaven, like springwater and sunshine and a sweet something that was simply her. The taste of her went immediately to his head in a hot rush of blood. *Take it easy, don't rush her* a voice in his head said, but the voice was dim, coming from far far away. Almost inaudible past the wild drumbeat of his heart. He wanted to pace the kiss, coax her mouth open gently, deepen the kiss by slow degrees, but the heat simply erupted in him in a volcanic upsurge.

One second their lips were touching and the next he'd widened his stance, pulled her close to him, and was holding her head for a deep taste of her, heady and spicy. Her tongue met his, and he jolted at the electric current that ran through him. His hand moved from her waist to her breast and felt the soft perfection of her. His thumb circled her nipple, and she whimpered. He pulled her even more tightly against him, angling his head for an even deeper taste of her...

"Hey, Charlotte!"

Charlotte gasped in his mouth and pulled away. They stared at each other, Matt gritting his teeth in frustration. He wanted back where he'd been seconds before—lost in her. Charlotte looked slightly shocked, pupils dilated until only a rim of gray the color of daybreak showed. Her mouth was wet and swollen from his. She was so desirable his teeth ached.

"Charlotte! Hey!" It was Perry Ensler, all in black, waving his arm wildly, walking with a short round man with long black hair and a goatee. *Laurel and Hardy,* Matt thought sourly. He had nothing against Perry Ensler except that he'd interrupted the best kiss Matt had ever had. And now that the spell was broken, he didn't think he'd be able to coax another one out of her—not with half the population of Baja streaming in through the huge doors set in the wall of the massive building barely visible in the distance.

Charlotte lifted a hand and waved at Ensler. He cupped his hands around his mouth, and shouted, "Catch you after the concert maybe!" Charlotte nodded, raised her hand, and smiled feebly. She stood still a moment, then blew out a breath.

It took her a moment to meet his eyes but she did, finally. Matt said nothing at all. It was her call, to acknowledge the kiss or not.

"Wow," she said finally, on a soft exhalation of breath.

Yeah, *wow* just about covered it.

Matt reached into the cabin of Lenny's Jeep and brought out Charlotte's shawl. He opened it and draped it over her shoulders, hands lingering for a moment, feeling the delicate shoulder bones underneath the skin. She lifted her hand to touch his briefly, then lifted it away. "We'd better get going," Matt said quietly, wishing the damned concert were over, and they could be alone. He took her arm and set off, following the endless stream of people.

Tall, ancient oaks whispered in the night breeze as they made their way through the winding, candlelit path, the sound mixing with the laughter and conversation of the other concertgoers. He heard Spanish, of course, and American English, but also snatches of French and German and some language that was either Swedish or Danish, he couldn't tell.

"Come on, honey." He guided her through the crowd, hand at her back, seated her, then took his own seat. Once he had them settled, he looked around. The Convento de San Agustìn was austere but eerily beautiful. By the flickering light of the torches, it looked otherworldly, like a spaceship from the past.

"Looks more like a medieval fortress than anything else," Matt said.

"It's got an interesting history, it's one of the oldest Spanish missions in Mexico, hence its ... primitive appearance." Charlotte smiled up at him. "You've never been out to the mission?"

He shook his head. Hadn't even thought of it.

The crowd murmured as three men and a woman filed out of a small door set in the mammoth wall.

"Oh look!" Charlotte exclaimed. "The musicians are coming out! I've heard that the cellist is excellent." She opened the program and sighed happily, running her finger down the program. "The String Quartet Number 17. I haven't heard that in years. Since college, in fact. This is going to be so wonderful."

Matt looked down at her. She was excited, happy, looking forward to the concert. She clearly *liked* this stuff. Hard as it was for Matt to believe, she truly enjoyed listening to live classical music. Her cheeks were pink with pleasure, that pretty mouth uptilted, eyes gleaming.

This was Charlotte Fitzgerald, he suddenly realized. This elegant, smiling, cultivated, happy woman. My God, this woman was utterly irresistible. What he'd been seeing was a woman down, at her lowest ebb, sapped of vitality. Already that woman had him tied in knots, but this one—this one brought him to his knees.

He picked up her hand, contemplating it for a moment. He could feel the delicate bones beneath the soft skin, all the miraculous elements of bone, tendon, muscle that made up her long, elegant artist's hands. He brought her soft hand to his mouth and kissed the back of it gently, as if he were a gentleman in a tux at the Met instead of a roughneck sailor in one of the two dress shirts he owned on a folding chair in the middle of nowhere.

He felt like a gent with a tux. He felt like a knight in shining armor with his lady love. Every cliché in the book—Jesus, that was him, right there. All wrapped up in a woman, heart skipping a beat when she smiled at him, willing—hell, more than willing—to ford rivers for her, climb mountains, slay dragons. Willing to kill for her. Certainly willing to die for her.

"Matt," she whispered, the torchlight flickering in her eyes. How it loved her face, caressing the mysterious hollows under her elegant cheekbones, that soft skin the color of moonlight. He turned her hand and pressed a kiss into the palm. She smiled at him and curled her hand closed, as if keeping the kiss inside.

Oh yeah. He'd do anything for her. Even sit on an uncomfortable chair and listen to long-hair music. Gah.

The musicians had all trooped onto the stage, which was empty except for four chairs and four music stands with sheets of music on them. The only extra light for them were four huge torches at the four corners of the large wooden dais that served as a stage.

They sat and tuned their instruments for a couple of minutes, then the violinist on the left suddenly straightened and tapped the music stand with his bow.

Inside a minute utter silence reigned. Three hundred people in the courtyard, and yet Matt could hear the wind soughing through the leaves of the bushes surrounding the cloister. The musicians picked up their bows, and Charlotte squeezed his hand in excitement, letting out a happy sigh.

Okay, this was it. By an act of heroism, Matt refrained from rolling his eyes and braced himself, totally in Stoic Mode. He'd done harder things in his life than sit through a boring hour of music. Shit, he'd stood watch thousands of times through the night. He'd hunkered behind a big rock for two days waiting for a convoy to pass. He'd lain on his stomach for nearly a week with only a thin plastic sheet under him, a plastic bottle to piss in, a plastic bag to shit in, and seven MREs, studying the movements in an enemy camp. Hell, most of life in the military was hurry up and wait...endlessly.

He could do this. He could especially do this with a happy, relaxed Charlotte by his side.

One of the violinists, clearly the leader, looked each of the others in the eye and gave a sharp nod.

Suddenly, in the space of a heartbeat, music filled the courtyard. It didn't sound as if it came from the musicians sawing away at their instruments. No, it seemed like it came from some mysterious otherworldly source—from the cool night air, perhaps, from the bright stars in the sky, from the dense, ancient stone walls and the rustling branches of the trees.

He had no idea how long the concert lasted. A minute. Forever. He lost all sense of time and of himself as he listened to the clear notes. The only thing he was always conscious of was Charlotte's hand in his, soft, warm, grounding him.

She seemed as caught up in the music as he was, leaning a little forward in her seat, head wobbling gently in time with the rhythms. Matt had never heard any of the pieces before and yet as soon as he heard the notes, it was as if he'd been listening to them all his life—instantly familiar, instantly a part of him. The notes shimmered in the air, as if they were starlight made sound.

After a time, the lead violinist met the other musicians' eyes, the music rose on a great crescendo, then stopped on a breath, leaving utter silence. As one, the musicians rested their right hands, bows upright, on their knees.

The silence lasted a heartbeat, two, then the audience erupted in ecstatic applause. Matt released Charlotte's hand—the only thing he'd do that for—and joined in.

The musicians suddenly grinned at the wild applause, and Matt realized how young they were. They'd seemed almost superhuman while playing—deathly serious, plugged into something higher and bigger than they were. But now he saw that they weren't much more than kids. Hugely talented kids who'd probably been practicing their instruments since they were five.

They were touched by magic, just as surely as Charlotte was.

He was stunned that he'd lost himself so much in the music. That had never happened before—music was something that had always been a take it or leave it kind of thing for him. It certainly never affected him emotionally. But now he felt shaken, as if sands had suddenly shifted beneath his feet, ripping open a hole in the ground, but instead of danger, the abyss that had opened up had showed him a new, shimmering reality, better and stronger than this one.

He came to as a sharp little elbow dug in his ribs. Charlotte was gazing at him, head tilted. "Well? Tell the truth, it wasn't that bad, was it?"

He swallowed. "No, no it—"

He stopped, unable to go on. He looked away sharply, so she wouldn't see how moved he was. What was going

on? He was utterly baffled by the swell of emotion in his
chest, almost too big to contain.

Get a grip.

When his throat loosened, and the bands around his chest
yielded, he took in a deep breath. "It was beautiful," he said
quietly, in answer to her question. "Truly beautiful. It was
like—like they were one person and one instrument."

"Yes," she said absently, shifting her knees as people
started getting up to leave, filing past them. All around
them was the sound of people talking, laughing, scraping
the chair legs across the flagstoned courtyard as they got
up and started moving toward the big gate. It all sounded
far away to Matt, who was still lost in the music, floating
in the darkness of the night, anchored only by the moon
and the stars. She seemed to sense that his silence was
unusual, because she gave him a sharp glance.

"You're surprised," she said, sounding surprised herself. She peered at him, eyes narrowed, studying him as if
she'd never seen him before. "You're surprised you liked
it. Tell the truth. You really enjoyed the music, and you
didn't think you would."

The disgruntled look he gave her made her laugh. The
sound rose in the night air and lifted his spirits. She didn't
laugh nearly enough.

"Admit it!" Charlotte crowed, looking like a beautiful
little she-devil. She jabbed him in the side again. "Come
on, tough guy. Admit it. No wonder you're looking like
someone punched you in the stomach. You loved it. So
here we have Mr. Macho, Mr. I'm-just-a-soldier, ma'am-
and-don't-know-nothing-else, who has discovered he has
an appreciation for art and has actually started his first
art collection and now finds out to his horror that he has

a taste for classical music." She shook her head, making a *tsk*-ing sound. "My heavens, who knows what's next? Maybe a passionate interest in fashion or interior design?" She laughed when she saw his expression.

Charlotte leaned forward and spoke softly into his ear. "I won't tell anyone, I promise. And I should talk. I've discovered that I like shooting people." She shook her head. "Who knew?"

CHAPTER NINETEEN

San Luis
April 28

The trip back to San Luis seemed to take forever and was over before Charlotte had time to gather her senses and decide what she was going to do about Matt.

They rode in silence, Matt giving increasingly lengthy sidelong glances at her as he drove them back. He drove the way he did everything physical—superbly. Charlotte watched the play of muscles in his forearm as he shifted gears in the ancient Jeep. The vehicle wasn't built for comfort, and the road was terrible, but Matt managed through sheer driving ability to smooth out the ride.

She was fascinated by his forearms and hands. They were powerful without being meaty—pure masculine grace. If she could, she'd make sketch after sketch of his hands alone—large, strong, nicked, and scarred but beautiful just the same. The very essence of male power.

It was hard to keep her eyes off him, so she forced herself to concentrate on the road instead. Though the moonlight was bright, the landscape was flat and featureless. She concentrated on the only thing visible, the faded yellow lines in the middle of the road, flickering in the headlights.

It was so hard not to look at Matt, she had to clench her fists, digging her fingernails into the palm of her hand. Everything about him fascinated her. She'd spent the entire afternoon immersed in the details of him—how his short dark hair grew in a whorl at the back of his head, how the ball of his shoulders strained the soft cotton tee shirt, how powerful his hands looked even in repose, how his dark eyes never lost that careful watchfulness, as if he was aware of everything at all times.

Oh, she was smitten. It was such an unusual feeling for her that it had taken her this long to realize it. And she was smitten with a man who was utterly alien to her, a man she'd never have even considered as a possible lover six months ago.

Charlotte was well aware that she had grown up pre-posterously privileged and wealthy, the beloved daughter of two doting parents. She didn't consider herself unduly spoiled, but by the same token she'd always just assumed that her life would take a straight, golden and pleasant path down to her future, and that that future included a loving husband, equally wealthy and privileged, children, trips to Europe, art and music in abundance.

The men she'd dated and the few lovers she'd had all shared more or less the same characteristics. They were witty and charming and well-read and well traveled. The places they went to all had museums, which they dutifully visited, unlike Matt, whose travels to her seemed to be exclusively to places "where the bad guys are" as he put it.

Matt was not her type. He was rough and grim, rather than witty. He had a take on the world that a year ago she would have called paranoid but which she now knew to be realistic—the world *was* full of bad people and danger. However, Matt was perfectly prepared, by training and character, to deal with it.

Charlotte Court would have found Matt intriguing for a minute or two, back in her old life, but would never have stuck around long enough to find out what he was really like. What made him tick under that stone-cold exterior. She preferred her men to share her interests, to have a little feminine streak to them, and Matt was unequivocally and entirely *male*.

But Charlotte Fitzgerald—ah, that was a different matter. Something had happened to her to change her beyond all recognition. Whether it was on the long, perilous trek across the country, a wounded fugitive, living by her wits, pushing herself farther than she'd ever thought she could go, or whether it was over the past two months in San Luis, living frugally, her life pared down to the essentials in this gorgeous place of elemental shapes and colors—whatever it was, she was a changed woman.

It was as if a ferocious wind had blown away all the trappings of Charlotte Court that she'd thought were her essence—her wealth, her place in society, her invulnerability—and left a stripped-down version of herself that rang true because it was bedrock. That stripped-down, essential Charlotte could survive on very little. She didn't need a mansion, servants, designer clothes, the company of other wealthy, privileged people like herself.

She'd become Charlotte Fitzgerald, survivor, who'd been through hell and survived. And she recognized in Matt a kindred spirit. He'd been through hell, too, and come out the other end even stronger than before.

They were in many ways alike, and if she hadn't been on the run, fighting for her life, she would never have known that.

Matt looked over again and their eyes met. Charlotte nearly gasped at the power of his gaze, like a punch to the stomach. It was an electric charge crackling between them, uniting them.

He picked up her hand and brought it to his mouth again. His lips were warm and soft, the skin around his mouth rough with heavy beard. As his lips touched the back of her hand, another jolt of electricity shot through her, and she finally recognized it for what it was—desire.

Desire was something she thought she understood. A man and a woman could have a good time in bed together—a nice, civilized time. A good meal, maybe a dinner theater, decent sex, followed by a nice glass of wine and good conversation.

That had nothing whatsoever to do with the punch to her senses when she met Matt's gaze. Desire flared in her, a swell of heat from her head to her toes. Her hand trembled in his. He felt it. Of course he felt it. He was preternaturally aware of what was going on in her, as if he were inside her skin, directing her responses. Matt didn't get that triumphant look men got when they knew they'd done what had to be done to coax you into bed. No, his face turned taut, sober, somber—as if they were embarking upon a serious life-or-death mission.

Maybe they were.

He kissed her hand again and carefully returned it to her lap to put both hands on the wheel as they entered the city limits of San Luis and he started the series of turns that would take them to her house.

The air in the cab was charged with energy, crackling with it. Charlotte felt alive in every cell of her body. She was aware of Matt next to her in every fiber of her being. It was as if she breathed him in with every breath she took.

She'd cheated death, time and again, over the past few months. Life wasn't always sweet, she knew that now, but it was there to be lived to the full, each moment a gift. Like now, in a dilapidated Jeep in Baja California, with a man she hardly knew.

And yet—she knew the essence of him. She knew he was brave and loyal and never played games. She knew he said what he meant and meant what he said. She knew he had an incredible streetwise intelligence that fascinated her, as if he'd seen it all and had filed it all away.

Matt parked behind Charlotte's house and killed the engine. He turned to her, big arm draped over the steering wheel. Again, that look like a punch. She didn't need to ask what he was thinking—she knew. With every look, with every touch of his hand to hers, she knew.

"We're here," he said quietly.

Yes, they were.

They were where they'd been heading since he'd rescued her from the black, clutching tentacles of the sea. Maybe they'd been heading toward this since the day she'd seen him outlined against the setting sun—a broken husk of a man taking strength from a wounded woman on the run.

He'd saved her life. In the most primitive way there was, deep in the bone and blood, she was his.

She couldn't take her gaze from his. The windows were down, and the sounds of the night air sounded loud in the silence of the cab. The soft splashing of the sea, revelers along the beach, a guitar strumming in a nearby house. The whites of his eyes gleamed in the darkness. He reached out a long finger and ran it down her cheek. Charlotte couldn't help the shudder that ran through her body. She lifted her hand and pressed his hand against her cheek.

"It's time, Charlotte," he whispered, and she nodded against his hand.

Yes. It was time.

Tijuana
April 28

Barrett parked the car and walked up and down the Avenida Revolucìon, feeling his way into the city. He'd done this hundreds of times before. When he tracked prey down to a specific city or town, he walked around the various sections of the city, using every bit of knowledge of the prey he had. He'd spend hours, senses wide open, seeing through the prey's eyes, thinking with the prey's head.

It worked, more often than not, particularly in wide-open places like Tijuana, where if you had a weakness, it was available to you in abundance, twenty-four/seven.

Too bad Charlotte Court didn't have any weaknesses, not in the usual sense. She didn't drink, do drugs, or need to mainline designer clothes and jewels. The only weakness she had that he could see was an almost neurotic need to paint and draw, especially under stress.

By evening, he was convinced that she wasn't in Tijuana. She might have spent the night, but the next morning, if she was capable of driving, she'd have lit out. Tijuana was not the place where she would settle down. Barrett was convinced of that by nightfall.

Barrett came to this conclusion in a small street just off the Avenida, sitting on a rickety chair out on the irregular paving stones, sipping a beer. A mass of guidebooks and maps was spread out on the little round plastic table, and the bottle of the local cerveza held down a pile of brochures against the rising evening breeze. He'd chucked the shiny black Feeb suit, the shiny brass Feeb badge for faded jeans and a tee—Fred Dugan, farm machinery rep out of Cleveland out for some fun in the sun, looking like every other *gringo* who'd just crossed the border.

The maps and guidebooks weren't there as part of a disguise. He was poring over the information, trying to find out where she'd have gone to ground. By the time the light started fading from the hemp-colored sky, Barrett thought he knew where she'd go.

San Miguel de Allende. A famous art colony, with more galleries than restaurants, full of foreigners. Founded in 1542. A good-sized city, elegant, filled with Italianate plazas. It had Charlotte Court written all over it.

The light was fading. If he wanted to make tracks, he had to get going. And yet he continued sitting, tracing the map of Mexico with his forefinger, stalling...

Something wasn't quite right...

He opened one of the brochures on San Miguel again. A music festival, ceramics and art courses, perfectly restored seventeenth century Spanish churches, a large expatriate population. Ken Kesey had lived there once. It was full of cute little cobblestoned streets with funky brightly colored adobe houses on each side. Christ, it even had something called Lifestyle Tours. In English. It was perfect.

What the fuck is wrong with this picture? What's wrong?

He continued touching the map, tracing the roads, his

finger slowly making its way from the northwesternmost portion of Mexico, Tijuana, down into the southern heart of the country, then back up, trying to figure out what was wrong.

His eye traversed the distance between Tijuana and San Miguel once more...

It was too far away, that's what was wrong.

That's what his subconscious had been trying to tell him. San Miguel was more than two thousand miles away, over sometimes narrow, twisting roads.

Barrett sat while the sky darkened, and the street lit up with a cornucopia of small lights. Salsa music drifted in from an open window above the taverna, and couples dressed for an evening out started emerging from the buildings. The sharp smell of women's perfume and men's cologne—the odors of a night out—mixed with the delicious smells coming from the back room of the taverna, and the sometimes-acrid whiff of sewer coming from an open grate. He sat, thinking it through.

Barrett was thoroughly male, forty-five years old, a soldier all his life. But he had an uncanny ability to put himself in his prey's shoes. So while the light drained out of the sky and raucous nighttime Tijuana replaced frantic daytime Tijuana, he turned himself into a twenty-six-year-old, beautiful, wealthy woman who was passionately interested in art.

He *was* Charlotte Court.

He was a pampered heiress on the run who had just made an epic escape across the continental United States, wounded and frightened. It was the kind of journey that would tax most people who hadn't had Special Forces training, let alone a civilian.

She'd just crossed the border into Mexico after a grueling trip through the snowy Midwest. God, that had had to give her a feeling of safety, of having somehow found sanctuary. The human animal can marshal vast reserves of adrenaline to keep going when life is at stake, but the longer the period of emergency panic, the greater the adrenaline depletion. Crossing that border, feeling safe, warm, anonymous for the first time in what must have felt like forever—she'd be exhausted, completely wiped out. Would she plan another long, cross-country trip? In a country she wasn't familiar with?

He turned it over in his mind, tuning out his surroundings, oblivious to the night sounds of a city of sin.

No, he thought suddenly. She wouldn't. She'd head in a straight line, where she didn't have to worry about directions.

And that would be straight down into Baja.

He'd head out at first light.

San Luis
April 28

Matt opened the door to Charlotte's house, letting it swing open and ushering her across the threshold with a hand to her back. They'd walked in silence, hand in hand, after parking Lenny's Jeep. They didn't need words. Matt didn't, anyway. He knew what he wanted.

Her. He wanted her, Charlotte. At the deepest level possible, she was his, and words wouldn't make it any truer.

The instant the door closed behind them, Charlotte turned in the circle of his arm and stepped forward until her breasts touched his chest and just like that she was in his arms, a slender column of pure fire, struggling to get closer to him.

Matt had had every intention of taking it slow, coaxing her into bed with him, but she blew those plans right out of the water. She took the kiss from zero to sixty so fast he nearly got the bends. Inside a minute, she was grappling with the buttons of his shirt, finally pulling his shirt apart, the buttons making little *ping!* sounds as they hit the tile flooring.

When she put her hands on him, it felt like fire. She burrowed her hands underneath his shirt, sliding them around his back, all the while pressing closer, closer...

Her mouth was a little honey trap—it was impossible to lift his mouth from hers. For a second there, he thought he should tell her to slow down, reassure her, do something with his mouth other than kiss her, but that was insane. What could he possibly tell her in words that his body wasn't telling her?

He was as hard as a pike, that muscle just one of the many muscles of his body that were hard with arousal. It didn't help that she was rubbing her hips against his, driving him insane.

He lifted his mouth from hers for a moment and looked down, thinking that he'd remember this moment for the rest of his life. She looked up at him, her face a pale perfect oval. Not so pale, no. Even by the dim light of the streetlamp outside, he could see that her cheeks were flushed, her lips red and swollen, her eyes dark with arousal.

He wanted this to be romantic, gentle, but his blood was up, and so was hers. In a second, they were on the bed, grappling, rolling, wild hunger in the blood. He lifted her up a little and slid the zipper down on the turquoise dress, pulling it off her shoulders and down. With it came bra, panties, sandals, and he was dumbstruck as he looked at her, naked in the moonlight, a pale, slim column of fire.

She opened her arms. "Come to me," she whispered.

Yes.

He slid into her, hard to soft, gritting his teeth as he lowered his face to hers, shaking with the effort to keep still so she could adjust to him. Her whole body lifted into his, those long slender legs hugging his hips, breasts brushing his chest. They watched each other, light to dark. "Now, Matt," she whispered.

He started moving in her.

San Luis
Early in the Morning, April 29

The window was open, and Charlotte could hear the waves plashing on the shore, keeping time with Matt's slow heartbeat. Her ear was directly over his heart. His heart had, as she would have expected, the slow beat of an athlete, almost one to her two beats. He also had the stamina of an athlete. The memory of last night made her smile.

It had been months—no, *years*—since she'd woken up with a smile on her face.

"I can hear you smiling," Matt said, his voice a deep rumble in his chest. His arms tightened around her, and she nestled more deeply against his shoulder. As pillows went, it was too big and too hard, but it had other advantages. It was the perfect position for her head so she could lie in his arms, boneless and replete.

And safe.

She felt utterly and completely safe, as if the world had

been purged of bad things. Or rather, that Matt would stand between her and the bad things in the world. She was lying half on him, one leg over his. One large hand moved lazily up and down from her backside to her neck, his hand warm, the skin calloused.

"I hope that smile is because of me," he rumbled.

"Oh, yeah," she sighed. Definitely. She didn't feel exactly carefree—her problems were like large black clouds far away on the horizon—but right now it was possible to think of nothing at all and it was such a delicious feeling. No fear, no planning, no worries—just an endless, floating now.

She drifted, content...

His stomach rumbled, waking her up. She laughed. "I guess that's body language for—get up and fix me breakfast."

"Depends." His voice was wary. "What do you have in the house?"

"Yogurt, an apple, and tea," she said primly. "If you want more, you'll have to go out and forage."

A deep, long-suffering sigh. His hand tightened in her hair. "Can't we keep more stuff to eat here? You're starving me. And here I am your very own sex slave and personal trainer. It takes calories to do that."

Charlotte ran the palm of her hand over his chest. It was such a sensual pleasure. The crisp chest hairs tickled her hand and under them was warm skin over heavy muscle. Every once in a while, her sensitive fingers came across ropy scar tissue. "No whining. The sex slave thing is very good, but speaking of being my own personal trainer..." Her finger found his nipple, a small, hard bead, and rubbed, pleased to feel a small shudder run through him.

He might be a very powerful man, but it turned out that she was a very powerful woman.

"Stop that," he ordered. "If you want to talk to me, that is." His head lifted from the pillow. "Unless you'd like to—"

Charlotte sighed and shook her head. The idea was lovely, but she was sore, and this closeness in bed was too...luscious to spoil with sex.

"Okay." His head fell back on the pillow. "So tell me what you want."

Charlotte ran a finger down the indentation between his pectorals, putting just enough fingernail into it to make him catch his breath. She was being naughty. She felt naughty, so totally unlike her, Ms. Cool. He was aroused—she could feel him against her thigh. He was good about it, he didn't push against her, he wasn't pressing for sex, but he'd like it. She'd like it, too, only later. Right now she was feeling languid and was enjoying tormenting him, just a little. It was like playing with a tiger you knew wouldn't attack.

"I was thinking," she said softly, walking her fingers back up his chest, "that now that I've slept with you, you have to cut me some slack with the swimming lessons and target practice. I get special treatment. Because, well...having surrendered my virtue and all, I deserve it."

There was a funny noise deep in his chest. It took her a moment to realize it was Matt laughing. "Sorry, honey," he said cheerfully. "Doesn't work like that. At *all*. God, none of us thought to sleep with the senior chief to get him to take it easy on us." He was silent a moment, then shook his head. "Wouldn't have worked, anyway. Gotta give you points for trying, though. Today you're going to start the crawl, and you're going to practice an hour and a half on the video game."

"But I've already killed El Gordo a thousand times!" Charlotte found it hard to believe that adolescent males could spend hours and hours shooting people in a video game. It was fun at first but got very old very fast. "So...what *are* the advantages to sleeping with you if you're not going to cut me some slack?"

The words were barely out of her mouth when he pulled her up on his chest, big hand clamped around her head, kissing her wildly. It was like lighting a torch to a bundle of dry grass. In an instant, Charlotte felt heat sparkle through her system, as if she'd walked naked in front of a blast furnace. Her skin prickled and burned everywhere she touched him. He'd somehow positioned her so that her legs opened to straddle him, knees wide open against his broad chest. While he ate at her mouth, he reached down and opened her sex over him, and the heat notched up even higher.

All thoughts flew straight out of her head. Robert gunning for her, a murder charge, her totally nonexistent future—gone. Gone under the assault of his mouth and hands. And when he lifted her up so she could see the heat in his eyes, the red along his cheekbones, his lips swollen— the very picture of an aroused male—the breath caught in her throat. She was upright only because his hands held her—one long arm bracing her back, one large hand spanning her lower belly. The hand emitted heat like a radiator, and she found it hard to distinguish between the heat of his hand and the heat her own body was generating lower down. She was one long flush, reaching from her face down to her loins.

Matt was an incredible turn-on. That long, strong, scarred body. Those dark, intense eyes filled with incandescent heat. The powerful hands, holding her so gently. The way he let her know he was hers—without any tricks or games.

Charlotte thought she knew enough about sex, but she hadn't a clue. It felt like her whole body was taken over by him. When he kissed her, and his tongue touched hers, her vagina fluttered. When he touched her breasts, the heat spread everywhere, even down to her curling toes.

He was watching her so intently she knew he could read her arousal in a thousand ways. Her heart beating so hard her left breast quivered. Her nipples, like little rocks, flushed dark red. The sheen of sweat covering her body. The slickness between her thighs.

They were both slick, the large head of his penis was weeping semen. Watching her eyes carefully, Matt started moving his hips, rubbing the length of his penis along the open mouth of her sheath. He understood she didn't want penetration right now, but God! this was just as exciting. He touched her breast, and she gasped. Immediately, she could feel a ripple run through the thick hard column between her legs. His hips picked up the rhythm as he searched her eyes deeply, seeming to walk inside her head to figure out what excited her.

It all did—the intense stimulation of her sex, the feeling of sitting astride something immensely powerful, his bellowing breaths, which opened her legs at each intake. The strokes increased in intensity, in speed, as great waves of heat rolled through her. His strokes became shorter, harder, less regular as he fell prey to the demands of his own body. With a soft cry, she convulsed just as Matt gave a loud groan and exploded. She could feel his climax coming between her legs as his penis swelled against her sensitive skin.

Charlotte fell, boneless, on top of him, breathing hard. He only had one arm around her, the other had fallen to his side as if he hadn't even the strength to hold her. He groaned again, as if he were dying, and she gave a half laugh.

They were plastered together by sweat and the amazing amount of semen that had come jetting out of him. The sharp distinct odor of sex rose, mingling with the unmistakable smell of Matt—musk and sea and clean sweat. It was all so *physical*. Raw and real and exciting as hell.

She turned her head slightly and kissed his neck. It was all she had the strength for.

"I think after that I deserve to have my El Gordo-killing time cut in half," she murmured.

Matt laughed.

CHAPTER TWENTY

San Luis
April 29

Charlotte waited until they were almost at the cantina, then touched Matt's arm. "I'll come in just a minute," she said, stopping. "I need to check something at the Internet café."

Matt frowned, his jaw muscles jumping wildly. When he frowned, it was something epic. Clouds gathered on the horizon, lightning flashed.

"Wait, I—"

She pushed at him gently. "Go on, now. You'll be late for your appointment, and your friend is waiting inside. I'll be by in just a few moments."

Charlotte smiled at him sunnily, blew him a kiss, and shot forward towards Café Flora before he could say anything. She'd waited until the last possible minute before his meeting with his old friend, knowing that Matt hated being late.

Sleeping with Matt had been a mistake, she knew that intellectually, though it didn't *feel* that way. It felt wonderful. But there are consequences to everything, and the fallout from going to bed with him was that he was even more proprietary toward her. She was going to have to guard her secrets much more closely now.

The young student who manned the desk smiled as she entered and pushed across a piece of paper with a code on it with a murmured *"Buenas dias, señorita,"* when he saw her walk in.

After typing in the code, Charlotte immediately Googled the *Warrenton Courier,* in the start of her little daily routine. She'd carefully read the *Courier,* check the headlines of the Web sites of the three local news stations, and Google Charlotte Court and Robert Haine. It made her feel so much better when nothing popped up. In five minutes she'd be out and slipping into the cantina before Matt had finished greeting his friend.

That was the plan, but when she accessed the Web site of the *Warrenton Courier* she froze.

DEAD TORTURED BODY OF COURT FAMILY MAID FOUND the headline blared.

Heart thumping painfully, Charlotte read the article through, read it again, then clicked onto the TV news sites. Her heart turned over in her chest as she saw a photograph, taken with a telephoto lens, of a naked body spread-eagled out under a huge tree, a pale blob of vulnerable flesh barely discernible as a human being behind yellow police tape.

All the news sources had the same information to impart. Early-morning joggers had literally stumbled across the dead body of Moira Charlotte Fitzgerald, housekeeper of the Court family. Moira Fitzgerald had been tortured, then killed.

As she read the reports, bile rose in her throat, and she had to swallow heavily in order not to throw up.

Each article contained a capsule account of the events two months ago—the murder of Philip Court by his daughter, who then proceeded to murder Imelda Delgado, a nurse in the hospital, and Charlotte Court's disappearance.

Charlotte sat back in the uncomfortable aluminum chair, trembling. It took her three tries with the mouse to click off, her hand sweaty and shaking. She could see herself reflected in the dark screen, her face a dead white oval, eyes wide.

She couldn't move, she could barely breathe.

Moira. Lovely, gentle, good-hearted Moira. *Tortured to death*.

The articles had been painfully clear. Moira had died in excruciating pain. The tips of her fingers had been cut off, the bones of her hands had been shattered—*forensic evidence points to a hammer* was the way one news article had put it—and her elbows and knees had been reduced to pulp. Charlotte found it hard to even imagine the pain Moira had suffered.

Slowly, feeling as if she were a thousand years old, Charlotte stood up. She had to lock her knees to do it. It took her several minutes before she felt she could move.

She was somehow responsible for Moira's death; she could feel it in her bones. No one could possibly want Moira dead. It was her connection to Charlotte that had brought her to the attention of a torturing murderer.

When she felt her legs could withstand her weight, she shuffled out of the Internet café, barely noticing the young student's frown as he watched her stumble across the room.

It took her several tries to open the door. Her hands felt numb.

Something terrible had come for Moira and it was now out for her.

"So," Tom Reich said as they sat at the table in the cantina. They'd both instinctively chosen the table in the farthest corner from the door, in a dark pocket. They sat at right angles, both facing the room.

"So," Matt nodded.

"Good to see you again."

"Likewise."

Finally, the waitress finished setting two cervezas on the table together with nachos and salsa and the menu and walked away.

Matt understood very well that nothing of any importance could be said while she was hovering around their table. He was cool with that. The waitress happened to be Mama Pilar's granddaughter and had lived in San Luis all her life, but still. Opsec was opsec.

Already the two of them meeting would have raised a little red flag up north. Operators seldom gathered in public in groups of more than two or three since 9/11.

Tom was looking at him, expression serious. "You're looking good. I know you were badly injured. What's your status now?"

Matt didn't even try to bullshit him. "I'm okay, came back pretty well, but I'm not as operational as I was. Get a little winded at times. Can't dive to more than a hundred feet." He kept his face totally impassive as he mentioned the career killer. A Navy SEAL who couldn't dive wasn't a SEAL.

"Tough break." Tom's gaze was direct, his expression understanding but not pitying. Exactly what Matt needed.

Matt shrugged. Life is tough. Suck it up. Their creed.

Tom searched his eyes. "So—you're out, I hear. They must have offered you a job with nonoperational status. They need boots on the ground now, but they also need brains in the offices."

Matt snorted. They *had* offered him a job, and he'd contemplated it for a nanosecond. "And be a REMF? No thanks."

Tom smiled. *Nobody* wanted to become a Rear Echelon Motherfucker.

"So...you happy here?" Tom looked around the cantina. "I walked around a little before coming here. It's a nice place. Might even be a good place to settle down. Lenny's shop looked full. You going to become a partner there?" The questions were casual, but his expression was anything but.

Matt shrugged again. "Nah. I'd like something a little more challenging than fishing and sports diving. But... I'm going to stay here...a while. I already told you. I've got...commitments."

Matt watched Tom's eyes widen at each hesitation. Soldiers don't hesitate, and they're not ambiguous or unclear when they speak. Matt had spent his adult life communicating facts in as clear a way as he could. His life and his men's lives depended on it. So Matt's hemming and hawing was enough to raise eyebrows.

"Okay." Tom leaned forward a little over the table. "I'll get right down to it, Matt. I have a proposition for you. A job. Ready for you whenever you want, as soon as your...commitment is over, because you'd need to relocate to San Diego."

This was it. Exactly as Matt had imagined. Tom's company was fast becoming legendary and would soon be one of the top security companies in the country and perhaps the world. An invitation to join him was something most men would covet. And Tom was one of the good guys. He looked Tom over. Becoming rich hadn't made him go soft in any way. He wasn't even dressed like a rich man, with his white cotton short-sleeved shirt and jeans, scuffed boots, and his Navy-issue diver's watch instead of a Rolex.

He was a good guy, and he was offering Matt a job, which he desperately needed. Matt was grateful, this was really good news, but...*damn!* Bodyguarding rich guys and wiring McMansions. That wasn't what he'd trained so long and so hard to do.

Still, it was his best option in this new life. There was no going back to the Teams. That dream was gone. Dead. *Suck it up.*

Feeling dead inside, Matt nodded. "For the moment I can't leave San Luis. But when I can—what does the job entail?"

"The best thing you can imagine." Tom's expression changed, turned gleeful. He dropped years, and for an instant looked like a kid instead of a thirty-six-year-old former soldier. "Listen up, Matt, this is big. It's something I've been thinking about and planning for a long time, and finally I've got things in place. I needed someone just like you, and now that I've got you, we can start." He shifted his beer aside and placed both big hands on the table, watching Matt's eyes. "We're going to re-create Red Cell."

Matt's heart gave a huge thump in his chest. God. *Red Cell!* The legendary team led by Marcinko, tasked with penetrating and testing security systems. There was a black hole where information about Red Cell should be, but enough info had escaped of the exploits of Red Cell to ensure their status forever as demigods. They'd been the best of the best, tasked with ferreting out security holes on nuclear submarines, military bases, and showing how top US officials were vulnerable to kidnappings. They'd left pompous and incompetent security managers red-faced and seething. They'd made enemies, but by God, thanks to the exploits of a small handful of very good men, the military's security readiness had doubled in a couple of years.

Red Cell. Hot *damn*.

Matt was wary of any news *that* good. "Can you—can we—do that? As civilians?"

"Oh yeah. It's a new ball game now, post 9/11. I've just signed a contract with Homeland Security to test the defenses of a couple of bases. And we're drawing up plans to penetrate a major port that's just been given half a billion dollars to beef up their security. So we're supposed to find out what the government's getting for its money. That's why I need *you*, Matt. I've got plenty of operatives on my payroll. Good guys, young, fast, strong. But I need a top-level planner, a strategizer. That's you. You were the best. That's it. I can't tell you any more until I know you're on board." He sat back. Tom was never much for words. He didn't have to be, his plan had a huge allure all its own.

The idea of re-creating Red Cell, of putting together the best, smartest team in the world to penetrate super-secure positions, to find the weak spots so they could be eliminated and strengthen his country's defenses... it was his dream job.

If it weren't for Charlotte, he'd have shook hands on the job on the spot. There was no doubt that this was as good as being a SEAL. Maybe even better. Matt itched to say yes, but he needed to talk to Charlotte, sound her out.

"Listen, I'm really interested, but I need to talk to someone first. I need to—oh, there she is." The door to the cantina opened and Charlotte walked in.

Tom's eyes widened and he gave a low whistle. "*That's* your commitment? Jesus, no wonder you're down here."

"Something's wrong." Matt stood abruptly as he saw Charlotte's face, bloodless with shock, and her outstretched hands. He reached her in two strides and folded her hands in his. They were icy-cold, and he held them between his own hands, trying to warm them. He clasped them tightly to slow the trembling.

She was shaking all over, and he finally just wrapped his arms around her. He had to hold her tightly to dampen down the tremors, she was shaking so hard. *Jesus, what happened?*

Matt's senses opened wide. He'd been on the alert for danger to his woman, but the surrounding environment had sent only low-level signals. But now he went to red alert.

"Charlotte, honey." He kept his voice low and reassuring. "What's the matter? Did someone hurt you?"

"Oh, Matt," Charlotte whispered. "Something terrible has happened." She could barely get the words out, slurring them as if she had hypothermia. It was almost as bad as when she'd fallen into the ocean.

"It's okay, honey, whatever it is," he murmured. "We'll take care of it."

"No." Her eyes were closed, tears turning the long lashes dark. She shook her head against his tee shirt, the tears leaving streaks. "Nothing will ever make it better." Her arms tightened around his waist.

"What's wrong?" Tom had come up behind him, face serious. "Is there something I can help with?"

"I don't know," Matt answered honestly. Charlotte was burrowing her head into his shoulder so hard it was as if she was trying to disappear into him. He eased her head away an inch. "Honey?" She was shuddering, eyes closed. "Sweetheart, listen to me." He eased her away another inch and waited until her eyes opened. The pupils were dilated, the irises a silver-gray rim surrounding them. "Whatever it is, I'm here. Listen, let's go home, so you can tell me what this is all about." He reached into his jeans pocket and left enough money to cover the meal they hadn't consumed.

"Do you need my help?" Tom asked soberly.

"I don't know." Matt looked at him then back down at Charlotte. "Honey?" he asked softly. "This is Tom Reich, from San Diego. He's ex-Navy. Tom's a really good friend and a good man to have at your back. Do we need his help?"

She looked carefully at him, then at Tom. She swallowed, breathing slowly. It took her a moment to answer, but when she did, the shakiness had left her voice. "I think—I think I need all the help I can get."

Matt opened her door with his key but stopped her from going into her house. He gave a glance at his friend Tom that as much as said *watch her* and entered her house, pulling out the big black gun she knew he kept on him at all times. Charlotte stood outside, blinking in the harsh sunlight. She felt weak and had to keep locking her knees; otherwise, she would have keeled over. Visions of the horrors Moira had suffered kept blasting through her, and a shudder took her each time. She felt a large, heavy hand on her shoulder. Matt's friend, Tom. She looked back and up at him. He wasn't quite as tall as Matt but had the same broad-shouldered, lean physique. He had dark blue eyes and dark blond hair, but except for the coloring, he was a replica of Matt. They didn't look alike but they shared a look. They had the same serious, watchful air and they held themselves in exactly the same way—as if ready for trouble at any moment.

He meant for his hand on her back to be reassuring, and the crazy thing was that it did reassure her. Matt was in her house and when he came back out she could be certain that there was nothing dangerous there. With Matt in front of her and Tom Reich at her back, she was just about as safe as a woman could be.

God, a year ago, choosing the company of men who made her feel safe wouldn't even have entered her head. And yet, right now, Matt and Tom Reich were exactly what she needed.

When she'd read about Moira, it was as if an enormous black abyss had opened up right in front of her toes, with ravening monsters at the bottom. This time recovering in San Luis had lulled her, made her almost forget that dangerous men were out to kill her. Slowly, the urgency of imminent danger had receded, and her thoughts had turned more and more toward trying to prove her innocence of the murder charge.

It turned out that the murder charge was the least of her worries.

Matt appeared on the doorstep, slipping his gun into the back of his jeans waistband, and nodded. "All clear."

He spoke to the man behind her, not to her. He stepped to one side, and Tom Reich put a hand to her back. It wasn't in any way a sexual touch. He'd sensed her unsteadiness and made sure she knew he was at her back.

Matt took charge. Within a minute, the three were sitting down, Matt next to her on the sofa and Tom on a chair facing them. Matt's arm was around her, heavy and warm. He looked at her, assessing. "We're ready when you are," he said quietly.

This was it. What Charlotte had been so afraid of— telling Matt her secrets and him turning her in to the police—seemed ridiculous now. She looked at Matt and his friend. They were watching her silently, soberly.

She held Matt's gaze and drew in a deep breath. "I—I don't really know where to begin, so I guess I'll just start with basics. My name isn't Charlotte Fitzgerald, it's Charlotte Court. And I live—lived in Warrenton, New York."

"Court," Tom said suddenly, eyes sharp. "Warrenton, New York. Any relation to Court Industries?"

Charlotte nodded wearily. "My family's. And now— mine, I guess."

Tom looked at Matt. "Scuttlebutt has it that Court Industries is going to sign a huge contract with the Pentagon. They've got this supersecret project. All I know is the name—Proteus."

At least Charlotte had an answer for that. "No," she said crisply, "it's not. My father and I both were against it."

"Yes," Tom replied, "it is. And soon. I keep my ear

pretty much close to the ground when it's a question of companies doing business with the Pentagon, and my sources are very clear on that. No one much knows what Proteus is, but word has it CI is going to make close to $8 billion off it."

Matt whistled and Tom nodded. That kind of money was worth killing for, to the right—or wrong—kind of person.

"Jesus," Matt said. He squeezed her shoulder gently. "Okay, honey, time to talk."

Matt and Tom let her tell the story her own way, both of them intently focused on her. Charlotte spoke until she was hoarse, but she knew that she'd said everything. Matt and Tom were as unpriestlike as any men she'd ever seen, but there was something of the confessional in the room. The quiet, the nonjudgmental attention, and above all, the sensation of unburdening herself of a huge weight.

Charlotte stopped for a moment. Both Matt and Tom were listening to her intently. She'd covered the ground up until February 20. This was the moment in which either Matt believed her or he didn't. She had no way of knowing which way it would go.

"Robert was obviously paranoid—he set up this immense security…thing inside the company. The head of security was this idiot called Conklin. Martin Conklin. He was just incredibly…annoying. He made this big thing about being a former soldier, though he wasn't anything like you, Matt. He kept saying he'd been in Special Forces…is that the right expression?" Charlotte looked up at Matt.

He slanted a glance at Tom, who had whipped out a Blackberry. "On it," he said, as he keyed something in. Two minutes later, he looked up and addressed Matt.

"Gunnery sergeant, accused of selling weapons off-base. Dishonorable discharge in 2004."

"Oh." Charlotte blinked, even more appalled at what Robert had done to her family's company. He'd hired a *thief* to be head of security. "My instincts were perfectly right, then. To tell the truth, I wasn't paying much attention. My father was getting worse by the day, and I was spending most of my time in the hospital." She stopped, took in a deep breath. This was it. Matt and Tom were watching her steadily, faces completely impassive. "On— on the twentieth of February, I went to visit my father. There was a snowstorm, and the temperature had dropped during the night. My car wouldn't start, and the maid lent me hers—an SUV, a Tahoe. She was so proud of that car. It was like a symbol of America and success to her, bless her. She's Irish and comes from a very poor family. Her aunt had been our maid forever and when she retired, she proposed her niece. We get—got on really well."

She was prattling, putting off the moment. Charlotte clenched her fists and chose her words carefully. If she closed her eyes, she could see the moment in the hospital, as fresh in her memory as if it happened yesterday.

"When I walked into Dad's room, I found Martin Conklin holding—" She swallowed. "Holding a pillow over his face. Dad's EKG was flatlined. Then I connected the dots and became absolutely furious. Conklin had this horrific *smugness* to him, as if he had a perfect right to snuff out my father's life. It enraged me and I grabbed the IV tree next to my father's bed and swung it at his head. It connected," she said with relish. "Hard."

Matt looked startled, his first expression since they'd entered her house. He reached over to raise her hand to his mouth. "Good girl," he murmured. Tom looked approving, too.

"Well, I don't know if I deserve congratulations because I didn't know I was going to do it until I did it, until I saw Conklin lying on the floor." The memory still gave her a hot rush of satisfaction. It heated her veins, helped her get over the numbing shock of Moira's death. "He had a gun with those cylinder thingies attached to the barrel—a silencer—and he shot me through the shoulder as I was running toward him."

Matt's jaw muscles were jumping, and his hand tightened painfully around her shoulder. She shifted, murmuring, and he let go with an oath.

"I knew the hospital inside out. I'd been practically living there for almost two years. I made it out via the service elevator and made it to Moira's SUV without encountering anyone else in Robert's security team."

Tom leaned forward. "You were shot in a hospital. Why didn't you just call a doctor?"

"Because I knew Conklin and this second man—I think his name was Renfert—would come after me. I was a witness to the fact that they'd killed my father, and they'd shot me. A doctor wouldn't be armed. They'd probably kill him, too. No, I decided to go to the police."

Tom sat back. "Smart thinking."

She sighed. "Not really. When I drove by, I saw Robert and a couple of his henchmen. They were outside, talking to the chief of police. It scared me. So I drove home."

They were listening to her with an intensity that was almost palpable, Matt unblinking. "They were there, too," she said softly. "Four armed men outside the gates of my home. I was in intense pain by that point, and I'd lost a lot of blood. I wasn't thinking too clearly. I thought I could make it to a friend's house, stay there for the night, have her call a doctor, and call maybe the FBI in the morning, but first I needed to stop at a gas station. And I saw—I saw on the evening news that I was wanted for murder."

"What?" both men exclaimed.

The astonishment in their voices gave her courage. She turned, trembling, to Matt, the words tumbling out of her. "They said that I was the one who killed my father and I shot a nurse who came in to stop me. Imelda Delgado. I knew her well, we'd become friends while she cared for my father. She was a very sweet woman of Filipino extraction. I couldn't believe they'd killed her. They said I did it." She looked at him, a leaden ball of grief and fear pressing against her chest, "I swear to you, I *swear* I had nothing to do with Imelda's death. And as for the thought that I'd kill my own father—" A harsh sob escaped her, and her throat closed up so tightly, no words could come out.

Matt had been sitting holding her hands, and now he moved forward. "Christ," he said, and folded her in his arms. Charlotte leaned into him so hard she wished she could simply tunnel right into him and absorb his strength through her skin.

"You must believe me," she said, her voice muffled against his tee shirt. "I didn't kill anyone, I couldn't—"

"God, honey, of course you didn't. There's no question of that." Though she wanted to lean her head against his shoulder forever, his hands eased her away from his chest so he could look her in the face. "Right now, I need for you to tell me the rest of the story, and I really need for you to tell me what spooked you so much." He shook her, just a little, as if to dislodge that huge boulder in her throat.

It worked. Somehow her voice came back. She pushed her hair away from her eyes wearily. "I—I didn't have much money with me and I knew enough not to use checks or my credit cards. I had barely enough money to get to Chicago, where my Great Aunt Willa lives. Lived. She passed away at the age of 91 during the Christmas holidays. I was her only heir, and I had the keys to her house. My house, now. I kept putting off flying to Chicago to settle the estate because my father was so ill. I knew Aunt Willa always kept a great deal of cash on hand, and I found where she kept it. The Midwest was in the middle of a snowstorm, I was running a terrible fever, and my shoulder hurt like the devil. All I could think about was escaping to some refuge somewhere warm. I didn't have my passport with me and even if I did, I was sure I'd be on some list at the airport. Wouldn't I?"

Matt and Tom nodded.

"I thought so. But I had Moira's brand-new American passport, and I knew I could make it into Mexico. I could even sort of keep my name. Moira's name is Moira Charlotte Fitzgerald. I often teased her about it. So... I drove cross-country and entered into Tijuana and just kept going until I was ready to faint. I think I was a little crazy with pain and fever when I arrived, but God was with me when I stopped at the cantina." She looked at Matt, so solid, so strong and squeezed his hand. "Three days later I saw you for the first time."

He folded her hand between his, the grasp warm and strong. "So what spooked you today?"

Charlotte jolted at the thought of Moira. Her chin quivered. "I've been following the local Warrenton news. I keep hoping that something will come to light to prove my innocence. I check every day. Today, it was all over the newspapers, and the Web sites of the TV stations."

A tear ran down her cheek, and her hands trembled. "What was, honey?" Matt asked, his voice gentle.

"Moira," Charlotte whispered. "Dead. Tortured to death."

"So it's settled," Tom finally said two hours later, while Matt gritted his teeth and barely refrained from punching his fist through the wall. *Settled, my ass.*

But the thing was—Tom was right. His logic was impeccable. Someone needed to go to Warrenton to investigate, and it couldn't be Matt. Matt wasn't willing to leave Charlotte's side, and Charlotte wasn't willing to go back until there was some evidence proving her innocence. And she was safer here than she would be in a place where there were men willing to torture a woman to death to get to her.

Jesus. Matt could contemplate danger coolly. All soldiers could. But the thought of Charlotte in those fuckers' hands—Charlotte being tortured—it made him break out in a sweat. No, she was staying right here and he had to, too.

Which left Tom.

"I can get there by this evening. There are people I can call in, and we'll nose around. I'm sure we can come up with something to prove Charlotte's innocence. Either the PD there has its head up its ass, or they're on the take. Because it doesn't sound like they have much of a case to make against Charlotte. Any halfway competent DA would throw the case out. So let me see what I can get. And then we call in the FBI and have Charlotte put in custody until her name is cleared and Haine is put in a cage."

Charlotte shuddered.

"Yeah." Tom shook his head at Charlotte. "It's a tough

break. But you won't have to stay in custody for long." He reached over to close his fist over her hand. "It'll be okay. You've got us on your side."

Charlotte smiled wanly at that. Matt just hoped that Tom was right—the trail was cold by now. But Tom had pulled miracles out of his butt before. And so had Matt.

"Here." Tom tossed him a sleek satiny gray plastic device. Matt caught it one-handed and slid it open. It was a cell phone. Tom had thumbed open his own, identical to the one Matt was holding, and punched in numbers as he walked into Charlotte's bedroom. The cell phone Matt was holding rang. He pressed the center button and all he heard was static.

"Press the red button on the lower-left-hand side and put it to your ear," Tom called. He did and the static disappeared. "We've got ourselves a secure comm system," he heard Tom say over the phone.

He was back in the room. "Don't use that cell phone for anything else. I'll call you when I have news. It's got a sixteen-bit encryption system at both ends. Really secure. Maybe the NSA could crack it, but it'd take them a month. In a month, you'll be busting your ass for me in San Diego, and Charlotte will be organizing a show at the Coronado." He started for the door.

"Listen, Tom," Matt said. Tom stopped and looked back at him. "Keep a list of what you're spending and I'll pay you back. And pay you for lost days of work." He said it without wincing. Tom was going to take a private jet to Warrenton, and four days of Tom's time was probably worth more than his yearly pension, but it didn't matter.

"Don't worry," Tom said, a big wide smile on his face. "I'll dock it from your pay."

CHAPTER TWENTY-ONE

La Paz, Baja Sur
May 5

As a former soldier, Barrett was very familiar with clusterfucks. You plan down to the minutest detail, you don't put a foot wrong, and yet everything goes south in a heartbeat in a perfect storm of bad luck. A loose bolt in the helicopter, a sudden sandstorm, an unexpected injury—it could be anything, and all that planning and work was worth crap.

There were lots of terms for it—SNAFU and FUBAR and goatfuck.

But the opposite can happen, too—an event so rare soldiers didn't even have a name for it. Pure blind good luck. Barrett was deep in the first when the second exploded right before his eyes.

He'd made his way slowly down the Baja peninsula, stopping at every town, big or small. He was Patrick Van der Elst, art collector from Arizona, and he went to every art gallery in every town until he wanted to vomit if he saw one more painting or sculpture or—God help him— "concept." He hit every art supply store and discovered

that Fabriano was a widely available make of art paper.
At the art supply stores he asked in a low-key way about a
friend of his who had said she was heading down to Baja
and had any *norteamericanas* settled in lately?

It was all done casually, *hey, no prob* because the last
thing he needed when a dead Charlotte Court—or whatever the hell she was calling herself—turned up, was the
police finding out that a *gringo* had been around asking
about her.

He started in the morning and ended when the last gallery closed, around midnight most of them. Then he'd get
into his rental and drive to the next town. And the clock
was ticking.

Barrett had made it down to La Paz, a fairly big city
on the tip of the peninsula, and he'd ticked off eight of
the twelve galleries in town and was thinking sourly
that maybe he should have gone straight to San Miguel
Allende after all, when *wham*. There it was.

A big three-foot-by-two-foot perfect rendering of Moira
Fitzgerald, painted by Charlotte Court. Even he could see
that.

"Nice, isn't it?" a voice asked from behind him. "The
artist is going to become a big name very soon."

Barrett turned to see a tall, gray-haired man checking
him out.

It was done discreetly, but it was unmistakable. Gays
creeped Barrett out, but he could certainly tuck that away
on a job. He smiled back and put some sex in the smile. The
man blinked and straightened, automatically patting his
gray ponytail. "I'm Perry Ensler, the owner of the gallery."

Barrett stuck out his hand and let the clasp last three
seconds too long. "Name's Van der Elst. Patrick. I'm on

vacation here and since my...partner has been insisting we start an art collection, I've been tooling around, poking my head in a few galleries here and there." He grimaced. "Crap, mostly, is what I've seen. But what the hell do I know? I sell swimming pools. But my partner, he's in banking and he's ambitious and he says we need an art collection so—" Barrett shrugged his shoulders and smiled into the guy's eyes. "Here I am."

"Well, you might not know much about art, but I'd say you have instinctive excellent taste, Patrick. This artist is our new star. I've just discovered her, and I've already sold half of what I bought from her. She works in several media, what are you looking for?"

Barrett allowed himself a blank look, which was actually genuine.

Ensler laughed. "Medium. What an artist uses. Oils, watercolors, pastels."

"Oh." Barrett put a sheepish look on his face. "I don't know what I'm looking for, except—I mean when you think of a painting you think of an oil painting, don't you?" He turned and pointed at the portrait of Moira. "I mean, what's that?"

"Oil." Ensler walked to the painting and touched the frame. "And I'm letting the painting go relatively cheaply because she's still unknown, but trust me, this painting will double in price in a year."

"So, who is she?" Barrett asked casually, leaning forward, ostentatiously reading out the signature in the lower-right-hand corner. "Charlotte Fitzgerald. How much is this one?"

Ensler stroked the frame, smiling. "You can have the

portrait for $12,000, and believe me it's a steal. Would you like to see other works of hers?"

Oh yeah. Barrett nodded.

Ensler walked him to the back room, where several sketches and watercolors were awaiting framing. "These are all hers," he said. "Haven't had a chance to frame them yet, they'll sell just as soon as I hang them, she's that good, eh? Excellent balance and composition, wonderful color sense, superb strokes in the oils, I think she's going to be huge."

Barrett tuned him out and focused on the work in front of him. He scanned each sketch and watercolor carefully, looking for clues to where she was. But the scenes were generic Mexico—sunrises, quick sketches of Mexicans, the sea at various times of day. Baja was a long, narrow peninsula, the sea was everywhere. There was nothing there that could in any way lead to Charlotte Court.

"Charlotte Fitzgerald, huh?" He injected a casual note of curiosity into his voice. "So where does she live? In Baja?"

"Ah ah ah, you naughty boy." Ensler gave him a coy look, forefinger wagging. "Bypassing the gallery is the oldest trick in the book. If you want a Charlotte Fitzgerald, you'll have to buy one from me. No going round the gallery owner."

You miserable little fuck, Barrett thought. He'd get the info, but he'd waste time, time he didn't have.

"Whoa there." He kept his face and voice pleasant. "Sorry, I wasn't thinking about that at all, but I guess you get a lot of that. Kind of like someone scouting a book in a bookstore, then buying it on Amazon, huh?"

"Precisely."

"Well." Barrett put his hands in his pockets, and jingled some coins. Casual guy thinking things over. His combat knife was in his right hand pocket, and his hand itched to bring it out *now*. One minute with the razor edge against that scrawny neck and he'd have the information he wanted. "I think her stuff is great, but I guess I better check with my partner. He's off doing some bank thing, and I can't get in touch with him. Say, do you close over lunch?"

Ensler smiled. "This is Mexico. We close from one to five."

Perfect. As far as Barrett could see, the gallery's security was shit. He had a four-hour window. This was going to be easy. He'd slide in and slide out, with no one the wiser. Ensler was bound to have Charlotte Fitzgerald's address on file.

"Great." He smiled. "If I can convince my partner, we'll come back around six, then, unless he's made other plans." His smile turned flirtatious. "Maybe when you close we can all go out for a beer together? My partner, he's really friendly."

Ensler's smile widened. "Oh, yeah."

Oh yeah. Tonight Barrett would catch up with Charlotte Court, now Charlotte Fitzgerald.

Four hours later, Barrett was outside Calle Verde 37, thoughtfully studying the doors and windows.

The door cracked open and Barrett turned to the side, cell phone open and at his ear. "Yeah, Bork, you heard me right. Get on the guy's case and make sure those orders are in by July." Dumb *gringo* tourist who couldn't leave the job behind.

A woman walked out of the house. Slender, pale blonde, very beautiful. Charlotte Court. Immediately behind her was a big guy who put his arm around her. He had dark, observant eyes that took in every detail.

Luckily, it was the time of evening in which Mexicans came out in force on the streets. There were at least twenty other people around. The big guy noticed them all, but Barrett didn't stand out in any way. He continued talking into his dead phone, eyes unfocused.

Still with his arm around her, the big guy walked Charlotte Court down to the beach.

Barrett didn't follow.

His time would come. Soon.

San Luis
May 7

"I need to ask you something," Matt whispered in her ear late in the evening two days later.

He wants to talk?

No way. Her heart was still racing, her muscles had turned to water and her brain to Cream of Wheat.

"Mfff," she answered into his biceps, pulling her hand out from under the covers to wag a forefinger back and forth. *No.*

Amazing how only minutes before she'd been supercharged with energy as they made love. Infused with it, tingling with it.

Her heart and her mind and her body had been completely open to him—as they had been since she'd confessed. Making love with him was all-consuming, it was as if he filled her heart and mind, not just her body.

She was still in mindless free fall from her climax,

lost in the sensations of her own body—and he wanted to *talk*?

Matt tightened his arms around her as he turned them over in bed. It was mean of him, because she'd actually had to move a muscle. Several muscles. But soon enough she was slumped on his chest, her head had found her favorite spot on his shoulder, and she was sliding deliciously from stunned pleasure to sleep when he lifted her up by the shoulders and shook her lightly.

The beast.

"Charlotte, open your eyes." She shook her head, eyes scrunched shut. "Come on, open those gorgeous eyes of yours." Annoyingly, he tapped her on the nose.

With a deep, heartfelt sigh, Charlotte opened her eyes and glared at him. "What?" she asked, aggrieved, and got an answering grin.

"We need to talk about what we're going to do when Tom comes back."

Charlotte laid her head back down on his shoulder, her new favorite place in the world, wide-awake now. "Depends on what he finds."

"He'll find what's necessary to clear your name. Tom's good. And we have to think beyond that, to what comes next."

What comes next. Who knew what came next? Charlotte could barely get her mind around the idea of Tom clearing her name. Matt's face had turned somber. Her answer meant a lot to him. But she had no answer.

"I have no idea what comes next, Matt," she said softly.

He angled his head so he could see her face. "Tom's job offer is a very good one." He watched her eyes carefully.

"His company's solid, and the money's good, too. There might even be a partnership down the line. It would mean relocating to San Diego, though. And I don't want to go alone. I want you to come with me."

There it was. She'd been expecting it, and she hadn't been able to come to a decision about what she'd say. At one level—*yes, I've never felt like this about a man before, of course I'll come with you*—was the obvious answer. But how could she say that? Her life was lying in shards around her. Even assuming Tom could clear her name—a megahuge assumption—there were a thousand things she needed to take care of in Warrenton. The company, the—

He'd been massaging her neck muscles, that large hand warmly rubbing, the long fingers reaching up to caress her scalp. His other hand had been travelling slowly up and down her back, but now, sneakily, he reached to cup her breast.

Heat zinged through her system, and her mind simply shut down as chills raced over her skin. Her stomach muscles clenched, and her breath caught when he absently rubbed the pad of his thumb over her nipple. Delicate intimate muscles clenched, as if she hadn't just had a shattering climax. Her body was completely out of her control. When had that happened?

She frowned, knowing her face was flushed with desire. "You're going to make me do whatever you want, and you're going to use sex to do it, aren't you?"

He made a low rough sound in his chest, a lion's growl. His eyes—those intelligent chocolate eyes—were slitted and focused on her. "Yeah, if it works, use it, I always say. So, coming back to—"

They both froze as the cell phone Tom had given him

rang. Matt had kept it constantly within reach these past two days, and all he had to do was stretch out his hand. He sat up, thumbed it open, and punched the red decryption button. "Yeah, talk to me."

Charlotte sat up, too, pulling the sheet up under her arms, shivering, the languor and heat of sex completely banished. She watched Matt's face but as usual, she couldn't read anything. He listened carefully, saying only "Uh-huh," at irregular intervals. Tom spoke for fifteen minutes, and Matt finally said, "Good job, Tom. I knew I could count on you," and flipped the cell phone closed.

"What? What?" Charlotte reached out to touch his arm, to anchor herself. Her heart was pounding, and it was hard to breathe.

Matt placed his hand over hers and it calmed her, a little. "Okay, this is what Tom found out. He has plenty of law enforcement contacts in the Northeast, and he called in some markers."

Charlotte shuddered at the thought of law enforcement officers studying her case. Tom would have to say where she was hiding. They could be already on their way here. She barely had time to panic before Matt squeezed her hand. "Tom went over the case with a good friend in the FBI. The friend was appalled at the behavior of the Warrenton PD.

"They ran a check on the gun that killed the nurse, though there were no prints. It had been wiped down. But the thing is—though the gun was unregistered, the bullet that shot Imelda Delgado matched a bullet found at the scene of an unsolved crime two years ago. A man had been shot in the kneecap. He was a recent hire at Court Industries—a low-level criminal who'd been boosting crates of material from the warehouse. Tom nosed around a little, and he found out that everyone suspected that the CI head of security—Martin Conklin—had kneecapped the guy as a warning to others, but the guy wasn't talking. Told the police he didn't recognize the man who shot him. Tom paid him a visit and was... persuasive. So the guy is willing to swear under oath that the man who shot him was Martin Conklin. And the bullet that was recovered from this guy matches the bullet that shot Imelda Delgado. Slam dunk. And once Conklin goes down, he'll take Haine with him. No one wants to do time for an asshole. Tom's FBI buddy says that... well, to use a technical term, you're home free."

Home free. Home. Free. Free to go home. A shudder began inside her, deep inside the core of her. The months of fear and grief and pain rose up like bile in her throat, her suddenly impossibly tight throat. A small sound escaped her, high and tight, a mewling whimper of emotion. Matt's arms went around her, pulled her close, his big hand covering her head, as if to protect her. Another harsh bubble of sound she couldn't suppress, and she broke down, crying out her rage and pain in great gulping sobs, crying so hard she could barely breathe.

Through it all, steady as a rock, Matt held her. He didn't shush her or try to make her stop crying, as if understanding she needed this outlet as badly as she needed the air she was gulping in. He didn't speak at all, simply held her tightly against him, offering the animal comfort of his body, instinctively knowing she needed the human contact as she was swept away on a tide of sorrow. One large hand covered the back of her head, the other anchored her waist, and his strength allowed her to let go.

She had no idea how long she cried—a minute? Ten minutes? She cried until there were no more tears, until the hot ball of grief in her chest subsided, until she could finally draw a deep breath.

Charlotte rested, spent, against Matt's hard shoulder, wet with her tears.

Her breathing finally slowed. "Better?" he asked quietly.

She nodded, surprised. Yes, it *was* better. It was as if she'd purged herself of something black and vile, something that had taken up an inordinate amount of space in her heart. The space was cleared now, and slowly the elements of her new life started to trickle in.

First, Matt. Warm, strong, steady. Intriguing. Beyond sexy. Matt was part of her life now. And that life included freedom to move, an actual future with Matt in it, instead of the living from day to day that had been her life for the past months.

"Are you ready to listen to me?" Charlotte felt Matt's chin move against her hair as he looked down at her. Amazingly, a big, white, laundered handkerchief smelling of starch appeared out of nowhere. Matt did handkerchiefs?

Charlotte sniffled and blew—well, honked—a little ashamed of the crying jag. She nodded and lifted herself up on her elbow. If he wanted to talk to her, he deserved to see her face.

"Okay," he nodded. "First off, I love you. I think that needs to be said up front. Just get it out there." He wiped the tears from under her eyes with his thumb. Charlotte's heart gave a huge thump. His eyes narrowed as he saw her reaction. "I didn't imagine that would be a huge surprise to you."

It wasn't surprise. It was recognition. The huge jolt

your system gives when your life moves on to another track and you've just noticed.

"I love you, too." She didn't even have to think of it. The words came welling up from deep inside her, and it was the truest thing she'd ever said.

He nodded again, his hard mouth lifted in a half smile. "Figured that might be the case. It makes what comes next a whole lot easier to say. I imagine you'll want to go home to Warrenton. We could leave tomorrow, if you want. I know that there will be...stuff you have to deal with. The FBI's going to want to talk to you. You'll probably have to testify, but that will be down the line. You've inherited a company, you'll have to do something about that. I'll be with you just as long as it takes. But when you've cleared the decks, I want you to know that we'll live wherever you want to live. If you don't want to relocate to San Diego, well, I can find a job just about anywhere."

His face wasn't totally unreadable to her anymore. It was impassive, yes, but there'd been a tightening of his features as he made his offer.

Her heart simply melted. The tears rolled down her cheeks, big fat ones that plopped on the sheet.

"Hey," Matt said, alarmed. "Jesus, what's the matter? I thought—"

She shut him up by leaning forward and kissing him, a soft brushing of lips, lifting away before he took control of it and they ended up rolling around in the sheets again. Sex with Matt was wonderful, but there were things she needed to say.

"I wouldn't mind living in San Diego at all. I don't care where we live, as long as I can be with you. I can paint anywhere. And in San Diego we can come down to San

Luis when we want. Maybe even buy a little house here. Maybe even this one."

"Yeah." He didn't even try to hide his relief. "Yeah, that's what I was thinking. So I guess that leaves just one more thing to wrap up?"

"Mm?"

He fumbled for her hand. To Charlotte's enormous surprise his hand trembled. That big, broad, brown hand shook. Amazing. He took in a deep breath. "Charlotte Court, will you marry me?"

Her mouth dropped open, and her mind went blank. Oh God, oh God.

They stared at each other. A bead of sweat formed on Matt's temple and slowly rolled down his face.

Marriage. *Marriage*. A lifetime with this man. This big, tough warrior, totally unlike any man she ever thought she'd marry.

Marriage. Children.

Marriage...

Yes. A thousand times yes.

The word couldn't make it past the boulder in her chest, so she nodded, the tears falling again, harder and faster than before.

She breathed in sharply and the word made it through her tight throat. "Yes, oh *yes!*" She threw herself at him.

He caught her.

San Luis
May 8

Barrett walked right by Charlotte Court on the marina.

Fuck! There were very few people out. His hand touched

his knife. One second. That's all it would take. One second, the knife sliding like butter between her ribs, puncturing the heart, and she'd drop like a stone. Or a quick slice to the femoral artery. By the time she looked down at the blood pumping out onto her white linen trousers, he'd be long gone. She'd bleed out before anyone could come to help her.

It could be so easy. A flick of his wrist, and she'd be stone dead.

He could even grab her, fall into the water with her, swim under the quay, and hold her under until she drowned.

None of these were even remotely possible as long as she was walking with the tall guy with the watchful eyes, who seemed to be with her twenty-four/seven. An operator. He walked like an operator. Either law enforcement or military.

The client had been clear that it couldn't look like murder. Two days ago, Barrett had sent the message to the bulletin board.

Found C in Mexico.

Haine must have been living with his computer because the answer came immediately.

Perfect. It must look like an accident.

So slicing and drowning were out of the question with the operator around. Slipping something in her drink to make it look like a heart attack?

Might be hard because she was looking so well. Fabulous, in fact. Barrett found it hard to believe this was a woman who'd been shot, a woman on the run from the authorities.

She was slightly pink from the sun, perfectly healthy, huge smile on her face turned up to the big guy walking beside her, holding her hand. Neither of them paid him any attention, which was good. But the operator seldom left her side, which was bad.

Well, if you have an obstacle and you can't get around it, you have to blast your way through it. Barrett had thought it through and he had a plan that included the operator.

Charlotte Court couldn't fall prey to a violent mugger and no one would believe she had had a heart attack or was sick enough to die.

But a love affair gone sour? Oh yeah. People believed anything of a beautiful woman. It was ingrained in human psychology. Beauties lead different lives, inspire greater passions, greater hatreds...

He had two cold guns. First shoot the operator, then her. Get their prints on the guns. It would work. Yeah. Charlotte Court, shot to death by her wrathful, jealous lover.

Anyone would believe that.

"Hurry it up, Matt," Charlotte called, making a neat pile of her underwear. They were leaving in a couple of hours. Lenny was going to drive them to Tijuana, where an FBI agent would meet them and take her and Matt across the border. They had tickets for the red-eye to Rochester, and tomorrow she'd be back home.

It would be horrible walking into her home and not having Moira, though. As soon as she was home, Charlotte was going to call Moira's family to ask about their burial preferences. If the family wanted, Moira could be buried in the Court family crypt.

Time was tight, and Matt was showering.

"Don't worry!" he shouted. "Unlike you, it will take me five minutes to pack."

Charlotte zipped her bag and placed it on a chair. They wouldn't have to stay more than a few days in Warrenton, Tom had said. He wanted Matt at work by next week, and had arranged for them to stay in a catered apartment in San Diego at company expense until they could find a house.

Charlotte was leaving most of her belongings here. Matt had promised her they could come down to San Luis his first weekend off. She started covering her paintings when she heard a knock at the door.

"Don't answer that!" Matt called, his voice muffled by the shower water. Charlotte rolled her eyes. If Matt had his way, whoever was out there would have to wait for Matt to finish showering, dry off, and get dressed. Matt's paranoia would have to stop at some point. He was going to have to tone it down if he wanted to live with her.

Start as you mean to go on.

She walked to the door and opened it. A thin blond man was standing there, checking her number. He saw her and started. "Oh! I h-hope I g-got the right n-number. Th-thirty-seven, Perry said. Are you Ch-Charlotte Fitzgerald?"

He was blinking in the bright sunlight, hands deep in his pockets.

Charlotte smiled. "Yes, I am, but I'm afraid I'm in a bit of a rush."

"M-May I come in? J-just for a moment? P-Perry Ensler s-sent me."

With an inward sigh, Charlotte stepped back. "Well, just for a moment."

"Th-thank you." He followed her in and looked around, eyes bright with interest. "Oh, m-my. P-Perry was right.

Such *talent*. N-name's Pete. Pete Cornwell. I c-collect s-sketches and bought several of y-yours at P-Perry Ensler's g-gallery in La P-paz. P-Perry d-didn't have any more of your s-stuff to sell, and he s-said to c-come directly to you."

Matt appeared in the doorway, hair wet, in jeans and tee shirt. The tee shirt clung to his wet chest. He hadn't even taken the time to dry. "You'll have to come back some other time," he said coldly.

The man looked alarmed at Matt's hostile tone. "S-sorry." He looked at Charlotte, Matt, then Charlotte again. "I g-guess this is a r-really bad t-time. B-but I'm d-driving back up to L-Los Angeles th-this afternoon and I did s-so want to b-buy s-some m-more s-sketches of y-yours b-before I g-go."

His stammer was getting worse and worse under Matt's cold stare.

"Okay. I can show you some of my sketches." She'd give this Pete Cornwell fifteen minutes to go through them, out of courtesy to Perry. It wasn't usual practice for an art gallery to make it easy for a customer to buy art directly from the artist. It was very gracious of Perry to point this man in her direction. He wasn't going to make a dime off the sales.

The portfolio with most of her sketches was on the sideboard. That sideboard made a very neat metaphor for her life melding with Matt's. In the top drawer, he kept two loaded pistols and a big black knife with a razor edge and a *groove* for blood. She'd never even heard of such a thing. *Just in case,* Matt had said when he'd put the weapons in the drawer.

Deadly weapons below. Her sketches above. Made for an interesting contrast.

Charlotte opened the portfolio, quickly chose twenty sketches. "Here," she said, "you can—"

Fast as a snake, the man's arm caught her around the neck and she felt a cold circle of metal against her temple. A gun had magically appeared in his hand. "Freeze!" he shouted.

Charlotte couldn't move. He held her in a chokehold. But he wasn't talking to her, he was talking to Matt.

"Weapons, on the floor. Hands up and behind your head. *Now!* Or she gets it right in the head." He ground the muzzle against her temple. Matt didn't move.

"Weapons. On. The. Floor. If you make me say it one more time, I'm putting a slug through her elbow."

The clatter of Matt's gun hitting the floor was loud in the suddenly quiet room. His eyes glittered almost coal black, his attention focused completely on the man holding her.

"Backup weapon, too."

"Don't have one on me," Matt growled. "I was taking a shower."

"What—what do you want?" Charlotte wheezed. The pain in her neck was excruciating. He was cutting off her airway. "Did Robert send you?"

"Shut up." His arm tightened, and she saw spots. It was entirely possible that she was going to die right now, choked to death. She brought her hands up and tried to pry his arm away, but it was like trying to shift a steel bar. She used her nails but couldn't find a purchase on the hard, ropy muscles of his forearm. He tightened his grip even more and she gasped, light-headed.

"You." The man addressed Matt. "Against that wall." His head jerked to the left.

Matt didn't move. "Let up on her first. No sense choking her."

The arm eased up slightly, and Charlotte gasped, finally able to breathe.

"Get over there," the man growled. "I need you against the wall. Right in front of me."

The oxygen infusion woke her up. Adrenaline coursed through her system. Her thoughts raced. She had to find some kind of advantage, some kind of leverage. *Think!* He hadn't killed her immediately. He could have. He could have shot them down immediately. The fact that he didn't meant that he had some kind of plan. He wanted this to go down in a specific way.

What did he want?

I need you against the wall. What a peculiar thing to say. This whole scene was utterly crazy. He was holding her tightly, watching as Matt slowly made his way to the wall.

Charlotte now saw that the man's hands looked odd. They...glistened. It took her a second to realize that he was wearing latex gloves. He'd planned this. All of this—it was part of some elaborate plan. And having Matt against the wall was part of it.

He was going to kill them both. Charlotte had found the love of her life, she was going to get married, and now this man was going to wipe them off the face of the Earth.

No! Not while she had a breath left in her. Matt was watching him fiercely but wouldn't make a move. Not as long as the man held a gun to her head. It was up to her.

Matt had reached the wall. The man was moving forward, toward Matt, pushing Charlotte in front of him. Maybe if she tripped or pretended to faint, she could make him lose his balance. All Matt needed was an opening. She'd seen how fast he could move. A second's opportunity, and he'd make his move.

The man took a step forward, and she could feel his muscles bunching for another step. *Now!*

Charlotte cried out, as if she'd stubbed her toe, and twisted, turning herself into a deadweight. It didn't work. Though he was thin, he was incredibly strong. He simply tightened his hold on her neck and lifted her as he took another step forward.

The hold had turned into a stranglehold. Red and black spots swam in front of her eyes. The room was turning gray, a rushing noise filled her ears.

She had to think of something fast before she passed out.

The sideboard! If she could somehow reach inside the drawer and pull out one of the pistols or even the knife. It was so sharp she could slice the tendons of his arm with it.

Charlotte stumbled again, heavily, and by the time he yanked her upright, she was so close to the sideboard she could almost touch it. Should she pretend to faint? Maybe—

Oh God! As soon as Matt moved to where he wanted him, the man swung the pistol from her head and aimed it at Matt. Charlotte watched in horror as his finger tightened on the trigger, squeezing gently—

Charlotte shoved at him with all her strength just as his finger pulled the trigger.

The gun went off in a roar, and Matt dropped like a stone, the wall behind him stained with bloodspatter.

Rage such as she had never felt before roared inside Charlotte, lighting a wildfire inside her. *He'd killed Matt.*

In a move faster than thought, she shoved at the man, pivoted, and opened the drawer in the sideboard, clutching the pistol.

The cold metal felt good in her hand, familiar. It gave her the power.

"Son of a bitch!" the man screamed, rounding on her, but by that time she had Matt's pistol pointed toward him, toward the man who had killed Matt.

She pulled the trigger—*bang bang bang bang bang bang*—aiming straight at his chest, walking toward him in a frenzy of fury so great, she kept pulling the trigger even after she'd finished the bullets, not hearing the click of the pistol on empty. Charlotte stood over him, panting, pistol still aimed at him. He wasn't moving.

He wasn't breathing.

She stood over him, teeth grinding, panting, waiting for the next move. If the miserable bastard so much as twitched a finger, she was going to club him upside the head with the pistol and crack his skull.

And then take the knife to him.

She hauled back and kicked him, so hard his body bounced. There was a small lake of blood spreading out from his back.

His eyes were open, staring unblinkingly at the ceiling. She kicked him again.

"Charlotte. Honey. He's dead." Matt's voice. God! He was alive! His voice woke her out of her trance, and she ran to him, sliding a little in the blood spreading out in a pool from where he lay.

"Matt!" she sobbed, kneeling in his blood. The bullet had gone through his shoulder. She didn't know whether it had nicked some important artery. There seemed to be so much blood! "Oh, God, Matt, don't die!"

He reached up and touched her cheek, smiling faintly. "Did...a number on that guy," he gasped. "Charlotte. My warrior princess."

And he fainted.

EPILOGUE

San Diego, California
A year later

My wife will be here shortly," Matt said through a clenched jaw for the bazillionth time. He looked yearningly out the big plate-glass windows of San Diego's trendiest art gallery, where Charlotte was having the opening of a one-woman show, hoping to catch a glimpse of her finally walking up the street.

It was the opening of her first show. A *vernissage* is what you were supposed to call it. *Torture* was what Matt called it.

Matt was being bombarded by questions he had no answer to, and the gallery owner wasn't being any help. He was too busy racking up sales. The little red dots that marked a sale had been sprouting on Charlotte's paintings like a rash of measles.

Where the hell *was* she? It wasn't like her to be late, certainly not for her own show. She'd been in a fever of excitement for months over it, painting up a storm, which had suited him because he was kept enormously busy working for Tom. They were both happily settled in San

Diego, in a big house in Coronado Shores filled to the rafters with Charlotte's work.

A tall, excruciatingly thin, very elegant lady drifted up to him in a cloud of perfume. She had a narrow face and lots and lots of teeth. She tapped him on his arm with a closed fan. "Excuse me," she said, her leathery face totally expressionless. He'd seen that a lot in women lately and had asked Charlotte about it. It shocked him when she said that women injected *botulism* in their faces for the wrinkles.

Botulism. The idea horrified him. He'd once risked his life to recover a strain of botulism in a canister headed for New York. Charlotte had laughed at his expression.

This lady might have injected the entire canister into herself because she could barely move her mouth.

"Does your wife work in gouache? I'd be very interested if she did."

"Nope," Matt responded. "She paints, she doesn't cook. No goulash." And made his escape outside.

It was a beautiful day, as most days were in San Diego. He took a deep breath, savoring the fresh air, away from the perfume, eau de cologne, hair gel, and hair spray inside.

For the millionth time, Matt thanked the gods that Charlotte was willing to live here with him. The month they'd spent in Warrenton testifying against Robert Haine and Martin Conklin had been miserable—cold and windy and rainy. If he never went back to Warrenton, it would be too soon.

The month had been worth it, though. It had taken all of Matt's willpower not to take a knife to Robert Haine. Even if he hadn't been able to slice him to bits, it had given him enormous pleasure to see him sentenced to twenty years hard time with no parole. The killer Haine had sent had recorded every word. Haine on film ordering Charlotte Court's death had sealed his fate.

Another good thing that had come out of that month had been the sale of Charlotte's shares to a consortium of young engineers. It had netted Charlotte an amazing amount of money, most of which she'd donated to a charity that gave art scholarships to poor students.

That was fine with Matt. He was making a bundle. They had more than they needed.

Actually, all he needed was Charlotte. Where was she?

There she was! After a year of marriage, his heart still leaped in his chest when he saw her. She was walking up the sidewalk, as beautiful as always. He frowned. She wasn't walking, she was…ambling. With no sense that she was half an hour late to the opening of her own show.

What the—?

Matt met her halfway and she took his arm, still at that strolling pace. "You're late," Matt said.

"Mmm," she answered, with a dreamy smile on her face.

"Ah, Charlotte?"

She turned that smile on him. "Yes?"

"Why are you late for your own show?"

"I had a doctor's appointment. It took longer than I thought."

"Jesus." He stopped abruptly, panic seizing him. "You're not sick, are you?" Just the thought of it made him break out into a sweat.

She laughed and tugged his head down for a resounding smack of a kiss. "No, darling, I'm not sick. As a matter of fact, I'm…embarking upon a new creative endeavour." She stuck her sharp little elbow into his side. "And it's a coproduction."

ABOUT THE AUTHOR

ELIZABETH JENNINGS has always loved words—big ones, little ones, fat ones, skinny ones. She's been a wordsmith all her life, as a simultaneous interpreter, translator, and now as a writer. She lives in southern Italy, which she loves, together with her wonderful, high-maintenance husband and son. Who could ask for anything more? To find out more about Elizabeth, you can visit www.elizabeth-jennings.com.

THE DISH

Where authors give you the inside scoop!

♥ ♥ ♥ ♥ ♥ ♥ ♥ ♥ ♥ ♥ ♥ ♥ ♥ ♥

From the desk of Michelle Rowen

Michael Quinn used to be a vampire hunter. Now, he's a very reluctant vampire in search of a magical cure for what ails him in LADY & THE VAMP (available now). He's nursing a bit of a broken heart after being on the losing end of a love triangle in my first two Immortality Bites titles, *Bitten & Smitten* and *Fanged & Fabulous*. He doesn't know that true love is just around the next corner, and she's got a wooden stake with his name on it. To help this tall, dark, and "fangsome" vampire bachelor on his quest for love, liberty, and the pursuit of a hot, blond mercenary named Janie, here is something that Quinn might encounter in your average, everyday vampire bar.

Top Ten Vampiric Pick-up Lines

1. "I don't drink . . . *wine*. But, how about a piña colada?"
2. "Hey, you! You, in the black!"
3. "Didn't I go to your funeral?"
4. "Baby, you don't look a day over 350!"
5. "You have a beautiful neck, mind if I bite it?"
6. "You look just like David Boreanaz!"

7. "Are you one of the children of the night? Would you like to be?"
8. "Where have you been all of my long, tortured existence?"
9. "You, me, a bag of blood. Whaddya say?"
10. "Is that a wooden stake in your pocket or is it . . . ? Okay, never mind."

Then again, perhaps Quinn should just steer clear of vampire bars for the time being. It's just a suggestion.

Happy reading!

Michelle Rowen

www.michellerowen.com

♥ ♥ ♥ ♥ ♥ ♥ ♥ ♥ ♥ ♥ ♥ ♥ ♥ ♥

From the desk of Marliss Melton

Dear reader,

It has been said that every novelist draws on what she knows and what her stories are, in some ways, autobiographical. So, reading any author's work is a bit like glimpsing the skeletons in her closet or her underwear hanging out to dry! This often-embarrassing phenomenon couldn't be truer for me than it is in DON'T LET GO (available now), the fifth book in my Navy SEAL series.

I've never been to Venezuela to do mission work like Jordan (the heroine of DON'T LET GO), but I did study abroad in Ecuador during college. I never adopted a child like the little boy Jordan wants to adopt, but I cherished my little Thai foster sister, who went on to be adopted in the United States. I've stood in her sister Jillian Sander's shoes, a widow with young children, hoping to carry her boys through their grief in the most positive way possible. I've watched a relationship develop between a fatherless boy and a man willing to fill a giant's shoes. But, most obviously, I've loved a man like Solomon McGuire, a man who is passionate in all things, secretly romantic, and sometimes hard to live with.

My second chance at love, my husband, most profoundly influenced the development of Solomon's character, from his black moustache to his New England dialect. Of course, I had to pair Solomon with a woman who resembles me, at least in regards to her hair color and the speed at which her baby was born. Not every reader is going to fall head over heels with this commanding character, but there'll be plenty who do. All I can say, ladies, is, "sorry, Solomon is all mine."

To see a real–life photo of my inspiration, just check out the photos page on my Web site www.

marlissmelton.com. And while you're there, check out a preview of my next SEAL Team Twelve book, featuring the blue-eyed, baldheaded Chief Sean Harlan.

Did I mention that my husband is also bald?

Yours truly,

Marli Meeton

♥ ♥ ♥ ♥ ♥ ♥ ♥ ♥ ♥ ♥ ♥ ♥ ♥ ♥ ♥ ♥ ♥

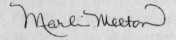

From the desk of Elizabeth Jennings

Dear reader,

Charlotte Court, the heroine in PURSUIT (available now), is a truly gifted artist, who perfected her craft in Florence, Italy. Art is her entire life until a murderer comes after her and she has to go on the run to Baja California. That's where she meets Matt, a former Navy SEAL, a rough, tough guy, who falls head over heels for her and is blown away by her talent.

Like Charlotte, I spent a number of years in Florence, Italy, immersed in an artistic environment. My mom worked at a US graduate school of fine arts—now, alas, defunct—in a beautiful villa nestled in the green hills just below Fiesole, Villa

Schifanoia. Legend has it that this was the villa where the young Florentine noblemen and women fled to avoid the plague in Boccaccio's *Decameron*.

We lived around the corner from a fabulous international art school that was in itself a small masterpiece. It was in a 16th century deconsecrated church in the Borgo San Frediano, simply a stunning place to study art. Just a glimpse inside felt like being magically transported back to a Greek or a Roman temple.

I'm arty, but not visually gifted like the students I grew up around. I love words. At the time, I was learning characterization, hooks, and motivation, studying the masters, going over the writing again and again and again, revising and rewriting until I got it right.

I founded a writer's group in Florence that met in the basement of the American church—quite an eclectic group of people. I was the only one writing romance and it did me good to pit myself against those who had no sympathy for or knowledge of the genre. It stiffened my spine. And, boy, did I learn how to tighten up my writing.

Since I was putting myself through this intense apprenticeship, exactly as a young Renaissance artisan working in a *bottega* or the young artists in that beautiful school, I had an enormous amount of sympathy for the work involved in becoming proficient at an art.

Charlotte Court was born then in my mind, all

those years ago. A beautiful woman, exceedingly gifted and hardworking, who lives for her art. I had her study at this wonderful art school. She was alive to me—her drive to paint and draw almost obsessive, yet totally understandable.

I have held Charlotte in my head and heart all these years, and in this, my eighth book, I have finally given her life.

She is put to the test in PURSUIT. Wounded and hunted, she shows immense courage and fortitude. I like to think that her art gives her strength and grace.

Happy reading!

Elizabeth Jennings

If you liked this book—
and like Romantic Suspense . . .
You'll LOVE these authors!!!

Karen Rose

*"Utterly compelling . . . high wire suspense that
keeps you riveted to the edge of your seat."*

—Lisa Gardner, *New York Times* bestselling author

Die For Me	*Have You Seen Her?*
(0-446-61691-5)	(0-446-61281-2)
Count to Ten	*I'm Watching You*
(0-446-61690-7)	(0-446-61447-5)
Don't Tell	*Nothing To Fear*
(0-446-61280-4)	(0-446-61448-3)

You Can't Hide
(0-446-61689-3)

Annie Solomon

"A powerful new voice in romantic suspense."

—*Romantic Times*

Dead Shot	*Like a Knife*
(0-446-61632-X)	(0-446-61230-8)
Blind Curve	*Dead Ringer*
(0-446-61358-4)	(0-446-61229-4)

Tell Me No Lies
(0-446-61357-6)

Want to know more about romances at Grand Central Publishing and Forever? Get the scoop online!

GRAND CENTRAL PUBLISHING'S ROMANCE HOMEPAGE

Visit us at www.hachettebookgroupusa.com/romance for all the latest news, reviews, and chapter excerpts!

NEW AND UPCOMING TITLES

Each month we feature our new titles and reader favorites.

CONTESTS AND GIVEAWAYS

We give away galleys, autographed copies, and all kinds of fun stuff.

AUTHOR INFO

You'll find bios, articles, and links to personal websites for all your favorite authors—and so much more!

THE BUZZ

Sign up for our monthly romance newsletter, and be the first to read all about it!